Charlaine Harris is the internationally bestselling author of several supernatural and mystery series, including the *Sunday Times* Number One bestselling *Sookie Stackhouse* books, filmed as the award-winning HBO® television series *True Blood*. She lives in a small town in southern Arkansas.

Toni L.P. Kelner is the Agatha Award-winning author of the *Where Are They Now?* and the *Laura Fleming* mysteries. She was awarded a Romantic Times Career Achievement Award, and her short stories have been nominated for the Agatha, the Anthony, the Macavity and the Derringer Awards. She lives in Massachusetts with her husband, fellow author Stephen P. Kelner, Jr. and their two daughters.

D0808233

Also by
Charlaine Harris and
Toni L.P. Kelner

HOME IMPROVEMENT
UNDEAD EDITION

EDITED BY

CHARLAINE
HARRIS

AND TONI L.P.
KELNER

AN APPLE FOR THE CREATURE

Jo Fletcher
BOOKS

First published by The Berkley Publishing Group (USA) in 2012
First published in the UK in 2012 by Jo Fletcher Books
This edition published in 2013 by

Jo Fletcher Books
an imprint of Quercus Editions Ltd.
55 Baker Street
7th Floor, South Block
London
W1U 8EW

CONTENTS

INTRODUCTION

Toni and I are absolutely qualified to edit this anthology of creepy school stories. After all, we both went to school for years. Like most creative kids, especially most creative smart kids who read heavily and enjoy learning, we had a bumpy time of it.

As a result, when the idea of a school setting came to us, it seemed a natural. There's always something happening under the surface in any given classroom. Some kids come from homes the rest of us couldn't even imagine, some teachers have their own secrets, and there are always dramas, ranging from does-he-like-me? to I-forgot-to-do-my-homework. Toni and I figured there are some dramas that might be a *little* more out of the ordinary.

We made our list (and checked it twice) of writers who'd give us something interesting, and we have been very happy with the results. Schools and students come in infinite variety, and in *An Apple for the Creature* you'll have a chance to run the gamut. Enjoy! Or you'll get detention.

—CHARLAINE HARRIS

Playing Possum

CHARLAINE HARRIS

A native of the Mississippi Delta, Charlaine Harris has lived her whole life in various southern states. Her first book, a mystery, was published in 1981. After that promising debut, her career meandered along until the success of the Sookie Stackhouse novels. Now all her books are in print, and she is a very happy camper. She is married and has three children.

I counted once. I counted twice. Yes! Twenty-three chocolate cupcakes with chocolate icing, liberally decorated with sprinkles. I put the cupcakes, one by one, into the shallow cardboard box I'd begged from the dollar store clerk. Of course I'd lined it with aluminum foil, and of course each little cake was in its own paper cup. A white sugar sprinkle rolled off, and I dropped it back onto the dark icing and gently pressed it down. I tried to ignore the siren song my bed was singing. I was up, and I had to stay up.

I'd been too tired to bake the night before. I'd gotten off work at midnight and had fallen into bed the minute I'd put on my nightshirt and brushed my teeth. Monday nights at Merlotte's Bar are usually pretty light, and I'd assumed the night before would follow suit. Naturally, since I'd hoped to get off a little early, last night had broken the pattern. Rural northern Louisiana is not a big tourist route, so we didn't get a whole lot of strangers in Merlotte's—but members of a Baton Rouge bikers' club had attended a huge motorcycle jamboree in Arkansas, and on their way home, about twenty of them had stopped to have supper and a few brews at Merlotte's.

And they'd stayed. And stayed.

I should have appreciated their patronage, since I have a partnership in the bar-slash-restaurant. But I hadn't been able to stop thinking about those twenty-three cupcakes I had to make, and calculating how long it would take me to mix, bake, and ice them. Then I'd figured how long it would take me to drive to Red Ditch, where my "nephew," Hunter Savoy, would be celebrating Labor Day with his kindergarten classroom. When I'd finally trudged in my back door, I'd looked at the recipe waiting optimistically on the counter along with the mixing bowl and the dry ingredients. And I'd thought, *No way*.

So I'd gotten up with the larks to bake cupcakes. I'd showered and dressed and brushed my long blond hair into a ponytail. I'd recounted the little goody bags, and boxed them, too. Now I was on my way; the boxes with the cupcakes and the goody bags carefully positioned on the floorboard of the backseat.

It's not that long a drive to Red Ditch, but it's not that easy a drive, either; mostly parish roads through rural areas. Louisiana isn't exactly known for its up-to-date road maintenance, and there were crumbling shoulders and potholes a-plenty. I saw two deer in time to dodge them, and as I drove slowly on a low-lying two-lane through a bayou there was a big movement in the reeds around its bank . . . big enough to signal "gator." This would be a fairly rare sighting, so I made a mental note to check out the bank on my way home.

By the time I parked in front of Hunter's school, I felt like it was already noon, but when I pulled my cell phone from my purse to check, I discovered the digital numbers read *10:03*. I had arrived at the time Hunter's dad, Remy Savoy, had told me the teacher had requested.

The Red Ditch school had once been a combination elementary and middle school. Since parish-wide consolidation, it was only a kindergarten for the children in the immediate area. I parked right in front of the wide sidewalk leading up to the dilapidated double doors. The yard was trimmed, but littered with pinecones and the odd bit of childish debris— a gum wrapper here, a crumpled piece of paper there. The low brown-brick building, clearly built in the sixties and not much changed since then, was quiet in the warm September sun. It was hard to believe the kindergarten was packed full of children.

I stretched, hearing my spine make some little crackling noises. Constantly being on my feet was taking its toll, and I was only in my twenties. Then I shook myself. It was not a day to think about a future of aching knees and feet. It was Hunter's day.

I couldn't gather my purse, the cupcakes in their broad, flat box, and the box of goody bags all at the same time. After a moment's indecision, I decided to take in the cupcakes first, rather than leave them in the warm car. I slung my big purse over one shoulder and lifted the cupcakes with both hands. I'd gotten them this far, and they still looked great. If I could just get them into the school and into the classroom without letting them slide around . . . I made it to the front door and up two shallow steps with no incident. By holding up the box as if I were delivering a pizza, I freed a hand to turn the knob, opening the door enough to use my butt to keep the opening wide enough for me and the box. It was a relief to step inside and lower my burden until I could grasp it with both hands. The door thunked shut behind me, leaving a wide bar of light lancing across the floor. Not exactly tight-fitting.

I'd been in the school before, so I knew the layout. I stood in a sort of lobby, the walls decorated with posters advising kids to wash their hands, to cover their noses with their crooked arms when they sneezed, and to pick up litter. Directly across from the double doors lay the school office. Classroom halls began to the right and to the left of the office, six classrooms on each hall, three to each wall. At the end of these halls were doors going outside to the playground, which was fenced in.

The school office had a big window, waist-high, through which I could see a woman about my age talking on a telephone. The window gave visitors a visual cue that they should check in. This was reinforced by a big sign (ALL VISITORS MUST SIGN THE SHEET IN THE OFFICE!). I knew that the proliferation of messy divorces was responsible for this rule, and though it was a pain, it was at least a half-ass security measure.

I'd had a fantasy that the school secretary would leap up to open the heavy office door, which stood to the left of the window. That didn't happen, and I managed it myself after a little juggling.

Then I had to stand in front of the secretary's desk, waiting for her to acknowledge me, while she continued to listen to her caller.

I had plenty of time to observe the young woman's curly brown hair and sharp features, somehow evened out by her almost freakishly round blue eyes. I was getting more and more impatient as she kept trying to speak into the phone, only to be steamrollered by whoever was on the other end of the line. I rolled my eyes, though I knew no one was watching; certainly not the woman, who was suppressing extreme agitation.

My flash of resentment was abruptly eclipsed when I realized that this conversation was anything but casual. All her thoughts were focused on the person she was arguing with, and she almost certainly didn't even register the live person standing right in front of her, getting more and more impatient. The door to the principal's office, to the left of the secretary's desk, was resolutely shut tight, though from behind it I could hear the light click of a keyboard. Principal Minter was working on something.

Meanwhile, I had time to read her secretary's nameplate. Sherry Javitts was having a very private conversation in a very public place. Not that it was a true conversation—the young woman was mostly listening to the diatribe pouring into her ears. She didn't know that I could hear it as clearly as she could, or at least catch an echo of it in her thoughts.

That's my big problem. I'm telepathic.

Sherry Javitts had a big problem of her own—an overpossessive and maybe deranged former boyfriend. She blinked and looked up at my unhappy face, finally absorbing my presence.

She interrupted the caller. "No, Brady," she said through literally clenched teeth. "It's over! I'm working! You have to stop calling!" And she slammed the phone back into its charger before she took a deep breath and looked up at me, making her lips curve in a ghastly smile.

"Can I help you?" Sherry said steadily enough, though I noticed her hands were shaking.

We were going to be civilized and ignore the incident. Fine by me. "Yes, I'm Hunter Savoy's aunt, Sookie Stackhouse," I said. "I've brought cupcakes for the Pony Room's Labor Day party."

She pushed a clipboard over to me. "Please sign in," she said. "Date, name, and time. Purpose of visit in that space, there."

"Sure." I put the cupcakes on top of a filing cabinet while I filled in the required information.

"I didn't know Hunter had an aunt," Sherry Javitts said. In a little town like Red Ditch, everyone would know the children's histories, even the history of relative newcomers like Remy Savoy and his little boy.

I needed to return to my car and get the box of goody bags, but I made myself give her a reassuring smile. (We were just strewing insincere smiles right and left.) "I'm not his actual aunt," I said. "Calling me 'aunt' is just easier. I was first cousin to his mama."

"Oh," she said, looking appropriately sober. "I'm so sorry for her passing."

"We sure miss her," I said, which was an out-and-out lie. Hadley had been in trouble all her life. Though she'd often tried to do the right thing, somehow that had never worked out. Bless her heart.

I waited for some kind of concluding remark, but Sherry Javitts was lost in her own thoughts, which revolved around a terribly threatening person named Brady, the self-same man she'd been arguing with. She didn't miss *him*.

"So," I said, a little more sharply than I'd intended, "I can go back to Hunter's classroom?"

"I'm sorry," she said, shaking her head. "Got lost in a cloud, there. Sure, go ahead."

"I'll have to come in and out at least once," I warned her.

"You go right ahead. Just sign out when the party is over." She was relieved I was leaving. At least this time, she was polite enough to rise and open the office door. Sherry was surprisingly tall, and she was wearing an unremarkable pale green dress that I envied only because it was a size 2.

I sighed as I thought of the chocolate cupcake I'd already had that morning.

I edged out of the small office with the cupcakes in my hands, glancing back through the big window to see Sherry Javitts, back in her chair, bow her curly head and put her hands over her face. That was sure the only way she was going to get any privacy in that fishbowl. The inner door of the office, the one to the principal's inner sanctum, opened even as I thought that.

I remembered meeting Ms. Minter at the spring open house. She was just as nicely dressed today in a tan pantsuit with a dark green scarf, a nice look with her warm brown skin. The appropriately clad Ms. Minter did not look happy, and I wondered if she'd overheard the furious conversation her secretary had had with Brady, whoever he was; husband, boyfriend, secret lover?

As I began walking down the corridor to the right of the office, I confess I was glad to be walking away from the fraught emotions. One of the most burdensome things about my condition is the constant bombardment of other people's personal woes. I can only block so much out; a lot seeps around the edges of my mental walls. I would much rather not have known about the Drama of Sherry and Brady. I shook the incident off and put a smile on my face, because I'd arrived at the Pony Room, second down on the right-hand side of the hallway. I didn't have a free hand to knock on the door, so it was lucky Ms. Yarnell spotted me through the rectangular window in the classroom door.

When I'd gone with Remy and Hunter to vet the kindergarten, we'd all liked the Pony Room the best, so I'd been relieved when Hunter had called to tell me Mrs. Gristede was going to be his teacher. Though I hardly knew her, both Hunter and I had learned telepathically that she was a nice woman who genuinely liked children. She was definitely a cut above the other teachers we'd encountered that night.

Unfortunately for everyone, two weeks before school opened Mrs. Gristede had been in a car accident, and her recovery was going to take her out for a whole half-year. Ms. Yarnell was her replacement and, according to Remy, she was working out pretty well.

While Mrs. Gristede was a short, round woman in her forties, Ms. Yarnell proved to be a short, round woman in her early twenties. Despite Ms. Yarnell's youth, she radiated the same pleasure in teaching, the same fondness for children that had so recommended Mrs. Gristede.

The kids seemed to love her, because there were at least six apples piled on her desk. There were different varieties, and some looked a little more battered than others, but I was impressed that she'd inspired such a traditional gift.

I had time to gather this positive first impression while Ms. Yarnell was holding the door for me. All the children were vibrating with excitement at this break in their routine (which had been so recently learned). I set down the box and my purse on a low worktable right inside the door when I saw Hunter dashing toward me.

"Aunt Sookie!" Hunter yelled, and I squatted so I could catch him in my arms. It was like being wrapped in a skinny, warm boa. Hunter was dark of hair and eyes like his mother—and like her, he was an attractive person, an advantage he would need since he'd gotten the family "gift."

I'm so glad you're here, he said silently.

"Hey, Hunter," I said, careful to speak out loud. I'd been trying to help Hunter learn to control his telepathy, which (sadly) meant teaching him to conceal his true nature. Children's emotions are so much purer, undiluted. I hated having to curb his natural exuberance.

You made the cupcakes, he said happily, right into my head. I gave him a gentle squeeze to remind him. "You brought cupcakes," he said out loud, grinning at me.

Lest you should think Hunter was a pitiful child with no one to love him—not only could Remy have followed instructions on a box of mix and opened a can of icing, but I was also certain that Remy's girlfriend, Erin, would have been thrilled to be asked to make treats for Hunter's first real school party. Though I didn't know Erin well, I knew she genuinely cared for Hunter. I didn't know why Hunter had picked me instead. Maybe he'd just wanted to see if I'd do it. Maybe, since I had to drive farther, I was the bigger challenge. Maybe he just wanted to be around someone like himself; we hadn't gotten to spend much time together since Hunter had started school. I confess that I'd been both surprised and secretly flattered when Remy had called to tell me, in a very tentative way and not within Hunter's hearing, that his son wanted me to attend the holiday celebration.

"Sure, I brought the cupcakes, silly. And if I can unwind you off me, I'll go back out to the car and get the rest of the stuff," I said. "You think Ms. Yarnell would let you help me? By the way, Ms. Yarnell, I'm Sookie Stackhouse."

Hunter detached himself and I stood up. He looked at Ms. Yarnell, hope all over his face.

She patted him on the head, turning to me with a warm smile. "I'm Sabrina," she said. "I'm filling in this semester for Mrs. Gristede, as I'm sure you know." Then her smile faded as she took me in.

I tried not to look as startled as she did. I was getting a strange vibe from Hunter's teacher, and she was getting the same sort of vibe from me. Well, well. This day was turning out to be extraordinary.

"I have a friend who's a lot like you," I said. "Her name's Amelia Broadway, she lives in New Orleans. Amelia belongs to a small group of people with the same interests." I didn't think any of the kids would know the word *coven*, but I didn't want to test that belief.

"I've met Amelia," Sabrina Yarnell said. "She's a sister under the skin. What about you?" Her voice was casual, but her eyes were not.

"Afraid not," I said. I truly have no magical ability of my own. (The telepathy had been given to me, by way of being a baby shower present to my grandfather.) But it would be silly not to tell her what she was already guessing. "I'm like Hunter," I said, patting him on the shoulder. His otherness could not have escaped the witch; he was too young to conceal it from a real practitioner.

"Can I go out to the car with Aunt Sookie?" Hunter asked, impatient with grown-up talk.

"Don't interrupt, Hunter," I said gently.

"Sorry!" Hunter squirmed, clearly worried that his bad manners might cost him a privilege.

"All right, Hunter, you go with your aunt, but you two come right back," Sabrina Yarnell said, giving me a level look to make sure I understood I wasn't getting permission to take Hunter to Dairy Queen for an Oreo Blizzard, or on any other unauthorized expedition. She was schoolteacher first, witch second.

"Not off school property," I agreed, smiling. "Mind if I leave my purse in here?"

When she nodded, I moved the cupcakes to the top of a filing cabinet, too high for any depredating little fingers. I stowed my purse on Ms. Yarnell's desk after tucking my car keys in my jeans pocket. "Come on, buddy," I said, holding out my hand to Hunter. He waved at his classmates, delighted to be the man of the hour. Most of the children waved back as if Hunter were leaving on a trip; they were clearly revved up by the prospect of the party. Maybe later, say by January, they'd be more blasé—but kindergartners, this early in the school year? Yeah, they were excited.

Hunter and I walked up the hall together, Hunter so full of the joy of it all that he was practically bouncing off the walls. I could hear the murmur of voices in each room. I caught glimpses of teachers and children through each rectangular window. The smell and sounds of school—did they ever change?

"Are you coming to Daddy's cookout Saturday?" Hunter asked, though he knew the answer. Since we were in a public place, he was taking care to talk out loud, which I appreciated, so I was gentle in my response.

"Hunter, you know already I have to work on Saturday. That's the tough part of being the boss, sort of. I have to fill in when other people can't be there." Because of a family wedding, two of our regular servers were going to be out on Merlotte's busiest day. "That's one reason I'm so glad I can be here now," I said. I wondered if I should stop at the office to explain that I had permission to take Hunter out the front door, but Ms. Minter and Ms. Javitts were having such an earnest conversation that I didn't want to interrupt them.

In fact, they looked so worried that I felt a flash of concern, myself. But I didn't want to involve Hunter in my anxiety, and I quickly blocked off my thoughts as I pushed open one of the front doors. "Who's going to be at you-all's cookout? Your daddy and Erin, I know. What about your great-uncle?"

Hunter told me about the few relatives and two distant cousins his own age who'd said they'd come grill hot dogs, too. They'd meet at the little Red Ditch park to play kickball and fly kites and throw Frisbees. He was describing his new dragon kite as I unlocked the car door and lifted out the box full of goody bags.

I'd bought the plastic bags stamped with horses (feeling proud that they fit in with the Pony Room theme!) at Wal-Mart, and I'd filled each one with candy, a tiny top, a harmonica, and a sheet of stickers on the advice of Halleigh Bellefleur, a schoolteacher friend. Maybe the twirl you had to give a top was too much for such little kids? Maybe I should have gotten something else? Oh, well, too late now. Hunter seemed pleased, which had been my goal. I let him carry the box, which he promptly tilted to one side.

"Whoops, we dropped one," I said, bending over to pick it up. "You think you can count them again for me? Make sure we have them all?"

"One, two—" Hunter began, and suddenly our heads snapped to

look in the direction of the turn into the parking lot. The screeching tires and the racing motor of an oncoming truck were telling both of us that something was wrong.

The pickup swerved into the parking lot and stopped with a spray of gravel in front of the school. We both squatted down, instinctively concealing ourselves. Luckily, there was a van parked between my car and the pickup, so Hunter and I had extra coverage. In Hunter's mind the van provided an impenetrable wall, and he felt much safer. I was not so optimistic, simply because I was larger and therefore more visible.

Maybe I was also more realistic.

If I canted myself at a strange angle I could see the driver's door of the pickup. It hadn't opened. I could glimpse the man behind the wheel. He appeared to be talking to himself, though maybe he had a cell phone in his farthest hand. He was wearing a Red Ditch Oil & Lube baseball cap and a plaid western-style shirt.

I glanced sideways at my nephew, torn between trying to absorb this new development and wanting to protect him. Hunter's eyes were wide and his face looked much older than a kindergartner's should. I could feel his fear beating against my own mind.

The pickup had parked in the BUSES ONLY area, designated by an unmistakable sign and yellow stripes on the pavement. That was lawless enough to rile any middle-class citizen, but that wasn't what had raised the hair on the back of my neck and made Hunter's face go dead white.

The man in the truck was batshit crazy.

I slapped my pocket, but I knew where my cell phone was—in my purse. In the Pony Room. All I'd brought out with me was my car key.

There were fields all around the school, except here in the front, on the west side. Small houses lined the two-lane street leading from Main to the school, but of the six or so dwellings, three were clearly empty right now, the occupants at work, if the lack of vehicles was a reliable indication. One of the others had a For Sale sign in front, and two were too far away for me to assess. If I took off for one of them, I might simply be wasting valuable time.

Damn. I *had* to go back into the school.

Was Hunter safer out here or inside? I could ease him back into the car, tell him to stay down. I had a mental montage of the sheriff's deputies showing up, bullets flying, Hunter hit by accident.

Okay, he had to come with me.

The people in the school had to be warned, especially Sherry Javitts. This man was surely the enraged Brady.

Sometimes I hated my telepathy. You'd think I could have gotten some talent that was useful for offense. I couldn't stop an armed man by thinking at him. But there was a defensive way it could be helpful.

Hunter, here's what we're going to do, I said silently. *You're going to walk into the school with me like we don't have a care in the world, and once we're inside you're going to run like a rabbit, right to the Pony Room. You're going to tell Ms. Yarnell to lock the door, a silly man is here.* "Silly" seemed inadequate, but "crazy" and "violent" and "probably armed" seemed too heavy for Hunter. I took a deep breath. *You and your friends are going to lie down on the floor, where no one looking through the door window can see you. Lie flat like pancakes, you hear?*

His head jerked once. *You come, too,* he pleaded.

I've got to warn the other people, I said. *I've got to try. You get to the room, you stay down, and you don't move, no matter what. Ms. Yarnell will take care of you all.* Sabrina Yarnell was capable of taking care of a roomful of children with both hands tied behind her back, but she couldn't stop bullets. At least, I didn't think so.

We were still squatting beside the open car door. Now, in the slowest way possible, Hunter and I stood up. I took another deep breath as I shut the car door.

Slow and easy, I reminded Hunter, and I smiled at him. It wasn't a good effort, but he smiled back in a very small way. We began strolling down the sidewalk to the front doors. I hoped, with the box of goody bags under my left arm, we made a convincingly casual scene. I put my free hand on Hunter's shoulder and squeezed gently. He looked up at me, no longer able to sustain even a neutral expression. Fear looked out of his dark eyes, and I had to work hard to force away my mental image of what I'd like to do to the man who'd ruined Hunter's happiness. With the box propped against one hip, I opened one of the old front doors.

We stepped inside, and it fell shut behind us. I knelt, handed the box to Hunter. I told him, *Scoot, darlin'. I'll see you in a minute or two. Now, run!*

The minute he started down the hall to the Pony Room, I stood and whirled around to look back through the window in the right front door. The crazy man was getting out of the truck, his mouth moving as he talked to himself. I knew he had a gun. I knew it, right from his head.

I spun back around to see Sherry Javitts blotting her face, the principal standing in the doorway of her own office. They were both staring out the office window at me, alerted by my odd actions and body language to the fact that something was very wrong.

"He's out there with a gun," I said as I pulled open the office door. "Call nine-one-one right now! Can we lock the doors?"

Without a word the principal hit a button and an almighty racket sounded throughout the school. "Lockdown alarm," she explained, grabbing a set of keys from right inside her office and hurrying to the entrance to shoot the deadbolt that secured the double doors. She stooped to push the floor bolt that held the left door in place. Once it was pushed down, she reached for the right one; but it didn't work.

Sherry was still gaping at me.

"Call the police," I said, biting back the word *idiot*. She picked up the phone. As she punched in numbers, her thoughts weren't coherent enough to decipher even if I'd had the time or inclination.

I didn't have to look outside to track Brady's progress. The turmoil in the man's brain got closer and closer until his chaos was beating inside my own head in time with his footsteps. He reached the front doors and began pounding on them.

Though they were bowing in, the doors held under Brady's initial assault. Ms. Minter spun on her heel and began running down the left-wing hall to lock the back doors leading to the playground. Sherry was staring at the way the doors were jumping. The phone was still in her hand. Someone on the other end was yelling.

"You need to hide," I said urgently. "If the doors give in, you have to be out of sight."

"But he might shoot someone else," she said. "He just wants me."

I didn't have time to figure out whether that was an incredibly brave thought or simply shock-induced honesty. "He doesn't have to get any-one," I said. "The cops will be here soon."

"Hardly any cops in Red Ditch," Sherry said, "as he's been remind-ing me every day for months." I could tell from her thoughts that Sherry was resolving to sacrifice herself. She felt surprisingly good about that; she would regain her pride and finally accomplish something big. A tinge of fatalism and self-righteousness colored this decision. If I've learned anything from years of hearing other people's most personal reflections, it's that we never do anything for only one reason.

I didn't want anyone to die today.

I spied a janitor's closet across from the school office. (I deduced this from the fact that a sign on the outside read JANITOR.) I grabbed the secretary's arm and hustled her over to it, opened the door, and shoved her inside. When Rachelle Minter came running back, presumably hav-ing locked the playground doors in both wings, I said, "Sherry's in there. Lock it," and she did it instantly. Then she stood and gasped for breath. The principal was not a runner, but she was a damn quick thinker.

I couldn't think of anything else to do. We'd locked the doors, we'd called the police, we'd hidden the target of the violence from the dealer of the violence.

It was like waiting for a tornado to touch down.

The principal and I stood side by side, our gazes fixed on the old doors with the ominous gap between them and the missing right-hand floor latch. Each time Brady crashed into the doors they spread a little farther apart before they rebounded into place. Though there was more play between the two doors than there should have been, the broken floor bolt would be the deciding factor.

"Maintenance guy didn't fix it," Ms. Minter gasped. "But who knew someone would try to kick the doors in?"

Abruptly, I wondered what the hell we were doing standing there. We weren't armed, and our mere presence would hardly be enough to deter Brady from whatever plan was in his crazy head. So far, he was absolutely bent on gaining entrance and finding Sherry.

"We better get out of the way!" I was surprised at how calmly I spoke, because my heart was racing like a motor on high. The unknown Brady had a lot of stamina. With every blow the doors bowed in more, rebounded more slowly. I grabbed Ms. Minter's hand and began to urge her back into the office.

I should have been concentrating; or maybe it wouldn't have made any difference, since Brady was moved by nothing more than rage and impulse. He hit the doors as hard as he could. Simultaneously, he fired twice through the gap between them. The boom of the gunfire was magnified in the little lobby. Even as I flinched, I felt a yank on my hand and I staggered.

Ms. Minter folded to the floor, still holding on to me.

Caught off balance, I sprawled to the floor with her, landing partly across her legs. I knew she'd been hit. There was shock and pain caroming from corner to corner in her brain. In a second, I could see the blood soaking her pantsuit. Her eyes were terrified.

"Oh, no," she said. "Oh, it hurts." Then she passed out.

I lay as still as though I were paralyzed. Had I been hit, too? I didn't think so, but I was so stunned I couldn't move.

I was facedown on the green linoleum, sprawled across poor Rachelle Minter's legs. She'd landed on her right side. I could feel the wetness as her blood pooled underneath me. Brady had continued his assault on the front doors after he'd fired. I could feel the surge of triumph in the gunman's brain. He was pretty sure we'd gone down, but I didn't think he could see us at the moment, and he didn't know if we were dead or not.

I could feel how wet the front of my T-shirt had become in a few seconds. Taking a big chance, I rolled over onto my side so I wasn't putting any more pressure on Ms. Minter. I lay as close to the wounded woman as I could. She wasn't dead yet. I could feel the life in her brain. Before I began my impersonation of a dead person, I opened my eyes a slit to look at myself. I was bloody enough to looked seriously wounded, perhaps even dead, as long as Brady didn't try to locate an actual bullet hole.

I made myself go totally limp. I told myself over and over, as I heard the doors finally spring apart, that he could not tell I was alive as long as I thought "limp and lifeless."

He won't shoot me. He won't shoot me. I begged God that Brady would not think a coup de grâce was necessary.

The school was eerily silent . . . to my ears, anyway. In my head, the panic of more than a hundred adults and children beat like an irregular drum. Clearest of all was the regret and terror of the woman in the closet only seven feet away from where I lay pretending to be dead. Sherry was almost incapable of coherent thought. I could totally understand that. At least I knew what was happening, but she was shut in that windowless tiny room, knowing that the man whose footsteps she could hear was there to kill her.

Then those footsteps were beside me. Brady was breathing harshly, rapidly; I could "hear" that he could not believe what he had done, that he knew that sometime in the future he would regret the deaths of the two women on the floor, that he was wondering where Sherry was, that *bitch*, she should be the one who was *dead*.

He screamed then, the sounded ripping from his throat as though he were being tortured. "Sherry," he bellowed. "Where the hell are you? I'm gonna shoot you, you whore! I'm gonna spray your guts all over the walls!"

Behind the wooden door Sherry was holding her breath and praying as hard as I had that he couldn't hear her breathe, couldn't smell her skin, couldn't see through the wall to where she was crouched among the cleaning products and rolls of toilet paper.

I couldn't move so much as a fingertip. I couldn't take a deep breath. *Limp,* I chanted to myself. *Limp, limp, limp.*

He kicked the wall about two feet away from my head, and then he cursed because he was wearing sneakers. It took every little sliver of will I could scrape together to keep myself from flinching.

I heard a siren . . . a lone siren. Though it sounded as sweet and welcome as a lover's greeting, I was conscious of a certain amount of disappointment. I'd half expected six sirens, or a dozen. I guess I'd been watching too much television. This wasn't Chicago or Dallas. This was Red Ditch. Some state troopers would be on their way, I was sure, but they wouldn't be able to arrive on the site instantly.

Maybe by the time they got here, this would be all over. But I couldn't imagine what the ending would be.

Brady stopped screaming threats and began trying doorknobs. Of course the one to the school office opened easily. He had a field day at Sherry's desk, tossing papers, throwing the telephone, causing as much chaos as he could. Though I knew he was intent on that destruction, I still didn't dare to move because the window overlooked the area where I lay. He might catch any slight movement of leg or arm.

Rachelle Minter was weaker now. I tried to imagine a plan that would save her; one that wouldn't include me getting killed, as well. I simply couldn't think of one. So I kept on playing possum.

The only thing I could do was worry. I spared a sharp moment of regret for Hunter. His day had been ruined, in the worst possible way. From now on, he'd remember his first-ever school party as an event of horror, and there was no way I could make that up to him.

I even had a second of sheer pique that the damn cupcakes were going to go to waste.

But mostly I worried about the children. If Brady started shooting into the rooms at random, sooner or later a child or a teacher would get killed. I had to think of a way to stop him.

Brady had resumed ranting and screaming, even when the siren abruptly cut off. I was so busy breathing shallowly and lying still that it took me a minute to dip inside his head, which was a virtual snake pit.

Brady had lost all his insulation; that was what I'd always called the civilizing influence that kept us from hitting other people when we were angry with them, stopped us from hawking and spitting on the floor of our grandmother's house, advised us to make an attempt to get along with coworkers. Maybe Brady had never had a lot of this insulation anyway. His mental and emotional entanglement with Sherry had stripped all this insulation away and all the wires in Brady's brain were hopping and sparking without any impulse control.

Brady was entirely human, but if I hadn't known better I'd have called him a demon.

The demons I'd known had been much better behaved. My sort-of-godfather, Desmond Cataliades, was mostly demon, and he wore civilization like a coat.

With no warning, Brady kicked me. I didn't know if he could sense an intruder in his head because he'd abandoned his semblance to a total human being, or if he simply felt like expressing his aggression. It was a huge effort to roll with the kick as if I weren't in my body.

Then Brady fired the gun into the office, and again I had to hold on to my possum persona with all the determination I could muster. I came *this close* to yelling out loud as the glass of the window shattered and rained down on me and Ms. Minter. Now some of the blood smearing me was my own.

I'd always assumed that to save my own life I could endure just about anything. I was finding that wasn't necessarily so. With Brady proving so completely unpredictable, I was fast approaching the jumping-up-and-screaming point.

If I'd been a genuine possum, my masquerade might have been easier.

He went past me again, screaming incoherently and slamming into every door he saw. I heard a door swing open, and I thought, *Oh no!* But the cleaning agent smell that wafted out told me *bathroom*, and I let out the breath I'd taken very slowly indeed.

The crazed man continued down the hall to the left of the office, and I heard not a sound from the teachers and kids trapped in those rooms. I opened one eye. Though my angle of vision prohibited me seeing very far down the right corridor, which I was facing, I could see that the teacher in the first room had taped construction paper over the window in her door. That was amazingly smart. In the room across the hall, apparently the kids had hidden out of sight of the window, and Brady said, "Where the hell are they?" He sounded merely puzzled. He sounded like a real person, for just a second.

I could get up and run out before he could catch me or shoot me, I thought. He had his back to me, his attention was definitely elsewhere, and if I scrambled up and leaped to the front doors I could be down the sidewalk and behind the cover of the cars before he could get to the doors and aim.

At least, I hoped I could.

And then I wondered about the lone police officer out in front of the school. I didn't know what kind of person he (or she) might be. He might be so shaken by the seriousness of the event that he was ready to shoot whoever came out the doors, especially a bloody stranger running directly toward the patrol car.

While I was doing my best impersonation of a dead person and listening as intently as I could to both Brady's physical actions and his mental chaos, I kept cudgeling myself to develop a plan. If I was out of his sight for a few seconds, should I move? Was staying right here the best policy? If I hid, where could that be?

Then I did something I should have done before. I reached out for Hunter.

Hunter? You okay?

There was a long moment of silence. *Aunt Sookie? Did he shoot you? We heard a gun.*

He didn't shoot me. I'm all messed up to look at, but I'm not hurt.

Who got hurt?

Ms. Minter is hurt, but I think she's going to be okay, I told him. I hoped I wasn't lying. She was still alive, anyway.

My cell phone is in my purse, honey, I told him. *If Ms. Yarnell doesn't have one, make sure she uses mine to call 911. There's a police car outside, but only one.*

Ms. Yarnell's been talking to 'em.

Great! *Tell her . . .* I began, but then I stopped. There was no way Hunter could relay messages without revealing his secret to all his peers.

Crap.

Tell her you need to borrow the phone to talk to your aunt, Hunter. Hold it to your ear. I'll be talking to you this way, but they'll think it's coming over the phone.

In a minute, he was back on the line—the telepathy line. *I think she knows,* he said, but he didn't sound worried about it. *What do you want me to tell her?*

Tell her Ms. Minter is down, but she's alive. I'm lying on the floor beside her. Ms. Javitts is locked in the janitor's closet. The bad man is named Brady, he was Ms. Javitts's boyfriend.

Why are you lying on the floor, Aunt Sookie?

I sighed, but I kept it in. This was not the best means of communication, but at least we were communicating. *I'm pretending to be hurt,* I explained.

You're playing possum.

Yeah, exactly, I said, relieved.

Ms. Yarnell says she needs a straight shot at him.

I puzzled over that. Was Ms. Yarnell telling me she needed a direct field of vision to our attacker, or that she needed no one in between because she meant to literally shoot him? (I put off worrying about an armed kindergarten teacher until later.)

I'd been thinking so hard I'd forgotten to listen for Brady. His feet were right beside me all of a sudden. I closed down everything inside. I was afraid he was going to kick me again, and the anticipation of the pain was almost as bad.

He needed to move three steps back to be in a direct line of sight from the door of the Pony Room. There was no way I could make that happen without moving. I tensed my muscles in preparation.

"No, Aunt Sookie!" screamed a voice down the hall.

Oh, God, *no*. Brady, shocked, stepped away from my prone form and turned to look down the hall in the direction of Hunter's voice.

Now! I said.

"Now!" Hunter said to Ms. Yarnell.

I heard a commotion in the hall. What the hell was the witch doing? I couldn't let Brady get close to the kids! I rolled from my left side to my stomach. Brady's back was to me, but he was about to start down the hall. I lunged across the intervening distance and grabbed his nearest ankle, the left. The minute my hands wrapped around it, I made up my mind he wasn't going anywhere unless he dragged me behind him.

Several things happened then; the front door eased open behind me. I caught a flicker of movement and a glimpse of khaki. But I had to reserve my attention for the man with the gun.

Brady looked down at me and shook his head, as though flies were buzzing around his face. I finally saw him clearly. He was a mess; he hadn't shaved in days and hadn't bathed, either. The plaid western shirt was torn, his jeans spattered with old paint. His sneakers were very worn. But they were able to cause damage when he kicked me, and he was making up his mind to do that again. He balanced on the foot I had pinned, and brought his right foot back to get some momentum. I yanked at his ankle and he had to put the foot back down to catch his balance.

"Bitch!" he yelled, and raised the free foot again to stomp on one of my arms. I ducked my head down as if that would help avert the blow.

I heard a thud and an exclamation from Brady as something hit him on his shoulder.

It rolled on the floor until it came to rest in front of the janitor's closet.

It was a big Red Delicious apple.

I could see past him. It had been thrown by Sabrina Yarnell, who was now holding out her hand to the open door of the Pony Room. One of the children tossed her another apple, a Fuji this time. That apple, too, came at Brady with deadly intent, and this time Sabrina nailed him in the head.

Brady forgot he wanted to stomp me. Suddenly, he was far more interested in finding out who was attacking him.

"Who are you?" he called to Sabrina. "I ain't here after you! Get back in that room."

But he'd been distracted just long enough. A hoarse voice behind me said, "Brady Carver! Drop the gun!" Brady's head whipped around at this new diversion, and though I was too anxious to keep my eyes on him to peek behind me, I figured the new entrant had to be the police officer.

Brady's face had gone through a startling variety of expressions in the last minute: bewilderment, resentment, anger. But now he settled on hostility, and he began to raise his right hand to shoot.

"I don't want to shoot you, Brady," said the voice, still hoarse with tension, "but you better damn believe I will do it, I will shoot you *dead*."

"Not if I get you first," Brady sneered. I was sure I was going to be spattered with Brady's blood, too, but the moment after, something amazing happened.

His right hand seemed to go numb. The fingers weren't able to retain their grip. The hand relaxed completely, and the gun fell from it to clatter to the floor close to my head. To my immense relief it did not go off, and I instantly released Brady's ankle to shove the gun across the floor in the direction of the police officer. I stayed still and low, though I sure wanted to get out of the middle of the floor and out of the line of fire. Just at the moment it seemed more important to keep the situation simple.

Sabrina was standing with her small plump hand extended in Brady's direction. She didn't look like a young schoolteacher at all. She looked like a ball of power and ferocity. I'd never seen a witch really look "witchy," but I practically expected to see Sabrina's hair stream back in an invisible wind while she kept Brady's arm immobile.

The police officer pushed the gun a little farther away from Brady with her foot—yes, the officer was a woman, a brief glance informed me. And then she was screaming, "Down! DOWN!" with the persistence of a banshee. To my amazement Brady Carver knelt two feet away from me, and I scrambled backward in an ungraceful sort of reverse crab walk. His arms jerked back behind him, ready for the cuffs. His face was full of astonishment, as if he could not believe he was doing this.

In short order, Brady was cuffed, useless hand and all.

Sabrina was staggering from the effort as she went back into her room in answer to an anxious chorus from the kids.

I tried to stand up. It took two attempts, and I had to lean against the wall.

A lot happened in the next few minutes.

The EMTs rushed in, and brave Principal Minter was loaded into an ambulance. Her keys were on the floor where she'd lain, and I pointed out to the police officer that Sherry needed to be released from the janitor's closet. The secretary was an emotional mess. She was taken to the hospital, too, to get something to calm her down.

By that time the state police had arrived.

The old school had never had so many guns under its roof.

All the people in uniform seemed relieved that the human damage hadn't been worse, though a few newbies were silently a bit disappointed that the situation had been resolved without their assistance. Brady Carver was marched out to a state trooper car to be taken off to the county lockup, one arm still flopping uselessly, and the police officer (Shirley Barr) got a lot of slaps on the back for subduing the shooter. Shirley Barr was an ex-military woman of color, and I figured that in the line of duty here in Red Ditch she didn't get too many chances to show what she was made of. She had to concentrate on not looking happy.

The parking lot began to fill with parents who had heard that something bad was happening at the school. With the principal and her secretary absent, there was no one to take charge until the school guidance counselor stepped up, driving over from the nearby high school to do the right thing.

Once I'd turned down an ambulance ride and I'd explained to the police why I'd been on the spot, no one seemed too interested in me. I went into the principal's bathroom, since there was no one to stop me, and I carefully wiped away all the visible blood—Ms. Minter's, and my own from the glass. My T-shirt was a mess, so I gave it to the policeman, who seemed to want it. I rummaged in the big box labeled "Donations" until I found a T-shirt that was way too tight but covered everything . . . just barely. It was better than being bloody.

I got a lot more attention from the state guys after I emerged in the tighter T-shirt.

But eventually I was able to walk back to the Pony Room to give Ms. Yarnell a hug. The kids were in surprisingly good spirits, which was a credit to their teacher. Hunter was just as glad to see me as he had been the first time I'd arrived that day, but he was definitely more subdued in expressing his pleasure. Ms. Yarnell had told the children that while they were waiting to find out what would happen the rest of the day, they might as well be celebrating Labor Day by partying.

A couple of the kids were too distressed, but most of them had gone along with the plan of singing the newly learned "America the Beautiful" and eating cupcakes. They'd poured out the contents of their goody bags as children ought to do. Hunter had gotten a thank-you hug from one little girl with about ten pigtails carefully composed in squares, and a big smile from a tousle-headed boy with cowboy boots. Hunter was doing his best to play a tune on his harmonica.

I hadn't spotted Remy out front, but then the police hadn't given me much of a chance to look. They were trying to take pictures of the lobby area and figure out the sequence of events.

They also seemed a little puzzled at some of the odder parts of the story.

They thought Sabrina had been suicidally lucky in throwing things at a shooter, and criminally irresponsible at opening the door of her room to step out into the hall. I didn't know if she'd even keep her job in Red Ditch after this. She was well aware of that possibility. "I couldn't let him keep on going," she said quietly, as we stood alone behind her desk.

"It bothers me that it took a lot of us to stop him," I confessed.

"Did any of us have a gun until the cop showed up?" she demanded.

"Did he have any restraint, any of the rules of morality or society, when he broke into the school?"

I eyed her with some curiosity. Sabrina was a much more philosophical witch than my friend Amelia. "No, he was purely the devil," I said. "He wasn't hiding anything. That was the real Brady."

"So we all had to show what we really were, too," she said quietly. "And look, we brought down the bad guy. And they don't suspect, none of them."

The inexplicable weakness in Brady's gun arm had been written down to some kind of heart event or even a stroke, and he would be having tests in the hospital after he'd been searched and booked at the jail. Several of the cops had even wished aloud that Brady *had* had a heart attack, one violent enough to kill him. They were eye-for-eye people . . . in their own, true hearts. And I didn't think anyone who had arrived on the scene, or even the officer who'd actually witnessed the event, knew that Sabrina's attack with the apples had been planned to make him look at her, give her magic a chance to weaken him. The police were convinced that only my grip on Brady's ankle had kept him from charging down to the Pony Room and killing everyone in there. They would never know what Sabrina and I really were. At least Ms. Minter would get credit for her outstanding presence of mind and courage; those were her true attributes.

I looked at Sabrina and smiled. "Well, you're right. We did our best with our own gifts. Now we've got to put them under wraps again. Someday, maybe, we'll get to be what we are."

There was so much we didn't know in this world. But looking at the children, some of them playing at the back of the room, some of them obviously distressed and ready to reunite with their parents, I could see that there was a future, that what kids were learning in classrooms all over America was not going to stop because sometimes kids experienced terrifying or simply unfamiliar stuff. . . .

Hunter's little friend, the boy in the cowboy boots, ran up to grab one of Ms. Yarnell's apples and threw it squarely at another little boy, just as he'd seen her do.

Yells of anger. Tears.

Yeah, some things about school would never change.

Spellcaster 2.0

JONATHAN MABERRY

Jonathan Maberry is a *New York Times* bestselling author, multiple Bram Stoker Award winner, and Marvel Comics writer. He's the author of a dozen novels in several genres and many nonfiction books on topics ranging from martial arts to supernatural folklore. Since 1978 he has sold more than twelve hundred magazine feature articles, three thousand columns, two plays, greeting cards, song lyrics, poetry, and textbooks. He founded the Writers Coffeehouse and cofounded the Liars Club, and is a frequent keynote speaker and guest of honor at major writers and genre conferences. Visit him online at jonathanmaberry .com and on Twitter (@jonathanmaberry) and Facebook.

--1--

"Username?"

"You're going to laugh at me."

Trey LaSalle turned to her but said nothing. He wore very hip, very expensive tortoiseshell glasses and he let them and his two-hundred-dollar haircut do his talking for him. The girl withered.

"It's . . . obvious?" she said awkwardly, posing it as a question.

"Let me guess. It's going to be a famous magician, right? Which one, I wonder? Won't be *Merlin* because even *you're* not that obvious, and it won't be *Nostradamus* because I doubt you could spell it."

"I can spell," she said, but there was no emphasis to it.

"Hmm. *StGermaine?* No? *Dumbledore? Gandalf?*"

"It's—"

He pursed his lips. "Girl, please don't tell me it really *is Merlin*."

Anthem blushed herself mute.

"Jesus save me." Trey rubbed his eyes and typed in MERLIN with slow sarcasm, each keystroke separate and very sharp. By the fourth letter Anthem's eyes were jumping.

Her name was really Anthem. Her parents were right-wing second gens of left-wing Boomers from the Village, a confusion of genetics and ideologies that resulted in a girl who was bait fish for everyone at the University of Pennsylvania with an IQ higher than their belt size. Though barely a palate cleanser for a shark like Trey. He sipped his pumpkin spice latte and sighed.

"Password?" he prompted.

"You're going to make fun of me again."

"There's that chance," he admitted. "Is it too cute, too personal or too stupid?" He carved off slices of each word and spread them out thin and cold. He was good at that. Back in high school his snarky tone would have earned him a beating—had, in fact, earned him several beatings; but then he conquered the cool crowd. Thereafter they kept him well-protected, well-appeased and well-stocked with a willing audience of masochists who had already begun to learn that anyone with a truly lethal wit was never—*ever*—to be mocked or harmed. In that environment, Trey LaSalle had flourished into the self-satisfied diva he now enjoyed being. Now, in his junior year at U of P, Trey owned the in-crowd and their hangers-on because he was able to work the sassy gay BFF role as if the trope were built for him. At the same time he could also play the get-it-done team leader when the chips were down.

Those chips were certainly down right now. Trey figured that Jonesy and Bird had gotten Anthem to call Trey for a bailout because she was so thoroughly a Bambi in the brights that even he wouldn't actually slaughter her.

"Password?" He drew it into a hiss.

Anthem chewed a fingernail. Despite the fact that she painted her nails, they were all nibbled down to nubs. A couple of them even had blood caked along the sides from where she'd cannibalized herself a bit too aggressively, and there were faint chocolate-colored smears of it on the keyboard. Trey made a mental note to bathe in Purell when he got back to his room.

"Come on, girl," he coaxed.

She blurted it. *"Abracadabra."*

Trey stared at the screen and tried very hard not to close the laptop and club her to death with it. He typed it in. The display changed from the bland log-in screen to the landing page for The Spellcaster Project.

The project.

It sounded simple, but wasn't. Over the course of the last eighteen months the group had collected, organized and committed to computer memory every evocation and conjuring spell known to the various beliefs of human culture, from phonetic interpretations of guttural verbal chants by remote Brazilian tribes to complex rituals in Latin and Greek. On the surface the project was a searchable database so thorough that it would be the go-to resource. A resource for which access could be leased, opening a cash flow for the folklore department. And, people would definitely pay. This database—nicknamed Spellcaster—was a researcher's dream.

Trey found it all fascinating but considered it immensely silly at the same time. He was a scientist, or becoming one, and yet his field of study involved nothing that he believed in. Doctors at least believed in healing, but folklorists were a notoriously atheistic lot. Demons and gods, spells and sacred rituals. None of it was remotely real. All of it was an attempt to make sense of a world that could not be truly understood or defined, and certainly not controlled. Things just happened. Nobody was at the controls, and nobody was taking calls from the human race.

And yet with all that, it was fascinating, like watching a car wreck. You don't want to be a part of it but you can't look away. He even went to church sometimes, just to study the people, to mentally catalog the individual ways in which they interpreted the religion to which they ascribed. There was infinite variation within a species, just as within flowers in a field. And soon he would be making money from it, and that was something he *could* believe in.

The second aspect of the project was Spellcaster 2.0, which began as Trey's idea but along the way had somehow become Professor Davidoff's. In essence, once the thousands of spells were entered, a program would run through all of them to look for common elements. Developmental goals included a determination of how many common themes appeared in spells and what themes appeared in a majority, or at least a significant number of them. The end goal was to create a perfect generic spell. A spell that established that there were some aspects to magical conjuring that linked the disparate tribes and cultures of mankind.

Trey's hypothesis was that anthropologists would be able to use that information, along with related linguistic models, to more accurately track the spread of humankind from its African origins. It might effectively prove that the spread of religion in all of its many forms stemmed from the same central source. Or—as he privately thought of it—mankind's first big stupid mistake. In other words, the birth of prayer and organized religion.

Finding that would be a watershed moment in anthropology, folklore, sociology and history. It would be a Nobel Prize no-brainer, and it didn't matter to Trey if he shared that prize, and all of the fame and—no doubt—fortune that went with it. Spellcaster was going to make them all rich.

"Okay," Trey said, "why are we here?"

Anthem chewed her lip. She did it prettily, and even though she was the wrong cut of meat for Trey's personal tastes, he had to admit that she was all that. She was an East Coast blonde with ice-pale skin, luminous green eyes, a figure that could make any kind of clothes look good and Scarlett Johansson lips. Shame that she was dumber than a cruller. He was considering bringing her into his circle; not the circle-jerk of grad students to which they both currently belonged, but the more elite group he went clubbing with. Arm candy like that worked for everyone, straight or gay. It was better than a puppy and it didn't pee on the carpet. Though, with Anthem there was no real guarantee that she was housebroken.

The lip-chewing had no real effect on him, and Trey studied her to see how long it would take her to realize it. Seven Mississippis.

"I've been hacked," she said.

"Get right out of town."

"And they've been in my laptop messing with my stuff."

"The spells?"

"Some of them, yes."

Trey felt the first little flutter of panic.

"I've been inputting the evocation spells for the last couple of weeks,"

Anthem explained. "One group at a time. Last week it was Gypsy stuff from Serbia, before that it was the preindustrial Celtic stuff. It's hard to do. None of it was translated and Professor Davidoff didn't want us to use Babelfish or any of the other online translators because they don't give cultural or—What's the word?"

"Contextual?"

"Right. They don't give cultural or contextual translations, and that's supposed to be important for spells."

"*Crucial* is a better word," Trey murmured, "but I take your point."

"I had to compare what I typed with photocopies from old spell books. After I finish this stuff Kidd will add the binding spells, then Jonesy will do the English translations. Bird's doing the footnotes, and I guess you'll be working on the annotations."

"Uh-huh."

"At first Jonesy dictated the spells while I typed, but that only really worked with Latin and the Romance languages because we kind of knew the spellings. More and more, though, I had to look at it myself to make sure it was exact. Everything had to match or the professor would freak. And there are all those weird little symbol thingies on some of the letters."

"Diacritical marks."

"Yeah, those." She began nibbling at her thumbnail, talking around it as she chewed. "Without everything just so, the spells won't work."

Trey smiled a tolerant smile. "Sweetie, the spells won't work because they're spells. None of this crap works, you know that."

She stared at him for a moment, still working on the thumb. "They *used* to work, though, didn't they?"

"This is science, honey. The only magic here is the way you're working that sweater and the supernatural way I'm working these jeans."

She said, "Okay." But she didn't sound convinced, and it occurred to Trey that he didn't know where Anthem landed on the question of faith. If she was a believer, then that was a tick against her becoming part of his circle.

"You were saying about the data entry?" he prompted, steering her back to safer ground.

Anthem blinked. "Oh, sure. It's hard. It's all brain work."

Trey said nothing to that. It would be too easy; it would be like kicking a sleepy kitten. Instead he asked, "So what happened?"

Anthem suddenly stopped biting her thumb and they both looked at the bead of blood that welled from where she'd bitten too deeply. Without saying a word, Anthem tore a piece of Scotch tape from a dispenser and wrapped it around the wound.

"Every day I start by checking the previous day's entries to make sure they're all good."

"And—?"

"The stuff I entered last night was different."

"Different how?"

"Let me show you." Anthem leaned past him and her fingers began flying over the keys. Whatever else she was or wasn't, she could type like a demon. Very fast and very accurate. The world lost a great typist when she decided to pursue higher education, mused Trey.

Anthem pulled up a file marked *18CenFraEvoc*, scrolled down to one of the spells, then tapped the screen with a bright green fingernail. "There, see? I found the first changes in the ritual the professor is going to use for the debut thingy."

Trey's French was passable and he bent closer and studied the lines, frowning as he did so. Anthem was correct in that this ritual—the *faux* summoning of Azeziz, demon of knowledge and faith—was a key element in Professor Davidoff's plans to announce their project to the academic world. Even a slight error would embarrass the professor, and he was not a forgiving man. Less so than, say, Hitler.

Anthem opened a file folder that held a thick sheaf of high-res scans of pages from a variety of sources. She selected a page and held it up next to the screen. "This is how it should read."

Trey clicked his eyes back and forth between the source and target materials and then he did see it. In one of the spells the wording had been changed. The second sentence read: *With the Power of the Eternal I Conjure Thee to My Service.*

It should have read: *With the Power of My Faith in the Eternal I Conjure and Bind Thee to My Service.*

"You see?" Anthem asked again. "It's different. There's nothing about the conjurer *believing*. That throws it all off, right?"

"In theory," he said dryly. "This could have been a mistype."

"No way," she said. "I always check my previous day's stuff before I start anything new. I don't make those kinds of mistakes."

The pride in her voice was palpable, and in truth Trey could not recall ever making a correction in any of her work before. The team had been hammering away at the project for eighteen months. They'd created hundreds of pages of original work, and entered thousands of pages of collected data. After a few mishaps with other team members handling data entry, the bulk of it had been shifted to Anthem.

"It's weird, right?" she asked.

He sat back and folded his arms. "It's weird. And, yes, you've been hacked."

"By who? I mean, it has to be one of the team, right? But Jonesy doesn't know French. I don't think Bird does, either."

Jonesy was a harmless mouse of a kid. Bird was sharper, but he was an idealist and adventurer. Bird wanted to chew peyote with the Native American Church and go on spirit walks. He wanted to whirl with the Dervishes and trance out with the Charismatics. Unlike Trey and every other anthropologist Trey knew, Bird was in the field for the actual beliefs. Bird apparently believed that everyone was right, that every religion, no matter how batty, had a clue to the Great Big Picture as he called it. Trey liked him, but except for the project they had nothing in common.

Would Bird do this, though? Trey doubted it, partly because it was mean—and Bird didn't have fangs at all—and mostly because it was disrespectful to the belief systems. As if anyone would really *care*. Except the thesis committee.

"What about Kidd?" asked Anthem. "It would be like him to do something mean like this."

That much was true. Michael Kidd was a snotty, self-important little snob from Philly's Main Line. Good-looking in a verminous sort of way. Kidd was cruising through college on family money and never pretended otherwise. Even Davidoff walked softly around him.

But, would Kidd sabotage the project? Yeah, he really might. Just for shits and giggles.

"The slimy little rat-sucking weasel," said Trey.

"So it *is* Kidd?"

Trey did not commit. He would have bet twenty bucks on it, but that wasn't the same as saying it out loud. Especially to someone like Anthem. He cut a covert look at her and for a moment his inner bitch softened. She was really a sweet kid. Clueless in a way that did no one any harm, not even herself. Anthem wasn't actually stupid, just not sharp and would probably never be sharp. Not unless something broke her and left jagged edges; and wouldn't that be sad?

"Is this only with the French evocation spell?" he asked.

"No." She pulled up the Serbian Gypsy spells. Neither of them could read the language, but a comparison of source and target showed definite differences. Small, but there. "I went back as far as the Egyptian burial symbols. Ten separate files, ten languages, which is crazy 'cause none of us can speak all of those languages."

"What about the Aramaic and Babylonian?"

"I haven't entered them yet."

Trey thought about it, then nodded. "Okay, let's do this. Go in and make the corrections. Before you do, though, I'm going to set you up with a new username and new password."

"Okay." She looked relieved.

"How much do you have to do on this?" Trey asked. "Are we going to make the deadline?"

The deadline was critical. Professor Davidoff was planning to make an official announcement in less than a month. He had a big event planned for it, and warned them all every chance he could that departmental grant money was riding on this. Big-time money. He never actually threatened them, but they could all see the vultures circling.

Anthem nibbled as she considered the stacks of folders on her desk. "I can finish in three weeks."

"That's cutting it close."

Anthem's nibbling increased.

"Look," he said, "I'll spot-check you and do all the transfers to the mainframe. Don't let anyone else touch your laptop for any reason. No one, okay?"

"Okay," she said, relieved but still dubious. "Will that keep whoever's doing this out of the system?"

"Sure," said Trey. "This should be the end of it."

--2--

It wasn't.

--3--

"Tell me exactly what's been happening," demanded Professor Davidoff.

Trey and the others sat in uncomfortable metal folding chairs that were arranged in a half circle around the acre of polished hardwood that was the professor's desk. The walls were heavy with books and framed certificates, each nook and corner filled with oddments. There were juju sticks and human skulls, bottles of ingredients for casting spells—actual eye of newt and bat's wing—and ornate reliquaries filled with select bits of important dead people.

Behind the desk, sitting like a heathen king among his spoils, was Alexi Davidoff, professor of folklore, professor of anthropology, department chair and master of all he surveyed. Davidoff was a bear of a man with Einstein hair, mad-scientist eyebrows, black-framed glasses and a suit that cost more than Trey's education.

The others in the team looked at Trey. Anthem and Jonesy on his left—a cabal of girl power; Bird and Kidd on his right, representing two ends of the evolutionary bell curve—evolved human and moneyed Neanderthal.

"Well, sir," began Trey, "we're hitting a few little speed bumps."

The professor arched an eyebrow. "'Speed bumps'?"

Trey cleared his throat. "There have been a few anomalies in the data and—"

Davidoff raised a finger. It was as sure a command to stop as if he'd raised a scepter. "No," he said, "don't take the long way around. Come right out and say it. *Own* it, Mr. LaSalle."

Kidd coughed but it sounded suspiciously like, "Nut up."

Trey pretended not to have heard. To Davidoff, he said, "Someone has hacked into the Spellcaster data files on Anthem's computer."

They all watched Davidoff's complexion undergo a prismatic change from its normal never-go-outside pallor to a shade approximating a boiled lobster.

"Explain," he said gruffly.

Trey took a breath and plunged in. In the month since Anthem sought his help with the sabotage of the data files her computer had been hacked five times. Each time it was the same kind of problem, with minor changes being made to conjuring spells. With each passing week Trey became more convinced that Kidd was the culprit. Kidd was in charge of research for the team, which meant that he was uniquely positioned to obtain translations of the spells, and to arrange the rewording of them, since he was in direct contact with the various experts who were providing translations in return for footnotes. Only Jonesy had as much contact with the translators, and Trey didn't for a moment think that she would want to harm Anthem, or the project. However, he dared not risk saying any of this here and now. Not in front of everyone, and not without proof. Davidoff was rarely sympathetic and by no means an ally.

On the other hand, Trey knew that the professor had the typical academic's fear and loathing of scandal. Research data and drafts of papers were sacrosanct, and until it was published even the slightest blemish or question could ruin years of work and divert grants aimed at Davidoff's tiny department.

"Has anything been stolen?" Davidoff asked, his voice low and deadly.

"There's . . . um . . . no way to tell, but if they've been into Anthem's computer then nothing would have prevented them from copying everything."

"What about the bulk data on the department mainframe?" growled Davidoff.

"No way," said Bird doubtfully. "Has that been breached?"

Trey dialed some soothing tones into his voice. "No. I check it every day and the security software tracks every log-in. It's all clean. Whatever's happening is confined to Anthem's laptop."

"Have all the changes been corrected before uploading to the mainframe?" asked Davidoff.

"Absolutely."

That was a lie. There were two hundred gigabytes of documents that had been copied from Anthem's computer. It would take anyone months to read through it all, and probably years to compare every line to the photocopies of source data.

"You're sure?" Davidoff persisted.

"Positive," lied Trey.

"Are we still on schedule? We're running this in four days. We have guests coming. We have press coming. I've invested a lot of the department's resources into this."

He wasn't joking and Trey knew it. Davidoff had booked the university's celebrated Annenberg Center for the Performing Arts and hired a professional event coordinator to run things. There was even a bit of "fun" planned for the evening. Davidoff had had a bunch of filmmakers from nearby Drexel University do some slick animation that would be projected as a hologram onto tendrils of smoke rising from vents in the floor around a realistic mock-up of a conjuring circle. The effect would be the sudden "appearance" of a demon. Davidoff would then interact with the demon, following a script that Trey himself had drafted. In their banter, the demon would extol the virtues of Spellcaster and discuss the benefits of the research to the worldwide body of historical and folkloric knowledge, and do everything to praise the project, short of dropping to his knees and giving Davidoff some oral love.

There were so many ways it could go wrong that he almost wished he could pray for divine providence, but not even a potential disaster was going to put Trey on his knees.

"Sir," Trey said, "while I believe we're safe and in good shape, we really should run Spellcaster 2.0 ourselves before the actual show."

"No."

"But—"

"You do realize, Mr. LaSalle, that the reason the press and the dignitaries will all be there is that we're running this in real time. They get to share in it. That's occurred to you, hasn't it?"

Yes, you grandstanding shithead, Trey thought. *It occurred to me for all of the reasons that I recommended that we not go that route.* He wanted to play it safe, to run the program several times and verify the results rather than go for the insane risk of what might amount to a carnival stunt.

Trey held his tongue and gave a single nod of acquiescence.

"Then we run it on schedule," the professor declared. "Now—how did this happen? By *magic*?"

A couple of the others laughed at this, but the laughs were brief and uncertain, because clearly this wasn't a funny moment. Davidoff glared them into silence.

Trey said, "I don't know, but we're doing everything we can to make sure that it doesn't affect the project."

The Spellcaster project was vital to all of them, but for different reasons. For personal glory, for a degree, for the opportunities it would offer and the doors it would open. So, Trey could understand why the vein on the professor's forehead throbbed so mightily.

"I've done extensive online searches," Trey said, using his most businesslike voice, "and there's nothing. Not a sentence of what we've recorded, not a whiff of our thesis, nothing."

"That doesn't mean they won't publish it," grumbled Jonesy, speaking up for the first time since the meeting began.

"I don't think so," said Trey. "The stuff on Anthem's laptop is just the spell catalog. None of the translations are there and none of the bulk research and annotations are there. At worst they can publish a partial catalog."

"That would still hurt us," said Bird. "If we lost control of that, license money would spill all over the place."

Trey shook his head. "The shine on that candy is its completeness. All of the spells, all of the methods of conjuration and evocation, every single binding spell. There's no catalog like it anywhere, and what's on the laptop now is at most fifty percent, and that's nice, but it's not the Holy Grail."

"I think Trey's right, Professor," said Jonesy. "We should do a test run. I mean, what if one or more of those rewritten errors made it to the mainframe? If that happened and we run Spellcaster 2.0, how could we trust our findings?"

"No way we could," said Kidd, intending it to be mean and scoring nicely. The big vein on the professor's forehead throbbed visibly.

Trey ignored Kidd. "We have some leeway—"

Jonesy shook her head. "The 2.0 software is configured to factor in accidental or missed keystrokes, not sabotage."

Shut up, you cow, thought Trey, but Jonesy plowed ahead.

"Deliberate alteration of the data will look like what it is. Rewording doesn't look like bad typing. If it's there, then all our hacker has to do is let us miss one of the changes he made and wait for us to publish. Then he steps forward and tells everyone that our data management is polluted . . ."

". . . and he'd be able to point to specific flaws," finished Bird. "We not only wouldn't have reliable results, we wouldn't have the perfect generic spell that would be the signpost we're looking for. We'd have nothing. Oh, man . . . we'd be so cooked."

One by one they turned to face Professor Davidoff. His accusing eye shifted away from Trey and landed on Anthem, who withered like an orchid in a cold wind. "So, this is a matter of you being stupid and clumsy, is that what I'm hearing?"

Anthem was totally unable to respond. She went a whiter shade of pale, and she looked like a six-year-old who was caught out of bed. Her pretty lips formed a lot of different words but Trey did not hear her make as much as a squeak. Tiny tears began to wobble in the corners of her eyes. The others kept themselves absolutely still. Kidd chuckled very quietly, and Trey wanted to kill him.

"It's not Anthem's fault," said Trey, coming quickly to her defense. "Her data entry is—"

Davidoff made an ugly, dismissive noise and his eyes were locked on Anthem's. "There are plenty of good typists in the world," he said unkindly. "Being one of them does not confer upon you nearly as much importance as you would like to believe."

Trey quietly cleared his throat. "Sir, since Anthem first alerted me to the problem I've been checking her work, and some of the anomalies occurred *after* I verified the accuracy of her entries. This isn't Anthem's fault. I changed her username and password after each event."

Davidoff considered this, then gave a dismissive snort. It was as close to an apology as his massive personal planet ever orbited.

"Then . . . we're safe?" ventured Bird hopefully.

Trey licked his lips, then nodded.

Davidoff's vein was no longer throbbing quite as aggressively. "Then we proceed as planned. Real test, real time." He raised his finger of doom. "Be warned, Mr. LaSalle, this is your neck on the line. You are the team leader. It's your responsibility. I don't want to hear excuses after something else happens. All I ever want to hear is that Spellcaster is secure. I don't care who you have to kill to protect the integrity of that data, but you keep it safe. Do I make myself clear?"

Trey leaned forward and put his hands on the edge of Davidoff's desk. "Believe me, Professor, when I find out who's doing this I swear to God I will rip his goddamn heart out."

He could feel everyone's eyes on him.

The professor sat back and pursed his lips, studying Trey with narrowed, calculating eyes. "See that you do," he said quietly. "Now all of you . . . get out."

--4--

Trey spent the next few hours walking the windy streets of University City. He was deeply depressed and his stomach was a puddle of acid tension. As he walked, he heard car horns and a few shouts, laughter from the open doors of sports bars on the side streets. A few sirens wailed with ghostly insistence in the distance. He heard those things, but he didn't register any of it.

Trey's mind churned on it. Not on why this was happening, but who was doing it?

After leaving Davidoff, Trey had gone to see his friend Herschel and the crew of geeks at the computer lab. These were the kinds of uber-nerds who once would have never gotten laid and never moved out of their mothers' basements—stereotypes all the way down to the Gears of War T-shirts and cheap sneakers. Now, guys like that were rock stars. They *got* laid. They all had jobs waiting for them after graduation. Most of them wouldn't bother with school after they had a bachelor's because the industry wanted them young and raw and they wanted them now.

These were the guys who hacked ultra-secret corporate computer systems just because they were bored. Guys who made some quick cash on the side writing viruses that they sold to the companies who sold anti-virus software.

Trey explained the situation to them.

They thought it was funny.

They thought it was cool.

They told him half a dozen ways *they* could do it.

"Even Word docs on a laptop that's turned off?" demanded Trey. "I thought that was impossible."

Herschel laughed. "*Impossible* isn't a word, brah, it's a challenge."

"What?"

"It's the *Titanic*," said Herschel.

"Beg pardon?"

"The *Titanic*. The unsinkable ship. You got to understand the mindset." Herschel was an emaciated runt with nine-inch hips and glasses you could fry ants with. At nineteen he already held three patents and his girlfriend was a spokesmodel at gaming shows. "Computers—hardware *and* software—are incredibly sophisticated idiots, feel me? They can only do what they're programmed to do. Even A.I. isn't really independent thinking. It's not intuitive."

"Okay," conceded Trey. "So?"

"So, what man can invent, man can fuck up. Look at home security systems. As soon as the latest unbreakable, unshakeable, untouchable system goes on the market someone has to take it down. Not wants to . . . *has* to."

"Why?"

"Because it's there, brah. Because it's all about toppling the arrogant assholes in corporate America who make those kinds of claims. Can't be opened, can't be hacked, can't be sunk. *Titanic*, man."

"Man didn't throw an iceberg at the ship, Hersch."

"No, the universe did that because it's a universal imperative to kick arrogant ass."

"Booyah," agreed the other hackers, bumping fists.

"So," said Trey slowly, "you think someone's hacking our research because he can?"

Herschel shrugged. "Why else?"

"Not to try to sell it?"

Some of the computer geeks laughed. Herschel said, "Sell that magic hocus-pocus shit and you're going to make—what? A few grand? Maybe a few hundred grand in the long run after ten years busting your ass?"

"At *least* that much," Trey said defensively.

"Get a clue, dude. You got someone hacking a closed system on a laptop and changing unopened files in multiple languages. That's *real* magic. A guy like that wouldn't wipe his ass with a hundred grand. All he has to do is file a patent on how he did it and everyone in corporate R and D will be lining up to blow him. Guy like that wouldn't answer the phone for any offer lower than the middle seven figures."

"Booyah!" agreed the geek chorus.

"Sorry, brah," said Herschel, clapping Trey on the shoulder, "but this might not even be about your magic spell bullshit. You could just be a friggin' test drive."

Trey left, depressed and without a clue of where to go next. The profile of his unknown enemy did not seem to fit anyone on the project. Bird and Jonesy were as good with computers as serious students and researchers could be, but at the end of the day they were really only Internet savvy. They would never have fit in with Herschel's crowd. Anthem knew everything about word processing software but beyond that she was in unknown territory. Kidd was no computer geek, either. Although, Trey mused, Kidd could afford to hire a geek. Maybe even a really good geek, one of Herschel's crowd. Someone who could work the kind of sorcery required to break into Anthem's computer.

But . . . how to prove it?

God, he wished he really could go and rip Kidd's heart out. If the little snot even had one.

The sirens were getting louder and the noise annoyed him. Every night it was the same. Football jocks and the frat boys with their perpetual parties, as if belly shots and beer pong genuinely mattered in the cosmic scheme of things. Neanderthals.

Without even meaning to do it, Trey's feet made a left instead of a right and carried him down Sansom Street toward Kidd's apartment.

He suddenly stopped walking and instantly knew that no confrontation with Kidd was going to happen that night.

The entire street was clogged with people who stood in bunches and vehicles parked at odd angles.

Police vehicles. And an ambulance.

"Oh . . . shit," he said.

--5--

Tearing out Kidd's heart was no longer an option.

According to every reporter on the scene, someone had already beaten him to it.

--6--

The following afternoon they all met in Trey's room. The girls perched on the side of his bed; Bird sprawled in a papasan chair with his knees up and his arms wrapped around them. Trey stood with his back to the door.

All eyes were on him.

"Cops talk to you?" asked Bird.

"No. You?"

Bird nodded. He looked as scared as Trey felt. "They asked me a few questions."

"Really? Why?"

Bird didn't answer.

"They came around here, too," said Jonesy. "This morning and again this afternoon."

"Why'd they want to see you guys?" asked Trey.

Jonesy gave him a strange look.

"What?" Trey asked.

"They wanted to see you," said Anthem.

"Me? Why would they want to see me?"

Nobody said a word. Nobody looked at him.

Trey said, "Oh, come *on*. You guys have to be frigging kidding me here."

No one said a word.

"You sons of bitches," said Trey. "You think I did it, don't you? You think I could actually kill someone and tear out their frigging heart? Are you all on crack?"

"Cops said that whoever killed him must have gone apeshit on him," murmured Bird.

"So, out of seven billion people suddenly I'm America's Most Wanted?"

"They're calling it a rage crime," said Jonesy.

"Rage," echoed Anthem.

"And you actually think that *I* could do that?"

"Somebody did," said Bird again. "Whoever did it must have hated Kidd because they beat him to a pulp and tore him open. Cops asked us if we knew anyone who hated Kidd that much."

"And you gave them *my* name?"

"We didn't have to," said Anthem. "Everyone on campus knows what you thought of Kidd."

And there was nowhere to go with that except out, so Trey left them all sitting in the desolation of his room.

--**7**--

The cops picked him up at ten the next morning. They said he didn't need a lawyer, they just wanted to ask questions. Trey didn't have a lawyer anyway, so he answered every single question they asked. Even when they asked the same questions six and seven times.

They let him go at eight thirty that night. They didn't seem happy about it.

Neither was Trey.

--8--

The funeral was the following day. They all went. It didn't rain because it only rains at funerals in the movies. They stood under an impossibly blue sky that was littered with cotton candy clouds. Trey stood apart from the others and listened with contempt to the ritual bullshit the priest read out of his book. Kidd had been as much of an atheist as Trey was, and this was a mockery. He'd have skipped it if that wouldn't have made him look even more suspicious.

After the service, Trey took the bus home alone.

He tried several times to call Davidoff, but the professor didn't return calls or emails.

The day ground on.

The Spellcaster premiere was tomorrow. Trey spent the whole day double- and triple-checking the data. He found nothing in any of the files he opened, but in the time he had he was only able to view about 1 percent of the data.

Trey sent twenty emails recommending that the premiere be postponed. He got no answers from the professor. Bird, Jonesy and Anthem said as little to him as possible, but they all kept at it, going about their jobs like worker bees as the premiere drew closer.

--9--

Professor Davidoff finally called him.

"Sir," said Trey, "I've been trying to—"

"We're going ahead with the premiere."

Trey sighed. "Sir, I don't think that's—"

"It's for Michael."

Michael. Not Mr. Kidd. The professor had never called Kidd by his first name. Ever. Trey waited for the other shoe.

"It'll be a tribute to him," continued Davidoff, his pomposity modulated to a funereal hush. "He devoted the last months of his life to this project. He deserves it."

Great, thought Trey, *everyone thinks I'm a psycho killer, and he's practicing sound bites.*

"Professor, we have to stop for a minute to consider the possibility that the sabotage of the project is connected to what happened to Kidd."

"Yes," Davidoff said heavily, "we do."

Silence washed back and forth across the cellular ocean.

"I cannot imagine why anyone would do such a thing," said the professor. "Can you, Mr. LaSalle?"

"Professor, you don't think I—"

"I expect everything to go by the numbers tomorrow, Mr. LaSalle."

Before Trey could organize a reply, Professor Davidoff disconnected.

--10--

And it all went by the numbers.

More or less.

Drawn by the gruesome news story and the maudlin PR spin Davidoff gave it, the Annenberg was filling to capacity, with lines wrapped halfway around the block. Three times the expected number of reporters were there. There was even a picket by a right-wing religious group who wanted the Spellcaster project stopped before it started because it was "ungodly," "blasphemous," "satanic" and a bunch of other words that Trey felt ranged between absurd and silly. The picketers drew media attention and that put even more people in line for the dwindling supply of tickets.

Bird, Jonesy and Anthem showed up in very nice clothes. Bird wore a tie for the first time since Trey had known him. The girls both wore dresses. Jonesy transformed from mouse to wow in a black strapless number that Trey would have never bet she could pull off. Anthem was in green silk that matched her eyes and she looked like a movie star. She even had nail tips over the gnarled nubs of her fingers. Trey was in a black turtleneck and pants. It was as close to being invisible as he could manage.

Davidoff was the ringmaster of the circus. He wore an outrageously gorgeous Glen Urquhart plaid three-piece and even with his ursine bulk he looked like God's richer cousin.

Even the university dons were nodding in approval, happy with the positive media attention following so closely on the heels of the murder.

The as yet unsolved murder, mused Trey. The cops were nowhere with it. Trey was pretty sure he was being followed now. He was a person of interest.

God.

When the audience was packed in, Davidoff walked onto center stage amid thunderous applause. He even contrived to look surprised at the adoration before eventually waving everyone into an expectant silence.

"Before we begin, ladies and gentlemen," he began, "I would like us all to share in a moment of silence. Earlier this week, one of my best and brightest students was killed in a savage and senseless act that still has authorities baffled. No one can make sense of the death of so wonderful a young man as Michael Kidd, Jr. He was on the very verge of a brilliant career, he was about to step into the company of such legendary folklorists as Stetson Kennedy, Archie Green and John Francis Campbell."

Trey very nearly burst out laughing. He cut a look at Bird, who gave him a weary head shake and a half smile, momentarily stunned out of all consideration by the absurdity of that claim.

"I would like to dedicate this evening to Mr. Kidd," continued Davidoff. "He will be remembered, he will be missed."

"Christ," muttered Trey. The stage manager scowled at him.

The whole place dropped into a weird, reverential silence that lasted a full by-the-clock minute. Davidoff raised his arms and a spotlight bathed him in a white glow as the houselights dimmed.

"Magic!" he said ominously in a voice that was filtered through a soundboard that gave it a mysterious-sounding reverb. The crowd ooohed and aaahed. "We have always believed in a larger world. Call it religion, call it superstition, call it the eternal mystery . . . we all believe in something. Even those of us who claim to believe in nothing—we will still knock on wood and pick up a penny only if it is heads up. Somewhere, past the conscious will and the civilized mind, the primitive in us remembers cowering in caves or crouching in the tall grass, or perching apelike on the limb of a tree as the wheel of night turned above and darkness covered the world."

Trey mouthed the words along with the professor. Having written them he knew the whole speech by heart.

"But what is magic? Is magic the belief that we live in a universe of infinite possibilities? Yes, but it's also *more* than that. It's the belief that we can *control* the forces of that universe. That we are not flotsam in the stream of cosmic events, but rather that we are creators ourselves. Cocreators with the infinite. Our sentience—the beautiful, impossible fact of human self-awareness and intelligence—lifts us above all other creatures in our natural world and connects us to the boundless powers of what we call the *super*natural."

From there Davidoff segued into an explanation of the Spellcaster project. Trey had to admit that his script sounded pretty good. He'd taken what could have been dry material and given it richness by an infusion of some pop-culture phrasing and a few juicy superlatives. The audience loved it, and they were carried along by a multimedia show that flashed images on a dozen screens. Pictures from illuminated texts. Great works of sacred art. Churches and temples, tombs and crypts, along with hundreds of photos of everything from Mickey Mouse as the Sorcerer's Apprentice to Gandalf the Grey. And there were images of holy people from around the world: Maori with their tattooed faces, Navajo shamans singing over complex sand paintings, medicine men from tiny tribes deep in the heart of the Amazon, and singers of sacred songs from among the Bushmen of Africa. It was deliberate sensory overload, accompanied by a remix mash-up of musical pieces ranging from Ozzy Osbourne to Mozart to Loreena McKennitt.

Then the floor opened and a gleaming computer rose into the light. It wasn't the department mainframe, of course, but a prop with lots of polished metal fixtures that did nothing except look cool. A laptop was positioned inside, out of sight of the audience. Smoke began rising with it, setting the stage for the evocation to come.

Suddenly four figures, two men and two women in black robes lined with red satin swirling around them, stepped onto the stage. Juniors from the dance department. They did a few seconds of complex choreography that was, somehow, supposed to symbolize a ritual, and then they produced items from within their cloaks and began drawing a conjuring circle on the floor. Other dancers came out and lit candles, placing them at key points. The floor was discreetly marked so the dancers could do everything just so. Even though this was all for show, it had to be done right. This was still college.

The conjurer's circle was six feet across, and this was surrounded by three smaller circles. Davidoff explained that the center circle represented Earth, the smaller circle at the apex of the design represented the unknown, the circle to his right was the safe haven of the conjurer; and the circle to the left represented the realm of the demon who was to be conjured.

It was all done correctly.

Then to spook things up, Davidoff explained how this could all go horribly, horribly wrong.

"A careless magician summons his own death," he said in his stentorian voice. "All of the materials need to be pure. Vital essences—blood, sweat or tears—must never be allowed within the demon's circle, for these form a bridge between the worlds of spirit and flesh."

The crowd gasped in horror as images from *The Exorcist* flashed onto the screens.

"A good magician is a scholar of surpassing skill. He does not make errors . . . or, rather, he makes only *one* error."

He paused for laughter and got it.

"A learned magician is a quiet and solitary person. All of his learning, all of his preparation for this ritual, must be played out in his head. He cannot practice his invocations because magical words each have its special power. To casually speak a spell is to open a doorway that might never be shut."

More images from horror movies emphasized his point. The dancer-magicians took up positions at key points around the circle.

"If everything is done just right," continued Davidoff, "the evocation can begin. This is the moment for which a magician prepares his entire life. This is the end result of thousands of hours of study, of sacrifice, of purification and preparation. The magician hopes to draw into this world—into the confined and contained protection of a magic circle—a demon of immeasurable wisdom and terrible power. Contained within the circle, the demon *must* obey the sorcerer. Cosmic laws decree that this is so!"

The audience was spellbound, which Trey thought very appropriate. He found himself caught up in the magic that Davidoff was weaving. It was all going wonderfully so far. He cut looks at the others and they were all smiling, the horrors of their real world momentarily forgotten.

Davidoff stepped into the Earth circle. "Tonight we will conjure Azeziz—the demon of spells and magic. The demon of *belief* in the larger world! It is he who holds all knowledge of the ways of sorcery that the dark forces *lent* to mankind in the dawn of our reign on Earth. Azeziz will share with us the secrets of magic, and will then guide us toward the discovery of the perfect spell. The spell that may well be the core magical ritual from which *all* of our world's religions have sprung."

He paused to let that sink in. Trey replayed the spell in his head, verifying that it was the correct wording and not any version of the mistakes that kept showing up in Anthem's computer. It all seemed correct, and he breathed a sigh of relief.

"Azeziz will first appear to us as a sphere of pure energy and will then coalesce into a more familiar form. A form that all of us here will recognize, and one in which we will take comfort." He smiled. "Join me now as we open the doorway to knowledge that belongs jointly to all of mankind—the knowledge that we do, in truth, live in a *larger world*."

As he began the spell, Davidoff's voice was greatly amplified so that it echoed off the walls. "Come forth, Azeziz! O great demon, hear my plea. I call thee up by the power of this circle! By thine own glyph inscribed with thy name I summon thee."

Suddenly a ball of light burst into being inside the demon's circle. Trey blinked and gasped along with the audience. It was so bright, much brighter than what he had expected. The lighting guys were really into the moment. The ball hung in the midst of the rising smoke, pulsing with energy, changing colors like a tumbling prism, filling the air with the smell of ozone and sulfur.

Trey frowned.

Sulfur?

He shot a look at the others. Which one of those idiots added that to the special effects menu? But they were frowning, too. Bird turned to him and they studied one another for a moment. Then Bird sniffed almost comically and mouthed: *Kidd?*

Shit, thought Trey. If that vermin had worked some surprises into the show, then he swore he would dig him up and kick his dead ass.

Onstage, Davidoff's smile flickered as he smelled it, too. He blasted a withering and accusatory look at the darkness offstage. Right where he knew Trey would be standing.

Davidoff reclaimed his game face. "Come forth, Azeziz! Appear now that I may have counsel with thee. I conjure thee, ancient demon, without fear and trembling. I am not afraid as I stand within the Circle of the Earth. Come forth and manifest thyself in the circle of protection that is prepared for thee."

The globe of light pulsed and pulsed. Then there was a white-hot flash of light and suddenly a figure stood in the center of the conjuring circle.

The crowd stared goggle-eyed at the tall, portly figure with the wisps of hair drifting down from a bald pate. Laser lights sparkled from the tiny glasses perched on the bulbous nose.

Benjamin Franklin. Founder of the University of Pennsylvania.

The demon smiled.

The audience gaped and then they got the joke and burst out laughing. The hall echoed with thunderous applause as Benjamin Franklin took a bow.

Trey frowned again. He didn't remember there being a bow. Not until the end.

"Speak, O demon!" cried Davidoff as the applause drifted down to an expectant and jovial silence. "Teach us wisdom."

"Wisdom, is it?" asked Franklin. There was something a little off with the prerecorded sound. The voice was oddly rough, gravelly. *"What wisdom would a mortal ask of a demon?"*

Davidoff was right on cue. "We seek the truth of magic," he said. "We seek to understand the mystery of faith. We seek to understand why man *believes.*"

"Ah, but wisdom is costly," said Franklin, and Trey could see Davidoff's half smirk. That comment was a little hook for when the fees to access Spellcaster were presented. Wisdom is costly. Cute.

"We are willing to pay whatever fee you ask, O mighty demon."

"Are you indeed?" asked Franklin, and once more that was something off-script. *"How much would you truly pay to understand belief?"*

None of that was in the script.

Goddamn you, Kidd, thought Trey darkly, and he wondered what other surprises were laid like land mines into the program. Anthem, Bird and Jonesy moved toward him, the four of them reconnecting, however briefly, in what they all now thought was going to be a frigging disaster. If Davidoff was made a fool of, then they were cooked. They were done.

Davidoff soldiered on, fighting to stay ahead of these new twists. "Um, yes, O demon. What is the cost of the knowledge we seek?"

"Oh, I believe you have already paid me my fee," said the demon Ben Franklin, and he smiled. *"My fee was offered up by vow if not by deed."*

He rummaged inside his coat for something.

"What's he doing?" whispered Jonesy.

Bird leaned close. "Please, God, do not let him bring out a doobie or a copy of *Hustler.*"

But that's not what Franklin pulled out from under his coat flaps. He extended his arm and turned his hand palm upward to show Davidoff and everyone what he held.

Davidoff's face went slack, his eyes flaring wide.

A few people, the ones who were closest, gasped.

Then someone screamed.

The thing Franklin held was a human heart.

--11--

Davidoff said, "W-what—?"

Bird gagged.

Jonesy screamed.

Anthem said, "No . . ."
Trey felt as if he were falling.

--**12**--

The demon laughed.

It was not the polite, cultured laughter of an eighteenth-century sci-entist and statesman. It was not anything they had recorded for the event.

The laughter was so loud that the dancers staggered backward, blood erupting from nostrils and ears. It buffeted the audience and the sheer force of it knocked Davidoff to his knees, cupping his hands to his ears.

The audience screamed.

Then the lights went out, plunging the whole place into shrieking darkness.

And came back on a moment later with a brilliance so shocking that everyone froze in place.

The demon turned his palm and let the heart fall to the floor with a wet *plop*.

No one moved.

The demon adjusted his glasses and smiled.

Trey whirled and ran to the tech boards. "Shut it down," he yelled. "Shut it all down. Kill the projectors. Come on—*do it!*"

The techs hit rows of switches and turned dials.

Absolutely nothing changed onstage.

"Stop that, Trey," said Ben Franklin. His voice echoed everywhere. Trey whirled.

"W-what?" he stammered.

"I said, stop it." The demon smiled. *"In fact, come out here. All of you. I want everyone to see you. The four bright lights. My helpers. My facilitators."*

Trey tried to laugh. Tried to curse. Tried to say something witty.

But his legs were moving without his control, carrying him out onto the stage. Jonesy and Anthem came with him, all in a terrified row. They came to the very edge of the circle in which the demon stood.

Bird alone remained where he was.

The audience cried out in fear.

"*Hush,*" said the demon, and every voice was stilled. Their mouths moved but there was no sound. People tried to get out of their seats, to flee, to storm the doors; but no one could rise.

Ben Franklin chuckled mildly. He cocked an eye at Trey. "*This performance is for you. All for you.*"

Trey stared at him, his mind teetering on the edge of a precipice. Davidoff, as silent as the crowd, stood nearby.

"*At the risk of being glib,*" said the demon, "*I think it's fair to say that class is in session. You called me to provide knowledge, and I am ever delighted, as all of my kind are delighted, to bow and scrape before man and give away under duress those secrets we have spent ten million years discovering. It's what we live for. It makes us so . . . happy.*"

When he said the word *happy* lights exploded overhead and showered the audience with smoking fragments that they were entirely unable to avoid. Trey and the others stood helpless at the edge of the circle.

Trey tried to speak, tried to force a single word out. With a flick of a finger the demon freed his lips and the word, "How?" burst out.

Ben Franklin nodded. "*You get a gold star for asking the right question, young Trey. Perhaps I will burn it into your skull.*" He winked. "*Later.*"

Trey's heart hammered with trapped frenzy.

"*You wrote the script for tonight, did you not?*" asked the demon. "*Then you should understand. This is* your *show-and-tell. I am here for you. So . . . you tell me.*"

Suddenly Trey's mouth was moving, forming words, his tongue rebelled and shaped them, his throat gave them sound.

"*A careless magician summons his own death,*" Trey said, but it was Davidoff's voice that issued from his throat. "*All of the materials need to be pure. Vital essences—blood, sweat or tears—must never be allowed within the demon's circle for these form a bridge between the worlds of spirit and flesh.*"

The big screens suddenly flashed with new images. Anthem. Typing, her fingers blurring. The image tightened until the focus was entirely on her fingernails. Nibbled and bitten to the quick, caked with . . .

"Blood," said Anthem, her voice a monotone.

Then Jonesy spoke but it was Davidoff's bass voice that rumbled from her throat. *"A learned magician is a quiet and solitary person. All of his learning, all of his preparation for this ritual must be played out in his head. He cannot practice his invocations because magical words each have their special power. To casually speak a spell is to open a doorway that might never be shut."*

And now the screens showed Jonesy reading the spells aloud as Anthem typed.

Trey closed his eyes. He didn't need to see any more.

"Arrogance is such a strange thing," said the demon. *"You expect it from the powerful because they believe that they are gods. But you . . . Trey, Anthem, Jonesy . . . you should have known better. You did know better. You just didn't care enough to believe that any of it mattered. Pity."*

The demon stepped toward them, crossing the line of the protective circle as if it held no power. And Trey suddenly realized that it did not. Somewhere, the ritual was flawed beyond fixing. Was it Kidd's sabotage or something deeper? From the corner of his eye Trey could see the glistening lines of tears slipping down Anthem's cheeks.

The demon paused and looked at her. *"Your sin is worse. You do believe but you fight so hard not to. You fight to be numb to the larger world so that you will be accepted as a true academic like these others. You are almost beyond saving. Teetering on the brink. If you had the chance, I wonder in which direction you would place your next step."*

A sob, silent and terrible, broke in Anthem's chest. Trey tried to say something to her, but then the demon moved to stand directly in front of him.

"You owe me thanks, my young student," said the demon. *"When the late and unlamented Mr. Kidd tried to spoil the results of your project by altering the protection spells, he caused all of this to happen. He* made *it happen, but not out of reverence for the forces of the universe and certainly not out of any belief in the larger world. He did it simply out of spite. He wanted no profit from your failure except the knowledge that you would be ruined. That was as unwise as it was heartless . . . and I paid him in kind."*

The demon nudged the heart on the floor. It quivered and tendrils of smoke drifted up from it. Trey tried to imagine the terror Kidd must have felt as this monster attacked him and brutalized him, and he found that he felt a splinter of compassion for Kidd.

"You pretend to be scholars," breathed the demon, *"so then here is a lesson to ponder. You think that all of religion, all of faith, all of spirit, is a cultural oddity, an accident of confusion by uneducated minds. An infection of misinformation that spread like a disease, just as man spread like a disease. You, in your arrogance, believe that because you do not believe, there is nothing to believe in. You dismiss all other possibilities because they do not fit into your hypothesis. Like the scientists who say that because evolution is a truth—and it is a truth—there is nothing divine or intelligent in the universe. Or the astronomers who say that the universe is only as large as the stones thrown by the Big Bang."* He touched his lips to Trey's ear. *"Arrogance. It has always been the weakness of man. It's the thing that keeps you bound to the prison of flesh. Oh yes, bound, and it is a prison that does not need to have locked doors."*

Trey opened his eyes. His mouth was still free and he said, "What?"

The demon smiled. *"Arrogance often comes with blindness. Proof of magic surrounds you all the time. Proof that man is far more than a creature of flesh, proof that he can travel through doorways to other worlds, other states of existence. It's all around you."*

"Where?"

The screens once more filled with the images of Maori with their painted faces, and Navajo shamans and their sand paintings; medicine men in the remote Amazon, singers from among the Bushmen of Africa. As Trey watched, the images shifted and tightened so that the dominant feature in each was the eyes of these people.

These believers.

Then ten thousand other sets of eyes flashed across the screens. People of all races, all cultures, all times. Cavemen and saints, simple farmers and scholars endlessly searching the stars for a glimpse of something larger. Something *there*. Never giving up, never failing to believe in the possibility of the larger world. The larger universe.

Even Bird's eyes were there. Just for a moment.

"*Can you, in your arrogance,*" asked the demon, "*look into these eyes and tell me with the immutable certainty of your scientific disbelief that every one of these people is deluded? That they are wrong? That they see nothing? That nothing is there to be seen? Can you stand here and look down the millennia of man's experience on Earth and say that since science cannot measure what they see, then they see nothing at all? Can you tell me that magic does not exist? That it has never existed? Can you, my little student, tell me that? Can you say it with total and unshakeable conviction? Can you, with your scientific certitude, dismiss me into nonexistence, and with me all of the demons and angels, gods and monsters, spirits and shades who walk the infinite worlds of all of time and space?*"

Trey's heart hammered and hammered and wanted to break.

"No," he said. His voice was a ghost of a whisper.

"*No,*" agreed the demon. "*You can't. And how much has that one word cost you, my fractured disbeliever? What, I wonder, do you believe now?*"

Tears rolled down Trey's face.

"*Answer this, then,*" said the demon, "*why am I not bound to the circle of protection? You think that it was because Mr. Kidd played pranks with the wording? No. You found every error. In that you were diligent. And the circles and patterns were drawn with precision. So . . . why am I not bound? What element was missing from this ritual? What single thing was missing that would have given you and these other false conjurers the power to bind me?*"

Trey wanted to scream. Instead he said, "Belief."

"*Belief,*" agreed the demon softly.

"I'm sorry," whispered Trey. "God . . . I'm sorry . . ."

The demon leaned in and his breath was scalding on Trey's cheek. "*Tell me one thing more, my little sorcerer,*" whispered the monster, "*should I believe that you truly are sorry?*"

"Y-yes."

"*Should I have faith in the regrets of the faithless?*"

"I'm sorry," he said. "I . . . didn't know."

The demon chuckled. "*Have you ever considered that atheism as strong as yours is itself a belief?*"

"I—"

"We all believe in something. That is what brought your kind down from the trees. That is what made you human. After all this time, how can you not understand that?"

Trey blinked and turned to look at him.

The demon said, *"You think that science is the enemy of faith. That what cannot be measured cannot be real. Can you measure what is happening now? What meter would you use? What scale?"*

Trey said nothing.

"Your project, your collection of spells. What is it to you? What is it in itself? Words? Meaningless and silly? Without worth?"

Trey dared not reply.

"Who are you to disrespect the shaman and the magus, the witch and the priest? Who are you to say that the child on his knees is a fool; or the crone on the respirator? How vast and cold is your arrogance that you despise the vow and the promise and the prayer of everyone who has ever spoken such words with a true heart?"

The demon touched Trey's chest.

"In the absence of proof you disbelieve. In the absence of proof a child will believe, and belief can change worlds. That's the power you spit upon, and in doing so you deny yourself the chance to shape the universe according to your will. You become a victim of your own close-mindedness."

Tears burned on Trey's flesh.

"Here is a secret," said the demon. *"Believe it or not, as you will. But when we whispered the secrets of evocation to your ancestors, when we taught them to make circles of protection—it was not to protect them from us. No. It was us who wanted protection from you. We swim in the waters of belief. You, and those like you, spit pollution into those waters with doubt and cynicism. With your arrogant disinterest in the ways the universe actually works. When you conjure us, we shudder."* He leaned closer. *"Tell me, little Trey, now that your faithless faith is shattered . . . if you had the power to banish me, would you?"*

Trey had to force the word out. "Yes."

"Even though that would require faith to open the doors between the worlds?"

Trey squeezed his eyes shut. "Y-yes."

"*Hypocrite,*" said the demon, but he was laughing as he said it. *"Here endeth the lesson."*

Trey opened his eyes.

--**13**--

Trey felt his mouth move again. His lips formed a word.

"Username?" he asked.

Anthem looked sheepishly at him and nibbled the stub of a green fingernail. "You're going to laugh at me."

Trey stared at her. Gaped at her.

"What—?" she said, suddenly touching her face, her nose, to make sure that she didn't have anything on her. "What?"

Trey sniffed. He could taste tears in his mouth, in the back of his throat. And there was a smell in the air. Ozone and sulfur. He shook his head, trying to capture the thought that was just there, just on the edge. But . . . no, it was gone.

Weird. It felt important. It felt big.

But it was gone, whatever it was.

He took Anthem's hand and studied her fingers. There was blood caked in the edges. He glanced at the keyboard and saw the chocolate-colored stains. Faint, but there.

"You got blood on the keys," he said. "You have to be careful."

"Why?"

"Because this is magic and you're supposed to be careful."

Anthem gave him a sideways look. "Oh, very funny."

"No," he said, "not really."

"What's it matter? I'll clean the keyboard."

"It matters," he said, and then for reasons he could not quite understand, at least not at the moment, he said, "We have to do it right is all."

"Do what right?"

"All of it," said Trey. "The spells. Entering them, everything. We need to get them right. Everything has to be right."

"I know, I know . . . or the program won't collate the right way and—"

"No," he said softly. "Because this stuff is important. To . . . um . . . people."

Anthem studied his face for a long moment, then she nodded.

"Okay," she said and got up to get some computer wipes.

Trey sat there, staring at the hazy outline of his reflection. He could see his features, but somehow, in some indefinable way, he looked different.

Or, at least he believed he did.

Academy Field Trip

DONALD HARSTAD

Don Harstad is a retired deputy sheriff who lives in Elkader, Iowa, with his wife of forty-eight years and two foundling beagles. Don is the author of several novels, including *Eleven Days*, *Known Dead*, *The Big Thaw*, *Long December*, and *Code 61*. This is Don's first short story, as well as his first venture into the paranormal. He found both experiences to be thoroughly enjoyable.

On Monday, June 7, 2006, a special one-week course began at the Iowa Law Enforcement Academy at Camp Dodge, just north of Des Moines. The course dealt with "Intelligence Techniques for Gathering Information from Nontraditional Sources, in Relation to Unusual and Unfamiliar Criminal Activities." The course, as with all the intelligence courses, was by invitation only. There were three instructors and eight experienced officers as students.

The three instructors were Agent Benjamin Young, Iowa Division of Criminal Investigation; Special Agent Norma Jensen, Federal Bureau of Investigation; and Deputy Sheriff George Bauerkamper of Dubuque County. All three had been involved in intelligence investigations regarding unusual crimes, and all had at least fifteen years in law enforcement.

The instructors and students assembled in a small classroom that was set some distance from the basic classes, and began precisely at 0900.

Agent Young began. "Okay, okay, hold it down." That got a laugh, as the room had been quiet. Young leaned on the podium, and said, "Okay. I know all of you. I don't think all of you know these two," and he gestured toward the man and woman behind him. "Norma there is with the FBI. George here's with the Dubuque County Sheriff's Department. They've done this type of investigation. They know their shit. That's why they're here. George busted a funeral home that was involved in necrophilia." That drew a couple of snickers. "Not quite what you might think," said Young. "George . . ."

The deputy stepped to the podium. He smiled. "Thanks, Ben. This wasn't a case of some undertaker boinking a stiff," he said. "This guy was pimping dead folks."

He had their attention.

"It was a joint task force, the undertaker in question being in central Iowa. I was fortunate enough," he said, with a wry grin, "to have one of his customers living in my county. This undertaker, he'd been renting the bodies to a group of necrophiliacs. Six in all. When he'd get their preferred sort of corpse, he'd make a couple of calls to the ones whose, ah, criteria had been met by the recently departed, and get five grand for an hour. Alone. With the deceased. Specials went for upwards of twenty-five thousand dollars for a night." He stopped, and glanced around the room. "Anybody want to guess what a special was?"

Nobody moved.

"A special meant that he'd deliver the departed to your home, and make the pickup when you were done."

"Jesus H. Christ," said the Cedar Rapids officer.

"Getting information on this dude was kind of interesting," said George. "We'll be discussing that later." He stepped back from the podium.

"Norma . . ." said Young, indicating it was her turn.

"The one I'm going to share with you," she said, stepping forward, "involved a man we referred to as the 'Tour Guide,' who scouted, obtained, and provided various resorts for the use of several cults in the Southern states, who practiced fun things like pedophilia, demonology, and cannibalism."

"Nice," said the woman detective from Iowa City. "Dealt with fraternities, did he?"

That got a laugh, including from Norma. "I think mostly they were the parents of the frat rats," she said. Another laugh. "Getting intel on him was a real challenge. Not even his clientele knew who he was, and almost none of them ever saw him. Payment in cash, at a dead drop." She smiled briefly. "No pun intended. Anyway, never the same place twice. Never even the same city. I got to travel lots and lots for that one."

"Okay, then," said Ben. "And to tie it in, I was involved in both investigations. So, now you've got an idea of what we meant by unusual. Anybody working on one of those right now?"

Nobody was.

"That's a relief. So, then we can concentrate on these cases. Okay, first of all . . ." He handed a stack of papers to the officer at the right front. "Pass these back. It's sort of a syllabus, but we've kept it pretty vague. Understandably."

"First thing we do," said Young, "is define the scope of the investigation. That changes a lot as you go. Then the geographical area, because of jurisdictional stuff. Then describe the offense as well as we know it, and describe any participants or other involved parties. That changes, too. Then we target the weak links, and go for them. Start the dominoes falling, until we get to the top. Just like all intel investigations. Always simple, always easy, and always successful, right?" That was the last laugh of the morning.

They broke for lunch, served in the academy cafeteria. The intelligence officers sat away from the fifty or so basic law enforcement recruits who were also in session, and mingled only at the salad bar. The three instructors hung back a bit, as the eight from their intelligence class went through the line.

"How ya think it's going so far?" asked Ben as they watched the class fill their trays.

"We got their attention," said George.

"You see the one I mentioned?" asked Norma.

"The one from Iowa City?"

"Yes. Detective Dillman. Louise Dillman. She's the one we want," said Norma. "Sure of it. Her chief agrees."

"Well, good enough, then," said Ben. "She's sure the right type."

"Really pretty," said George.

Norma elbowed him. "Not pertinent. Dirty old man."

"Not dirty," he said, affectionately. "Pretty isn't pertinent as a qualifier, but it's gotta be difficult to blend those looks into the general population, though. That's what I meant."

"I've seen her undercover," said Ben, "and trust me, you wouldn't recognize her."

"Really?" said Norma. "Then how did you know it was her?"

"The way she nibbled my ear," said Ben.

"You're both awful."

"Who's got the dirty mind, here, I ask you? No, really, though. All made up, straight black hair, not blond like it is now. Fake piercings. Fake tattoos. Tank top. Boots. Wouldn't recognize her unless she showed you her ID."

"Memorable, huh?" said Norma. "Working Johns undercover?"

"Not really. Posing as an art major, working burglaries from student housing."

The rest of Monday and all of Tuesday and Wednesday were taken up by flowcharts, relational databases, Facebook and Twitter accounts, blogs, alerting reports to be forwarded to the intelligence analysts, and the need to know and right to know criteria for this type of investigation. Dull, often repetitious, but vital to maintaining the confidentiality and restricting the dissemination of the material they would be developing in such cases. All examples, however, were taken from actual cases, and that helped alleviate the boredom.

Ben's closing statement at 1630 hours on Wednesday consisted of three sentences: "Tomorrow we do the media relations stuff in the morning, and then we split up and do some practical stuff in teams. Normal street dress. Have ID, but don't display it."

The eight students had been under a rather loose surveillance themselves, and had been dividing up into groups of three and five to go out to dinner, and then entertain themselves for the evening. The group of three tended to go to a movie, while the group of five tended to party at local bars until closing time. Detective Louise Dillman, of the Iowa City Police Department, was a prominent member of the latter group.

As the instructors gathered for their own supper and entertainment, they discussed Detective Dillman.

"How do we want to handle breaking the news to her?" asked George.

"We," said Norma, "thought you should be the one to do it."

"Oh, nope. Not me." George looked at his two friends. "Well, then, why me? Ben, you could do it easily. Norma, you'd be perfect for the job. I'm just an old fart with some stories."

"But you discovered it."

"You were right there, right after Ben. Hell, it couldn't have been more than an hour or so."

"Yeah. But you were there first, and you'd be the best for this. First-hand is always best."

George sighed. "How much do I drop on her?"

"Just lay it out, within reason," said Norma. "Ben and I'll take the others on the field trip. You just get her in a quiet place, and then take her to where she can observe while you talk. That ought to do it."

"What if I become aware," asked George, "as this thing goes down, that we're wrong about this?"

"About her, you mean?"

"Yeah, Ben. About her. Her qualifications. That's why you should do this."

"Norma and I picked her," said Ben. "Too close to the subject. Got to be you."

"And if you decide she's not the one we want, then just slow it down, or minimize it, or whatever, and get out of it gracefully," said Norma. "That's what I meant by within reason. But that's not gonna happen, my boy. She's our girl."

George held up his beer glass. "That's me, old graceful." He took a drink. "Here's to you being right," he said.

"You have doubts?" asked Norma. "Seriously?"

George leaned back, and looked at both of them. He was silent for a few moments, and then heaved a sigh. "Oh . . . no. Not really. I think we've got the right one. Just, you know, err on the side of caution sort of stuff."

"Of course." Ben pushed the chip bowl toward George. "Have some."

"Remember to bring your gun?" asked Norma.

"Always do, Mom." George picked up a chip.

"Don't start the mother crap," said Norma. "We just want you to be safe. Take her in close, but not too close. She's got to be allowed time to think."

"Got a plan," said George. "I'm gonna rely on my instincts."

Norma shook her head. "Not that . . . please, not that."

"It'll be fine," said George. "Not to worry." He cleared his throat. "How about 'Ma'?"

"Thin ice," said Norma.

"Just in case, better charge up your cell phone," said Ben. "I've got a walkie-talkie for you, too. Radio's much better if things go to hell on ya."

"Thanks."

Thursday, after a nutritious, if bland, academy lunch, the three instructors introduced their class to two new instructors from the DCI. With lots of hustle and bustle and by the shuffling of assignments, it was doubtful that any of the class was particularly aware that only Detective Dillman had been paired with George.

"What we gonna do, boss?" asked Dillman.

"Call me George. Well, we're gonna take my car, for starters. Hop in."

"Where we headed?"

"Buckle up," he said. "You drive like I do, it's just smart."

She did so. "We assigned to some really bad guys?"

"Possibly one of the worst."

He stopped at the intersection with the main base road, and glanced at her to see what effect that had had. He met the gaze of large blue eyes that seemed just a bit wider than usual. She was judging him, as well.

"You're serious."

"I am." He pulled out, and headed for the highway.

"Cool."

"I hope so," he said. "It might be very late before we get back. You have any appointments, or plans to go out, or anything?"

"Just pizza, whenever we get back."

"Okay. Well," he said, turning south toward the interstate, "it starts gettin' late, just call whoever it is and make an excuse."

"Sure."

"You got your gun?"

"Yep. You think I actually might need it?"

"Never can tell," said George.

"Oh, cool," she said. "Don't get me wrong, but this classroom routine was getting to be a little . . . ah . . ."

"Dull?"

"Yeah."

"This ought to take care of that," he said. He took the East 80 on-ramp. "Everything from now on is completely classified. Class I Confidential. No notes. Not now, not afterward. You remember it all. No report to a superior. Somebody asks you for one regarding today, you refer 'em to me or Ben or Norma. Okay?"

"Yes." She sounded more serious now.

"Nobody else in this class is getting this briefing. Nobody. Understood?"

"Yes." Her brow wrinkled, but she didn't say anything else.

"I'm taking you all the way back to Iowa City," he said. He turned to look at her. "Surprised?"

"Ah, yeah." After a pause, she said, "I mean, I got that place wired, you know? Not sure there's anything you can show me there that I don't already know."

"Wait and see," he said. "What I'm going to show you is something behind some of the things you know, and maybe some of the things you take for granted."

"What if somebody from my department spots us?"

"You're taking me around to show me some stuff for class," said George. "Examples of your work."

She half giggled. "Wish I'd known you in high school." She scooched down in her seat as far as the belt would allow. "Okay. What're we gonna see?"

"For starters, I'll show you, or prove to you, or substantiate everything I'm going to tell you."

"Okay."

He drove in silence for a moment. "What do you know about vampires?"

The silence resumed. He glanced over at her again, and saw her brows knit, her eyes regarding him with some suspicion.

"Anything?"

She finally said, "Well, just what I see in the movies, I guess."

He could tell from the tone of her voice that she was marking time, just to see where this was going.

"They're real."

"No, they're not."

"Yes," he said. "They are."

"Shut up!" She paused, and he said nothing. "You're serious?"

"Absolutely."

"You mean, you know, live-action role players and that shit, right?"

"Nope. Real. Absolutely, positively real."

"Oh, bullshit."

"Nope. True. Real. I've seen what they do. I've even seen one or two. We've been working this case for better than three years now."

"Three years?"

"They're what you might call elusive," he said.

"You actually . . ." she said, and then paused. "Okay, you want me to believe there are blood-sucking demons out there?"

"Well, they don't suck blood," he said. "At least, not as far as we know. Now."

She sat in silence for about two miles. He didn't look over, but he could feel her eyes on him. Finally she spoke.

"I gotta say, that, you know, if it wasn't for your credentials, if it wasn't for the fact that this is an official class, if it wasn't for the fact that I know there are some investigations that most of us never hear about, if . . ."

"Accepted. Disclaimer accepted. Really don't expect you to buy in all the way, not all at once. Just keep an open mind today, all right? We just don't do theoreticals, not at this level."

She laughed. "Oh, yeah. Right."

After a few moments, he began to explain the history of the investigation. How it had begun with a report presented to an Iowa State Medical Examiners' annual meeting, where it had been reported that there had been a surge in the deaths of undergraduates at the University of Iowa in Iowa City, at Iowa State University in Ames, at Loras College in Dubuque, and at the University of Northern Iowa in Cedar Falls.

"I mean, it wasn't like the black plague was getting started up or anything," he said. "But there were six students among them in the first year, five in the second, and eight in the third. All undergraduate females. All discovered deaths, all unexplained circumstances, and all with an unidentified substance in the system that was discovered, they told us, pretty much by accident. Not toxic, as far as they could tell. None of the stuff like Special K, or any known narcotic or stimulant substances. Nothing on the list of controlled substances."

"So, what did it turn out to be? I mean, I know those lab people. They had to identify it. Or at least make it a new classification. That's the way they work," she said.

"Close as they've come so far," he said, "is that it's something like sort of a narcotic, or hypnotic, or whatever effect. Apparently naturally occurring stuff."

"Pardon?"

"Yeah, sorry. I didn't do all that well in chemistry. Closest they've come, they say, is kind of like a very exotic mammal's venom."

"What?" She had been startled, and it just kind of slipped out.

"That's what they say."

"You've just gotta be shittin' me." She paused, then said, "Really? What kind of mammal? Hell, there *aren't* any venomous mammals. . . ."

"Kind of mammal? What, you think I'm some sort of biologist? Exotic, like I said. Best I can do for you. Anyhow, that's as close as they can come," he said. "We know where it came from, though, that's for sure."

He drove on a few seconds. He glanced over and saw she was consulting her BlackBerry.

"Callin' somebody?"

"Nope, on the 'net . . . Well, damn. There *are* venomous mammals. Shrews, for instance. Who knew?" She lowered her BlackBerry. "Point for you."

"Okay . . ."

"So, these vampires are, like, related to shrews?"

"Could be. Maybe by marriage?" He smiled.

"You gonna tell me or what? What they really are."

"Vampires."

She gazed at him for several seconds. "The truth."

"Like I said. Vampires."

"Okay," she said with a laugh. "This is some kind of initiation thing, right? Next is UFOs and crop circles?"

He shook his head. "We'd never play games with an officer who was armed. Not when you'd maybe have to use it. We're not screwing around, and we're not screwing with your head. I just told you that."

"Yeah . . . in so many words, I guess you did."

They drove in silence again for a bit. "Remember the case you handled, about six months back? A girl named Claire . . . uh . . . B something."

"Claire Bennington," she said. "Freshman from Newton. Found in her dorm room, dead. Unattended. No apparent causes . . ."

"They attributed her death to 'exhaustion,' or some medical term for that," he said. "But absolutely not anorexia. Too short-term for that. None of the eating disorders. Right?"

"Yeah." Louise thought back. "The body was discovered in the victim's dorm room, just like you said. We got called by the medical examiner's office because it was an unattended death. In a nearly fetal position, wrapped snugly in her sheet and blanket, with her pillow on her head, and her face turned to the wall. There were no marks of any remarkable sort on the body, except some small creases in her skin where it pressed into the sheets. Her lower side was mottled purple. Postmortem lividity, it was called, and it clearly indicated that she had died in that position." Her voice had become mechanical, as she remembered. "The kid, Claire, was eighteen, with streaked blue and red hair. Faded blue flannel pajama bottoms covered with SpongeBob SquarePants, athletic socks, and a new Hawkeye sweatshirt." She paused again, thinking. "Totally normal kid. Toxicology came back negative. Nothing. No blood alcohol, no dope in her or in the room, no prescription drugs other than some sinus medication used by her roommate. According to her driver's license, she had been five feet six, and weighed 133 pounds. When they weighed the corpse, she came in at 102 pounds. Emaciated. Totally skin and bones. We asked around. Her parents hadn't seen her for three months, but got phone calls about three times a week. When they were interviewed, provided no history of any eating disorders. Neither did her local doctor. The autopsy revealed no anomalies anywhere. She was a perfectly healthy, dead eighteen-year-old. Best we had to go on was her roommate said that Claire had been listless recently. Said that she had urged Claire to go to Student Health, because it might be mononucleosis. So I checked. No record of her going to Student Health. The pathologist ruled out mono anyway." She snorted. "Along with anything else specific. Said it was a toss-up between sudden adult death syndrome and total exhaustion. In other words, they hadn't a clue."

"Great."

"Yeah. I admit it, that one bothered me. My niece had the same pajama bottoms."

"Ah."

"They told us that most cases of chronic fatigue really don't have a discoverable root cause. Ranges from depression to overworking to dope to, well, none of it was present in the workups. Not anything specific." She looked over at him. "How'd you get interested in her?"

"Her case was referred to us," said George. "Well, not referred, so much as her blood, kind of, got in the hands of one of our forensic pathologists. At the request of the pathologist in Iowa City. Our folks discovered minute traces of that venomlike stuff."

"Why wasn't I told about that?" asked Louise, suddenly angry.

"You just were," said George. "And keep it to yourself, because not even your local pathologist has been told."

"It was murder, then," she said.

"Well, sort of."

"You can't sort of murder somebody!"

"Well, as it turns out, yes, you sort of can."

She stared at him, waiting for an explanation.

"Well," he said, "the attorney general's office thinks there may be an outside chance that this critter may not actually be doing this intentionally. You know, kisses a girl, she goes all gaga, and whatever it is thinks, gee, I'm a great kisser."

"Seriously?"

"Not as far as I'm concerned, anyway. But it's something we have to settle before we can make it a crime. Act and the intent, ya know. Whatever we're dealing with has to know, or reasonably anticipate the effect, and then do it anyway. Then it's murder."

They drove on, into a sky darkening with rain clouds. A thunderstorm, coming in from the northwest, was beating them to Iowa City.

"You're gonna keep telling me it was a vampire who did these," said Louise. "Right?"

"Yeah." George looked over at her. "Because it was."

She stared at him. "*You* are fuckin' *nuts*."

"There are times when that would be a comfort," he said, seriously. "You're being told this because we hope you can be instrumental in our investigations. I know it's not easy to buy in to this, but you pretty much have to, because it's true."

"Right." She pursed her lips. "Okay, so why are we headed to IC?"

"To show you the next victims, we think. The student body has lots of, ah, susceptible people."

"So you know who is doing this?"

"We have, ah, indications. High degree of probability. We don't have enough to support a charge against it, or him, or whatever. Not yet. But we will."

"Give me a minute," she said.

A light rain began as they were passing the Williamsburg Interchange, and she spoke again. "Okay. Background."

"Thought you'd never ask," he said. "That whole venomlike diagnosis thing? That got it started. It was referred to CDC in Atlanta. They told us, well, what to look for."

"It's nationwide?"

"Not quite. But they've found the same evidence in seven states. They described the circumstances of all the victims, including their social activities. Turns out that this venom shit is an STD, more or less."

"Let me get this. . . . This vampire dude, he has venom instead of semen? He screws them to death, right? Come on. That's just gross."

"Oh, no. Just has to be direct contact with mucous membranes. That's how the predator—because that's what they are, predators—that's how the predator transmits it. A kiss . . . getting saliva in contact with a mucous membrane, that's all it takes. The gland that secretes the venom, or whatever, seems to be located right alongside the salivary glands. They say that a normal autopsy would never discover 'em." George attempted to lighten it up just a bit. "Hell, I suppose it can be transmitted if it spits in your eye."

She sighed, loudly. "Just when I think I can get a grip on this, you toss something else in."

"Think how we felt as it developed," he said. "And it gets worse. The CDC people say that the specimen they have there, male, is just about completely sterile. And they tell me that if he was gonna mate with another like him, they'd have a . . . well the term they finally gave me was a *mule*."

She just stared.

"We've never seen a female, but we think they exist. CDC believes they'd be the same, though. Fertility-wise. So they need to mate with humans."

"I knew we'd get to the sex thing. I knew it."

"Not the way you think. They need to have lots of, you know, episodes, before they can have a successful reproduction. So they just keep doing it, and that's what gets the victims into an overdose kind of state. With the venom. And they just can't recover."

"That," said Dillman, "makes no sense at all. If they were pregnant, then they'd kill them, and that would be the last thing they'd want."

"CDC thinks pregnancy brings some kind of immunity. Fetus is immune, of course, and it transfers to the mom through the blood or something." He glanced over at her. "Hey, that's just what they said. Beats the shit out of me altogether."

"So, like, it's federal? And accidental to boot?"

"First, that *does* explain why Norma is at the academy this week, doesn't it? We don't usually rate having the FBI as a participant." George moved into the right lane. "No accident, though. This critter, it uses people, exhausts them, burns them up for what it considers their failure. The sample at CDC said that he'd get furious after so many attempts with a gal and he'd just step up the frequency in kind of a rage. He had to know what the result would be. Sometimes in just a few months. Sometimes over a period of years, depending on its particular whim, I guess." He swerved right to get to their exit. "I have no idea how it works. The medical folks probably do. I do know that the chronic fatigue is the most remarkable symptom. It can really be deadly without, you know, being the cause of death. Three here in Iowa we believe just zonked out when driving. Killed in the wrecks, or died shortly after. One died when, according to witnesses, she just seemed to be in a daze and stepped out into traffic without looking. The baseline here is that we find out about it when the victim dies. So far, we've never examined a living victim, because we just can't know who they are." He took Exit 244, bringing them into Iowa City on Dubuque Street. The rain had become steady, and the background sounds of the wipers were a kind of comforting accompaniment. "The Iowa victims so far have all been female, under twenty-five, attractive, eager, and more trusting than not. Look around . . . see any potential victims?"

"We have a couple thousand freshmen who that would fit, every year."

"Exactly. Where else would you find a similar group?"

"Any university town."

"And that's where we find these critters. Vampires, for want of a better term. But there are those who think that it's just exactly what they are, or at least what's referred to in some of the legends."

"Why Iowa?"

He snorted. "Well, ya know," he said, confidentially, "we're a simple folk." Old joke. "But for real . . . not so many cops, not so many nut cases. Nut cases, we find, tend to spoil their game. You actually get nut-case vampire hunters, for one thing. Weird people. That's why they've kind of migrated out from the major metro areas, and headed for flyover country." George turned right on Church, then left on Clinton. They were passing a row of dormitories on one side of Clinton, and some fraternity houses on the left. As they reached the first dorm, they slowed. "That's where she lived, right?"

"Currier Hall," said Louise. "Top floor, above the entrance there."

He glanced at his watch. They were early. "Want to see where we think she was first contacted?"

"You know that?"

"We think so," he said. They drove on.

"So, let me get this straight, nobody has ever actually *seen* one of these things, right?"

"Oh, no. No, I told you, they've been seen, all right. Twice by me, even," he said. "Not socially, though, if that was what you meant."

"Screw social," she said. "Why didn't you arrest them?" There was very strong skepticism in her voice, and he knew they had a way to go.

"Did. One of 'em. It ain't easy, trust me. It, or he, wasn't very happy being found, okay?" He remembered the manlike creature. They'd cornered it in an enormous home improvement store, of all places. Just on the outskirts of Dubuque. They'd been following him at a distance for several nights, and when they saw him drive around behind the closed store and cut a hole in the wire fence, it looked like they had him in a righteous bust. What he was doing in there they had no idea, nor why he wanted to steal instead of simply buying whatever he needed. They called for backup, and got a sheriff's car, a state patrol car, and two Dubuque PD cars, all with a single officer. They put an officer on each side of the huge place, in case he saw them coming and made a break for it. They stationed the Dubuque County deputy near the hole in the fence, and then George and his partner went in. The vampire had apparently heard them approaching, and made for the rear exit. They'd been in hot pursuit when he'd slammed out the back door and was confronted by a Dubuque police officer. All hell had broken loose, and the city cop and George's partner had been severely injured. George had tried to hold him at gunpoint, and the creature had decided to go its own way. He'd charged George, heading toward the cornfield behind the store, and George had shot him. Eight times. "Had to shoot him."

"Didn't die, though. Right?" There was sarcasm in her voice.

"Oh, no. Should have died. Hit him lots of times. It was really messy, and he really fought it. But you're right. Didn't die, though."

"Immortal," said Louise.

"That's not true. Just live a long time, and really hard to kill," he said. "Remember the Des Moines detective, shot a guy in the chest six times, the guy strangled him while he was trying to reload? That was meth, but it's the same sort of deal."

"So you busted him?"

"For attempted murder and burglary. It was really strange, okay? I mean, we were having to do so many reports about shots being fired, not to mention somebody actually getting shot . . . we didn't get to examining the store's security tapes for three days. When we finally did, we were lookin' for what he was actually doing in there. Found a young female employee standing back by the manager's office. She was waiting for him. We were sure of it. I mean the store was closed, had been for hours."

"Oh. But you got him for it?"

"Not for being a vampire. We thought about giving that a shot, but the prosecutor said we couldn't get it to fly, and we'd just blow the investigation. The vampire just did seventy-two hours in the hospital, believe it or not. Under very close guard. Then jail, then in front of a judge, then to Security Mental Health down here in Iowa City, for his pre-placement evaluation." He laughed. "That was a hoot! Anyway, then the Feds sort of got him on loan, all legally, and he's the one now down at CDC in Atlanta."

"What did his attorney have to say about that?"

"Nothing. Court-appointed. Justified, since he or it wouldn't cough up any information regarding his finances. That would have given up his name, and he didn't want to do that. His choice. The exam upon admission to Security Mental Health, so they can tell what institution to put him in? Well, that showed he or it wasn't quite human, one way or another. Something extra or missing in his DNA, ya know? That's a tough one, because we can only charge humans, okay? Everything else in the law we just turn over to animal control." He said that with a grin. "So, anyway. We took the matter to the AG, and they took it to a judge who has a kind of confidential court. Just like the federal judges, you know? The ones who hear select terrorism cases? Like that."

"You might need to show me a transcript of that."

"In my briefcase, backseat. Go ahead."

"You brought it with you?"

"It's one of the things I would need, if I was in your position. To convince me." He turned, and they crossed the Iowa River. "It wasn't easy getting that out of the files," he said, as she opened his briefcase. "Don't lose it."

"Yeah, right." She began to read, and he pulled into a restaurant parking lot. She looked up. "Mondo's? He lives *here*?"

"Oh, hell, no. I'm hungry, and thought we could sit in the lot while you read the file, and then go in and get something. Love their Italian sausage sandwiches. We've got time."

He shut the car off, and rolled down the windows. The rain had made everything smell fresh and clean, and he liked the sound of the cars as they went by on the Coralville Strip, splashing through the puddles.

She finished the transcript in about fifteen minutes, and returned it to his briefcase.

"Redacted a lot, didn't they?"

"You mean those black lines? Yeah. Just names and places, though."

"I noticed the prisoner being referred to as John Doe 6822. No name?"

"Not that he'd give. We're sure he had, well, identities. Giving them up, that might just enable us to trace activities. So he didn't. I never said they were stupid." He opened his car door. "Hungry?"

There weren't many in the grill at that hour, and they got an isolated table.

"It mentions one that was killed," she said. "The transcript."

"Yeah. Missouri."

"No details, though. How *do* you kill one?"

George chuckled. "They're pretty straightforward down in Missouri. Blew his head off, if I remember right. Shotgun."

"Ah." She scanned the menu. "I'll have whatever you're having," she said. "Gotta hit the restroom."

During the meal, he asked her if there had been anything she remembered from the Claire Bennington case that, now that she knew who or what had killed her, might have been important but previously overlooked.

"Numph," she said, her mouth full of sandwich.

"DCI labs handled the processing?"

"Most of it."

He nodded, and cut off another section of sandwich. "You believing this, yet?"

She chewed silently, swallowed, and then said, "Beginning to."

"Wanna see where it lives?"

"You bet. Ah, but can we keep calling it 'he'? Easier to get my mind around, okay?"

"Sure. Whatever you want. I call it 'he' most of the time, myself. But they're a lot easier to deal with if you call 'em 'it.' Easier to comprehend, after a while. But 'he' it is."

Back in the car, she tried to lighten it up a bit. "Is there gonna be a test over this?"

"Strictly pass-fail."

"How will I know?"

"Been thinkin' about that," he said, backing out of the parking place.

"Not up to me alone, but I tell ya what. If I tell you I'm recommending to Ben and Norma that you be added to the task force, then you can figure you're in."

As they went back over the Iowa River and approached the old state capitol building up on its hill, he said, "Ever been to the Museum of Natural History, up over there?"

"Macbride?"

"Yep."

"Only once. Unusual place. That where he lives?"

"Nope. Just making conversation." He turned left, went straight past the Memorial Union, and into the parking ramp on the right. He took the automated ticket, and found a place fairly close to the exit. "Let's walk from here. Just for a few minutes. We got a little time to kill, yet."

She wanted to ask just what he was waiting for, but didn't.

Everything near the campus of the University of Iowa seems to be uphill. George announced that, due to his advancing years, they would walk more slowly than the students, who seemed to fly up the hills with little or no effort. As effortlessly as Louise, he noticed, whose long legs seemed to prefer a faster pace. As they went up, he asked her what she'd want to be when she grew up.

"Never really intend to," she said, smiling. "Call me later."

He smiled back. "But when and if you do?"

"Well, back in high school, I wanted to be Indiana Jones," she said.

"Really?"

"Yep. Hat and whip and all. No S&M crap. Just wanted to be Indy."

"Cool."

"Majored in history, looking for a minor in archeology. Changed to English, because it was easier and, well you know. If you're majoring in history, you only have two choices . . . make it or teach it."

"So they say." They were nearing the top of the hill. The stopped at the top, ostensibly to let George get his bearings, but really to let him catch his breath. "So you're an English major, huh?"

"No. Got interested in people again, so I changed my major to sociology. That was crap. So I got back to history, and stayed there. Kind of hiding where classes were cool until I could graduate and get on with things."

George was beginning to like her.

"How in hell did you get into cop work?"

"Paid better than being a high school teacher," she said. "At least this way, somebody gives you some shit, they only do it once."

"Got that right." They had crossed Market Street to their left, and walked a short bit on Capitol Street when he stopped. "This is a place you should be aware of."

"What?"

"It, or he, spends a bit of time here, late at night."

"This is the chemistry building," she announced patiently.

"Yep. Was called Chem Dent in my day. Dentistry was here then, too. But this is the place."

"There's just no freakin' way. It's classrooms and labs."

"Oh, there's a reason. There's . . . okay, you gotta stop staring at it. Let's walk a bit farther. He's likely not in there now, anyway. Trust me, we don't want to corner him in there without a TAC team."

They began walking north.

"Okay, look," she said. "You expect me to believe that he lures freshmen girls to the chemistry building in the middle of the night, seduces them, transfers venomlike stuff as an STD thing, and then makes them his, what? Slaves? In the fuckin' chem building? You ever *smell* that place?"

It must have been the way she said it, because George found himself laughing.

"This isn't funny!"

"No, no. I know." He drew a deep breath. "It's just I didn't realize how screwy it sounded. Ah. Well, anyway, no, he also has a house. But he doesn't, well, live there. We think he *lives* in a subbasement area beneath the chem building."

"How . . . ?"

"We've done some surveillance. Not a lot, but enough to get baseline data."

"So who on my department worked with you?"

That was a fair question, George thought. "Nobody on Iowa City PD. Your Johnson County sheriff gave us a hand."

She didn't seem too happy about that. Jealous of her jurisdiction, and wanted a piece of the action. George was beginning to like her a lot.

"Let's head back to the car," he said.

"So how does he get to students?" she asked. "Hang around in bars?"

"Nope. He's an artist." He watched her face for a reaction. There was none.

"He teach it?" she asked, as they walked.

"Not as far as we know. Not for the U of I anyway. He does art stuff. Specifically, drawing people."

"Drawings from life, or something like that. Sketching people. That'd kind of figure," she said. "No pun intended."

"Think back," said George. "What was the Claire girl's major?"

"Art," said Louise. "She was an art major."

"He runs an art supply store," said George. "Has a couple of art grad students working for him there. They're the conduit to the students, and the store is where lots of the art majors get supplies. Cheaper than some of the other stores, they tell me."

"He's in retail?"

"Enterprising, too," said George. "He's gotta eat. Walk beside me, and make like we're, oh, buddies of some sort. Head down like we're discussing some really academic thing." She did. He began to tell her about the intelligence workup on this creature, in a very conversational tone, and being very watchful for anybody passing too close. He explained how they'd been investigating leads for two years.

"When you get to watching him on a regular basis, you'll notice he doesn't drive. No DL. Walks or bicycles just about everywhere. We think he didn't want to get a driver's license because, one, it makes him give an ID. Two, you get stopped for some traffic stuff, that's getting noticed. Ninety percent of all citizens' only contact with law enforcement is through traffic incidents. That, and you get in a wreck, you might even get hurt. Not safe to go to an ER. Last thing it wants is to be rendered unconscious in a crash. Wake up in the ER and wonder just what tests they might have run."

They walked on.

"Got him with four bank accounts, under four different identities, with four separate banks, two accounts a year, for two years. Then we lose the trail. None of the accounts are as large as we think his main account should be. You know how that goes. Launders stuff. I'm not into that, really, but that's just what they tell me."

"Right."

"Most everything you hear about vampires isn't true. They can go out in the light. They just don't like to, because, apparently, when the natural end gets near, diseases start popping up, okay? And, like, with everything else they have to worry about then, skin cancer erupting like acne is something they'd rather not deal with."

"Sure."

"They can be killed just like anything else we'd get involved with. No stakes required. Nothing like that. Crucifixes don't mean diddly. Holy water just gets 'em wet. Garlic has no effect whatsoever, except they can smell you a mile away. They don't change into bats, and they can't fly or anything like it. Although the one I shot jumped pretty good."

They were back at the car. "Look down there, to the bottom of the chem building . . . see that steel door? Near the corner."

She did.

"That's where he gets in. That's where he comes out. About all we know at this point. You might want to check further into that."

She nodded. "Sure."

He glanced at his watch. "What say we go look at the art supply store, and then I'll show you the house."

The store, in an old, one-story building that looked like a corner grocery that had lost its usefulness, had "Ernesto's Art Supply" painted in the window.

"Ernesto?" she asked. "It's Ernesto? Hell, I drive by this place every day."

"Ernesto Miska. That's it. Ah, him."

"Well . . . shit. I've been in that store. A theft report, a couple of years back. Shit, I've met him."

"Know where he lives?" asked George as they drove by the store.

"No. No reason to. I'm sure we've got his address. . . ."

"Over here," he said, turning left. "Right here . . . the light gray one."

He indicated a normal-looking, two-story, wood frame house, with a wide porch and a gabled roof indicating an attic space. There was a small one-car garage nestled on the side, with one of those old paved driveways that consisted of two narrow, parallel concrete tracks. There were old trees throughout the neighborhood. The house did not stand out at all.

"There, huh?"

"Yep." He drove to the end of the long residential block, and turned around. "We'll park here. Wait for him to come home. Just to let you get a look at him in case he's changed his appearance since the burglary case."

"Thanks."

He reached back onto the floor of the backseat, and produced a nylon binocular case, which he handed to her.

"Use these."

After almost a minute's silence, while Louise removed the binoculars, removed the lens caps, focused for the distance, and observed for a few moments, she said, "I'm gonna buy in to this. The more I think about it, the more sense this makes. Claire Bennington," she said softly. "She really was an art major. That's the key for me."

"Good."

"What do you want me to do?" she asked, still peering through the binoculars.

"Gather intelligence," he said. She could hear the smile in his voice.

She put the binoculars in her lap. "I know that. How about something more here? A line of inquiry would be nice. Just a suggested one. To get me started."

"We'd kind of like you to get to know him. Can you draw?"

"Not for shit," she said. She drummed her fingers on the binoculars. "I suppose I could pose, or something. They always need a model."

"We were thinking more along the lines of shopping in his store," said George. Although, thinking about it, he realized Louise would make a fine model. "Getting naked for somebody is always . . . chancy." He chuckled.

"Hey, I was ready to give my all," she said. "Make a note of that."

"Consider it done." He looked directly at her. "Do not, and I mean never, try to get somebody undercover. Not with this . . . whatever he is. You or anybody else. They seem to be pretty cop aware, most of the time. You get somebody to go under for you, you write 'em off. They get that venom crap in 'em, and they're probably just plain done."

"Somebody inside the store, though?"

"We've given up on that. These things are pretty slick. Pick up on it right away, probably. Keep him at arm's length."

"Okay."

"You'll be talking pretty regularly to one of us, probably Ben. If you think you want to do something like a snitch inside, don't do it without permission from him."

"Sure. Okay. Yes, sir. Got it."

He shook his head ruefully.

Two figures came around the corner at the far end of the block. Even at that distance, and with his naked eye, George could discern that one was pushing a bicycle and the other was carrying a load of some sort.

Louise put the binoculars to her eyes, and said, "It's him. It's Ernesto." She paused, and then said, "And some girl. She's a treat. Black hair with a purple streak. Tacky blue jeans with fake wear holes. Stupid black tennis shoes. Emo look, if I ever saw it. Art student, I'll bet."

"Let me see," said George.

She handed him the binoculars. He looked closely. The "man" looked to be somewhere between thirty and forty, moustache, about six feet tall, with close-cropped dark hair. He, too, was wearing faded blue jeans but without the holes, tennis shoes, and a light blue, sleeveless hooded sweatshirt. "Yeah, it's our target." He shifted his gaze. The girl was slender, long-legged, with black and purple hair, just as Louise had described. A good five eight, she had rather dark eyes, and for a moment he thought she was wearing sunglasses. It must have been makeup, he thought. She was carrying quite a bit of stuff over her shoulder and under her left arm. A big, flat, thin, white object, which he thought might be a canvas; a backpack with one strap over her shoulder; and a contraption made of tubular steel. "Walking his bike, the girl's carrying the load. A tripod?"

"The chrome legs, right?"

"Yep," he said, passing the binoculars back.

"Easel, I'd think." Louise peered through the binoculars again. As the couple got closer, she said, "Oh, no way . . . she's carrying groceries, too. Oh, cute. Two piercings in her lower lip. Snakebites. What a slut."

"Don't judge," said George, startled at the intensity of her remark.

"Don't mind me," said Louise, as she continued to watch. "I just get tired of bailing those idiots out when they get in trouble."

The couple stopped in front of Ernesto's house. "Oh no, shit," said Louise, as the pair started up the front steps. "She's going in with him. Easel, sketch pad and shoulder bag and all. Yep. See him let her go up the steps first? What a freaking gentleman; he's just checking out her butt. And she knows it, I can tell you that. Shit."

"How old you think she is?" asked George.

"Under twenty. There they go, right on in, honey. Just put your stuff down, and take off your clothes. I'll be right with you. . . ." She looked at George as the door closed behind Ernesto and his girl. "He's gonna do her. I can tell just by the way she went up the steps, she's good to go."

"You can?" That, he couldn't help thinking, would be a very useful talent. "Maybe just, you know, she's there for supper or something?"

"Yeah, right."

"Tell ya what," he said. "Let's stick for a little while, okay? See if she comes out anytime soon."

"Hell, let's just kick the door in and bust his ass," said Louise ruefully. "Just kidding. Hey, I'm sorry I got so worked up. Won't happen again."

"No problem," said George, and he meant it.

They waited. From their vantage point, they had a fair view into the house through what seemed to be a large bay window in a living room, and a well-glazed area they took to be a porch or dining room. They were unable to see much in either room because the ambient light was still much brighter than the interior of the house.

"Maybe," said Louise, "we could just call, and ask them to turn on a light?"

"Give 'em time."

About thirty minutes later, a light came on in what they had taken for a dining room, and they saw that it was actually the kitchen.

"Great kitchen," said George.

"Yeah." Louise had grabbed the binoculars again. "He apparently cooks with his shirt off," she said.

"Saves on laundry, I guess."

"Oh, for shit's sake," she said. "She cooks topless, too! That asshole!"

"Can I see? Just for verification."

She handed over the binoculars. He looked, and handed them back. "Nice."

She grabbed the binoculars, and as she brought them to her eyes, she said, "Nice what?"

"Oh, just nice," said George. "Like they say, wouldn't toss her out of bed for eating crackers."

"Yeah, right . . ."

"Check out the tattoos," he said. "Anything you recognize?"

"On her?"

"Yeah, didn't see any on him."

"Just a sec . . . just a floral thing on her right arm, upper. Oh, sure. Sure. Wouldn't you just fuckin' know, she's got a red rose on her left boob. How daringly unique."

"Well, speaking personally," said George, "I haven't encountered all that many. . . ."

"Oh, it's that phony art-student look. They all do stuff like that. Especially the young ones. Nobody understands them. They're just having such deep emotions. They're going to be different, just like all the other girls with dyed hair, and snakebites, and rose tatts on their boobs. Different just like everybody else who's unique and misunderstood, and oh so very creative. Give me a break."

"I take it you don't have any tattoos," said George.

Louise put down the binoculars, took a deep breath, and handed them to him. "Just my badge number on my ass," she said, with a laugh. "Sorry about the rant. You just gotta work in a university town for a few years, you get that way, that's all. Same crap, always new to them."

George thought she'd recovered rather nicely. He put the binoculars to his eyes. "What're they having for supper?"

"Men." She looked around her, deliberately avoiding Ernesto's house. She reached out and he gave her the binoculars. "Hey . . . there's a guy over here, in this house, and he's got binoculars, too! He's lookin' right into the kitchen from his second floor. . . ."

"Let me see," said George. He looked, and then said, "Well, roses and boobs seem to attract an audience." He grinned and handed the binoculars back to Louise.

"Disgusting," she said, and didn't look back at the man in the house again.

The light was fading fast. "What say we head back to Des Moines?"

Louise nodded. "Sure."

They pulled slowly away from Ernesto's, and as soon as they had turned the corner, George said, "Not quite hungry yet. You?"

"We just ate," she said, deep in thought. After a moment, she asked a question.

"I'm supposed to work this alone, right?"

"For now. Low-key," he said. "You need any assistance, you can call the task force member nearest you, and they'll help out."

"What if I need help in a hurry?"

"Make sure you don't," he said. "You're just gathering information. But you need help really fast, call anybody you can. We can clean up the details later, if necessary. Don't endanger yourself over this. Okay?"

She nodded, and neither of them spoke for at least ten miles.

"I better call my buds," she said, "and tell them I'll be late." She pulled her cell phone from the front pocket of her blue jeans.

George glanced over while she dialed, and noticed how the blue light from the phone made her look quite young.

"Hi, it's me," she said. "I'm just headed back in to DM, so it'll be a while. Yeah. No, I'll probably catch up at Ho Jo's." There was a pause, then, "Oh, yeah. See you then." She terminated the call.

"How'd you manage to choose me?" she asked.

"You were recommended."

"Who?"

"I have no idea," he said. "Need-to-know only. I just got tapped for the briefing part."

"Oh."

"Glad I did," he said. "Nice to know you. Nice to have you on board."

"Thanks," she said.

Back in Des Moines, he let her off at the academy parking lot, where she'd left her car.

"I'll be in touch," he said.

"Yeah, okay." As she reached her car, she turned and waved.

Still in the lot, George called Ben. "Done. Where you want to meet?"

George found Ben and Norma at the Rock Bottom Restaurant and Brewery, just off University Avenue in West Des Moines.

"How'd it go?" asked Ben.

"Not bad," said George. "Couple of surprises, but not bad overall. I think she'll do."

"Tell her anything she didn't already know?"

"Twice, I think. I'm pretty damned sure she didn't know we had captured one, and shipped him alive and well to CDC in Atlanta. Had to tell her that, to substantiate what we knew and how we got it. She asked about them being immortal. I told her about the one they blew away in Missouri. I think that surprised her."

"What about her and the target?" asked Norma. "How'd she handle that?"

"Well," said George, "about how you'd think. I'm not sure if she had any real idea what was going on with him, with the venom and that stuff. She almost blew her cover, though, I think. Just for a second. But," he said, with some disappointment in his voice, "she seems like just about any other addict. Either denying the facts, or thinking she's the one to beat it through willpower. Won't get her, any way you cut it." He shrugged.

"What with that hypnotic crap, who knows? She probably won't ever wake up to the real danger until she's dead." He reached for some Doritos. "Anyway . . . We did the general stuff, the case history, all that. Then I showed her that art supply store he runs, and she managed to be surprised. Said she'd handled a theft case there, 'bout two years ago."

"That's what her boss told us," said Ben.

"Yeah. Sticking to the truth always helps. So, I asked her if she knew where his house was, she said she didn't, so we went there, too. Drove by, then up to the end of the block, and parked so we could see the approach he'd take. She did just fine there, too."

Norma nodded, took a sip of her drink, and said, "Cool one, huh."

George nodded. "She's good. But then he comes walkin' his bike home, and he's got this sweet young thing with him. She started to misfire right about then. Covered pretty good. Then him and the gal go on into the house, and she started to sound kind of pissy."

"Really?" Norma leaned forward. "Like, how?"

"Well, Ernesto let the gal go up the porch stairs in front of him, Louise says something about how he was just checking out her backside."

"That's it?" asked Ben.

"Nope. Then she said the gal was pretty much beggin' for it." George took a sip of his beer. "Can women really tell that sort of thing?"

"Why do you ask?" Norma had a sly smile on her face.

"Be a handy thing to learn," said George.

"We can discuss that later. What else did she say?"

"Well, we watched the place for a while, and she was right back to normal, and then the lovebirds show up naked in the kitchen window. At least topless. I mean," he said, "as far down as we could see without gettin' out of the car and standing on the roof."

"No shit?" Ben laughed.

"Yeah. She got real upset about them being naked. The gal had a rose tattooed on her left breast, and that got Louise really testy."

Ben nodded. "Sure."

"Then, you know the surveillance we got goin' on Ernesto next door? Damned if she didn't spot our man upstairs, with binoculars. Better get that to him, and get his ass out of there. Ernesto finds that out, I wouldn't want to be there."

"Crap, we better do that tonight," said Ben, and took out his cell phone.

"Already called it in," said George. "I think I covered it pretty well, but I thought we shouldn't take chances on this dude."

The food arrived, and the conversation changed to the weather for a minute or two.

Alone again, Norma asked, "She made three cell calls, you want to know to who and when?"

George nodded.

"Around three ten," said Norma, consulting her BlackBerry, "she called Ernesto at his store. Said she was in Iowa City, that she had a task force member with her, and that it looked like things were going well."

"When she was in the john at Mondo's," said George. "I thought it might be something like that. Hated to stop there, but we were way too early for Ernesto to go home, and I wanted her to see him."

"Then, about eight fifteen. You were outside Iowa City then."

"She had to call her friends back at the Academy," said George. "Tell 'em she was gonna be late. I was right there. Who was she really talking to? Ernesto?"

"You bet. He told her he needed to see her when she got back."

"I'll bet."

"Then, about the time you called Ben, she was on the phone to Ernesto again. She said, and I quote, 'I'm in.' Then she called him an 'asshole' and asked if 'the little slut with the tattoo on her boob' was still there."

"Pissed, like I said."

"So," said Ben. "What do we think?"

"I think we got our inside snitch with Ernesto," said George. "She just don't know it."

"Now, we decide how to utilize her the best way," said Norma.

They were silent again as they ate. Each was thinking about the fate of Detective Louise Dillman.

"She must have been turned just about the time she talked to Ernesto at that theft call a couple years back," said Ben. "So we can confirm that all his victims don't die within eighteen months."

"The docs think that he just, you know, gets her about every two or three weeks. They say the venom substance is persistent, but seems to wear off a little with time, so he has to hit her again every once in a while to keep her under control." Norma winced. "Unless she gets knocked up."

"Her department health records say she's on the pill," interjected Ben.

"Let's hope she stays on 'em. She must be willing, though. To keep the relationship active."

"Trust me," said George. "She is. The way she reacted when she saw the other girl. . . . I was kinda gettin' to like her," he said. "She's not all bad, you know?"

"Bright, ambitious, and a good cop," said Ben. "Until Ernesto got hold of her."

"You tell her about that coed who died in her own bed? The unexplained death she covered?"

"Yep."

"And . . . ?"

"Well, I'm just not sure," announced George, after a moment. "She seemed genuinely surprised, okay? But, God, she had to at least suspect, after she got involved with Ernesto. Don't you think?"

After another silence, George asked the question that had been bothering him all the way back from Iowa City. "You think, like, she got put in some sort of rehab unit, she might, you know . . . ?"

"Completely recover?"

"Yeah, Norma. Completely."

Norma shook her head. "They tell me that it's progressive. Nonreversible. It can slow way down, but it's always eating. They're not really sure how long it takes in the absence of the vampire, but they suspect she'd go into a coma and die within five or six years."

"And still head over heels for Ernesto?"

"Apparently so."

George toyed absently with his food for several seconds, and then became aware he was doing so.

"Oh, sorry. It's just a shame, though. Ya know?"

"It is," said Norma. "She's pretty much dead and doesn't know it. We've either lost her already, or are going to lose her soon, regardless how you cut it. Not that I'm not compassionate, but look on the bright side. She's going to be planting some false information in Ernesto's head for us. At least we can get some use out of her this way. Before she crawls off and dies." She looked at both men, who were silent. "There, that's settled. Can you pass the rolls?"

Sympathy for the Bones

MARJORIE M. LIU

**Marjorie M. Liu is an attorney and a *New York Times* bestselling author
of paranormal romances and urban fantasy. She also writes for Marvel
Comics. For more information, please visit her website at www
.marjoriemliu.com or follow her on Twitter @marjoriemliu.**

The funeral was in a bad place, but Martha Bromes never did much care
about such things, and so she put her husband into a hole at Cutter's,
and we as her family had to march up the long stone track into the hills
to find the damn spot, because the only decent bits of earth in all that
place were far deep in the forest, high into the darkness. Rock, everywhere else, and cairns were no good for the dead. The animals were too
smart. Might find a piece of human flesh in the yard by the pump with
sloppiness like that. I'd seen it myself, years past. No good at all.

The leaves had gone yellow and the air bit cold, whining shrill like
the brats left behind the dead, trudging slow beside their weeping mother.
Little turds, little nothings. Just blood and bone, passed on from a father
who was a cutter, a stone lover, mixing his juice inside a womb that was
cold and sly. I did not like Martha. I did not like her husband, either.
Edward Bromes was a hard man to enjoy, in any fashion. I cried no tears
that he died.

Later that night, I burned the doll that killed him.

Next morning, frost; first kiss of winter. I added layers of wool, and
laced my feet and legs into boots lined with rabbit; gathered my satch-
els, took up a tin can I hung from the hook at my belt, and marched

from the rotten timber shack into a silver forest, glittering, spiked with light and a chill.

Persimmons had fallen overnight and the deer had not got to them. Quick business, but careful; those thin orange skins split open at the hint of a tense finger, and I ruined more than I cared to admit. Popped them in my mouth to hide the evidence. Spit out the seeds into my palm, and tucked them into the satchel where I kept the needle and thread. The rest, what was perfect and frostbit, I carried in the can for old Ruth.

She was knitting when I came upon her, sitting on her slanting porch as though the cold was nothing to withered flesh. Crooked broken teeth, crooked smile that might have been pretty but for the long scar pulling her bottom lip.

"Clora, you brought me sweets," she cooed, setting aside her yarn. "Enough for pudding?"

I placed the tin can into her hands, which were scarred with needle pricks. "Not yet. Maybe tomorrow."

She caught my wrist before I could pull away. "And the ashes?"

I knew better than to hesitate. No good to pretend I was happy, either. Obedience was enough. Obedience was the same as falling on knees, like the Sunday regulars the preacher took down to the river to pray at the cross and handle the Lucifer snake he kept in a pine box.

I dug into the satchel and pulled out a small packet of folded calico, sewn shut with my finest black thread stitches. Ruth's smile widened, and she snatched it from my hand—holding it up to her nose and closing her eyes with pleasure.

"Good," she said, finally. "Edward had it coming for what he did to you."

I grunted, walking past Ruth into the cabin, unable to look into her eyes.

"Clean your needles," Ruth called after me. "Time for lessons, Clora."

I lit the fire, and while the flames leapt and scrambled within the stove, I relieved the burden of needle and thread: slender bone daggers punched with holes; and rough spools, collapsed with lichen-dyed browns and a rich burgundy soaked from sumac-bobs; thin as a strangler's wire and finely made—by my own hands, hours spent at the fixing of such binding threads.

The needles still had blood on them. I sat down at the table, wet the bone with a dash of apple vinegar poured from a flask in my satchel, and scrubbed hard with the pad of my thumb. Skin to bone, trying to summon the proper devotion. I was still scrubbing, whispering, when Ruth limped into her home.

Her own needles gleamed white as snow, hung around her neck like a fan of quick fingers.

"Not saying their names right," she said, leaning so close the great bulk of her breasts touched my back. "Need to show your kin the proper respect, Clora. All my teachings to no account, otherwise."

And then her hand fell upon my hair, warm as the fire burning, sinking into my skull behind my eyes, and she said, "Try again tomorrow. Right now we got a poppet to make. Some Buck Creek girl set her eye on a cutter man from the quarry, and her mother wants him gone."

I spread the needles over the table. "Maybe he loves her."

Ruth snorted, and drew away. "Her mother brought a cutting of his hair."

Nothing more needed saying.

The ground was still soft over Edward's grave.

His brothers were too lazy to pack him down hard, or even lay stone on top, which was what he would have wanted, being a cutter at the quarry for most of his adult life. I took a stroll past Martha's cabin on the way to the hill, making sure she was home.

Wives were odd sometimes. Over the years, I'd seen a few who couldn't pull themselves from the graves of lost men, sitting up all through the day and night with Bibles, crosses, or nothing to hold but their skirts and faces, weeping and praying like God would give them a resurrection, like maybe their men were as good as Jesus and would be risen. Seemed to me that was arrogance bordering on sin, but not one that was any worse than murder.

Martha was home. I stood at the edge of the forest, staring at her lit windows, watching her make circles all around her kitchen. I could have gone closer, but the old coonhound was tied to the porch, and even though he knew me, there was no sense in sparking the possibility of him making an unattractive sound.

The forest sang at night, trills and clicks, and whispers of the wind in the naked rubbing branches. Coyotes yipped and somewhere close a fox screamed like a woman, making my skin crawl cold even though it was nothing to fear.

The shovel was heavy on my shoulder. So was the ax.

I found the grave before moonrise and started digging. Took hours. I didn't focus as I should. Kept thinking about Edward Bromes, and my last view of his body before his brothers slid him into the pine box: pale, stiff, eyes sewn shut.

I thought about other men, too.

I had to jump down into the hole, standing waist-high in loose dirt as I used the ax to pry apart the soft, cheap wood. Martha had insisted on something finer than a muslin shroud, but each groan of those splitting planks made my heart beat harder until I was breathless, expecting to hear shouts, dogs barking. The night was all as it should be, though: empty, quiet, crisp with frost.

Edward smelled a little, but no worse than other corpses. I looked down at him with nothing but a small tallow candle to enhance my sight, but that was more than enough. I had sewn the stitches myself to close his eyes, prepared the body for burial under the watchful, too watchful, gaze of his wife, and now we were met again and he was still dead, but with a purpose.

I cut off his right hand, wrapped it in oilskin, and reburied him.

By sunrise I was home, and had just enough time to wash up before I went for another day of lessons with old Ruth.

Think what you will, but I had no real family. Mother dead from the influenza, father run off with a woman who clerked for the big boss at the quarry. Gone ten years, and maybe he'd thought a six-year-old daughter would be cared for by relations, but a good hunting dog would have been more welcome, and was; old Tick, a bloodhound come down from Kentucky as a puppy, brought to heel by an uncle after my father run off, and I still recall Martha and Edward and another aunt being angry about the inconvenient loss.

I was another mouth to feed. By the time Ruth found me, I had no shoes, no coat, and my hair had to be shorn to the scalp because of lice and fleas. I still remember the sores on my legs and arms: insect bites scratched to infection; and the vinegar baths and salt scrubs, and willow-bark tea forced down my throat for weeks, weeks after Ruth took me in and clothed me like a doll in soft dresses.

"Clora, my sweet," she'd say, and I loved her for it. Decided, in that pure childlike naivete kin to wishing on a star, that I would do anything for her, I'd care for her, I'd be hers in body and soul.

It was the soul part I hadn't realized would be a problem.

The poppet for the mother of the Buck Creek girl took three days to make.

I cut cloth from one of the old burlap bags folded by the fireplace, and took up a smaller, sharper finger-blade to shear out the shape of a man. Twice I did this, using the first as a pattern that I traced with a stick of coal. Ruth had taught me to do the same with twisted roots and vines, formed to take a human shape; or dried corn cobs or clay; but cloth had advantages that Ruth had spelled into me, such as it could be sewn into a vessel filled with all the sundry items a good hoodoo needed: blood and bones, and cuttings of hair; dried fluids from a man's loving, trapped on cloth; mushrooms, feathers, shell, and stone. Little bits of power in the right hands with the right intent and desire, making a sympathetic echo that might correspond to a living human body.

"Need to fix that red stitch," Ruth told me, as I sewed. "Fix it or start over."

I pulled the bone needle back through the hole as Ruth turned away to her own sewing: a doll as long as my forearm, with a real face embroidered in her finest threads: black hair, blue thread dyed from woad for his eyes, a strong nose identified by a crooked line.

"Haven't told me who that's for," I said, quiet.

"Hush." Ruth put a fat persimmon in her mouth, and began sucking on it. "You'll make another mistake. All my teaching will be for naught if you keep up this way."

I gave her a small smile, but with my eyes averted. I only made mistakes when I had a mind to do so. Ruth might say she wanted me strong, and I'd tried to please her in that way before I realized better—before I seen a look she couldn't hide on the day I sewed a hoodoo that made a man burst his brain with apoplexy before I finished the last stitch. Us at the spring market in the valley, sitting under a tree, and all it was supposed to be was a lesson in seeing the hoodoo make a man itch. Not die.

So, I made mistakes after that. Small ones. Enough to make me look weak.

Not from guilt.

I wanted to survive.

I walked the poppet down to Buck Creek on the fourth day. It was cold and bright, and the closer I got to the bottom of the valley, the more houses I saw deep in the woods—and in the distance, the winding track of the dirt road that somewhere bled north into a larger road, and larger, beyond which I'd never seen.

I didn't need Ruth's directions to find the right home, built into the side of a rocky hill cleared of trees. I could hear the creek, but the chickens were louder, scratching in a large pen guarded by a hound gone gray at the muzzle. The mother was out in the yard splitting firewood, cheeks red from exertion and the chill, her bare hands the same color. Her smile was tight-lipped when she saw me, but I didn't take it hard. Asking for a bad act was the same as committing it, and didn't matter how it was done: God would be all for the remembering, when the final day was come.

"Didn't expect you so soon," she said.

"Soon as done," I replied, looking around. "Is your daughter here?"

Her gaze hardened. "Off to the quarry. She brings that man his lunch. Won't be reasoned with, no matter how hard I come at her."

"Shame," I said, wondering at how much I sounded like Ruth. "Terrible she won't believe you. About his way with women, I mean."

"I only want what's best for her. Plenty of fine men, without Betty making eyes at a no-good. If he gets her with child . . ." The mother made a disgusted sound, and leaned the ax against the cutting block. "God's work that Margaret down at the Bend heard of his wandering eye before I let it go too far."

God's work, maybe. My work, certainly. Rumors could cast a spell just as powerful as needle and thread.

I began to pull the poppet from my satchel, but the mother stiffened and took a step back.

"Not out here," she said, looking around as if a crowd from church had gathered in the trees. "Not here."

We went inside. Her cabin was dark, but it smelled like warm bread and coffee. She offered me none of that, except a handful of crumpled bills that looked like the right amount, though it was hard to tell. I didn't count them. Ruth knew how to handle a cheater, well and good, which this woman surely knew.

I laid the poppet on the table. "You sure you want to do this yourself?"

The mother hesitated. "What does it take?"

"Burn it," I said. "Or stab it. Twist its head to break his neck. Anything you do will kill him, slow or fast."

She went pale. "That's the Devil's work."

I offered back her money. "You said you wanted him gone."

The mother stared at the doll and took a long, deep breath. I waited, already knowing the answer.

When I left her home, I carried the poppet in my satchel—and the money, too.

I walked toward the quarry.

The man was easy to find, as he was lunching with a girl no older than me, sixteen at best, pretty as morning with long blond hair and a face that might have been her mother's, if her mother had ever been young and happy.

I watched them from the edge of the woods and ate my own lunch: a soft-boiled egg, a bit of bacon between some bread. Tapped my feet and rubbed my hands, trying to stay warm, watching the man and girl smile and laugh and make lovey-dovey with their eyes—and me, wondering all the while what that would feel like, wishing and afraid, but mostly wishing.

The girl left with a laugh and kiss. The man watched her go. His eyes, for her only. If he had ever wandered, I was certain he would never wander on her.

I started walking before he did, making my way through the woods so that I was waiting for him on the trail down to the quarry. He took his time, and was whistling when he saw me—though that stopped when he said, "Miss?"

Nothing hard in his face. Nothing bad, as was believed. The girl was right to love him. I had known it for weeks now, from the first time I seen them together.

I put my hand in the satchel, on the rough skin of the burlap doll. "I've come to warn you, mister."

He frowned. "Who are you?"

"Someone who knows old Ruth," I said, and something cold and small entered his eyes, natural as the ill, bone-chilling breeze passing around us on the trail. Ruth was like that breeze in these parts, known and accepted, and respected out of fear. Most granny women were, like as in the blood, born from the old country that was still rich in the veins of those who had settled these hills and valleys. Fear of a hoodoo woman was natural. Fear was how it had to be.

"Ruth has her eye on you," I said. "When it comes, it'll be her doing."

He paled. "Done nothing wrong. Don't even *know* her."

I stepped back into the woods. "Remember what I told you. It was Ruth who ordered it."

"Wait," he began, reaching for me. I slipped away, but he did not try to follow. Instead he ran up the trail, away from the quarry. Chasing the girl, I thought. She was something he wanted to live for.

I pulled out the poppet, and twisted its head clear around.

The man was buried two days later, and the night after I slithered into that proper cemetery and dug for him. If he was watching from on high, I didn't mind. I sawed off his hand, and wrapped it up tight.

=====

I was good at digging for the dead. Ruth started me at the age of twelve, from necessity. It was time. I'd become a woman, my first bleed, and needles couldn't be made from any old bone. So my own mother was first, and my grandmother after her—followed by *her* mother. Nothing less would do, Ruth said, and I believed her though it made me cry. Took a long while, too, and lucky for me my relatives were buried in the family plot, out in the hills where no one ever came.

All for sympathy, was something else Ruth taught me. Bones had to be sympathetic to make a hoodoo stitch work its wiles, and nothing was more in sympathy than a line of women, from mother to daughter and backward to beyond. Never mind any strife that might have pressed between generations. Who was left living mattered most to the dead. According to Ruth, that was me.

Though it seemed, as it had for some time, that it wasn't just the bones of those come before that might matter in the stitching. Any bone, from a body with desire, might have a say in the power of a hoodoo.

Any bone at all.

Now, there were stories come down from the hills that I remembered being told even as a child, and the telling of them was still rich on the tongues of the people who settled in the valley and high country, away from the quarry. Tales of the banshee and hag-riders, and the little folk who Ruth thought she could consort with, though I'd never seen anything but a raccoon sip the milk she left out, nights. I don't know if I believed in such tales, though I respected the possibility, given the power of the needle and stitch, which had to come from somewhere—and if not the world of the spirit then maybe God, though I did not think He would approve the use for which His gift had been put.

It certainly was not for God that I was a conspirator to murder. And I had no confidence that He had a greater hold of my soul than Ruth.

Took me four years to realize something might be shifty, and by then I was ten. I got it in my head to go raiding some jar of sweets that Ruth kept just for herself, and it wasn't a minute after my first bite of pepper-

mint that the pain started in, right in my stomach. I doubled over thinking I'd been stabbed, sure to find blood, but nothing was there but the
certainty that my insides were going to spill outside.

Calling for Ruth did no good. She was standing right there, watching. Holding a doll made of pale cloth, large as a swaddled babe and
cradled in her arms with a fork jabbed into its belly.

Ruth's eyes, satisfied and cold. "Been soft on you. And now you try
to steal from me. After everything I done to keep you whole."

Well, it took me a week to walk after that.

But it gave me time to think.

That new doll, with the blue eyes and crooked nose, remained a silent
presence. Ruth worked on it with a steadiness I'd not seen in years, taking care with every stitch, mumbling devotionals over her needles before
she'd even thread them. I watched her clean those bone daggers each
morning, and when it came time to fill that doll with the hoodoo, she
made me go outside in the cold and practice my embroidery, claiming a
need to concentrate in peace. It was no consequence to me. I knew what
she was doing. Capturing a soul was no secret, even though she'd never
taught me the way of it.

"Power makes you greedy," Ruth said, seven days after needling that
first stitch. "I'm no innocent in that regard, as you well know."

I was standing beside the fireplace, bent over a tin pail that held a
mixture of cow urine, fermented these last three weeks, and the smashed
hulls of black walnuts. Preparing dye for the thread, spun with my own
hands from wool shorn from the sheep that Ruth kept in a pen on the hill.

"Look at me," she said.

The doll was in front of her on the table, soft limbs stretched out,
soft body embroidered with runes and blooms and glimpses of eyes peering from behind twisting vines. I looked for only a moment and then
settled on Ruth, who was eyeing me all speculative. I kept still.

"You have never been greedy," she said, finally. "Never saw a sign
of it in your eyes, and I been looking for years, since I showed you that
first stitch."

"I don't want what you have," I said truthfully.

Ruth grunted, and pushed herself off the chair. "Good girl."

I hesitated. "Never asked who taught *you*."

Oh, the smile that flitted across her mouth. Made me cold.

"My teacher," Ruth murmured, stroking the bone needles laid out on the table. "My own granny, with her wiles. My mother had no gift for the stitch, but there was something in me, from the beginning."

Her gaze met mine. "Same as I saw in you."

My cheeks warmed. "No use for it, except killing. That's no life, Ruth."

"Better life than what you were headed for." Her fat fingers flicked through the air above the blue-eyed poppet. "Would have been in a grave. Nothing to show for living. Nothing to show those sympathetic bones."

I looked down at my needles, spread across the table. Each one born from a hand, hands whose names I knew: Lettie, Polly, Rebecca. Mother, Grandmother, Great-Grandmother.

And now I knew the names of other bones from other hands.

All in sympathy.

It'd been years since Ruth had ventured off her land, but that afternoon she put on a woolen skirt and coat that moths and mice had been chewing on for a decade, pinned up her long gray hair, and buttoned her blouse until those needles hanging around her neck were hid. Not that showing them would have made folks any less uncomfortable. Ruth walking amongst the good Christians of the valley might be enough to thin the blood of that hollering preacher himself.

We were real silent until the end, just before she limped out the door, and she looked back and said, "There's a man come to my attention. You go home now, come back tomorrow."

"You need help?" I asked, but she raised her brow at me, made a clucking nose, and walked on out. The poppet was in a cloth bag that swung from her shoulder.

I followed her, soon after.

Ruth had a fast limp. I had to hustle to catch up. Not that I wanted to get too close, but there was some investment on my part, and so I took a different trail that was roundabout and uneven, steep—too difficult for Ruth to walk, though I myself was too fast, sliding and flirting with loose rocks underfoot, and low-lying branches that might have taken my eye or broken my nose if I hadn't been quick to duck. All for good, though. I reached the bottom of the trail, certain I was first and Ruth, somewhere above, still huffing and puffing.

I kept to the woods, lungs tight as I forced down deep breaths of cold air, and made my way to a small log cabin settled in a clearing where a man stood on the covered porch, rocking a baby. A stone cutter, still dusty from the quarry, staring at his child like she was sunshine and angels, and so much sweetness I had to look away.

I took another breath, and walked from the woods.

"Clora," he said, with a tired smile, kind as could be. "Been some time."

"I'm sorry for that, Paul." I hoped he couldn't hear the thickness of my voice. "How's Delphia?"

Paul glanced over his shoulder at the cabin's closed door. "Pain's lessened, I think. That tea you brought seemed to help her sleep. But it's this one," and he paused, holding his babe a little tighter, "that's gotten fussy."

"Etta," I murmured, peering into blue eyes that were just like her father's.

"Oh, but it's nothing," said Paul, just as gently, and kissed her brow. "I'm just glad I'm fit to care for her. What with . . ."

He stopped. I looked away again, toward the woods. His wife was dying, eaten up by scirrhus in her breasts. No stitch could cure her of those tumors. Maybe, if caught early. But not by the time I heard. Not for nothing did I think it fair the needle could kill or control, but when it came to healing a mother, all that power was to no account.

"It won't be much longer," I said quietly.

Paul's jaw tightened. "Then just me and Etta. Been thinking of leaving the quarry when that happens, maybe to find work in one of the towns up north. Cutting stone is too dangerous. Can't let nothing happen to me now."

I glanced down at the baby. "You have something to live for."

Paul made a small sound. "Come inside, Clora."

"Can't." I backed away, shaking my head. "Ruth is coming."

He frowned, holding his daughter tighter. "You shouldn't spend so much time with that witchy woman. You'll get the taint on you."

"Too late," I said, making his frown deepen. "And didn't you hear me?"

"Heard." Paul gave me a disapproving look. "Got nothing to fear from an old woman. Why she visiting, anyhow?"

"Your wife sent a note. She got it in her head that Ruth could cure her."

His brow raised. "Can she?"

"No." I stepped off the porch, nearly falling, and suddenly it was hard to see past the tears blurring my eyes. "She's going to hurt you, Paul. I want you to remember that. It was *her* doing."

Her doing, not mine. Her doing, even though it was me that put the idea in Delphia's head, even though I was the one who carried the note, that note that told a story of how much a woman would give to live just a while longer so that she might not leave behind a little daughter and a good man. A good man who loved her with all his soul, she said.

I knew the interest Ruth would have in a man like Paul: so good, so true. Nothing rarer. Nothing more powerful.

I walked away, and as he called my name, the baby cried.

It got done, just as I knew it would, and the stain was on my hands sure as if I'd taken a knife and cut Paul's heart.

I heard of his death from Martha, who stopped by my shack because she was terrible lonely—terrible, to come visiting a girl she'd never wanted—but even if the words hadn't come from her mouth, I'd seen the doll on Ruth's special shelf where she kept other poppets filled with death's power, and I had to turn away, not wanting to look too deep into those embroidered blue eyes. Not because I was reminded of Paul, but because all I could think of was his daughter who would soon be alone. Delphia wouldn't last the week, Martha said. Blamed the shock of losing her husband.

Sure, I'd known that, too, even if I hadn't wanted to think on it.

Wasn't just power that made people greedy, but desperation. And I'd had plenty of that building inside me, years on end.

The night Paul was buried, I went and stole his hand.

Now, I was guessing that the dead might know the truth of things, that I was no innocent and that my soul was in the shadow, but I hoped these men might also recall those words I'd spoken at the end—to Edward, too—that it was Ruth, Ruth, Ruth that made the spell that killed them. They might be sympathetic, as such, to my plight. A gamble, but one worth taking.

I made the needles from their bones. One full week it took to extract and carve, and polish—and pray as I had never prayed—but when I had my little daggers I began sewing the doll.

The cloth I used was old. Old enough that I'd had to dig up my mother, grandmother, and great-grandmother for it. The oldest of them was a white wedding gown, turned brown with age; and then a black dress torn up with holes; and last, a gown made of muslin that tore so easily, I held my breath when I added it to the patchwork of poppet flesh.

Days I practiced stitches with Ruth, and nights I stitched to kill her, embroidering a fantasy of freedom upon the skin of the doll: an open road leading to its heart, and the blue sky, and birds with their wings outstretched. Black thread held the joints, but everywhere else, color sapped from forest dyes, from the walnut and woad, safflower and goldenrod, mixed double, double, to toil and trouble.

I poured my heart into the making of that poppet. I poured what was left of my soul. And when I was done, or near so, I cut open my arm to spill my blood upon its guts: strands of hair I'd gathered, sneak-like, over years in Ruth's home; persimmon seeds she'd spit from her mouth into the yard; and chicken bones where her teeth left marks. Epsom salts for freedom, and blue salt for healing; gray talcum powder to protect from evil; and last, dirt from the graves of my mothers. Dirt from the graves of the men, along with a finger from each of their hands.

And when I was done I set a shroud upon the thing, because its eyes seemed to watch me, and I could not stand the judgment already waiting, on high and low, and inside my heart where there was no peace and never would be, even if I got what I wanted.

Even so.

"There's something different about you," Ruth said, setting down some knitting as I approached her cabin. The morning sun was on her: hair silver as frost, her skin pale, and those bone needles shining white around her throat.

"I'm tired," I said. "Been thinking."

"Dangerous." Ruth heaved herself from the rocking chair and went inside. "I'll make you tea."

She said those words with kindness. I'd heard them a million times. Comforting, warm. Ruth, who had rescued me. Ruth, who had raised me as her own. Ruth, who had been my teacher and friend.

When she turned her back on me I reached inside the satchel, grabbed the poppet, and squeezed.

Her back arched so wild she went up on her toes, a rattling cry tearing from her throat. I squeezed harder and heard a cracking sound. Bone, breaking.

Ruth crumpled, slamming down with a thud that rattled the entire porch. For a moment she was completely still, and then her fingers twitched, and her hands and arms began to move, and she clawed at the planks, panting for air. Her legs remained still.

I took a long deep breath, and climbed the steps. My heart pounded. Dark spots floated in my vision. Ruth tried to grab my foot, hissing curses at me, but I sidestepped and went into the cabin.

I gathered the dolls on the shelf, including one with my name embroidered over the heart. My hands burned when I touched it, dizziness sweeping down, but I swallowed hard and held the doll close—burning, burning—and went back outside.

"I'll kill you," Ruth whispered, gaze burning with hate. "I should have killed you years ago."

"You held the leash and thought that was enough."

Foam touched her lips. "I *cared* for you."

I held up the doll she had made to control me. "Not in the right way."

"You would do the same!" Ruth tried to grab me again as I walked past her to the yard. I dumped the dolls on the hard frost, and then reached into the satchel for Ruth's poppet. I went back and showed it to her, crouching a safe distance away. Her eyes narrowed, and even with her back broke I saw those wheels turning, how she examined every stitch, searching for a flaw. But of course there was none. If I'd done one thing wrong, I'd be dead and she would be kicking my corpse into the refuse pile for the pigs to eat.

"Impossible." Ruth tore her gaze from the poppet. "I own you."

"I found sympathy." I pulled down my collar to reveal two necklaces of bone needles hanging from my neck. "Just enough."

Her eyes widened. "Those men."

I said nothing, and the silence was terrible and heavy, heavy on me because I saw myself in that moment; me, in Ruth's place, sprawled on the porch with a broken back and some other girl standing over me, ready to take my place with a fury. Future or not, it chilled me.

"Oh, God kill you," Ruth whispered. "God kill you, and the Devil, too."

"In time," I said, and twisted the poppet's head.

Freedom should have a tingle, some flash of light, but I felt no different afterward. Maybe I wasn't free. Maybe being free of Ruth wasn't the same thing at all.

I burned all the dolls, except mine. I was too much a coward to tempt my own death, though I deserved it in a mighty way. Shadow of death over my heart, waiting, waiting, for the needle and thread. Wicked stitchery.

I wanted to learn a different kind.

Ruth, I burned with the dolls. I broke her needles.

But I kept her house.

A week later, I heard word that Delphia had passed. No relatives nearby to care for the baby, and no one stepped in to take claim. I waited, to be sure, and then went down into the valley to take the girl. I did not ask.

I held out my arms, and there was something in the way those folk looked at me, something I'd never seen before except when they looked at Ruth, but I supposed I finally had her eyes.

I took the child in, but the only doll I made for her was stitched for play, with a needle from her father's hand.

Things would be different, I promised.

All for sympathy for the bones.

Low School

RHYS BOWEN

Rhys Bowen currently writes two historical mystery series: the Molly Murphy novels, featuring a feisty Irish immigrant sleuth in 1900s New York City, and the lighter, funnier Royal Spyness series about Lady Georgiana, thirty-fifth in line to the British throne in the 1930s. Rhys's books have received many award nominations and she has won thirteen major awards, including Agatha, Anthony and Macavity as well as Reader's Choice for Best Mystery Series. Her books are definitely traditional mysteries so she loves writing short stories where she can reveal her inner dark and evil side. Rhys is a transplanted Brit, now dividing her time between California and Arizona, where she goes to escape the harsh California winters.

"Where are your two number-two pencils, properly sharpened?"

I looked up at a man who had a face like a skeleton—sunken eyes, skin stretched over cheekbones, thin humorless mouth. His glasses were perched on the end of a long nose and he was almost bald, too, completing the skeletonlike effect. He was wearing a grayish-white, short-sleeved button-down shirt with ink stains around the pocket, and a tie onto which egg had dripped at some stage. The word *schoolteacher* formed in my mind at the same moment that he repeated the question.

"Your two number-two pencils? Properly sharpened?" He paused, those colorless sunken eyes staring at me now with distaste. "You do have your two number-two pencils, properly sharpened, I hope?"

I patted my side, then looked around me. "I don't seem to have brought a purse."

He made the sort of tut-tutting noise I'd only read about before and gave a big dramatic sigh. "Not a good start to our first day, is it? The instruction sheet clearly told you that two number-two pencils would be required and that they should be properly sharpened as there is no sharpener available in the examination room."

"I don't think I received . . ." I stammered. "I don't remember receiving any kind of instruction sheet."

"Everybody is sent the instruction sheet in preparation for their first day," the man said. "Clearly you chose to disregard the instructions. I shall have to report this to Ms. Fer."

"Ms. Fur?"

"Our principal. And no, it is not spelled *fur* like the animal's hair. It is *Fer* from the Latin 'to do' or 'to make,' as I'm sure you know, being a student of the subject."

I nodded.

"I'm afraid Ms. Fer will not be pleased. Oh, dear me, no. We expect everyone here to obey the instructions to the letter."

I shrugged. "Well, I'm sorry but I don't remember receiving any instruction sheet. I guess it must have been lost in the mail. And I can't make pencils appear out of thin air."

He reached into his shirt pocket. "As it happens, I do have a pencil I can lend you, just for today," he said. "To help you out this once. Until you know the ropes. But I expect it to be returned immediately after the examination, you understand. And don't break the point because there is no way to sharpen it in the examination room."

I stared at his pocket, blinked, then stared some more because I could have sworn there had been no pencil sticking out of that pocket before but now there appeared to be several. He handed it to me solemnly, as if he were bestowing a great gift. Then he glanced at his watch. "You'd better hurry. Showing up late for the examination is something that wouldn't be so easily forgiven. Go on. Off you go."

"Where is the exam room?" I asked. My heart was racing now.

"Didn't bother to read that either, I see," he said, looking down at me as if I were a hopeless case. "Not a good start, Miss Weinstein. Not what we expect here. It's room six hundred and sixty-six. Off you go then. Hurry."

He pushed open a door for me and I stepped through into a long hallway. It was dark and dingy, lined with lockers and with doors spaced at intervals along either side. From behind these doors came the occasional murmur of voices. But the hallway was deserted. Nobody to ask where I should go. Where the hell was I anyway? I tried to remember but my brain remained fuzzy. My nose twitched at the familiar smells—chalk and books and old sweaty socks and food left to go bad in forgotten lunch bags.

"High school!" I said out loud. That's where I was. I was in a high school, but certainly not my own. My school was all glass and brightly lit hallways with murals on the walls. This one hadn't had a paint job in years, nor had a janitor been around with a broom for decades, judging by the drifts of trash in the corners. I stopped walking. So what was I doing here? Why couldn't I remember? The word *accident* formed itself at the back of my consciousness. Something to do with an accident. That was it—I'd been in the hospital. A bad accident, obviously, since I appeared to have lost my memory. Perhaps my parents had decided to send me to another school until I could catch up with the work I had missed. Perhaps I was only here to take an exam I had missed—the SATs? A college entrance exam? But wait—hadn't I already taken my SATs? Or had that just been a practice test?

My stomach had tied itself into knots at the mention of the word *exam*. I couldn't be late for an exam, whatever it was. I broke into a run, feeling my shoes, which were somehow too big at the heels, slipping off as I ran. Why was I wearing heavy, unfashionable shoes and not my usual heels? I tossed that thought from my mind. The only thing that mattered at this moment was to find the exam room and be on time.

I was never late for anything. I always aced exams. Honor student. Class president, that was me. And whatever this exam was, I'd ace it and get back to my own school and my old life because I sure as hell wasn't staying in a dump like this. I almost skidded on a tossed banana peel. A door opened and a boy came out. Before I could ask him where I'd find the exam room he glanced in both directions, then took off at a run down the hall and disappeared into the gloom through more double doors at the other end. I glanced up as I saw a movement to my right. A girl was walking beside me—a dumpy, overweight girl with an awful haircut, an atrocious hand-knitted purple sweater and a long droopy skirt. Honestly, how could some people be so clueless about fashion sense? Didn't she realize her clothes made her look like a pathetic, sagging balloon? No wonder she was sneaking along, cutting class. I would, too, if I looked like that.

I lifted my hand to brush my hair from my face and the girl did the same thing at the same time. I took a step forward and she had vanished. I stopped, stepped backward and she appeared again, looking at me with a puzzled expression.

"Wait," I said and I saw her mouth move in sync with mine. Cautiously I lifted one hand, and to my horror she did the same. Was she making fun of me or what?

"Listen, you," I said and took a threatening step toward her. She did the same. I froze as I realized I was staring into a mirror. This dumpy, clueless, disgusting person had to be me. I looked down and saw this was true. I was wearing a purple hand-knitted sweater and a long shapeless skirt. And as I touched the rough yarn of the sweater I remembered my mother making it for me. She was always knitting me things until I told her that there was no way I was ever going to be seen dead in something she made for me again. But that was after Sally Ann helped me lose weight and taught me how to dress.

So why had I gone back to looking like this? When had I put on all this weight I'd taken all that trouble to lose? And why wasn't I even bothering to wear makeup? The accident—I thought. It must have been a really bad accident and I must have been in the hospital for a while and put on weight while I was there and my old clothes were the only things that would fit me. But would I ever have left the house willingly looking like this? I tried to remember getting ready this morning, eating breakfast, driving or taking a school bus, but no memories would come. I really was in a bad way, but I was sure of one thing: when I got home tonight I was going to burn these icky clothes and go on a crash diet until I looked like myself again.

Then I remembered the examination. That was more important right now than worrying about the way I was dressed. I peered through the half darkness to see if the rooms were numbered, but they were not. How was I supposed to find the six hundred hall if I didn't know where I was now?

Simple, I thought. I'd find the office and have someone show me the way. And if I was late for the exam, they'd understand that I was new. At least I could make myself a bit more presentable before anyone saw me. I could slick back my hair and roll up that long skirt and perhaps I was wearing a T-shirt under the sweater. I ducked into a girls' bathroom at the end of the hall and coughed as the smell of smoke met me. The air was so thick with smoke that the lighting created a red haze through which the shape of the sinks and the stalls beyond were only indistinct shapes. Then I saw that I wasn't alone. Four girls, dressed in black, were lounging against the basins, smoking. They were all in tight, tight jeans and black T-shirts with skulls and similar scary images on them. They looked up with cold, predatory eyes as I came in. As the biggest one, wearing a studded leather jacket, turned to me, a trick of the reddish shadows almost made it look as if she had a tail. I gasped.

"Well, look what the cat just brought in," she said. Two others straightened up.

"What do you think you're doing, fatso scum?" The one in the studded jacket stepped right in front of me and blew smoke in my face. "Are you totally clueless? Don't you know that this is the GothChix bathroom? Nobody else comes in here, not if they know what's good for them. The last stupid girl said she really had to go, so could she possibly use the toilet. And you know—we let her. Well, actually we flushed her head down the toilet. And she was so scared she wet herself, remember?"

She looked to her friends for confirmation and they nodded, grinning.

"But her head wasn't quite as round as yours. Yours would probably get stuck and the janitor would have to come and get you out."

"Or she'd have to walk around with a toilet on her head all day," someone else commented. "I'd like to see that."

The other girls laughed.

"Wanna try?" She moved closer again.

"Look, I'm sorry," I said, holding up my hands in front of me as if to ward off a blow. "I didn't know. I'm new here. I don't belong."

"She's right about that. She belongs at a bag ladies' convention," one of the other girls said. She gave me a shove, sending me sprawling into the big girl. The studs on that jacket dug into my cheek and I gave a cry of pain. They laughed again.

"What's your name, bag lady?" she asked.

"It's Amy. Amy Weinstein."

"We won't forget it, Amy Weinstein. We don't like the look of you. You better watch yourself."

Some of my innate spunk was resurfacing. "You can't talk to me like that. I'll report you to the principal."

For some reason this made them roar with laughter. "Oh, that's a good one," one of the girls said, wiping her eyes.

"If she really wants to go see the principal, then good luck to her," another said.

The big girl grabbed my sweater front and dragged me close to her. "I'll tell you one thing, girl. You show your face in here again and we'll pull out your eyelashes, one by one. Got it?" She gave me a hearty shove that sent me ricocheting off the basins and staggering into the tiled wall. "Now get lost."

I fled, disgusted at myself for not standing up to them. The hallway was still deserted and opened into another, identical hallway. I must be really, seriously late for that exam by now. I wondered if I dared to report those girls and what they might do to me if I did. One thing's for sure, I thought as I hurried forward, peering into the darkness that seemed even deeper in this hallway, there is no way I'm staying here. What were my parents thinking, sending me to a place like this? If it's just one exam I'm supposed to take here, then fine, but I'm sure as hell not coming back.

Then a thought flashed across my consciousness. An image of a grave and I'm dressed in black and . . . my father is dead. I went to his funeral. I stopped walking and stood, frowning as I tried to make sense of this fact. How could that be? I tried to picture that funeral but nothing would come. A bell rang, jangling loudly above my head. Doors opened and students streamed out, making me feel like a salmon swimming upstream. I was pushed and jostled around as they hurried past.

"Wait," I called. "I'm trying to find the six hundred hall. Room six hundred and sixty-six."

They acted as if they hadn't heard me. Their faces went past me in a blur. The hallway cleared until it was deserted again. I decided I should follow them—at least I'd have a chance of finding a classroom with someone in it before the next period started. As I walked on down the hall I heard the sound of knocking—a hollow hammering sound. It seemed to be coming from one of the lockers. I went over and listened. As well as the knocking I heard a muffled voice yelling, "Help, let me out."

I opened the locker door and a small skinny boy half fell out. He was naked, wearing his underpants over his head. I helped him to his feet.

"Here," I said, taking his underpants off his head. "You'd better put these on quickly. I won't look." I turned away.

"Thanks," he said. "I've been in there since last night. I thought I was going to pass out from lack of air."

"What happened to your clothes?" I looked in the locker.

"The jocks took them. I expect they've dumped them in the trash and they've been burned by now."

"Come on," I said. "I'll take you to the principal's office and you can report them. And you can telephone your parents for more clothes."

"Are you crazy? I'm not going anywhere near the principal's office," he said. "I'm not that stupid. I'll see if I can find something to fit me in the lost and found." He started down the hall, but then turned back. "Thanks for rescuing me."

"You should seriously report this. It's not right. Bullies should be punished."

"Happens all the time," he said. "If you're small they pick on you. Bullies rule here. You're either the predator or the prey. And you'll be prey, just like me."

"Then transfer to another school."

For some reason this made him grin. "You must be new," he said.

"I am, and I'm supposed to be taking an exam, in the six hundred hall."

"Room six-six-six?" he asked and made a face.

I nodded. "Can you tell me where it is? I'm already late."

"Oh no. You'd better run. That direction. You keep going until the very end, then up the stairs to the top floor. It's a long way. I hope they won't give you detention on your first day."

"Is detention that bad?"

He nodded silently. "The worst. It's . . . down there, you know? You don't want detention. Trust me."

He scurried away in the opposite direction and I started to run again.

It was hot and stuffy here and the sweater was way too thick and itchy. I felt perspiration trickling down under my arms and checked to see what I was wearing under that sweater. Nothing. Not even a bra. And it appeared that I had not used any deodorant because I stank. What was the matter with me—who let me leave the house dressed like this? I reached the end of the hall and as I pushed open the swinging doors into a stairwell another smell hit me. The faint odor of rotten eggs. Probably the science lab, I thought. An experiment gone wrong or students playing a trick on the science teacher by mixing the wrong chemicals.

I started up the stairs. The staircase was in almost total darkness and I kept going, up and up. I would never get to the exam at this rate. What would happen if I failed it? Or if they wouldn't even let me take it because I was so late? Would that mean I couldn't go back to my old school, or I'd fail my college entrance exam? I counted the floors and came at last to what had to be the sixth. How come a school this large didn't even have an elevator? It must take forever to get between classes. My feet echoed on the vinyl floor and back from the tiled walls. *Clomp, clomp, clomp.* A door opened suddenly and an angry face looked out. A woman's face, birdlike with a big nose and cold reptilian eyes.

"You, girl—what do you think you are doing?" she snapped. "Disturbing my examination."

I glanced up at the door. The numbers 666 were now glowing over the door frame.

"I'm supposed to be here," I said. "I'm to take this exam but nobody told me how to find the room. I'm sorry I'm late."

"You will be sorry, if you don't complete the exam in time," she said. "What's your name?"

"Amy Weinstein."

"Ah, yes. We were expecting you." The smile on her face was not welcoming, but instead expressed malicious delight. "Amy Weinstein who thinks a lot of herself. Thinks she's the cat's whiskers. Overachiever—am I right?"

"I'm a good student," I said. "I worked hard for everything I achieved. My parents didn't have the money to send me to a good college so I had to get a scholarship."

I paused as I said the words. Had I already gotten into college? In which case this exam meant nothing and I didn't have to worry about it.

"We'll see how well you do here," she said. "You'd better not waste any more time. You do have two number-two pencils, properly sharpened?"

"I have one," I said. "The man at the door lent it to me. I didn't receive any instructions. Or I might have done, but I've been in an accident and lost my memory."

"That's a poor excuse for failure, isn't it? Go on in and take a seat at an empty desk. You'd better work fast because you only have an hour left. You wouldn't want to find yourself in remedial classes, I'm sure."

"Remedial? I'm in the gifted program. I'm in Advance Placement English."

"At your old school, maybe. Here the rules are a little different." And she smiled again. She took me by the arm and propelled me inside. Her fingers dug into my flesh like talons.

The room was much bigger than I had suspected from the outside. It stretched away into more gloom with row after row of desks at which students were scribbling furiously. Nobody even looked up as I passed them to take my place.

"Begin immediately," the bird-woman said and I turned over the sheaf of papers that lay on the desk.

Algebra, the first one was headed. Algebra, I thought. It's been ages since I did algebra. How long had it been, exactly? So long ago I couldn't remember studying it at all. Why couldn't they have told me the subjects in advance? Then I could have studied up.

I focused on the first problem. If x and then a squiggly sign I didn't recognize to y, and then a + b in brackets, can we say that z is greater than x is? I blinked, stared at it again. It made no sense, even if I did know what that squiggly sign meant. Surely you couldn't have so many unknowns in one problem. But the other kids seemed to be working away as if they weren't fazed at all.

I moved on to the second question. Draw a graph to show that x/y might tend toward infinity in the circumstances z squared is less than 100. Again it made no sense to me. I had done well enough in algebra, surely, but I'd never encountered anything like this. The thought struck me that perhaps this was some kind of advance placement exam for math whizzes. Well, that wasn't me, anyway. I'd never claimed to be a math whiz. My strengths had always been in the arts—reading, writing, history, languages, that was where I shone.

I turned over the algebra sheet and flipped ahead to see how much of the exam was math. Then I heaved a sigh of relief as I saw pages of writing ahead. World history. Good. I'd ace this part.

> Discuss the treaty of Nebrachshazar in fourth-century BC and how it affected the development of cuneiform writing for the Babylonian people.

> Are we justified in saying that there was peace in Persia in the year AD 731?

> Which Chinese emperor did more to hinder the spread of the Taoist philosophy—Yin Fu Cha or Tse Wong Ho?

My heart was racing now. My throat was so dry I couldn't swallow. I didn't know any of this stuff. I'd never learned it. Our version of world history didn't stretch much beyond the Spanish conquests in the New World and some more memorable kings of England.

Another subject. There must be another subject I could do. English. Right. There was an English paper.

> Which little-known imitator of Shakespeare also wrote a play that took place in Windsor? In what ways was it similar to the Merry Wives? Discuss the passages that were borrowed from Shakespeare.

> Give examples of seventeenth-century treatises with a Roundhead slant and contrast them to similar works favoring the Cavaliers.

> Early-twentieth-century Bulgarian Romantic poets—what do they all have in common?

"This is stupid!" I almost said the words out loud, then swallowed them back at the last moment. There was not one question I could begin to answer. I was going to fail hopelessly. I would be put in remedial classes with all the dummies I so despised. I saw myself clearly—sitting in class while some idiot asked a dumb question and the rest of us had to wait while the teacher explained it all over again. Now I'd be in class with kids like that.

No, I wouldn't. This had gone on long enough. I wasn't going to stick around here one moment longer. I'd go to the office, call my parents and tell them to come and get me. I rose to my feet.

"Where are you going?" the bird-woman demanded.

"I'm not staying," I said. "I don't want to be here. This school isn't right for me."

"Not as smart as you thought you were, huh?" she said. "Fine. I'll tell the principal that you refused to take the entrance exam. I'm sure she'll be wanting to meet with you anyway. We don't tolerate lack of cooperation here."

"Ooh, she'll get detention," someone hissed.

"Who said that?" The bird-woman looked up sharply. "You, boy. Did I say no talking after the examination has started or not?"

"Yes, ma'am, you did."

"Then take your things and go. Your chance to redeem yourself has just ended."

"But I didn't mean . . ." he stammered. "Just let me finish it. I almost had it finished this time."

"Rules are rules. Go." She pointed at the door.

"You can't expect me . . . You can't make me . . ." he blurted out. "It's not fair, you know." His face looked a picture of misery. No, more than misery, torment. But he dragged his feet all the way to the door and it clanged shut behind him.

"Anybody else have something they'd like to say?" She turned back to the room.

Heads went down and everyone scribbled frantically.

"I have something I want to say," I said. "This isn't the Dark Ages. You don't get the best out of students by intimidating them."

There was a collective gasp.

"Oh, we will enjoy having you here, Miss Weinstein," the bird-woman said. "We will find you a delightful challenge."

"Too bad, because I'm not staying." I walked to the door and went to pull it open. It wouldn't budge. That boy had opened it easily enough and there didn't appear to be any kind of lock.

I turned back to the teacher and she was grinning now, her face lit up with amusement. "You don't get it yet. You will. Now go back to work. *I* say when this exam is over."

I stood by the door. "Would you please open this door. I want to go home."

"Unfortunately we don't always get what we want, do we?" she said, going back to the papers on her desk. "We get what we deserve."

"I don't deserve to be treated like this. None of us do."

She glanced up briefly. "Have you never treated others as if they were beneath you? Have you never gloried in your power over them?"

"No, never." I blurted out the words but an image flashed across my mind—and I heard someone say, "Texas Chemicals versus Rodriguez." What on earth did that mean? And yet it seemed vaguely familiar, something I had heard or read about before.

The bird-woman went back to her work and I went back to my desk. I turned over the next page hopelessly. Then suddenly I saw questions that I could do. U.S. Government and Constitution. I looked down the page.

What preceded the constitution, and why was it unworkable?

Yes, I could do this. I started to write furiously.

Which amendment . . . Yes, I knew that. I'd obviously just found the few stupid pages before and now I was back on track. They'd see that I knew my stuff—after all, if anyone knew about Congress, it should be me, right? I stopped writing and frowned at this thought. Why should I know about Congress?

"Ten more minutes," the bird-woman said.

I went back to writing and then there was a snapping sound and the finely sharpened tip of my pencil broke off. I stared at it in dismay. I tried to write with the stub but it was impossible.

A bell rang, jangling loudly above our heads.

"Leave your papers on the desk and file out in silence," the bird-woman said.

Reluctantly I left my unfinished government paper and joined the line. I saw a couple of kids take a look at me and then snigger. I joined them as they walked back down the six hundred hallway to the stairwell and fell into step beside a studious-looking girl. She was wearing glasses and was dressed in a dorky manner, like me, so at least I figured she'd be someone I could talk to.

"Hi," I said. "What was that exam all about? I mean, did you know that crazy stuff?"

"Oh, yes," she said. "I read the study sheets ahead of time. It was a cinch." She went to walk on ahead of me.

"Wait," I said. "I'm new here and I don't like it."

"Don't like it?" She looked as if she was about to smile. "That's funny. Do you think anyone likes it?"

"Then why put up with it? There are plenty of better high schools around. Normally, I go to Oakmont. It's great. Very modern. Very academic."

"I don't know of any Oakmont."

"Near the civic center and the freeway."

"I don't know what you're talking about. This is the high school."

"Well, I'm not staying. Can you tell me the way out?"

"Way out?" She looked puzzled.

"Yeah, the way out."

"The way out?" she repeated, and she started to laugh.

"What's wrong with you? Do you happen to have a cell phone on you so I can call my parents?"

"Cell phone?"

There was something seriously strange about this girl, or about this school, or both. "The office then, so I can call my parents to come and get me."

"Nobody can come and get you, don't you know that yet?" She pushed past me and almost ran to escape from me. I followed her down the stairs, staying close to the handrail because a tide of students was coming up.

"Out of the way, freak." A boy in a letter jacket deliberately knocked into me. Luckily I held on or I'd have gone tumbling down.

This is like a nightmare, I muttered. Nobody will tell me how to get out. An exam with questions I can't possibly answer. Then I stopped halfway down a flight of stairs, making those behind me barrel into me and start cursing. And I actually laughed. A nightmare. Of course. It was the classic nightmare that had plagued me all my life—the exam I was perennially late for. The exam with questions I couldn't possibly answer. The strange building with no way out. That was it. I was dreaming. Now it all made sense. I'd been in some kind of accident and I was in a coma or something. And I'd wake up and everything would be back to normal again.

I finished the flight of steps with an almost jaunty tread. All I had to do was keep reminding myself that it was all a dream and I could handle anything. The students now seemed to be streaming along a different hallway.

"Where is everyone going?" I asked, hopeful that it might be the end of the school day and time to go home.

"Lunch, stupid," a skinny freckled-faced boy said.

I followed along, although I didn't feel hungry. The cafeteria was a huge subterranean room that echoed with noise, the clash and clatter of plates competing with the shouts of students. What's more, it smelled terrible, like drains and boiled cabbage. I stood in line with the rest and inched my way toward a counter. Someone took a tray, so I did. A plate was banged down in front of me.

"Stew?" a helper behind the counter asked, and before I could answer, a great ladle of grayish, glutinous stuff was slopped into my plate. The helper gave me a toothless grin. "Vegetables?" she asked and dropped some gray boiled cabbage on top of the congealed mess.

"Wait," I said, fighting back revulsion. "Is there a choice? Pizza maybe?"

The toothless grin widened. "Do you want it or not?"

I was pushed forward to where an old woman sat at a cash desk. "Five dollars," she said.

"Five dollars? For this—" I went to say "crap," then swallowed down the word at the last second. Then I remembered. "I don't have my purse with me."

"No matter. Put it on your tab, Miss Weinstein."

How did they all know my name with all these thousands of students?

I carried my tray and looked around for a place to sit. Hostile stares or stupid giggles greeted me. I found an empty table far in a corner and sat down. I'd really have to do something about the way I looked. If this was a dream, I'd dream myself better looking. Better still, I'd dream Sally Ann into my dream and she could help me get back to my real self. I sat alone at that table and thought wistfully of Sally Ann, the first real friend I ever had. The only one who cared about me when I was a fat, clueless freshman and other kids picked on me or teased me. If it hadn't been for her, I'd never have changed. I might not even have lived because when she came into my life I was seriously thinking of suicide. I'd started reading up on how many pills it takes to kill a person and I'd begun stealing my mother's sleeping pills and my dad's heart medication. Then she'd arrived and suddenly everything was fine.

"Hey, you." A figure loomed over me. She was a gorgeous blonde, wearing a cheerleading outfit. "You're sitting in my seat."

"I didn't realize we had assigned seats," I said.

Her friends had come up behind her now, more cheerleaders and a couple of jocks in letter jackets. They burst out laughing.

"Are you totally clueless?" the blonde said. "This is the table we want and so you move. Got it?"

"Why should I have to move?" My fighting spirit had returned.

"Because we say so and we count and you're nothing. Go on, beat it."

"And if I won't move?"

"I do this," the girl said and before I could dodge she grabbed my head and rammed it down into my plate. Hot rancid fat went up my nose and I coughed and gagged. I fought to sit up as she held me down.

"Let her up, Tracy. Or she might die," one of the other girls said and they roared with laughter.

The girl released me. "Got the message?" she said. "Go on, get lost."

I got to my feet, wiping my eyes with my hand because I didn't seem to have a napkin.

"You guys need to learn that bullying is not acceptable," I said. "I'm going right now to report you to the principal and to make an official complaint." I looked around, noticing that the cafeteria had become suspiciously quiet and that other kids were watching us. I turned to them. "What's wrong with this place?" I demanded. "Don't you realize that it's so much nicer if we all get along? If we can't be kind to each other in a school, in a community—what chance do nations ever have to live in peace because the whole of society is at war. Gangs, cliques, police brutality—what do they achieve except to make one person feel superior and others angry and inadequate?"

There was dead silence and the thought struck me that I'd made this speech before. I saw myself on a podium and the crowds were cheering and applauding. "I made this speech when I was running for Congress," I said and even as the words came out I realized how ridiculous they sounded. The kids burst out laughing. I was about to go and find a bathroom that wasn't inhabited by a wolf pack when someone near me called out, "Hey, Joshua! Dave's looking for you."

And it was as if I'd been struck by lightning. Dave. That name meant something to me—I'd been married to Dave and our baby son had been named Joshua. Suddenly I saw it all clearly—the apartment on the Upper East Side and the sun streaming in through the window with the view of Central Park and Dave saying, "It's no use. It's not working, Amy. You're married to your ambition, not to me." Then he put a hand on my shoulder. "It was never the same after Joshua died, was it?"

I stepped out into a deserted hallway, digesting this vision. I wasn't really in high school. I was grown up and I'd been married and Dave had left me because Joshua had died and he couldn't handle it. And I was a successful lawyer who was running for Congress. And I wore high heels and designer suits and had my hair styled by the best stylist in the Village. And I remembered the accident now—driving too fast because I was late and the van that came unexpectedly from my left. . . .

A hand grabbed my shoulder. "The principal wants to see you," a voice said. "This way."

"Fine," I thought. What could the principal do to me? I'd tell her she was only a figment of my imagination and pretty soon I'd wake up.

Down the stairs we went. It was hot and stuffy down here and it

crossed my mind to wonder why the principal chose this part of the
school for her office. The boy who had been escorting me knocked on a
door. It read, "Ms. Fer. Principal."

"Enter," said a voice.

"The girl you wanted, Ms. Fer," the boy said and shoved me inside.
Ms. Fer was sitting at a polished mahogany desk. She looked like an
older version of me—immaculately dressed in a black suit and white
blouse, hair streaked with gray but perfectly cut, face still unlined, gold
pin in her lapel, long red fingernails.

I was horribly conscious of how I must look—the purple sweater now
streaked with congealing stew, my hair sticky, my face a mess.

"I don't really look like this," I said. "Some bullies jammed my face
into my plate."

"I heard you caused a disturbance in the cafeteria." Her voice was
low, smooth and commanding.

"I caused? Listen, I was sitting there, minding my own business."

"I hear you've been nothing but trouble since you arrived, unpre-
pared, this morning. We don't tolerate troublemakers here."

"Then expel me. I'm not staying anyway. And if you really want to
know, this isn't the real me. I'm not even a high school student any longer. I'm grown-up and successful and I look great and you're just in my
hallucination, so I don't really care what you say."

"So you never really looked the way you do now?" She leaned forward as if she was interested.

"Well, yes, I guess I did. When I first went to high school I was overweight and a dork and clueless about clothes and I had no friends. And
people picked on me, just like here."

"You were desperately unhappy."

"Yes."

"So much so that you were thinking of taking your own life."

"Yes. How did you know that?"

"But you decided not to."

"I made a friend. And she took me under her wing. She rescued me."

"Tell me about this good friend of yours."

She leaned forward, smiling encouragingly, seeming to give the
impression that she was on my side, a pal.

I found myself smiling, too, at the memory. "Her name was Sally Ann. She was Chinese American—really attractive and petite—and spunky. She wasn't afraid of anyone. You should have seen the quick answers she came up with to the bullies and jocks. She could wipe the floor with them."

"A bad girl, then?"

"No, not bad. Stretched the rules a bit. Taught me how to sneak out of class undetected, how to write my own excuse notes. That kind of thing. Oh, and taught me how to smoke. But nothing too terrible. It was just that my whole world changed when she took me under her wing. She told me she could make me popular like her and it was true. By the time she left, I was in with the popular kids and I never looked back."

"A good friend indeed."

"Yes, but . . ." My smile faded. "She left suddenly and she never said good-bye. So all my life I wondered what happened to her . . . whether she got pregnant or into some other kind of trouble? She had a bad home life, she told me, so I wondered if there was something with her parents that forced the family to leave or made her run away." I paused, a clear image of Sally Ann coming into my brain. She was laughing as we climbed up the hill behind my house together, her black hair blowing out in the wind. Not a care in the world. And the next Monday she hadn't shown up for school. "If only she had contacted me, I'd have wanted to help her," I finished.

"Tell me about the time she made you the offer to help you become popular," Ms. Fer said.

Suddenly I could see it clearly, almost as if a movie were playing inside my head. She is sleeping over at my house and she says, "You know, you could be really pretty and you're smart. All you need is a little help. I could lend you some clothes that are too big for me, and help you diet and teach you how to act cool like me. In no time at all I guarantee you'd be popular."

"Are you serious?" I ask.

"Trust me. It will be a cinch."

"I'd do anything," I say.

She laughs. "You mean you'd sell me your soul and your firstborn child?"

I'm laughing, too. "And anything else you'd like. Willingly."

She takes a piece of paper. "We have to do this formally," she says and she sticks a pin into my finger. "Ow," I say as a drop of blood falls onto the paper. "Go on, sign your name," she says, and I do it. Then she signs hers.

I look up and realize that Ms. Fer has been watching the same scene unfold. "And what happened after that?"

"You know," I said, "it all happened like she said. She came to my house with these fabulous clothes and I lost weight and I really did become popular. Next year I made the cheerleading squad and then student council, and I was homecoming princess. I never looked back. I wished many times that she could have seen me and I could have thanked her."

"So you went from strength to strength," Ms. Fer said quietly. "Straight A's in college, Harvard Law School and then you got a reputation as a dynamite lawyer who would stop at nothing to win a case, not even if it meant ruining lives, wrecking companies and homes."

"I wouldn't put it that way," I said, frowning. "I like to win, that's for sure. I was being paid to win cases."

"What about Bradley versus that steel company? What about the Emerson case?"

My frown deepened. "They were unfortunate, but those people were in a downward spiral anyway." Then I looked up. "How do you know about them? Have you been following my career?"

"Oh, I know everything about you, my dear," she said. "Remember that piece of paper you signed? I happen to have it here." She handed it to me. "I, Amy Weinstein, hereby give my soul and my firstborn child to my friend Sally Ann in return for learning how to become gorgeous and successful and popular." There was my signature, written in dark brown dried blood, and under it, *Accepted. S.A. TAN.*

I looked up in horror. "It says Satan." I could hardly get the words out. "Are you trying to tell me that she—that she was the devil in disguise?"

"What do you think?" Ms. Fer asked evenly. There was the hint of a smile on her face.

Anger welled up inside me.

"She tricked me. That was terrible. She got me to sign my soul away through trickery."

Ms. Fer shook her head. "You said you would have done anything and at that moment you would have given anything to her, even your soul."

"But I was a stupid kid. That's totally unfair."

"Whoever said that Satan had to play by the rules?" she said. "And Satan doesn't have to have horns and a red face. He has to appear in a form that humans find seductive, otherwise he'd have few converts. You needed a best friend—a spunky, pretty best friend."

I stared at her, openmouthed, as something else occurred to me. "My firstborn child," I whispered. "Joshua. He was born perfect. Nothing wrong with him. And then a few hours later he suddenly stopped breathing for no reason. The doctors said something about underdeveloped lungs, but you should have heard him cry when he was born. He had a loud, perfect cry."

"Yes, he did, didn't he," she said. "I did hear his cry. A lovely little fellow. I actually had a glimmer of remorse about taking him. But a contract is a contract, as you yourself said many times in court."

For the first time I saw her name plaque on her desk. Ms. Lucy Fer.

"Am I in hell?" The words came out as a whisper.

"What do you think?"

"Either I'm still in a coma after that accident and this is a horribly real hallucination or . . ."

"You're not in a coma any longer," she said. "You never woke up. You slipped away and I was waiting for you."

"But that's not fair," I said. "I can't be in hell. Hell is for bad people—criminals, murderers."

"You're a murderer."

"I am not."

"The auto accident that sent you to us. You plowed into a van carrying a family. A mother and her three children. One of them was a baby of three months old. The van caught fire. They were all trapped inside and died a most horrible death."

"But it was an accident. You said so yourself. I didn't want to kill anybody."

"But you ran the red light because you were in a hurry. You didn't want to be late, did you? So you took the risk."

I winced as she said the words. The full memory had come back to me now. I could see myself, gripping that steering wheel, my face consumed with anger. The bastard. The underhanded, sneaky bastard. How could he pull a trick like that?

"I couldn't be late. I was told at the last minute that my opponent had shown up unexpectedly at the county fair and was going to make a speech. Sneaky tactics. He knew I was scheduled to speak there that afternoon. So I had to be there when he spoke to defend myself."

"So you thought you could flout the law and run a red light."

"Look, I'm sorry it happened but that van must have jumped the light, too."

Ms. Fer shook her head. "On the contrary. The van could not have jumped anything. It was so old it could only creep along. It lacked the acceleration to get out of your way when it saw you coming. The family was poor, you see. The father had lost his job when your law firm put his company out of business. I believe you represented the bank in court on that one, didn't you? And won your case yet again?"

"I was paid to win cases," I said. "I was good at what I did. And I worked for whomever retained us."

"Big business," Ms. Fer said. "Chemical companies. Tobacco. Multinationals."

"They paid well."

"They destroyed lives. Texas Chemicals versus Rodriguez. You remember that one?"

Funny, that had been the thought that had popped into my head once before today. I nodded.

"Family lost three children to leukemia directly linked to outflow of toxic waste, correct?"

"It was not proven that there was a link."

"YOU managed to prove that there wasn't a link."

I stared at her angrily. "I was no worse than anyone else trying to make a good living. And I was running for Congress, for pete's sake. I wanted to help my country."

"You wanted to fuel your ambition. That relentless, driving ambition. You had to be best, top dog, didn't you? It's no use, Amy Weinstein. You can't hide anything from me. You see, I made you what you are. I saw a good brain and a desire to prove yourself and I molded you. You've always been my creature. Always been destined for here."

"So is this farce of a high school the preliminary for hell? Do I have to graduate over again? Do I get some better-looking clothes?"

She smiled now. "Oh, no, my dear. You don't get it, do you? This is hell. Your hell. For ever and ever."

I smiled back now as a thought struck me. "Did it not occur to you that now that I know where I am, now that I know the ropes, I can survive here pretty well? I used to be a hot shot at my high school. I can become that again. I can look good and speak out against unfairness and get other kids to rally around me. I'm a natural leader, you know."

"You became a natural leader after you had given me your soul."

"So? Does it matter when I found my voice?"

"Very much. You see, you've now gone back to what you were before I transformed you. From now on every morning will be a new day for you. You'll start the day knowing nothing—lost, blundering, pathetic without your number-two pencil to take the exam—just the way you were when Sally Ann found you at your old high school." She watched the panic growing in my eyes, and the satisfied smile spread across her face. "Every now and then you'll have a flash of memory, just to remind you what you have lost. But as time goes on, these memories will fade until all you'll know is that you're the new girl at this school—the fat girl, the misfit. Every day. For the rest of eternity."

I stared at her. "Is there no way out?" I whispered. "No way to redeem myself? There is good in me, you know. A real desire to help. I could do good."

"Too late, Miss Weinstein," she said. "Your future was sealed when you sold me your soul. Now you'd better hurry. It wouldn't do to be late for PE class."

I got up and tried desperately to think. Some way out. There was always an escape clause.

"Wait," I said, turning back to face her. "That contract. In the state of New York a minor cannot enter into any manner of contract without the consent of a parent and the signature of same parent. We were in the state of New York when that contract was signed. Hence it is null and void. That contract does not exist, Ms. Fer."

I reached across the desk, took the sheet of paper and tore it in half.

I saw a flicker of amusement go through those narrowed eyes. "You obviously don't read the small print, Miss Weinstein," she said. "That statute does not apply to contracts signed in blood. The laws governing those contracts are far older than the state of New York. They go back to the dawn of humanity."

"I don't agree," I said. "A contract signed in the state of New York is governed by the laws of that state. And a contract signed under coercion or pretense can be disputed in any state."

"Oh, I shall enjoy having you here, Miss Weinstein," she said. "Such an enjoyable challenge. Most poor wretches simply resign themselves to their lot." A bell sounded in the hallway outside. "Now you had better hurry. The PE teacher is not as tolerant as I am."

I came out of her office into the hallway that was already swarming with students. I joined the throng but my brain was already racing. I wasn't going to let her beat me. There was always a loophole. There had to be a celestial court to which I could appeal, and when they heard how she had tricked me, they'd judge in my favor. I had never lost an important case in my life and I wasn't about to lose this most important one!

I strode out now.

"Hey, watch it," one kid said as I bumped into him.

"You watch it yourself," I answered. A plan was already forming in my head. First step was to get out of these awful, ugly clothes. I'd go into the locker room and help myself to some better items while everyone was at PE. Supplement those from the lost and found. Find myself a locker to hide the stuff away, in case I found myself dressed like this tomorrow. Oh, and steal a hairbrush, too. Surely everything was fair game in hell?

And then? I'd have to work quickly while my mind was still razor sharp. There must be other students like me, sentenced unjustly, tricked into being here. I'd find them and motivate them. We'd form a movement.

It would grow until the whole school was behind me. And we'd take over the school, and I'd represent each of them in the celestial court and we'd win.

You're going down, Ms. Fer, I vowed to myself. I found the library and pushed open the door. I had some planning to do, and some studying. If I had to take those tests again tomorrow, I planned to ace them. I'd be prepared.

I'd already stolen two number-two pencils, properly sharpened, from Ms. Fer's desk.

Callie Meet Happy

AMBER BENSON

Amber Benson is an actor, filmmaker, novelist, and amateur occultist who sings in the shower. Best known for her work as Tara Maclay on *Buffy the Vampire Slayer*, she is the author of the Calliope Reaper-Jones series for Ace Books and the middle-grade ghost story *Among the Ghosts*. She is also the codirector (with Adam Busch) of the feature film *Drones*. She can be stalked on her blog—amberbensonwrotethis .blogspot.com—and on Twitter and Facebook.

Calliope Reaper-Jones felt like an idiot.

No, that wasn't right. *Idiot* was too vague a term.

Calliope Reaper-Jones felt like . . . *a dunce*. Yes, that was more apropos.

A dunce. The kind that sat in the back corner of the classroom with her face to the wall, a large conical cap affixed firmly to her head, trying not to cry as all the other kids pointed fingers and laughed uproariously at her.

It was an odd feeling, one Callie hadn't encountered in more than a dozen years primarily because it was a sensation uniquely specific to the elementary school experience, something about the amazing cruelness of small children and the amazing ability of adults to look the other way.

"Miss Reaper-Jones?"

The use of her name, out loud and in front of the whole class, made Callie jump. Eyes refocusing, she returned her attention to the problem at hand, pressing the mute button on her (really distracting) internal monologue so she could concentrate.

"I, um, well—" she stammered, feeling the imaginary dunce cap settling farther down the crown of her head.

"Yes, Miss Reaper-Jones? Spit it out."

The blood rushed to her cheeks in a florid burst.

"I didn't really, uh, do the reading you assigned."

Silence from the peanut gallery.

If the proverbial pin *had* dropped, you would've heard the sound of it bouncing on the linoleum, twice, before rolling underneath one of the classroom's desks where it would've stayed, unmolested, until some random day in the faraway future when a janitor came to sweep it away.

Surveying the crowd and trying not to let their hostile stares sting, Callie decided there was actually nothing peanut-y about the assortment of oddities and misfits who had somehow, over the course of their service to Death, Inc., never learned to call up a wormhole and were, thusly, stuck in the same Remedial Wormhole Calling class as Callie.

How to describe her peers?

Angry was a good descriptive word. *Annoyed* was another. *Peeved* could also be added to the list. The group fell short of the index-finger-pointing (and elementary school laughter) Callie's brain had conjured up earlier . . . but just barely.

"I don't understand your inability to do your homework, Miss Reaper-Jones," the teacher said, shaking her head.

A tall, shaggy-haired Asian woman with a beaked nose and fleshy jowls that fluttered like gills whenever she spoke, Mrs. Gunwhale—as she'd asked the class to call her—was partial to bruise-colored, diaphanous muumuus that made her bloated appendages appear larger and rounder than they actually were.

"You're a grown woman—and one in a leadership position, no less," Mrs. Gunwhale continued, the frown she wore speaking volumes about the hostility she'd engendered toward Callie, a student she'd decidedly labeled "indolent."

While Mrs. Gunwhale may have been sorely mistaken about most things, she wasn't wrong about the many leadership responsibilities Callie had to shoulder in order to run Death. Since her dad had been murdered and she'd inherited the presidency of Death, Inc.—who'd have thunk Death would be run like a corporation—Callie's world had done a one-eighty. There wasn't time in her rigorous schedule for indolence these days. Overseeing Death, Inc., and being the de facto "Not So Grim

Reaper" was running her ragged, keeping her so damn busy she was having a hard time focusing on anything that wasn't directly work-related.

Like homework.

"Well, that's why I didn't do it," Callie said, aware that the whine in her voice would make her no friends. "There was a Death board meeting and then I had to go to Hell, talk to Cerberus—"

"Everyone here is a commuter student." Mrs. Gunwhale breathed. "They all hold full-time jobs and, yet, they still find time to do their homework."

"That's right," a girlish falsetto chimed in from the front row.

Callie glared at the owner of the voice, a wispy woman with a halo of bright orange, dandruff-laden hair, and found herself wishing she could use her Death powers to give the woman—the teacher's pet, of course—a little kick in the direction of an early grave.

Stop that right now, Callie thought as she mentally scolded herself for thinking such horrible thoughts. *Bad, bad, bad,* bad *Death!*

Part of the responsibility of possessing special powers—like the power of bestowing life and death—was learning to be judicious about how you applied them. You weren't supposed to just lay waste to every Tom, Dick, or Harry (or teacher's pet) that got on your nerves. You were supposed to be wise like King Solomon and split the baby in half—

She paused, realizing she'd gotten the stupid analogy wrong.

"Cutting the baby in half is never the intended outcome—" Callie mumbled to herself.

"Miss Reaper-Jones, stop mumbling. I'm trying to have a pertinent conversation with you!"

"Pertinent?"

"Yes, pertinent," Mrs. Gunwhale said, enunciating every word. "Pertinent as to whether you continue in my class or not."

Where there was once silence, now came a snicker from the aforementioned peanut gallery. Callie turned her head, trying to catch the culprit in the act, but only encountered a wall of stony faces, their slack jaws and dead eyes as bland as the faux wood-grain paneling that decorated the four walls of the modular classroom. The class was meeting in a "temporary" trailer that normally housed a second-grade class in a

Jamaica, Queens, elementary school (it'd been on-site since 2001, so the "temporary" part was a joke), but at night it was leased out—for an undisclosed sum—to the University of Supernatural Studies Extension Program. Though it was nice to be back in the tri-borough area (it was almost Manhattan!), the gray on gray on brown—ash-colored linoleum-tiled floors, brown fake wood-grain Formica desks two sizes too small for any adult bottom to command, dirty-gray dry-erase boards lining the washed-out, smoky walls—was pretty damn depressing.

And if the decor was not conducive to teaching adults how to call up wormholes, then Callie could only imagine the adverse effect it would have on fidgety second graders attempting to learn fractions. No wonder kids hated to go to school—if Callie had been shunted into a classroom like this one (no matter how nice and kid-friendly the teacher had tried to make the temporary digs), she'd probably have come out of the system totally illiterate.

"Miss Reaper-Jones?" Mrs. Gunwhale bellowed, her aggressive baritone filling Callie's head like the thundering boom of cannon fire.

As much as she wanted to tell Mrs. Gunwhale where she could shove her Remedial Wormhole Calling class, she knew she needed to master wormhole calling if she wanted to run Death, Inc., and not be laughed at by her employees—including the six numb nuts she was trapped in the modular trailer with for the next four nights' worth of classes.

Steeling herself for the worst, she took a deep breath and said:

"I would like to stay in your class."

"And . . . ?"

Mrs. Gunwhale's dark eyes blatantly telegraphed that she would need to see a little begging from her recalcitrant pupil before she relented and let Callie stay in the class.

Callie sighed, her hands tied. It was imperative that the head of Death, Inc., be self-sufficient and capable of traveling around the Afterlife on her own, without her Executive Assistant calling up wormholes for her like she was some kind of nincompoop. If she didn't suck it up now and somehow master the art of wormhole calling, she was giving her enemies the advantage, allowing them the opportunity to petition the Death board to recall her from her new job.

"*Please*, I would like to stay in your class?" Callie choked out, the obsequiousness of the word making her feel nauseous.

A look of triumph spread across Mrs. Gunwhale's face. Exultant, she lifted her sausage arms into the sky like airborne blimps—and then the ungainly woman shocked everyone by doing a graceless twirl on the linoleum floor, causing both the gill/jowl flaps around her jaw and the muumuu she had on to flutter with happiness.

"That's the first step, Miss Reaper-Jones," Mrs. Gunwhale trilled. "Admit I'm the boss and that you are mine to mold and we're getting somewhere."

Callie gave a mirthless chuckle, trying to appear game, but like an aggressive baby kraken, the obnoxious, juvenile part of her personality had already awoken and was now itching to start planning Mrs. Gunwhale's disemboweling.

"Why don't you come up to the front of the class, Miss Reaper-Jones, and try opening a temporary hole in reality—"

It took Callie a moment to comprehend that, against her will, she was once again being foisted into the spotlight. Actually, she realized, looking around at the smirking faces of her fellow classmates, she'd never left said spotlight since she'd begun the class two days earlier. She didn't want to be paranoid, but she was getting the rather distinct impression the other students didn't like her very much . . . or rather, they didn't like that she was in charge of Death, Inc., and, for all intents and purposes, was their boss.

And it wasn't like she'd *wanted* to take the class in the first place.

Two weeks prior, Callie had discovered that her Executive Assistant, Jarvis, had enrolled her, without her permission, into the course. He'd assumed she'd attend without too much fuss because it met in New York City, one of her most favorite places in all of the world. Of course, what he'd neglected to inform her was that it took place not in Manhattan, but in Queens—which was like telling someone she'd won a trip to Hawaii, then dropping her off in Lompoc, California.

To make herself feel better, and to shake her growing paranoia, Callie imagined the tongue-lashing she would give Jarvis when she got back to Sea Verge, the familial mansion she shared with her sister,

Clio, and their hellhound puppy, Runt—and, boy, was it gonna be a doozy.

"We're waiting. . . ."

Callie looked up to find the long shadow of Mrs. Gunwhale looming over her.

"Okay," Callie said as she eased herself out from behind the kid-sized desk and stood up, her left leg numb from being squeezed too tightly against the metal bar that connected the chair to the desktop.

Limping over to the front of the classroom, she stopped in front of the stained dry-erase board and waited for Mrs. Gunwhale to give her further instructions.

"Now, if you'd done the reading I'd assigned you," Mrs. Gunwhale said, gathering up the fabric of her muumuu and resting her generous backside against the corner of her rectangular desk, "you'd know that there are small, subatomic particles called neutrinos that *appear* to travel faster than the speed of light, but in reality, they are using *wormholes* in order to burrow in and out of the fabric of time/space—"

Callie's attention began to waver, her inner monologue taking over with a vengeance as Mrs. Gunwhale droned on and on about neutrinos.

How am I supposed to pay attention when the woman is doing Science Speak? Callie grumbled to herself—and then, her mind distracted: *And what the hell is with that damn mole??*

The mole in question belonged to Mrs. Gunwhale, and the more the teacher talked, the more the blackened growth on the tip of her nose began to take on an otherworldly presence. Large and irregularly shaped, it seemed to bend and stretch of its own accord, as if it were doing mole calisthenics in order to beef itself up, escape Mrs. Gunwhale's elongated proboscis, and go in search of a more attractive host . . . like Calliope Reaper-Jones!

Eeeek!

Shuddering, Callie ripped her mind away from scary-mole-contemplation-land just as Mrs. Gunwhale stopped speaking.

"Neutrinos," Callie said before Mrs. Gunwhale could quiz her. "I get it."

Even though she didn't have a clue what she was talking about.

"Good," Mrs. Gunwhale replied, rubbing her hands together expectantly. "Now show us."

Attempting to remember all the things Jarvis had imparted to her about wormhole calling over the past year—and the things she'd learned during the first two sessions of Mrs. Gunwhale's boring class—she closed her eyes and tried to imagine a place, any place.

I just want to go someplace like *here, but* not *here,* she thought. *Someplace happy!*

In her imagination, she saw the modular classroom bend around her, space and time becoming as pliant as the bellows of a giant accordion while unseen hands expertly folded the gray and brown drabness of the room like a blank piece of origami paper. The hostile faces of her classmates abruptly disappeared inside the reformation, the space continuing to morph until finally even Mrs. Gunwhale's laserlike gaze was stripped away . . . and then, for the first time ever, she felt her mind open like a lotus flower, all the free-floating strands of thought and magic and imagination coming together in a pinpoint of golden-hued light.

I'm doing it, she thought, her heart beginning to hammer excitedly. *I'm calling up a goddamned wormhole!*

It was as if a bantam sun had exploded around her, blinding her just as she opened her eyes to behold her creation. Only there was nothing to see once her irises had readjusted, the evanescent glare having left her eyeballs feeling dry and burnt.

All around her was cold, empty night.

The stars appeared above her, blinking into existence one at a time until the universe was once again filled with their twinkling light. Callie felt the cold wetness of snow engulfing her, her breath racing in and out of her lungs in feverish bursts as she tried to collect herself.

"Are you okay there? You hit the ground really, really hard."

Dragging her eyes away from the night sky, Callie saw a pale-faced young woman in a bubblegum pink wool hat and scarf standing above her, cascading blond curls of hair poufing out around her face like lemon cotton candy. Her cornflower blue eyes were filled with concern, her powdery-rose lips turning down at the corners while she considered the image of Callie lying like a bag of discarded refuse in the chilly slush of a snowbank.

"I think I'm okay," Callie said, sitting up slowly so all the blood in her head didn't rush out in a flood, leaving her woozy. "Where am I?"

"What did she say?" another voice chimed in and Callie turned around to see its owner, a tall brunette with a turned-up nose that bore a thick spackling of freckles across its bridge. She was standing on the far side of the snowbank wearing a dark blue hoodie pulled taut over her head and tied tightly at the base of her throat in a futile attempt to keep out the cold.

The blond girl shook her head, looking up at the brunette quizzically.

"She wanted to know where she was," she replied, wrinkling her pretty nose.

"How hard did she hit her head?" the brunette asked.

"I'm fine. My head is fine. I'm just freezing my ass off," Callie interjected, wishing she'd had the forethought to put on a snowsuit instead of the light blue wrap dress she'd shimmied into that morning. "And when the hell did it start snowing?"

"Um, are you kidding?" the blonde said. "It's been snow central for like three months."

Callie tried to stand up, holding on to the blonde for support as she struggled not to slip in the slush, her very inappropriate footwear—a pair of Jimmy Choo peep-toe pumps—making it hard for her to keep her balance.

"That's not true," Callie said, letting the blonde's arm go as she managed to finally right herself. "There was no snow on the ground when I got here earlier tonight."

September had been unseasonably warm for the East Coast, with highs in the sixties and seventies, so this bit about snow being on the ground for the past three months was pure bunk. Besides, there'd been no hint of snow in the air when she'd arrived at class, let alone was it possible for that much snow to have fallen in the hour since she'd—

Callie paused mid-thought as she realized that no matter where she set her eyeballs, there were no modular classrooms anywhere in her vicinity. In fact, no classrooms or administration buildings or gyms or anything else that might evoke the grounds of an elementary school.

"Okay, where the hell am I?"

The blonde blinked.

"You're in Queens, New York."

The brunette nodded her agreement.

"But that's not possible. Where is PS 181?"

"What's a PS 181?" the blonde asked curiously.

Exasperated, Callie sighed.

"It's an elementary school where I was taking—"

She paused, realizing she'd almost divulged more information than she'd intended to.

"—um, an adult education class."

The two young women gave her a funny look. Then the brunette, who was proving to be far more officious than the blonde, said, "Agatha, I'm gonna go over by that tree and I want you to tell me what you sense."

"All right, Happy, I'll give it the old college try, but you're gonna have to stand pretty far away," Agatha replied, pointing to a copse of trees that was about a hundred feet from where they were standing. "Probably over there to start with."

Happy—Callie had a hard time associating the name with the serious-looking brunette—nodded, wrapping her arms around herself as she left the confines of the sidewalk and began the slow trudge through the snow toward the trees. The blonde, Agatha, gave Callie a honey-sweet smile and reached out, taking one of Callie's frozen hands in between her own warmer ones.

Squeezing her eyes shut, Agatha seemed to be concentrating on the physical connection between them, but it didn't appear she was having much luck.

"Still too close," she murmured under her breath just as Happy arrived at the predetermined spot.

"*Keep going?*" Happy called out from beneath the wide shadow of the tree line.

"Yep, keep going!" Agatha replied, eyes still closed, pink mouth in a firm line.

Callie watched as Happy shook her head, then turned around and started crunching through the snow again, passing the snow-topped pines and heading farther out into the woods.

Woods? What woods were there in Jamaica, New York? The place was a veritable concrete jungle—Starbucks and bodegas on every corner, houses and apartments taking up whole city blocks. Yet, as far as the eye could see, she found nothing but trees and a thin line of a freshly cleared road beside the snow-covered sidewalk they were standing on.

"What are you doing?" Callie asked after a few more seconds of protracted silence, but Agatha only shook her head.

"Just give me one more minute."

Callie stood there, shivering in the pitch-black night, her teeth chattering in double time as she tried not to lose her patience. She wanted to know where in the heck the wormhole had taken her, but she was starting to get the horrible feeling it wasn't so much a "where?" as it was a "what?" kind of a question.

"Um, so I'm starting to get the feeling that—"

"Shh!" Agatha shushed her, then she squeezed Callie's fingers so tightly it felt like the meaty bits of muscle might burst through their fleshy casings like overcooked sausages.

"Anything?" Happy cried from another spot a few yards away from the original stand of pine trees.

Agatha didn't answer, but her eyelids fluttered.

"*No way!*" she breathed, eyes flying open to look at Callie—to *really* look at her, almost as if she were some alien specimen trapped inside a bottle of formaldehyde.

"What did you say?" Happy yelled, but Agatha's rigid stance had piqued her interest, and she was already making her way back toward them through the snow, the crunching of her boots a riot of sound in the muted hush of the wind and the flickering buzz of the streetlights.

"*Who are you?*" Agatha breathed, the look of wonderment on her face disconcerting.

"I'm Calliope Reaper-Jones," Callie said to peals of Agatha's laughter.

"No, silly," the other girl said, playfully punching Callie in the arm. "Who are you *really?*"

Well, that's a loaded question, Callie thought.

"I mean, your aura is on fire," Agatha continued. "You have the craziest vibrations I've ever seen."

No shit, Callie thought, wondering just how much Agatha was able to sense about her—and if she'd been able to pick up Callie's connection to Death, Inc.

"And what are *you* really?" Callie asked, turning the mock interrogation on its head. "One of those crazy psychic ladies who goes around giving people annoying psychic readings that they don't want?"

"Agatha's no Cassandra." Happy snorted, having reached them just in time to overhear Callie's last comment. "She's an aura reader . . . and a pretty damn effective one, too."

"This gal's full of psychic ability," Agatha said, turning to Happy. "I mean, I don't think I've ever met anyone whose aura was so fully charged—"

"Look, I'm *not* psychic, but, you know what, I *am* freezing," Callie interrupted, the real fear of becoming hypothermic making her cranky. "Is there somewhere warm we can go?"

"Well, we were on our way to a very exclusive acting master class," Agatha began, but Happy cleared her throat loudly.

"No, *you* were going to a master class. I was only going to watch you take it."

Agatha pouted, her large heart-shaped lips turning down at the corners again.

"But you said you'd participate!"

"I did not," Happy sputtered, looking put upon. "There is no way in hell I'm taking that class. No way, no how."

"As cute as the witty banter is, ladies," Callie said, the cold making it hard to feel her face. "I need to get somewhere warm before I turn into a Popsicle."

The two girls gave each other an inscrutable look, then Happy nodded. "Okay, we'll take you with us, but on one condition."

Callie nodded.

"Okay, whatever you want. Just get me to a fire."

"You have to tell us what you are!" Agatha chirped, unable to wait for Happy to get the words out. "You're like Pat Boone or something, dropping out of the sky like he did in that movie *The Man Who Fell to Earth*."

Pat Boone? Callie thought, shuddering on the inside. *I think someone is in dire need of a pop culture tutorial.*

"No, if I were *David Bowie*, I wouldn't be in this situation." Callie sighed, daring either one of them to contradict her. "But I think I'll save any and all explanations until we're out of the snow."

"Then follow us," Happy said, crawling over the snowbank so she could join them on the sidewalk. "It's just down the street."

Down the street was a relative term, especially when you were hobbling around in a pair of peep-toe pumps in the snow.

After ten minutes of walking, and freezing, they left the darkened woodland landscape behind them and stepped out into a better-lit suburban street. Only there were no tract homes here, no cookie-cutter little boxes or white-picket fences neatly arranged in a row along the curve of the street. Instead, there was a sprinkling of older Victorian homes, all decorative curlicues and clapboard siding in a myriad of pastel colors.

Interstitial bits of broken Gothic wrought-iron gating separated the lots, which were large and overgrown, and deciduous trees, denuded of their autumnal skins, giddily waved their skeletal branches back and forth in a hobgoblinlike greeting.

"Is that a cemetery?" Callie asked, her eyes resting on a lot at the top of the street where a hulking Victorian mansion sat vigilant over the rest of the neighborhood, its side yard crowded with a bevy of headstones, in various states of neglect.

"Looks like it," Happy said, her words ripe with distaste.

"Is that where we're going?" Agatha asked, looking to Happy for the answer as they continued their procession through the snow.

The wind and precipitation had picked up as soon as they'd started walking, dusting the sidewalk with a thin layer of wet powder that made the trek almost unbearable for Callie. Finally, Happy and Agatha had taken pity on her, each girl taking an arm and helping her navigate the quickly accumulating sludge.

"I think this is it," Happy replied, pausing long enough to pull a piece of lined notebook paper from the back pocket of her jeans. "We're going to 4316 East Elm Street, so, yeah, it looks like the right number."

"You're kidding me. You're taking an acting class there?" Callie said in between shivers as she pointed up at the Victorian monstrosity that loomed above them.

"Oh, I know it looks scary, but it won't be once we get inside. I promise," Agatha said, eyes sparkling with excitement. "Count Orlov only offers this master class once every three years and he chooses a new, haunted setting each time. Believe me, it's so exclusive, it's . . ."

Apparently, Agatha couldn't think of a word that was more exclusive than *exclusive* and let the sentence trail off. Callie looked over at Happy, who shrugged.

"So maybe this is a dumb question, but why didn't you guys just drive here?"

"Orlov's rule," Agatha said, rolling her eyes. "Everyone has to park back at the Waldbaum's grocery store parking lot, so they can then come humbly on foot to seek the count's instruction."

"That's why you were walking?"

"Isn't it a lovely gesture? All that humbleness in one place." Happy grimaced.

"Happy, don't be mean," Agatha said, her blue eyes flashing. "Count Orlov is a very humble person! Besides, I don't pay you to make jokes at my expense."

"I'm Agatha's personal assistant," Happy said, answering Callie's unspoken question.

"My untouchable personal assistant—"

"Untouchable?" Callie asked.

"Don't be stupid," Agatha said, looking bored. "Everyone knows an untouchable is someone who absorbs psychic power. They're like a negative psychic. Everyone who's anyone has one."

Callie didn't like being called stupid. It was a word she found highly distasteful—and it made her want to dig in her heels right there on the sidewalk and not move another inch.

"I still have no idea what you're talking about," Callie said, feeling frustrated by the conversation. "And it's not stupidity. It's a lack of local knowledge. Your world is *way* kookier than mine."

"Which leads us back to our bargain—" Agatha chirped, but Callie shook her head.

"No divulging of information until I'm between four walls and a roof," Callie said, slipping in the snow. "Which actually brings me to another question: What's this Orlov dude gonna say when an uninvited guest shows up with you guys?"

It appeared Agatha hadn't thought of this eventuality, but luckily, Happy was on top of things. She pulled a cell phone from her pocket and pressed On, the screen lighting up even before her finger had released the button.

"I was thinking I could call you a taxi once we got there—"

"No! You'll get us kicked out of the master class!" Agatha shrieked, reaching for the cell phone, but only managing to knock the electronic device out of Happy's hand, where it bounced once on the sidewalk and fell into the street.

"Agatha was asked not to bring any electronic recording devices with her," Happy offered in explanation, stepping off the curb and out onto the snow-covered asphalt, the knees of her jeans getting wet as she bent down to collect the tiny black cell phone from the snowy gutter.

She pressed the On button again, but this time the screen—which had a new jagged crack across it—stayed black.

"You broke it," Happy said, giving Agatha a nasty look, but the blond girl was made of Teflon, and Happy's distress slid right off her.

"Good, now we won't get in any trouble."

Happy tried the On button one more time, without any luck, then she slid the unresponsive phone back into her pocket, a sour cast to her face.

"Well, I guess you're stuck with us for a little while longer," Happy said as she and Agatha left the safety of the sidewalk and began the long climb up the icy set of rickety wooden steps leading to the Victorian mansion.

Callie—shivering, wet, and miserable to the core—took a deep breath and exhaled slowly before setting her foot on the first step and following the girls skyward. The steep, winding stairway would eventually deposit them on the Victorian's large wraparound porch, but the climb to the summit was treacherous. With each successive step, Callie felt her legs shake harder, the heels she wore making it necessary for her to use the stair's splintered handrail to keep herself upright, every handhold eliciting a small yelp of pain as the wood broke off and inserted itself into the skin of her palms.

"This sucks!" Callie yelled up at the girls, who were far ahead of her, having managed the wayward stairs with the ease of two little mountain goats.

Callie realized if she wanted to reach the porch sometime in that century, she was going to have to accept the possibility of frostbite and take her shoes off. Reaching down, she released one foot from its calfskin prison, then the other, stuffing both shoes under her left arm so she could continue the climb in splinter-free bliss, her ability to balance intact again.

Why am I even doing this? Callie asked herself. *Why don't I just open up a wormhole and get the hell outta here?*

The answer was very simple. No matter how many times she closed her eyes and willed a wormhole into being, she just couldn't seem to make anything happen. For some reason her Death abilities were limited here in this strange new world she'd unwittingly come to inhabit. She wasn't capable of creating even a *spark* of magic—and she didn't know if it was because she'd bumped her head on the ground when she'd been unceremoniously deposited in this alternate version of Queens or if her new environment was the culprit. Either way, she was kinda screwed, as far as making a quick getaway was concerned.

"Hurry up!" Agatha called down to her.

Callie wanted to say something snarky in return, but she was too out of breath from the climb to do anything but clamber up the last few remaining stairs and heave her tired self onto the porch.

"I hate . . . this house . . . already," Callie wheezed, as, barefoot, she leaned her forehead against the wooden railing.

"Are you okay?" Happy asked, touching Callie's shoulder.

"Just. Out. Of. Breath."

Callie continued to lean against the railing while somewhere in her unconscious awareness, she heard Agatha knock on the front door, heard it open, and then, to her utter relief, found the three of them being shepherded into the light of the house's front foyer.

"Thank God," Callie breathed, as warmth enfolded her like a blanket.

The room was small and cramped; red velvet Victorian print wallpaper covered the otherwise bare walls while a red shag runner bisected the polished dark-wood floor, splitting the space in two. There was only one other exit, a dark-wood door cut into the wall directly opposite the front entrance.

A tall woman in a camel pantsuit, her long blond hair piled haphazardly on top of her head, stood in front of this other door, a hand placed delicately on either hip. To her right sat two fawn-colored spindle chairs wedged between a drop-leaf side table with a dying potted plant on its top and an antique coatrack, but she didn't offer anyone a seat. In fact, she didn't look too happy to see them at all.

"You're late . . . and you've brought an uninvited guest," the woman said, her voice a growl.

Agatha, not one to be intimidated by anyone, mirrored the woman's stance.

"We found this poor girl wandering in the woods. We couldn't just leave her there, could we?" she replied, incredulous.

The woman backed down immediately.

"Well, I'm sure you couldn't just leave her out there . . . Miss Averson, is it?"

Agatha nodded, pleased the woman had recognized her.

"I'm Fiona O'Flagnahan, Count Orlov's associate. And my daughter, Heather, is a huge fan of your television show."

This pleased Agatha even more.

"It's so exciting to meet a fan of the show," she purred, totally ignoring the fact that it was the woman's daughter, and not the woman, herself, who liked her work.

Angelic features lit from within, she reached out and took the woman's arm, squeezing it.

"Would you like an autograph? I can do that for you, no problem," Agatha continued, turning to Happy and snapping her fingers.

"Can we get this woman an autographed photo?"

"I left my bag in the car. Count Orlov's orders," Happy said, shrugging helplessly.

Agatha turned back to the woman.

"Give my untouchable assistant your name and address and we'll get publicity to pop one in the mail pronto."

The woman smiled, impressed that Agatha possessed an "untouchable" assistant—*whatever that meant,* Callie thought—and gave Happy her address, spelling out her daughter's name twice, so Agatha would be sure to write it correctly. When she was finally done, the woman turned her attention back to Callie.

"Why don't we get your friend to the sitting room where we have the fire going?" the woman said. "That ought to warm her up a bit."

"I just want to call a taxi," Callie said, her lips beginning to fade from a garish eggplant to a healthier pale peach now that she was inside.

The woman crooked an eyebrow and shook her head.

"But that's not possible. There are no electronic devices in this house. Not even a microwave or a computer." She finished with a flourish of her hand as if she were Vanna White flipping a vowel.

Callie turned to glare at Happy.

"Hey," she said, "don't look at me. I'm just the assistant."

After that pronouncement, it didn't appear there was anything else left to say on the subject.

"This way," Fiona intoned, as she opened the door behind her and led them out into a long hallway, which, at first glance, seemed to go on forever, but as they followed Fiona down its path, shortened so Callie could see the end.

"Wow, this place is huge," Callie said, bare feet padding on the soft, crimson shag runner that had continued with them from the foyer into the hallway.

"It once belonged to the painter Edgar Allan Poe—" Fiona said as she led them deeper into the belly of the house.

"I think you're mistaken. Edgar Allan Poe wasn't a painter, he was a poet and writer," Callie said, interrupting the flow of Fiona's discourse, so that the older woman turned around to glare at her.

"Um, painter," Agatha said, dropping a little vocal fry at the end of the word *painter.*

"I may have hit my head back there, but not hard enough to change the fact that Edgar Allan Poe was a writer."

Callie looked to Happy, who was quickly becoming her touchstone in a world where she felt totally alien and out of place, but Happy merely shook her head.

Okay, Callie thought, *so apparently Edgar Allan Poe is a painter now. Great.*

It was beginning to feel like Callie had stumbled into a play that no one had given her a copy of the script to read beforehand—and since she wasn't too keen on improv, she was having a really hard time keeping up. From now on, she was just gonna keep her mouth shut and work on figuring out a way to call up a wormhole so she could get home.

"Fine, whatever," Callie said, dropping the subject.

Fiona took this as a cue to resume her monologue.

"As I was saying," she continued, brushing a strand of blond, straw-like hair off her forehead, "Edgar Allan Poe and his child bride, Virginia, moved into this house in 1846, along with her mother and one servant. . . ."

As Fiona droned on, she led them still farther into the interior of the house. The hallway was clearly the mansion's main artery from which doors, like capillaries, branched off into hidden rooms and other unseen spaces—and, though it was a two-story dwelling, there didn't seem to be a stairway anywhere on the premises, which was definitely odd.

There's way more to this house than meets the eye, Callie mused, but kept the thought to herself.

As they continued onward, it got darker, the flickering of the candle-light sconces that lined the walls—the only light source in the house—making it hard to see what might be lurking in the shadowy corners or even underfoot.

"This place is spooky," Callie whispered to Happy while, ahead of them, Agatha happily chattered away at Fiona.

"I didn't want Agatha to accept the count's invitation," Happy whispered back, "but she was adamant."

"Are you sure this guy is on the up-and-up?" Callie asked, pausing midstride to slide her shoes back on. The darkness was giving her the creeps and she did *not* want to step on something crunchy or slimy in bare feet.

"I did some research—" Happy began, but was cut off when Fiona came to an abrupt stop in front of a locked door—one that looked no different from any of the other ten doors they'd passed on their way to this one.

"Here we are," Fiona said, pulling a small bronze key from a chain around her neck and inserting it into the door's lock. "Count Orlov is waiting for you inside."

This she directed at Agatha, who clapped her hands together, then turned back and gave Happy and Callie a big, sloppy wink.

"Yippee! I'll see you guys later!"

And then she was pushing past Fiona, her feet dancing with excitement as she crossed the threshold and disappeared into the darkness of the room. Happy, who didn't look at all like her name at that moment, started to protest, but Agatha was already gone, Fiona slamming the door shut on her retreating back.

"There we go," Fiona said, slipping the key back into the lock and turning it twice. "Now, let's get the two of you settled."

She gestured for Happy and Callie to follow her as she continued down the hall, and though neither of the girls wanted to go with her, neither could figure out a way to refuse the invitation.

As they walked, the darkness inside the house became as pervasive as the cold and wet outside the house, and Callie couldn't help wishing she was lying back in the snow making snow angels or freezing to quasi-death (she was immortal, so it would be Popsicle City, not Death Town) instead of traipsing through the creepy old Victorian mansion.

"The sitting room is just beyond this door. There's a fire already in the grate," Fiona said, her voice sending the silence skittering away into the corners. "All you have to do is go inside."

They had come to the end of the hallway and only one more door remained to be opened—and a narrow, sickly looking doorway it was. The whole bottom right side of the molding appeared to have been shredded into pieces, like someone, or something, had clawed unsuccessfully at it for days or weeks—or even years—until finally they, or it, had just given up and faded away.

Fiona continued to beckon them forward, her blond updo and camel-colored suit looking oddly sinister in the candlelight—and that was when Callie decided she wasn't going to go anywhere near the door, regardless of who she offended.

She knew that there was something terribly wrong with the mansion and with Fiona and with everything else they'd experienced since they'd stepped inside the house. If she and Happy were foolish enough to open the decrepit door at the end of the hallway, then any negative outcome that occurred would be of their own doing. She didn't know if Happy was going to appreciate where her thoughts were leading her, but she hoped so . . . because Callie had been hoodwinked too many times in her life not to recognize a setup when she saw one.

"Nope. Not gonna happen," Callie said, holding her ground in a pair of dirty Jimmy Choos. "I think we're gonna go back down this hall and you're gonna use that little key of yours to open the door to the room you stashed Agatha in—"

The words had no sooner left Callie's mouth than Fiona was scrambling for the doorknob, using the element of surprise to try to open the door before Callie and Happy realized what she was doing.

"Not in this lifetime!" Callie cried as she dove for Fiona's waist, wrapping her arms around the older woman's middle and toppling them both onto the red shag runner.

Fiona was a spitfire, almost bending in half in order to dig her French-manicured nails into Callie's throat, cutting long crimson gashes into the girl's otherwise pristine flesh. The "Girl Who Would Be Death" cried out in pain, losing her grip on her opponent as she tried to stanch the flow of blood from her wounded neck.

"Don't you dare!" Callie heard Happy scream, then she watched as the tall brunette launched herself at the wily woman in the camel-colored suit, the two of them rolling across the floor.

The blood was flowing fast and loose from Callie's throat, but she ignored it. Dropping her hand from her throat—it was useless there; her body would heal of its own accord without any external help—she flipped herself onto her belly, slip-sliding in the puddle of blood that'd gathered underneath her, while a few feet away from her, she saw Happy punching Fiona, hard, in the solar plexus.

"I see . . . that you . . . don't need . . . my help," Callie wheezed, finally managing to pull herself up alongside the brunette, who seemed to be rather enjoying the pummeling she was giving the older woman.

"I think she's incapacitated now," Happy said, as Fiona's green eyes rolled up behind her eyelids and she stopped struggling.

"I think so," Callie said, appreciating the quick work Happy had made of Count Orlov's associate. "Let's grab the key and get out of here."

Happy nodded, grasping the chain around Fiona's neck and giving it a good yank.

"The bitch tried to bite me," Happy said, as she pocketed the key, then looked down at her hoodie, which was streaked with Callie's blood and Fiona's saliva.

"That's disgusting," Callie said, reaching into the pocket of her dress and pulling out a moist towelette. "Moist towelette?"

Happy stared at the neat white package, disbelief in her eyes.

"You gotta be kidding me."

Callie shook her head.

"I never kid about hygiene. Here, take one."

Happy accepted the packet, tearing it open and fishing the moist towelette from its innards.

"What about you? You're losing a lot of blood," Happy said, pointing at Callie's throat.

"I'm . . ." She paused, not sure what to say—a last-minute impulse brought out the truth.

"I'm immortal and I'm pretty sure I come from an alternate universe. Just FYI."

Happy snorted. "Of course you are and of course you do."

"Now I've told you all about me so we're even-steven," Callie said, starting to laugh a little hysterically.

"It's not funny," Happy continued, helping Callie to her feet. "I think there's a powerful telepathic illusionist running this show—someone we've dealt with in the past. And if that's the case, then Agatha's in a whole heap of trouble."

"A telepathic what?" Callie asked as she followed Happy back down the hallway.

"Illusionist. Someone who can manipulate matter, affect people's minds," Happy replied. "And they can wreak all kinds of havoc if left unchallenged. Especially this guy. He's obsessed with Agatha and has a serious bad attitude to boot."

"That's not good," Callie said, shuddering.

"No, it's not."

When they reached what they thought was the door Agatha had disappeared through, Happy thrust the key into the lock, but it jammed, not wanting to go in.

"Wrong door," Callie murmured. And then she slumped forward, grasping for the wall as her body went limp and rubbery.

"Callie!" Happy cried, grabbing the other girl around the waist and slowly easing her to the ground.

"I feel so . . . woozy," Callie said, eyes fluttering as, for the second time in her life, she realized she *might* actually be dying.

It had almost happened once before, when she'd been poisoned with promethium—every immortal had a killing weakness, one that was totally unique to them, and Callie's just happened to be promethium—but she'd been careful to stay far, far away from the stuff since then.

"Is there . . . promethium?" Callie choked out, fear etching her gut like acid.

"Promethia-what?" Happy cried, confused. "I thought you said you were immortal. You're still bleeding like a stuck pig!"

With a shaky hand, Callie reached up and put her fingers to her neck. Sure enough, the wound had not closed, but, instead, was continuing to leak her lifeblood out onto the rug.

And then it dawned on her.

"It's you, Happy," Callie said, finally understanding why she hadn't been able to call up a wormhole while she was in this alternate universe. "You inhibit psychic ability . . . what we call 'magic' in my universe. And it means that you're blocking . . . my immortality."

"Shit," Happy said, backing away from Callie.

"No, no . . . come back," Callie said. "I just need to stop the flow of blood for now. Give me . . . your hoodie."

Happy unzipped her jacket and slid out of it, handing it to Callie.

"Pressure," Callie breathed, lifting the hoodie to her neck. "Put pressure on the wound."

It was obvious she was much weaker than she'd realized because

Happy had to take the jacket and wrap it around the wound for her, securing the makeshift tourniquet in place by tying the sleeves into a tight bow.

"I think that should work," Happy said, sitting back on her heels to admire her handiwork.

"Feel better . . . already." Callie sighed, giving Happy a weak smile as the other girl helped her to her feet.

"God, I hope so," Happy said, her face wan. "Now let's find Agatha."

With Callie holding on to Happy's arm for support, the girls continued down the hallway. This time it seemed luck was on their side, because the next door they tried was the right one, the key sliding into the lock and turning with a satisfying *click*.

"Okay," Happy said, grasping the doorknob with her right hand. "One, two . . . three!"

She threw the door open and Callie screamed as she realized they were teetering on the threshold of a yawning abyss.

"It's not real," Happy said calmly, reaching out a hand so that it hung in the empty air before them.

Suddenly the yawning abyss disappeared, almost as if it had never existed at all, and in its place, they discovered a bare octagonal room with an army cot in one corner and a chamber pot half hidden underneath it.

"Happy!" Agatha cried, jumping up from the cot and racing over to them. "I knew you'd rescue me! Count Orlov never came—I don't even think the invitation was really *from* him—and then the door was locked and I couldn't get out . . . Ew, what happened to your hoodie?"

Happy, who was used to Agatha's one-track mind, brushed off the hoodie comment with, "Harold's here."

"What?" Agatha said, her blue eyes wide with disbelief.

Happy looked grim.

"I think he's orchestrated this whole thing in order to make good on his promise to turn you into a collectible."

All the color drained from Agatha's face.

"Oh, no," she said, looking ill.

"This isn't like an ex-boyfriend thing, is it?" Callie asked.

"No!" Both Happy and Agatha shouted at the same time.

"Sorry I asked," Callie said, glad her snarkiness was returning because it meant she wasn't gonna be dying anytime soon.

"He's a film producer whose career was ruined by a film that Agatha happened to star in—" Happy began.

"I told him it was a bad script," Agatha chimed in.

"He blames her completely for the failure," Happy continued. "And he promised to turn her into a collectible doll because he said her performance in the film was as stiff and fake as one."

"He's working all this stuff from a remote location so you can't zap his psychic powers, Happy," Agatha said angrily.

"I would expect so," Happy agreed, and at those words, the floor beneath them started to shake, the army cot flipping onto its side as the chamber pot went flying.

"All right, time to get out of here," Callie said, gripping Happy's arm for support.

"But what if we're trapped?" Agatha moaned, tears springing to her eyes.

"Agatha!" Happy said, her brow furrowed in consternation. "Stop trying to create unnecessary drama."

Agatha's eyes instantly cleared and she shrugged.

"Well, drama seemed appropriate for the situation, but if you'd rather I not—"

"I'd rather you not, actually," Callie said as she followed Happy through the door that led back out into the hallway, the house beginning to disintegrate around them.

At first, Callie thought she was imagining the house's destruction, but as they ran, she saw the ceiling and walls starting to flake into charred black bits that rained down on their heads like volcanic ash.

"The house is a telepathic illusion from Harold's mind," Happy said. "So it can't hurt us."

She was right. As soon as they reached the front foyer, the final bits of the false image dissipated and they were met with a wash of black soot that settled onto their heads in soft, delicate clumps. . . . Only when Callie brushed the stuff away from her face, she realized that it wasn't soot covering her head. It was snow.

And then she started to shiver.

The remains of the abandoned mansion were skeletal. Curved wooden beams reminiscent of a naked rib cage exposed the rotting interior to the snowy sky, while corroded siding sloughed off its exterior in swaths like dead skin from a corpse. The red shag runner Callie had snuggled her feet into proved to be nothing more than decaying dirt and leaves, the front foyer merely an empty room without a front door.

The woman they'd called Fiona had managed to make her escape during all the craziness—and Callie wondered if there was any truth to the story she'd told about the daughter and the autograph. And if so, was the address she'd given Happy real?

Once they'd surveyed the decaying house, it hadn't taken a genius to understand why Fiona had been so adamant that Callie and Happy leave by the back exit: If they'd followed her directions, they'd have plummeted to their deaths via the deep ravine that lay directly behind the property.

As the girls trudged back to the Waldbaum's parking lot clearly the worse for wear, Callie realized it was just dumb luck that no one had gotten killed. Harold—or whoever the mastermind was, if Happy's hypothesis was incorrect—had been very clever in using the house as their staging ground, luring Agatha and Happy into a trap via an invitation to a master acting class with the great acting coach Count Orlov—something Agatha's ego couldn't resist. It was only by the most random of coincidences—asking the wormhole to take her to a "happy place," which the universe translated as "take me to a place where Happy lives"—that Callie had stumbled into the story and wrecked the bad guy's plan.

When they reached the parking lot, Agatha's red Maserati was the only car left in the lot. As Happy unlocked the doors, Agatha threw her arms around Callie's shoulders and gave her a pythonlike squeeze.

"I'm so glad we met you. If you're ever in New York or L.A. and need a place to crash . . ."

Agatha released her, and Callie smiled.

"Agatha, like I tried to explain before," Happy said, exasperation thick in her voice, "Callie comes from another universe—"

"Whatever," Agatha said, rolling her eyes as she climbed into the driver's seat and snagged the keys from her assistant. "Like I said: My casa is your casa."

Smiling, she jammed the keys into the ignition, the car roaring to life underneath her nimble fingers. As Agatha gunned the engine, Happy rolled down the passenger window and Callie hobbled over, trying not to let her teeth chatter as the snow settled all around her like dew.

"If you hadn't dropped out of the sky when you did . . ." Happy said, but she didn't need to finish the thought. They all knew Callie's surprise arrival had stacked the cards in their favor . . . at least this night.

"It was just dumb luck," Callie said, shrugging.

"Are you sure we can't drop you somewhere?" Happy asked, but Callie shook her head.

"I think the sooner you get out of here, the faster I can heal myself and get where I need to go."

"Well, thank you for everything. Seriously," Happy said, giving Callie a warm smile. "And good luck getting ho—"

Happy didn't get to finish her good-bye because Agatha chose that moment to jam her foot on the gas, the candy-red Maserati speeding off into the shimmering white night in a cloud of exhaust.

As the car rounded the bend and disappeared into the darkness, Callie's wounds began to close.

Callie took a deep breath and then a blinding golden light filled her soul and she was gone. With a sigh, she wondered why it'd taken her so long to figure this whole wormhole thing out in the first place.

Oh, well, Callie thought. *At least I've got the hang of it now.*

Callie opened her eyes to find herself back in Mrs. Gunwhale's modular classroom, her classmates staring at her, gape-mouthed. She knew she must've looked like a bloody mess, but she didn't care. She'd started this Remedial Wormhole Calling class with zero hopes of ever learning anything, and now she'd found that she'd conquered the entire syllabus.

It was a thrilling feeling—and she could go back to Death, Inc., tomorrow with her head held high and her ego ten times bigger than it'd been the day before.

Mrs. Gunwhale opened her blowhole to speak, but Callie raised her hand for silence.

"I just want to say thank you, Mrs. Gunwhale, and thank you, fellow students, for absolutely nothing."

Callie smiled, her strength returning in leaps and bounds.

"Now, if you'll excuse me," she said, grinning, "I'm going home. I've got a business to run."

And without another word, Callie called up a wormhole and disappeared into the night, never to see the modular classroom at PS 181 again for as long as she immortally lived.

Iphigenia in Aulis

MIKE CAREY

Mike Carey is the author of the Felix Castor novels and (along with Linda and Louise Carey) *The Steel Seraglio*. He has also written extensively for comics publishers DC and Marvel, including long runs on X-Men, Hellblazer and Ultimate Fantastic Four. He wrote the comic book *Lucifer* for its entire run and is the co-creator and writer of the ongoing Vertigo series The Unwritten.

Her name is Melanie. It means "the black girl," from an ancient Greek word, but her skin is mostly very fair so she thinks maybe it's not such a good name for her. Miss Justineau assigns names from a big list: new children get the top name on the boys' list or the top name on the girls' list, and that, Miss Justineau says, is that.

Melanie is ten years old, and she has skin like a princess in a fairy tale: skin as white as snow. So she knows that when she grows up she'll be beautiful, with princes falling over themselves to climb her tower and rescue her.

Assuming, of course, that she has a tower.

In the meantime, she has the cell, the corridor, the classroom and the shower room.

The cell is small and square. It has a bed, a chair and a table in it. On the walls there are pictures: in Melanie's cell, a picture of a field of flowers and a picture of a woman dancing. Sometimes they move the children around, so Melanie knows that there are different pictures in each cell. She used to have a horse in a meadow and a big mountain with snow on the top, which she liked better.

The corridor has twenty doors on the left-hand side and eighteen doors on the right-hand side (because the cupboards don't really count);

also it has a door at either end. The door at the classroom end is red. It leads to the classroom (duh!). The door at the other end is bare gray steel on this side but once when Melanie was being taken back to her cell she peeped through the door, which had accidentally been left open, and saw that on the other side it's got lots of bolts and locks and a box with numbers on it. She wasn't supposed to see, and Sergeant said "Little bitch has got way too many eyes on her," but she saw, and she remembers.

She listens, too, and from overheard conversations she has a sense of this place in relation to other places she hasn't ever seen. This place is the block. Outside the block is the base. Outside the base is the Eastern Stretch, or the Dispute Stretch. It's all good as far as Kansas, and then it gets real bad, real quick. East of Kansas, there's monsters everywhere and they'll follow you for a hundred miles if they smell you, and then they'll eat you. Melanie is glad that she lives in the block, where she's safe.

Through the gray steel door, each morning, the teachers come. They walk down the corridor together, past Melanie's door, bringing with them the strong, bitter chemical smell that they always have on them: it's not a nice smell, but it's exciting because it means the start of another day's lessons.

At the sound of the bolts sliding and the teachers' footsteps, Melanie runs to the door of her cell and stands on tiptoe to peep through the little mesh-screen window in the door and see the teachers when they go by. She calls out good morning to them, but they're not supposed to answer and usually they don't. Sometimes, though, Miss Justineau will look around and smile at her—a tense, quick smile that's gone almost before she can see it—or Miss Mailer will give her a tiny wave with just the fingers of her hand.

All but one of the teachers go through the thirteenth door on the left, where there's a stairway leading down to another corridor and (Melanie guesses) lots more doors and rooms. The one who doesn't go through the thirteenth door unlocks the classroom and opens up, and that one will be Melanie's teacher and Melanie's friends' teacher for the day.

Then Sergeant comes, and the men and women who do what Sergeant says. They've got the chemical smell, too, and it's even stronger on them

than it is on the teachers. Their job is to take the children to the classroom, and after that they go away again. There's a procedure that they
follow, which takes a long time. Melanie thinks it must be the same for
all the children, but of course she doesn't know that for sure because it
always happens inside the cells and the only cell that Melanie sees the
inside of is her own.

To start with, Sergeant bangs on all the doors, and shouts at the
children to get ready. Melanie sits down in the wheelchair at the foot of
her bed, like she's been taught to do. She puts her hands on the arms of
the chair and her feet on the footrests. She closes her eyes and waits. She
counts while she waits. The highest she's ever had to count is 4,526; the
lowest is 4,301.

When the key turns in the door, she stops counting and opens her
eyes. Sergeant comes in with his gun and points it at her. Then two of
Sergeant's people come in and tighten and buckle the straps of the chair
around Melanie's wrists and ankles. There's also a strap for her neck:
they tighten that one last of all, when her hands and feet are fastened up
all the way, and they always do it from behind. The strap is designed so
they never have to put their hands in front of Melanie's face. Melanie
sometimes says, "I won't bite." She says it as a joke, but Sergeant's people
never laugh. Sergeant did once, the first time she said it, but it was a
nasty laugh. And then he said, "Like we'd ever give you the fucking
chance, sugarplum."

When Melanie is all strapped into the chair, and she can't move her
hands or her feet or her head, they wheel her into the classroom and put
her at her desk. The teacher might be talking to some of the other children, or writing something on the blackboard, but she (unless it's Mr.
Galloway, who's the only he) will usually stop and say, "Good morning,
Melanie." That way the children who sit way up at the front of the class
will know that Melanie has come into the room and they can say good
morning, too. They can't see her, of course, because they're all in their
own chairs with their neck-straps fastened up, so they can't turn their
heads around that far.

This procedure—the wheeling in, and the teacher saying good morning, and then the chorus of greetings from the other kids—happens seven
more times, because there are seven children who come into the classroom

after Melanie. One of them is Anne, who used to be Melanie's best friend in the class and maybe still is except that the last time they moved the kids around (Sergeant calls it "shuffling the deck") they ended up sitting a long way apart and it's hard to be best friends with someone you can't talk to. Another is Steven, whom Melanie doesn't like because he calls her Melon-Brain or M-M-M-Melanie to remind her that she used to stammer sometimes in class.

When all the children are in the classroom, the lessons start. Every day has sums and spelling, but there doesn't seem to be a plan for the rest of the lessons. Some teachers like to read aloud from books. Others make the children learn facts and dates, which is something that Melanie is very good at. She knows the names of all the states in the United States, and all their capitals, and their state birds and flowers, and the total population of each state and what they mostly manufacture or grow there. She also knows the presidents in order and the years that they were in office, and she's working on European capitals. She doesn't find it hard to remember this stuff; she does it to keep from being bored, because being bored is worse than almost anything.

Melanie learned the stuff about the states from Mr. Galloway's lessons, but she's not sure if she's got all the details right because one day, when he was acting kind of funny and his voice was all slippery and fuzzy, Mr. Galloway said something that worried Melanie. She was asking him whether it was the whole state of New York that used to be called New Amsterdam, or just the city, and he said, who cares? "None of this stuff matters anymore, Melanie. I just gave it to you because all the textbooks we've got are twenty years old."

Melanie persists, because New Amsterdam was way back in the eighteenth century, so she doesn't think twenty years should matter all that much. "But when the Dutch colonists—" she says.

Mr. Galloway cuts her off. "Jesus, it's irrelevant. It's ancient history! The Hungries tore up the map. There's nothing east of Kansas anymore. Not a damn thing."

So it's possible, even quite likely, that some of Melanie's lists need to be updated in some respects.

The children have classes on Monday, Tuesday, Wednesday, Thursday and Friday. On Saturday, the children stay locked in their rooms all day and music plays over the PA system. Nobody comes, not even Sergeant, and the music is too loud to talk over. Melanie had the idea long ago of making up a language that used signs instead of words, so the children could talk to each other through their little mesh windows, and she went ahead and made the language up, or some of it anyway, but when she asked Miss Mailer if she could teach it to the class, Miss Mailer told her no really loud and sharp. She made Melanie promise not to mention her sign language to any of the other teachers, and especially not to Sergeant. "He's paranoid enough already," she said. "If he thinks you're talking behind his back, he'll lose what's left of his mind."

So Melanie never got to teach the other children how to talk in sign language.

Saturdays are long and dull, and hard to get through. Melanie tells herself aloud some of the stories that the children have been told in class. It's okay to say them out loud because the music hides her voice. Otherwise Sergeant would come in and tell her to stop.

Melanie knows that Sergeant is still there on Saturdays, because one Saturday when Ronnie hit her hand against the mesh window of her cell until it bled and got all mashed up, Sergeant came in. He brought two of his people, and all three of them were dressed in the big suits, and they went into Ronnie's cell and Melanie guessed from the sounds that they were trying to tie Ronnie into her chair. She also guessed from the sounds that Ronnie was struggling and making it hard for them, because she kept shouting and saying, "Let me alone! Let me alone!" Then there was a banging sound that went on and on and Sergeant shouted, "Shut up shut up shut up shut up shut up!" and then other people were shouting, too, and someone said, "Christ Jesus, don't—" and then it all went quiet again.

Melanie couldn't tell what happened after that. The people who work for Sergeant went around and locked all the little doors over the mesh windows, so the children couldn't see out. They stayed locked all day. The next Monday, Ronnie wasn't in the class anymore, and nobody seemed to know what had happened to her. Melanie likes to think that Ronnie went through the thirteenth door on the left into another class, so she might come back one day when Sergeant shuffles the deck again. But what Melanie really believes, when she can't stop herself from thinking about it, is that Sergeant took Ronnie away to punish her, and he won't let her see any of the other children ever again.

Sundays are like Saturdays except for the shower. At the start of the day the children are put in their chairs as though it's a regular school day, but instead of being taken to the classroom, they're taken to the shower room, which is the last door on the right, just before the bare steel door.

In the shower room, which is white-tiled and empty, the children sit and wait until everybody has been wheeled in. Then the doors are closed and sealed, which means the room is completely dark because there aren't any lights in there. Pipes behind the walls start to make a sound like someone trying not to laugh, and a chemical spray falls from the ceiling.

It's the same chemical that's on the teachers and Sergeant and Sergeant's people, or at least it smells the same, but it's a lot stronger. It stings a little, at first. Then it stings a lot. It leaves Melanie's eyes puffy, reddened and half-blind. But it evaporates quickly from clothes and skin, so after half an hour more of sitting in the still, dark room, there's nothing left of it but the smell, and then finally the smell fades, too, or at least they get used to it so it's not so bad anymore, and they just wait in silence for the door to be unlocked and Sergeant's people to come and get them. This is how the children are washed, and for that reason, if for no other, Sunday is probably the worst day of the week.

The best day of the week is whichever day Miss Mailer teaches. It isn't always the same day, and some weeks she doesn't come at all. Melanie guesses that there are more than five classes of children, and that the teachers' time is divided arbitrarily among them. Certainly there's no pattern that she can discern, and she's really good at that stuff.

When Miss Mailer teaches, the day is full of amazing things. Sometimes she'll read poems aloud, or bring her flute and play it, or show the children pictures out of a book and tell them stories about the people in the pictures. That was how Melanie got to find out about Agamemnon and the Trojan War, because one of the paintings showed Agamemnon's wife, Clytemnestra, looking really mad and scary. "Why is she so mad?" Anne asked Miss Mailer.

"Because Agamemnon killed their daughter," Miss Mailer said. "The

Greek fleet was stuck in harbor on the island of Aulis. So Agamemnon put his daughter on an altar, and he killed her so that the goddess Artemis would give the Greek fleet fair winds and help them to get to the war on time."

The kids in the class were mostly both scared and delighted with this, like it was a ghost story or something, but Melanie was troubled by it. How could killing a little girl change the way the winds blew? "You're right, Melanie, it couldn't," Miss Mailer said. "But the Ancient Greeks had a lot of gods, and all kinds of weird ideas about what would make the gods happy. So Agamemnon gave Iphigenia's death to the goddess as a present, and his wife decided he had to pay for that."

Melanie, who already knew by this time that her own name was Greek, decided she was on Clytemnestra's side. Maybe it was important to get to the war on time, but you shouldn't kill kids to do it. You should just row harder, or put more sails up. Or maybe you should go in a boat that had an outboard motor.

The only problem with the days when Miss Mailer teaches is that the time goes by too quickly. Every second is so precious to Melanie that she doesn't even blink: she just sits there wide-eyed, drinking in everything that Miss Mailer says, and memorizing it so that she can play it back to herself later, in her cell. And whenever she can manage it, she asks Miss Mailer questions, because what she likes most to hear, and to remember, is Miss Mailer's voice saying her name, Melanie, in that way that makes her feel like the most important person in the world.

One day, Sergeant comes into the classroom on a Miss Mailer day. Melanie doesn't know he's there until he speaks, because he's standing right at the back of the class. When Miss Mailer says, ". . . and this time, Pooh and Piglet counted three sets of footprints in the snow," Sergeant's voice breaks in with, "What the fuck is this?"

Miss Mailer stops, and looks round. "I'm reading the children a story, Sergeant Robertson," she says.

"I can see that," Sergeant's voice says. "I thought the idea was to educate them, not give them a cabaret."

"Stories can educate just as much as facts," Miss Mailer says.

"Like how, exactly?" Sergeant asks, nastily.

"They teach us how to live, and how to think."

"Oh yeah, plenty of world-class ideas in *Winnie-the-Pooh*." Sergeant is using sarcasm. Melanie knows how sarcasm works: you say the opposite of what you really mean. "Seriously, Gwen, you're wasting your time. You want to tell them stories, tell them about Jack the Ripper and John Wayne Gacy."

"They're children," Miss Mailer points out.

"No, they're not," Sergeant says, very loudly. "And that, that right there, that's why you don't want to read them *Winnie-the-Pooh*. You do that, you start thinking of them as real kids. And then you slip up. And maybe you untie one of them because she needs a cuddle or something. And I don't need to tell you what happens after that."

Sergeant comes out to the front of the class then, and he does something really horrible. He rolls up his sleeve, all the way to the elbow, and he holds his bare forearm in front of Kenny's face: right in front of Kenny, just an inch or so away from him. Nothing happens at first, but then Sergeant spits on his hand and rubs at his forearm, like he's wiping something away.

"Don't," says Miss Mailer. "Don't do that to him." But Sergeant doesn't answer her or look at her.

Melanie sits two rows behind Kenny, and two rows over, so she can see the whole thing. Kenny goes real stiff, and he whimpers, and then his mouth gapes wide and he starts to snap at Sergeant's arm, which of course he can't reach. And drool starts to drip down from the corner of his mouth, but not much of it because nobody ever gives the children anything to drink, so it's thick, kind of half-solid, and it hangs there on the end of Kenny's chin, wobbling, while Kenny grunts and snaps at Sergeant's arm, and makes kind of moaning, whimpering sounds.

"You see?" Sergeant says, and he turns to look at Miss Mailer's face to make sure she gets his point. And then he blinks, all surprised, and maybe he wishes he hadn't, because Miss Mailer is looking at him like Clytemnestra looked in the painting, and Sergeant lets his arm fall to his side and shrugs like none of this was ever important to him anyway.

"Not everyone who looks human is human," he says.

"No," Miss Mailer agrees. "I'm with you on that one."

Kenny's head sags a little sideways, which is as far as it can move because of the strap, and he makes a clicking sound in his throat.

"It's all right, Kenny," Miss Mailer says. "It will pass soon. Let's go on with the story. Would you like that? Would you like to hear what happened to Pooh and Piglet? Sergeant Robertson, if you'll excuse us? Please?"

Sergeant looks at her, and shakes his head real hard. "You don't want to get attached to them," he says. "There's no cure. So once they hit eighteen . . ."

But Miss Mailer starts to read again, like he's not even there, and in the end he leaves. Or maybe he's still standing at the back of the classroom, not speaking, but Melanie doesn't think so because after a while Miss Mailer gets up and shuts the door, and Melanie thinks that she'd only do that right then if Sergeant was on the other side of it.

Melanie barely sleeps at all that night. She keeps thinking about what Sergeant said, that the children aren't real children, and about how Miss Mailer looked at him when he was being so nasty to Kenny.

And she thinks about Kenny snarling and snapping at Sergeant's arm like a dog. She wonders why he did it, and she thinks maybe she knows the answer because when Sergeant wiped his arm with spit and waved it under Kenny's nose, it was as though under the bitter chemical smell Sergeant had a different smell altogether. And even though the smell was very faint where Melanie was, it made her head swim and her jaw muscles start to work by themselves. She can't even figure out what it was she was feeling, because it's not like anything that ever happened to her before or anything she heard of in a story, but it was like there was something she was supposed to do and it was so urgent, so important, that her body was trying to take over her mind and do it without her.

But along with these scary thoughts, she also thinks: Sergeant has a name, the same way the teachers do. The same way the children do. Sergeant has been more like the goddess Artemis to Melanie up until now; now she knows that he's just like everyone else, even if he is scary. The enormity of that change, more than anything else, is what keeps her awake until the doors unlock in the morning and the teachers come.

In a way, Melanie's feelings about Miss Mailer have changed, too. Or rather, they haven't changed at all, but they've become stronger and stronger. There can't be anyone better or kinder or lovelier than Miss Mailer anywhere in the world; Melanie wishes she was a Greek warrior with a sword and a shield, so she could fight for Miss Mailer and save her from Heffalumps and Woozles. She knows that Heffalumps and Woozles are in *Winnie-the-Pooh*, not the *Iliad*, but she likes the words, and she likes the idea of saving Miss Mailer so much that it becomes her favorite thought. She thinks it whenever she's not thinking anything else. It makes even Sundays bearable.

One day, Miss Mailer talks to them about death. It's because most of the men in the Light Brigade have just died, in a poem that Miss Mailer is reading to the class. The children want to know what it means to die, and what it's like. Miss Mailer says it's like all the lights going out, and everything going real quiet, the way it does at night—but forever. No morning. The lights never come back on again.

"That sounds terrible," says Lizzie, in a voice like she's about to cry. It sounds terrible to Melanie, too; like sitting in the shower room on Sunday with the chemical smell in the air, and then even the smell goes away and there's nothing at all forever and ever.

Miss Mailer can see that she's upset them, and she tries to make it okay again by talking about it more. "But maybe it's not like that at all," she says. "Nobody really knows, because when you're dead, you can't come back to talk about it. And anyway, it would be different for you than it would be for most people because you're . . ."

And then she stops herself, with the next word sort of frozen halfway out of her lips.

"We're what?" Melanie asks.

"You're children," Miss Mailer says, after a few seconds. "You can't even really imagine what death might be like, because for children it seems like everything has to go on forever."

There's a silence while they think about that. It's true, Melanie decides. She can't remember a time when her life was any different from this, and she can't imagine any other way that people could live. But there's something that doesn't make sense to her, in the whole equation, and so she has to ask the question.

"*Whose* children are we, Miss Mailer?"

In stories, she knows, children have a mother and a father, like Iphigenia had Clytemnestra and Agamemnon. Sometimes they have teachers, too, but not always, and they never seem to have Sergeants. So this is a question that gets to the very roots of the world, and Melanie asks it with some trepidation.

Miss Mailer thinks about it for a long time, until Melanie is pretty sure that she won't answer. Then she says, "Your mom is dead, Melanie. She died before . . . She died when you were very little. Probably your daddy's dead, too, although there isn't really any way of knowing. So the army is looking after you now."

"Is that just Melanie," John asks, "or is it all of us?"

Miss Mailer nods slowly. "All of you."

"We're in an orphanage," Anne guesses. The class heard the story of Oliver Twist once.

"No. You're on an army base."

"Is that what happens to kids whose mom and dad die?" This is Steven now.

"Sometimes."

Melanie is thinking hard, and putting it together, inside her head, like a puzzle. "How old was I," she asks, "when my mom died?" Because she must have been very young, if she can't remember her mother at all.

"It's not easy to explain," Miss Mailer says, and they can see from her face that she's really, really unhappy.

"Was I a baby?" Melanie asks.

"A very tiny baby, Melanie."

"How tiny?"

"Tiny enough to fall into a hole between two laws."

It comes out quick and low and almost hard. Miss Mailer changes the subject then, and the children are happy to let her do it because nobody is very enthusiastic about death by this point. But Melanie wants to know one more thing, and she wants it badly enough that she even takes the chance of upsetting Miss Mailer some more. It's because of her name being Greek, and what the Greeks sometimes used to do to their kids, at least in the ancient times when they were fighting a war against Troy. At the end of the lesson, she waits until Miss Mailer is close to her and she asks her question really quietly.

"Miss Mailer, were our moms and dads going to sacrifice us to the goddess Artemis? Is that why we're here?"

Miss Mailer looks down at her, and for the longest time she doesn't answer. Then something completely unexpected and absolutely wonderful happens. Miss Mailer reaches down and *she strokes Melanie's hair.* She strokes Melanie's hair with her hand, like it was just the most natural and normal thing in the world. And lights are dancing behind Melanie's eyes, and she can't get her breath, and she can't speak or hear or think about anything because apart from Sergeant's people, maybe two or three times and always by accident, nobody has ever touched her before and this is Miss Mailer touching her and it's almost too nice to be in the world at all.

"Oh, Melanie," Miss Mailer says. Her voice is only just higher than a whisper.

Melanie doesn't say anything. She never wants Miss Mailer's hand to move. She thinks if she could die now, with Miss Mailer's hand on her hair, and nothing changed ever again, then it would be all right to be dead.

"I—I can't explain it to you," Miss Mailer says, sounding really, really unhappy. "There are too many other things I'd have to explain, too, to make sense of it. And—and I'm not strong enough. I'm just not strong enough."

But she tries anyway, and Melanie understands some of it. Just before the Hungries came, Miss Mailer says, the government passed an amendment to the Constitution of the United States of America. It was because of something called the Christian Right, and it meant that you were a person even before you were born, and the law had to protect you from the very moment that you popped up inside your mom's tummy like a seed.

Melanie is full of questions already, but she doesn't ask them because it will only be a minute or two before Sergeant's people come for her, and she knows from Miss Mailer's voice that this is a big, important secret. So then the Hungries came, Miss Mailer said—or rather, people started turning into Hungries. And everything fell to pieces real fast.

It was a virus, Miss Mailer says: a virus that killed you, but then brought you partway back to life; not enough of you to talk, but enough of you to stand up and move around and even run. You turned into a monster that just wanted to bite other people and make them into

Hungries, too. That was how the virus propagated itself, Miss Mailer said.

So the virus spread and all the governments fell and it looked like the Hungries were going to eat everyone or make everyone like they were, and that would be the end of the story and the end of everything. But the real people didn't give up. They moved the government to Los Angeles, with the desert all around them and the ocean at their back, and they cleared the Hungries out of the whole state of California with flame-throwers and daisy cutter bombs and nerve gas and big moving fences that were on trucks controlled by radio signals. Melanie has no idea what these things are, but she nods as if she does and imagines a big war like Greeks fighting Trojans.

And every once in a while, the real people would find a bunch of Hungries who'd fallen down because of the nerve gas and couldn't get up again, or who were stuck in a hole or locked in a room or something. And maybe one of them might have been about to be a mom, before she got turned into a Hungry. There was a baby already inside her.

The real people were allowed to kill the Hungries because there was a law, Emergency Ordnance 9, that said they could. Anyone could kill a Hungry and it wouldn't be murder because they weren't people anymore.

But the real people weren't allowed to kill the unborn babies, because of the amendment to the Constitution: inside their moms, the babies all had rights. And maybe the babies would have something else, called higher cognitive functions, that their moms didn't have anymore, because viruses don't always work the same on unborn babies.

So there was a big argument about what was going to happen to the babies, and nobody could decide. Inside the cleared zone, in California, there were so many different groups of people with so many different ideas, it looked like it might all fall apart and the real people would kill each other and finish what the Hungries started. They couldn't risk doing anything that might make one group of people get mad with the other groups of people.

So they made a compromise. The babies were cut out of their mommies. If they survived, and they did have those function things, then they'd be raised, and educated, and looked after, and protected, until one of two things happened: either someone came up with a cure, or the children reached the age of eighteen.

If there was a cure, then the children would be cured.

If there wasn't . . .

"Here endeth the lesson," says Sergeant.

He comes into Melanie's line of sight, right behind Miss Mailer, and Miss Mailer snatches her hand away from Melanie's hair. She ducks her head so Melanie can't see her face.

"She goes back now," Sergeant says.

"Right." Miss Mailer's voice is very small.

"And you go on a charge."

"Right."

"And maybe you lose your job. Because every rule we got, you just broke."

Miss Mailer brings her head up again. Her eyes are wet with tears. "Fuck you, Eddie," she says.

She walks out of Melanie's line of sight, very quickly. Melanie wants to call her back, wants to say something to make her stay: *I love you, Miss Mailer. I'll be a warrior for you, and save you.* But she can't say anything, and then Sergeant's people come. Sergeant's there, too. "Look at you," he says to Melanie. "Fucking face all screwed up like a tragedy mask. Like you've got fucking feelings."

But nothing that Sergeant says and nothing that Sergeant does can take away the memory of that touch.

When she's wheeled into her cell, and Sergeant stands by with his gun as the straps are unfastened one by one, Melanie looks him in the eye. "You won't get fair winds, whatever you do," she tells him. "No matter how many children you kill, the goddess Artemis won't help you."

Sergeant stares at her, and something happens in his face. It's like he's surprised, and then he's scared, and then he's angry. Sergeant's people can see it, too, and one of them takes a step toward him with her hand halfway up like she's going to touch his arm.

"Sergeant Robertson!" she says.

He pulls back from her, and then he makes a gesture with the gun. "We're done here," he says.

"She's still strapped in," says the other one of Sergeant's people.

"Too bad," says Sergeant. He throws the door open and waits for them to move, looking at one of them and then the other until they give up and leave Melanie where she is and go out through the door.

"Fair winds, kid," Sergeant says.

So Melanie has to spend the night in her chair, still strapped up tight apart from her head and her left arm. And it's way too uncomfortable to sleep, even if she leans her head sideways, because there's a big pipe that runs down the wall right there and she can't get into a position that doesn't hurt her.

But then, because of the pipe, something else happens. Melanie starts to hear voices, and they seem to be coming right out of the wall. Only they're not: they're coming down the pipe, somehow, from another part of the building. Melanie recognizes Sergeant's voice, but not any of the others.

"Fence went down in Michigan," Sergeant says. "Twenty-mile stretch, Clayton said. Hungries are pushing west, and probably south, too. How long you think it'll be before they cut us off?"

"Clayton's full of shit," a second voice says, but with an anxious edge. "You think they'd have left us here, if that was gonna happen? They'd have evacuated the base."

"Fuck if they would!" This is Sergeant again. "They care more about these little plague rats than they do about us. If they'd have done it right, we didn't even need to be here. All they had to do was to put every last one of the little bastards in a barn and throw one fucking daisy cutter in there. No more worries."

It gets real quiet for a while after that, like no one can think of anything to say. "I thought they found a cure," a third voice says, but he's shouted down by a lot of voices all at the same time. "That's bullshit." "Dream on, man!" "Onliest cure for them fuckin' skull-faces is in this here clip, and I got enough for all."

"They did, though," the third voice persists. "They isolated the virus. At that lab in Houston. And then they built something that'll kill it. Something that'll fit in a hypo. They call it a *phage*."

"Here, you, skull-face." Sergeant is putting on a funny voice. "I got a cure for you, so why'n't you come on over here and roll up your sleeve? That's right. And all you other cannibal motherfuckers, you form an orderly line there."

There's a lot of laughter, and a lot of stuff that Melanie can't hear clearly. The third voice doesn't speak again.

"I heard they broke through from Mexico and took Los Angeles." Another new voice. "We ain't got no government now. It's just the last few units out in the field, and some camps like this one that kept a perimeter up. That's why there's no messages anymore. No one out there to send them."

Then the second voice comes in again with, "Hell, Dawlish. Brass keep their comms to theirselves, like always. There's messages. Just ain't any for you, is all."

"They're all dead," Sergeant says. "They're all dead except us. And what are we? We're the fucking nursemaids of the damned. Drink up, guys. Might as well be drunk as sober, when it comes." Then he laughs, and it's the same laugh as when he said, "Like we'd ever give you the chance." A laugh that hates itself and probably everything else, too. Melanie leans her head as far to the other side as it will go, so she can't hear the voices anymore.

Eddie, she tells herself. Just Eddie Robertson talking. That's all.

The night is very, very long. Melanie tells herself stories, and sends messages from her right hand to her left hand, then back again, using her sign language, but it's still long. When Sergeant comes in the morning with his people, she can't move; she's got such bad cramps in her neck and her shoulders and her arms, it feels like there's iron bars inside her.

Sergeant looks at her like he's forgotten up until then what happened last night. He looks at his people, but they're looking somewhere else. They don't say anything as they tie up Melanie's neck and arm again.

Sergeant does. He says, "How about them fair winds, kid?" But he doesn't say it like he's angry, or even like he wants to be mean. He says it and then he looks away, unhappy, sick almost. To Melanie, it seems like he says it because he has to say it; as though being Sergeant means you've got to say things like that all the time, whether that's really what you're thinking or not. She files that thought next to his name.

One day, Miss Mailer gives Melanie a book. She does it by sliding the book between Melanie's back and the back of the wheelchair, and tucking it down there out of sight. Melanie isn't even sure at first that that's what just happened, but when she looks at Miss Mailer and opens her mouth to ask her, Miss Mailer touches a finger to her closed lips. So Melanie doesn't say anything.

Once they're back in their cells, and untied, the children aren't supposed to stand up and get out of their chairs until Sergeant's people have left and the door is closed and locked. That night, Melanie makes sure not to move a muscle until she hears the bolt slide home.

Then she reaches behind her and finds the book, its angular shape digging into her back a little. She pulls it out and looks at it.

Homer. *The Iliad* and *The Odyssey*.

Melanie makes a strangled sound. She can't help it, even though it might bring Sergeant back into the cell to tell her to shut up. A book! A book of her own! And *this* book! She runs her hands over the cover, riffles the pages, turns the book in her hands, over and over. She smells the book.

That turns out to be a mistake, because the book smells of Miss Mailer. On top, strongest, the chemical smell from her fingers, as bitter and horrible as always: but underneath, a little, and on the inside pages a lot, the warm and human smell of Miss Mailer herself.

What Melanie feels right then is what Kenny felt, when Sergeant wiped the chemicals off his arm and put it right up close to Kenny's face, but she only just caught the edge of it, that time, and she didn't really understand it.

Something opens inside her, like a mouth opening wider and wider and wider and screaming all the time—not from fear, but from need. Melanie thinks she has a word for it now, although it still isn't anything she's felt before. Sometimes in stories that she's heard, people eat and drink, which is something that the children don't ever do. The people in the stories need to eat, and then when they do eat they feel themselves fill up with something, and it gives them a satisfaction that nothing else can give. She remembers a line from a song that Miss Justineau sang to the children once: *You're my bread, when I'm hungry.*

So this is hunger, and it hurts like a needle, like a knife, like a Trojan spear in Melanie's heart or maybe lower down in her stomach. Her jaws start to churn of their own accord: wetness comes into her mouth. Her head feels light, and the room sort of goes away and then comes back without moving.

The feeling goes on for a long time, until finally Melanie gets used to the smell the way the children in the shower on Sunday get used to the smell of the chemicals. It doesn't go away, exactly, but it doesn't torment her in quite the same way: it becomes kind of invisible just because it doesn't change. The hunger gets less and less, and when it's gone, all gone, Melanie is still there.

The book is still there, too: Melanie reads it until daybreak, and even when she stumbles over the words or has to guess what they mean, she's in another world.

It's a long time after that before Miss Mailer comes again. On Monday there's a new teacher, except he isn't a teacher at all: he's one of Sergeant's people. He says his name is John, which is stupid, because the teachers are all Miss or Mrs. or Mister something, so the children call him Mr. John, and after the first few times he gives up correcting them.

Mr. John doesn't look like he wants to be there, in the classroom. He's only used to strapping the children into the chairs one by one, or freeing them again one by one, with Sergeant's gun on them all the time and everything quick and easy. He looks like being in a room with all the children at the same time is like lying on an altar, at Aulis, with the priest of Artemis holding a knife to his throat.

At last, Anne asks Mr. John the question that everybody wants to ask him: where the real teachers are. "There's a lockdown," Mr. John says. He doesn't seem to mind that the children have spotted him for a fake. "There's movement west of the fence. They confirmed it by satellite. Lots of Hungries coming this way, so nobody's allowed to move around inside the compound or go out into the open in case they get our scent. We're just staying wherever we happened to be when the alarm went. So you've got me to put up with, and we'll just have to do the best we can."

Actually, Mr. John isn't a bad teacher at all, once he stops being scared of the children. He knows a lot of songs, and he writes up the words on the blackboard; the children sing the songs, first all at once and then in two-part and three-part harmonies. There are lots of words the children don't know, especially in "Too Drunk to Fuck," but when the children ask what the words mean, Mr. John says he'll take the Fifth on that one. That means he might get himself into trouble if he gives the right answer, so he's allowed not to; Melanie knows this from when Miss Justineau told them about the Bill of Rights.

So it's not a bad day, at all, even if they don't have a real teacher. But for a whole lot of days after that, nobody comes and the children are alone. It's not possible for Melanie to count how many days; there's nothing to count. The lights stay on the whole time, the music plays really loud, and the big steel door stays shut.

Then a day comes when the music goes off. And in the sudden, shocking silence the bare steel door slams open again, so loud that the sound feels like it's shoving its way through your ear right inside your head. The children jump up and run to their doors to see who's coming, and it's Sergeant—just Sergeant, with one of his people, and no teachers at all.

"Let's do this," Sergeant says.

The man who's with him looks at all the doors, then at Sergeant. "Seriously?" he says.

"We got our orders," Sergeant says. "What we gonna do, tell them we lost the key? Start with this bunch, then do B to D. Sorenson can start at the other end."

Sergeant unlocks the first door after the shower room door, which is Mikey's door. Sergeant and the other man go inside, and Sergeant's voice, booming hollowly in the silence, says, "Up and at 'em, you little fucker."

Melanie sits in her chair and waits. Then she stands up and waits at the door with her face to the mesh. Then she walks up and down, hugging her own arms. She's confused and excited and very, very scared. Something new is happening. She senses it: something completely outside of her experience. When she looks out through the mesh window, she can see that Sergeant isn't closing the doors behind him, as he goes from cell to cell, and he's not wheeling the children into the classroom.

Finally her door is unlocked. She steps back from it as it opens, and Sergeant and the other man step inside. Sergeant points the gun at Melanie.

"You forget your manners?" he asks her. "Sit down, kid."

Something happens to Melanie. It's like all her different, mixed-up feelings are crashing into each other, inside her head, and turning into a new feeling. She sits down, but she sits down on her bed, not in her chair.

Sergeant stares at her like he can't believe what he's seeing. "You don't want to piss me off today," he warns Melanie. "Not today."

"I want to know what's happening, Sergeant," Melanie says. "Why were we left on our own? Why didn't the teachers come? What's happening?"

"Sit down in the chair," the other man says.

"Do it," Sergeant tells her.

But Melanie stays where she is, on the bed, and she doesn't shift her gaze from Sergeant's eyes. "Is there going to be class today?" she asks him.

"Sit in the goddamn chair," Sergeant orders her. "Sit in the chair or I swear I will fucking dismantle you." His voice is shaking, just a little, and she can see from the way his face changes, suddenly, that he knows she heard the shake. "Fucking—fine!" he explodes, and he advances on the chair and kicks it with his boot, really hard, so it flies up into the air and hits the wall of the narrow cell. It bounces off at a wild angle, hits the other wall and crashes down on its back. Sergeant kicks it again, and then a third time. The frame is all twisted from where it hit the wall, and one of the wheels comes right off when Sergeant kicks it.

The other man just watches, without saying a word, while Sergeant gets his breath back and comes down from his scary rage. When he does, he looks at Melanie and shrugs. "Well, I guess you can just stay where you are, then," he says.

The two of them go out, and the door is locked again. They take the other kids away, one by one—not to the classroom, but out through the other door, the bare steel door, which until now has marked the farthest limit of their world.

Nobody comes, after that, and nothing happens. It feels like a long time, but Melanie's mind is racing so fast that even a few minutes would feel like a long time. It's longer than a few minutes, though. It feels like most of a day.

The air gets colder. It's not something that Melanie thinks about, normally, because heat and cold don't translate into comfort or discomfort for her; she notices now because with no music playing and nobody to talk to, there's nothing else to notice. Maybe it's night. That's it. It must be night outside. Melanie knows from stories that it gets colder at night as well as darker.

She remembers her book, and gets it out. She reads about Hector and Achilles and Priam and Hecuba and Odysseus and Menelaus and Agamemnon and Helen.

There are footsteps from the corridor outside. Is it Sergeant? Has he come back to dismantle her? To take her to the altar and give her to the goddess Artemis?

Someone unlocks Melanie's door, and pushes it open.

Miss Mailer stands in the doorway. "It's okay," she says. "It's okay, sweetheart. I'm here."

Melanie surges to her feet, her heart almost bursting with happiness and relief. She's going to run to Miss Mailer. She's going to hug her and be hugged by her and be touching her not just with her hair but with her hands and her face and her whole body. Then she freezes where she is. Her jaw muscles stiffen, and a moan comes out of her mouth.

Miss Mailer is alarmed. "Melanie?" She takes a step forward.

"Don't!" Melanie screams. "Please, Miss Mailer! Don't! Don't touch me!"

Miss Mailer stops moving, but she's so close! So close! Melanie whimpers. Her whole mind is exploding. She drops to her knees, then falls full-length on the floor. The smell, the wonderful, terrible smell, fills all the room and all her mind and all her thoughts, and all she wants to do is . . .

"Go away!" she moans. "Go away go away go away!"

Miss Mailer doesn't move.

"Fuck off, or I will dismantle you!" Melanie wails. She's desperate. Her mouth is filled with thick saliva like mud from a mudslide. She's dangling on the end of the thinnest, thinnest piece of string. She's going to fall and there's only one direction to fall in.

"Oh God!" Miss Mailer blurts. She gets it at last. She rummages in her bag, which Melanie didn't even notice until now. She takes something out—a tiny bottle with yellow liquid in it—and starts to spray it on her skin, on her clothes, in the air. The bottle says Dior. It's not the usual chemical: it's something that smells sweet and funny. Miss Mailer doesn't stop until she's emptied the bottle.

"Does that help?" she asks, with a catch in her voice. "Oh baby, I'm so sorry. I didn't even think. . . ."

It does help, a little. And Melanie has had practice at pushing the hunger down: she has to do it a little bit every time she picks up her book. This is a million times harder, but after a while she can think again and move again and even sit up.

"It's safe now," she says timidly, groggily. And she remembers her own words, spoken as a joke so many times before she ever guessed what they might actually mean. "I won't bite."

Miss Mailer bends down and sweeps Melanie up, choking out her name, and there they are crying into each other's tears, and even though the hunger is bending Melanie's spine like Achilles bending his bow, she wouldn't exchange this moment for all the other moments of her life.

"They're attacking the fence," Miss Mailer says, her voice muffled by Melanie's hair. "But it's not Hungries, it's looters. Bandits. People just like me and the other teachers, but renegades who never went into the western cordon. We've got to get out before they break through. We're being evacuated, Melanie—to Texas."

"Why?" is all Melanie can think of to say.

"Because that's where the cure is!" sobs Miss Mailer. "They'll make you okay again, and you'll have a real mom and dad, and a real life, and all this fucking madness will just be a memory!"

"No," Melanie whimpers.

"Yes, baby! Yes!" Miss Mailer is hugging her tight, and Melanie is trying to find the words to explain that she doesn't want a mom or a dad, she wants to stay here in the block with Miss Mailer and have lessons with her forever, but right then is when Sergeant walks into the cell.

Three of his people are behind him. His face is pale, and his eyes are open too wide.

"We got to go," he says. "Right now. Last two choppers are loaded up and ready. I'm real sorry, Gwen, but this is the last call."

"I'm not going without her," Miss Mailer says, and she hugs Melanie so tight it almost hurts.

"Yeah," Sergeant says. "You are. She can't come on the transport without restraints, and we don't got any restraints that we can use. You come on, now."

He reaches out his hand as if he's going to help Miss Mailer to her feet. Miss Mailer doesn't take the hand.

"Come on, now," Sergeant says again, on a rising pitch.

"I'm not leaving her," Miss Mailer says again.

"She's got no—"

Miss Mailer's voice rises over Sergeant's voice, shouts him into silence. "She doesn't have any restraints because you kicked her chair into scrap metal. And now you're going to leave her here, to the mercy of those animals, and say it was out of your hands. Well damn you, Eddie!" She can hardly get the words out; she sounds like there's no breath left in her body. "Damn—fuck—rot what's left of your miserable fucking heart!"

"I've got to go by the rules," Sergeant pleads. His voice is weak, lost.

"Really?" Miss Mailer shouts at him. "The rules? And when you've ripped her heart out and fed it to your limp-dick fucking rules, you think that will bring Chloe back, or Sarah? Or bring you one moment's peace? There's a cure, you bastard! They can cure her! They can give her a normal life! You want to say she stays here and rots in the dark instead because you threw a man-tantrum and busted up her fucking *chair*?"

There's a silence that seems like it's never going to end. Maybe it never would, if there was only Sergeant and Miss Mailer and Melanie in the room: but one of Sergeant's people breaks it at last. "Sarge, we're already two minutes past the—"

"Shut up," Sergeant tells him. And then to Miss Mailer he says, "You carry her. You hold her, every second of the way. And you're responsible for her. If she bites anyone, I'm throwing you both off the transport."

Miss Mailer stands up with Melanie cradled in her arms, and they run. They go out through the steel door. There are stairs on the other side of it that go up and up, a long way. Miss Mailer is holding her tight, but she rocks and bounces all the same, pressed up against Miss Mailer's heart. Miss Mailer's heart bumps rhythmically, as if something was alive inside it and touching Melanie's cheek through her skin.

At the top of the stairs, there's another door. They come out into sudden cold and blinding light. The quality of the sound changes, the echoes dying suddenly. Air moves against Melanie's bare arm. Distant voices bray, almost drowned out by a mighty, droning, flickering roar.

The lights are moving, swinging around. Where they touch, details leap out of the darkness as though they've just been painted there. Men are running, stopping, running again, firing guns like Sergeant's gun into the wild, jangling dark.

"Go!" Sergeant shouts.

Sergeant's men run, and Miss Mailer runs. Sergeant runs behind them, his gun in his hand. "Don't waste rounds," Sergeant calls out to his people. "Pick your target." He fires his gun, and his people fire, too, and the guns make a sound so loud it runs all the way out into the dark and then comes back again, but Melanie can't see what it is they're firing at or if they hit it. She's got other stuff to worry about, anyway.

This close up, the smelly stuff that Miss Mailer sprayed on herself isn't strong enough to hide the Miss Mailer smell underneath. The hunger is rising again inside Melanie, filling her up all the way to the top, taking her over: Miss Mailer's arm is right there beside her head, and she's thinking *please don't please don't please don't* but who is she pleading with? There's no one. No one but her.

A shape looms in the darkness: a thing as big as a room, that sits on the ground but rocks from side to side and spits dirt in their faces with its deep, dry breath and drones to itself like a giant trying to sing. It has a door in its side; some of the children sit there, inside the thing, in their chairs, tied in with straps and webbing so it looks like a big spider has caught them. Some of Sergeant's people are there, too, shouting words that Melanie can't hear. One of them slaps the side of the big thing: it lifts into the air, all at once, and then it's gone.

Sergeant's arm clamps down on Miss Mailer's shoulder and he turns her around, bodily. "There!" he shouts. "That way!" And they're running again, but now it's just Sergeant and Miss Mailer. Melanie doesn't know where Sergeant's people have gone.

There's another one of the big rocking things, a long way away: *a helicopter,* Melanie thinks, the word coming to her from a lesson she doesn't even remember. And that means they're outside, under the sky, not in a big room like she thought at first. But even the astonishment is dulled by the gnawing, insistent hunger: her jaws are drawing back, straining open like the hinges of a door; her own thoughts are coming to her from a long way away, like someone shouting at her through a tiny mesh window: *Oh please don't please don't!*

Miss Mailer is running toward the helicopter and Sergeant is right behind. They're close to it now, but one of the big swinging lights turns and shows them some men running toward them on a shallow angle. The men don't have guns like Sergeant does, but they have sticks and knives and one of them is waving a spear.

Sergeant fires, and nothing seems to happen. He fires again, and the man with the spear falls. Then they're at the helicopter and Miss Mailer is pulled inside by a woman who seems startled and scared to see Melanie there.

"What the fuck?" she says.

"Sergeant Robertson's orders!" Miss Mailer yells.

Some more of the children are here. Melanie sees Anne and Kenny and Lizzie in a single flash of one of the swinging lights. But now there's a shout and Sergeant is fighting with somebody, right there at the door where they just climbed in. The men with the knives and the sticks have gotten there, too.

Sergeant gets off one more shot, and all of a sudden one of the men doesn't have a head anymore. He falls down out of sight. Another man knocks the gun out of Sergeant's hand, but Sergeant takes his knife from him somehow and sticks it into the man's stomach.

The woman inside the copter slaps the ceiling and points up—for the pilot, Melanie realizes. He's sitting in his cockpit, fighting to keep the copter more or less level and more or less still, as though the ground is bucking under him and trying to throw him off. But it's not the ground, it's the weight of the men swarming on board.

"Shit!" the woman moans.

Miss Mailer hides Melanie's eyes with her hand, but Melanie pushes the hand away. She knows what she has to do, now. It's not even a hard choice, because the incredible, irresistible human flesh smell is helping her, pushing her in the direction she has to go.

She stops pleading with the hunger to leave her alone; it's not listening anyway. She says to it, instead, like Sergeant said to his people, *Pick your target.*

And then she jumps clear out of Miss Mailer's arms, her legs propelling her like one of Sergeant's bullets.

She lands on the chest of one of the men, and he's staring into her face with frozen horror as she leans in and bites his throat out. His blood tastes utterly wonderful: he is her bread when she's hungry, but there's no time to enjoy it. Melanie scales his shoulders as he falls and jumps onto the man behind, folding her legs around his neck and leaning down to bite and claw at his face.

Miss Mailer screams Melanie's name. It's only just audible over the sound of the helicopter blades, which is louder now, and the screams of the third man as Melanie jumps across to him and her teeth close on his arm. He beats at her, but her jaws are so strong he can't shake her loose, and then Sergeant hits him really hard in the face and he falls down. Melanie lets go of his arm, spits out the piece of it that's in her mouth.

The copter lifts off. Melanie looks up at it, hoping for one last sight of Miss Mailer's face, but it just disappears into the dark and there's nothing left of it but the sound.

Other men are coming. Lots of them.

Sergeant picks up his gun from the ground where it fell, checks it. He seems to be satisfied.

The light swings all the way round until it's full in their faces.

Sergeant looks at Melanie, and she looks back at him.

"Day just gets better and better, don't it?" Sergeant says. It's sarcasm, but Melanie nods, meaning it, because it's a day of wishes coming true. Miss Mailer's arms around her, and now this.

"You ready, kid?" Sergeant asks.

"Yes, Sergeant," Melanie says. Of course she's ready.

"Then let's give these bastards something to feel sad about."

The men bulk large in the dark, but they're too late. The goddess Artemis is appeased. The ships are gone on the fair wind.

Golden Delicious

FAITH HUNTER

Faith Hunter writes urban fantasy: the Skinwalker series, featuring Jane Yellowrock—*Skinwalker, Blood Cross, Mercy Blade, Raven Cursed*, and *Death's Rival* in October 2012—and the Rogue Mage series, featuring Thorn St. Croix, a stone mage in a postapocalyptic, alternate reality—*Bloodring, Seraphs, Host*, and *Rogue Mage RPG and World Book*. This short story, "Golden Delicious," takes place in the Skinwalker series, after *Raven Cursed*, and between the short story in the e-compilation *Cat Tales* and *Death's Rival*. When she isn't writing, Faith likes to make jewelry, run whitewater rivers (Class II and III), and RV with her hubby and their rescued Pomeranian dogs.

Rick's face was still tender, though the bruising was already yellow and the scabs had fallen off, revealing pink, healed skin. When he was human, it would have taken days to reach this stage of healing, but it had been less than twenty-four hours since he was sucker-punched. There were very few good things about being infected with were-taint, but fast healing was on that short list.

"He was trying to hurt you, yet you held back." Soul glanced at him from the corners of her eyes. "It didn't go unnoticed."

He pushed on his teeth. They were no longer loose. "I'm betting he was a bully in high school," he said. "Not used to a guy forty pounds lighter and three inches shorter taking him down."

Soul's full lips lifted slowly. "Without breaking his jaw, his knees, or dislocating his shoulder, all of which you could have done." She made a left, turning onto a side road. Shadows covered them in the dim confines of the company car. "You taught him a valuable lesson. There are things out there that are bigger, faster, and won't care if he carries a PsyLED badge.

"Speaking of things bigger and faster than human, walk me through it again," she said, shifting their discussion as easily as she shifted gears.

"Human-sense evaluation, initial technology, followed by enhanced senses," Rick said. "Then the pets and more tech as needed."

From the back, Pea twittered and Brute growled. Pea was a juvenile grindylow, Rick's pet and death sentence rolled up in one neon-green-furred, steel-clawed, kittenlike cutie. The werewolf taking up the backseat was stuck in wolf form, thanks to contact with an angel, and he didn't like being called a pet, which meant that Rick did so every chance he got. The wolf hated leashes, his traveling cage, and eating from a bowl on the floor, but it wasn't like he had a choice. Since Brute couldn't shift back to human and had no thumbs, he had two options: accept the leash and being treated like a dangerous dog, or sit in a cage all day. He'd gone for the partial-freedom route, which meant partnering with Rick LaFleur. Rick, who hadn't been human in two months himself, was at the training facility for the Psychometry Law Enforcement Division of Homeland Security—called PsyLED Spook School by the trainees.

The three composed a ready-made unit, a triumvirate of nonhuman specialists. If they could learn to work together. So far, that didn't look likely. The werewolf might not be responsible for Rick's loss of humanity, job, and girlfriend, nor for the total FUBAR'd mess his life had become, but Brute had been part of the pack that kidnapped and tortured him. Rick didn't like the wolf or want him around, but like Brute, he had no choice right now. PsyLED had specifically requested them together, and had refused to accept Rick as a solo trainee. It was a package deal or no deal.

Soul said, "Treat this as if it's a paranormal crime and you're the first investigator on-site. If you spot something out of the accepted order, hold it for the proper time. You'll find that by training your investigative skills to work to a specific but fluid formula, you'll actually gain a freedom of thought processes that will work well in the field." Soul pulled into a driveway.

"This training site is the most difficult you will encounter during your time here. In the last two months, three students signed their Quit-

Forms and left the program after seeing the site." Her eyes narrowed, the skin around them crinkling. "And I can't explain why this particular crime scene has been so difficult on them." She turned off the car.

The small ranch house was dark, crime-scene tape over the sealed doors, plywood over the windows. The grass was six inches high, the flower beds needed weeding. "Assuming that the grass was cut in the week prior," Rick said, "we're looking at maybe eight weeks since the crime."

Soul looked at him strangely. "You're the only one who even glanced at the outside of the house."

"I was a cop," he said, feeling the loss in his bones. "We look at everything."

Soul grinned, losing years and making him wonder again about her. She could have been thirty or fifty, tribal American, Gypsy, mixed African and European, or a combo. "I knew getting an undercover cop in this program was going to work. That's why I asked to be your mentor."

That was news. Soul was one of the top three mentors at Spook School, and Rick hadn't known how he'd been paired with her.

Soul opened her door, using the interior lights to twist a scrunchy around her platinum hair to keep it out of the way. "The neighbors called nine-one-one when they heard screaming and a dog howling. It was the second night of the full moon, nearly eight weeks ago. The first officers on the scene secured the area, called Medic, made arrests based on the evidence, and then called PsyLED."

Rick stepped to the driveway and opened the back door for the pets. Brute leaped out—leash-free this time because there were no humans around—his white fur bright in the nearly full moon. Pea clung to his back, smiling, showing fangs as big as Brute's. Most people saw a green-dyed kitten when they saw her. It. Whatever. Pea was as playful as a kitten, and could get lost chasing a ball of twine for hours, but if he or Brute stepped out of line and risked passing along the were-taint to a human, she'd kill them without hesitation. That was her job.

"You stay by the door until I'm ready," Rick instructed. Brute scowled and emitted a low growl. This wasn't the first time they'd been over this. The last time Rick had brought it up, Brute had walked over to his instruction manual and lifted a leg. Rick had just barely saved the manual from a nasty drenching. Now, he held the wolf's eyes as the growl began to build.

Eventually, they'd have to deal with the question of who was in charge, and the wolf would have to accept beta status, acquiesce to Rick as alpha. Soul looked down at the wolf. "You're part of Rick's investigative team," she said, her tone cold. "I will not have silliness." Brute dropped his ears and whined, submissive, and Rick shook his head, wishing he knew her trick. Soul lifted her long skirts above the dew-damp grass and led the way to the door. She unlocked it and stood back, her fingers laced together.

Rick pulled on a pair of black nitrile gloves and flipped on the inside light. There was no furniture in the room, but it was far from empty. "It's a witch-working, salt-circle, internal pentagram composed of feathers, river-worn rocks, tiny moonstones, and dead plants. Two pools of blood in the pentagram suggest a blood rite, but it's an odd combo for one. Blood rites usually require full, five-element mixed covens." He stepped away from the front door, moving sun-wise, or clockwise, a foot outside the circle, to avoid activating any latent spells. "We have five practitioners, from four of the elements—air, water, two moon witches, and oddly, the death-magic branch of earth witches." Death-magic was rare, little-known, and almost never practiced. Adepts were considered dangerous by other witches, because they used dying things to power workings, and when nothing around was dying, they would steal the life force of the living. In Spook School, he had learned how they worked. They were not nice people.

In the corner, standing with Soul, Brute was growling again, the basso so deep it was more a vibration on the air than actual sound. His mentor put a hand to the wolf's head, and Brute hunched, his shoulder blades high. Pea was staring at the circle, her eyes wide, one paw-finger at her mouth. It was the animals' first crime scene, and Rick could imagine how awful the sights and smells must be to them.

"The composition of practitioners made for a lopsided but feasible working," Rick said. "The death witch was coven leader, sitting at the north, with a moon witch to either side, and air and water at the base, which made for the best balance the coven could get in during the full moon.

"The scorch mark in the center of the circle suggests they called up a demon, likely one that was moon-bound. If they called up a demon, it was for something bad, and I haven't heard of anything happening that might be demon-born."

Soul tilted her head, acknowledging his analysis, but not giving him more information.

"The salt ring is broken in three places, which suggests that the working was completed or was interrupted in such a way that there's no residual power remaining. If this was a fresh crime scene and no one had been into the room, the first thing I'd do is verify with the psymeter that the working is not active. Do you want me to go ahead and do that?"

Soul said, "Not now. Proceed."

Rick studied the circle. "Because of the blood-magic, I'd call in Psy-CSI to take trace matter and blood samples to be held for possible DNA in the event that we have humans to compare, and in the event that this was a fatal crime."

Soul nodded, expressionless. "The investigators did so."

"Photographs, samples of each of the elements used, fingerprints, blood spatter workup—" Rick stopped. He was standing at the air point, studying the blood pattern. It was smeared and splattered over a large area, maybe four feet, but not puddled, as it would have been had the witch collected the blood in a bowl and then spilled or poured it. He bent closer and saw hairs in the blood. There were three, with more in the blood in the center of the circle, a lot more, some in small clumps. Stress caused some animals to lose hair. "—and speciation of the hairs," he finished after a brief pause. "Then I'd search the rest of the house. Shall I bother? It smells empty." Spook School knew everything about his situation, had tested his sensory perceptions extensively during his interview phase. Soul knew he had much better senses than a human, even in his current state.

Soul shook her head.

"End of human eval." Rick dropped to one knee in a tripod position, weight on knee, feet, and one hand. He sniffed in short, quick inhalations. An electric shock slammed through him, triggering the memories. Werewolf. He gasped, the jolt of pain and terror whipping through him. He managed a breath, then another, breathing deeper, forcing the fear and panic away with each breath. The witches had sacrificed a werewolf on the full moon. Rick opened an evidence packet. With a pair of tweezers, he picked up the hair closest. "Each hair is three inches long, pale at the root, fading to gray, and black at the tip."

Soul watched, assessing his reaction. She had known. Of course she had known. Except for Brute, this was the first were he had scented since the attack, the kidnapping, and the subsequent torture by the Lupus Pack in New Orleans. And his reaction to it was part of what would make or break his qualification and acceptance into PsyLED.

Slowly he lowered the hair into the evidence bag, fighting down the panic attack. He had thought he'd conquered the PTSD. Not so. The scars and the mangled tattoos on his shoulder and upper arm ached, feeling blistering hot, though they weren't. He forcibly relaxed, breathing slowly to decrease the fight-or-flight response brought on by the scent. The words clean and concise, his brain actually still functioning, Rick said, "Presumption: Speciation of blood in the center of the circle was revealed to be werewolf blood. Second presumption: It bit the air witch, badly enough to transmit the were-taint."

At the words, Pea launched herself from Brute's shoulders and scampered across the room, leaping, crabbing sideways; she disturbed nothing. Brute followed slowly, but outside the circle, the overhead light throwing odd shadows, the darkest ones pooling under the werewolf. His growl, until now only a vibration, grew in volume. Rick realized that Brute had already detected the other werewolf, had known what had happened here from the moment they entered the room, and had been kept calm only by Soul's hand on his head. Rick would have to learn to read Brute in the field—assuming they passed the training

Pea stopped at the center of the circle and scraped at the dried blood with one scalpel-sharp claw. She brought it to her nose and sniffed. She sneezed, hard, covering her tiny mouth with a paw, then raced to the dried blood at Rick's feet. Brute and Pea stood, nose-to-nose, sniffing.

Slowly, Brute moved to the center of the circle and sniffed again. His ears went back and the vibration of his werewolf growl filled the room, seeming to bounce off the walls into Rick's chest. Brute's pale, crystalline eyes stared up at the former cop, his growl increasing in volume before falling away into a whine. If Rick hadn't known better, he would have thought the wolf was feeling worried, concerned. But three seconds spent with an Angel of the Light could have been no cure for Brute's cruelty.

Pea stepped over the salt circle and put her forelegs on Rick's jeans-clad shin, staring up at him. Her tail twitched, her face mournful. "Yeah," he said to her, stroking her once in comfort. "We're too late. Maybe weeks too late." He looked at Soul. "Did the witch turn?" Soul pressed her lips together and didn't answer. Rick figured that info was need-to-know, and trainees were the lowest on the information ladder.

On his hands and knees, Rick circled the room, sniffing, letting the scent signatures settle into his brain, new memories, new associations. Rick turned to Brute. "You're up." The werewolf held Rick's eyes with a predator's intensity. This was something they had worked out the first day of school, a Q&A to keep them from having any Timmy-fell-down-the-well moments of attempted communication. "Take scent signatures of the subjects." Brute snarled at him, but walked slowly around the circle, sniffing at each spot where a witch had knelt during the working. When he was finished, the wolf sat down again, waiting for the confirmatory questions.

"All the witches were female," Rick said.

"You can tell that by scent?" Soul interrupted, surprised.

Rick held up a finger, watching the wolf. There weren't many male witches because they tended to die at puberty, but it was always wise to confirm. The wolf nodded, which was a strange gesture on the animal.

"Were all the witches related?" Rick asked.

Brute shook his head.

"Two were related," Rick said.

Brute nodded once.

"This witch"—Rick indicated a point on the pentagram—"and that one."

Brute nodded again. Most covens were related by blood, even if widely spaced on the family tree.

Soul's eyes gleamed and her nostrils widened. Rick could hear her heart rate increase. "Very good," she murmured.

Pea stood on her hind feet, asking to be held. Rick boosted her up and Pea balanced across one shoulder, her tail curling around his neck, her furry cheek next to his. She didn't purr, exactly. It was more part-purr and part-croon, rhythmical, musical, and harmonic.

Soul crossed the room, walking widdershins, or counterclockwise. When she reached him, she buried her hand in Brute's ruff, scratching his ears. The werewolf sighed in happiness. "None of the other trainees did half as well, not even the witches, and they had a better handle into magic-working than you will ever have. Starting a week late, you are better at this than any of the others." A half smile curled her lips. "Don't tell them I said so."

"Psymeter," he said, not responding to the compliment. Rick knew that, in his case, being the best was not a guarantee that his triumvirate would graduate and go on to be PsyLED agents. They had other issues. Lots of other issues.

Soul lifted the strap of the bulky device from around her head. The training units were older models, having been pulled from field use when the agency got lighter-weight, more compact ones, but the older models still worked. Rick stepped outside, clipped the box to his belt, and turned the unit on. He zeroed it to the outside magical ambience, which should have been close to zero. The meter needle fluctuated and settled safely in the green zone. This particular device had been calibrated just for his unit, taking into account their magical energies, which had higher-than-human readings.

He deliberately did not look up at the sky. Tomorrow night was the first night of the full moon and he got weird close to the full moon, wanting to sit and stare up at it. For hours. Yeah. Weird.

Rick stepped back inside and instantly the meter spiked. Rick stopped and looked at Soul. The meter wasn't reacting to her—Soul showed up as human though she definitely was not—but to something else in the room. "It's redlining. This far out time-wise from a working, it should be a low yellow, max."

"What might that signify?"

"Several possibilities. The working was interrupted. The working is still active, which means they transferred the working to an amulet. Or it had a delayed result yet to be released. But I don't see signs of anything magically active, so which was it?"

Soul shook her head. "We don't know yet." Rick handed Soul the psymeter and she touched Brute's shoulder, which came to her waist. The gesture was part scratch and part something metaphysically calming, which made Rick once again wonder what Soul was. Fairy? Elf? The wolf started panting and closed his eyes.

Rick said, "I want to see the crime-scene photos, mug shots, and the notes of the OIC and the IO."

"Why?" She sounded sincerely curious, not if-I-ask-a-question-he'll-learn-something curious. "What do you think that the officer in charge and the investigating officer might have missed?"

"I don't know. But the meter's still redlining. I might see something that the rest of you missed, or something in the photos might hit on what I smelled or saw. I might draw a different conclusion or ask a different question. I want to see all that because tomorrow night is the start of the full moon. And we might have a werewolf out there."

Soul stared at him, her black eyes speculative. They were even blacker than his own Frenchy-black eyes, and usually they sparkled, throwing back the light like faceted black onyx. But tonight they were somber. Soul pulled a cell phone from a pocket in her gauzy skirt and punched in a number. "Have the on-call administrator call me back ASAP." She closed the cell.

Rick studied the circle once more. "Did our people make the three openings in the salt?"

That enigmatic half smile lit her features again. "No. It was that way when we found it." Soul's platinum ponytail slid to one shoulder and stayed there when she raised her head. She was graceful, small, and curvy in all the right places. He wanted to know more about her, but he also understood that the relationship between trainee and mentor was one of strictly enforced professionalism. There weren't a lot of law enforcement jobs open to someone who carried the were-taint. He wasn't going to blow his chance to work for PsyLED by giving the wrong signals. He'd made too many mistakes where women were concerned. He'd lost his humanity because of that. He turned and went outside.

The light inside the house went out behind him and he heard Soul lock the door. He could count the tumblers if he wanted to. Cat hearing was part of the enhanced senses he'd gained when he was bitten by a black were-leopard.

Soul's cell tinkled, New Age musical chimes. She walked away, opened it, and instead of saying hello, said, "Mariella. Thank you for returning my call."

"How did your wonder boy do?" Mariella Russo, the instructional administrator, asked.

Though Rick had never met the IA, he'd remember that voice. It sounded rough as splintered wood, as if she smoked four packs of cigarettes and drank a pint of rotgut whisky every day. Soul knew he had acute senses, but she never acted accordingly and he'd learned a lot of interesting things by listening. He turned away so Soul couldn't read his face. Pea nuzzled his cheek and he stroked her, absently. Brute was a white shadow off to the side, glowering at him.

"Our best PsyLED investigators took two weeks to determine what his unit deduced in only twenty minutes," Soul said. "And, thanks to his law enforcement training, he added observations that the other trainee units missed. It will be in my report. He wants the crime-scene photos, mug shots, and the notes of the OIC and the IO. I am recommending he be given access."

"This situation is far too delicate and volatile for a trainee to have that sort of entrée," Russo said. "So the answer is no, Soul."

"Rick LaFleur didn't turn or go insane at the last full moon," Soul said. "He survived it. Intact. He may see something we missed. Or he may know something he doesn't realize he knows until the memory is triggered or the association falls into place."

"What Chief Smythe needs from him is the name of the witch who created his counter-spell music. Get that and we'll reconsider."

Rick went cold. Was that why he had been invited to train at PsyLED? Because the department wanted access to his friend, an unknown witch, one not in the databases? Or access to a charm no one had ever heard of before—one that controlled the pain brought on by the full moon? And most important, why would Liz Smythe want it?

Pea made a twitter of concern and he stroked her gently. "It's okay, Pea." But it wasn't. Not by a long shot.

"The chief administrator can ask for her own information," Soul said. "Come on. Let Rick see the crime-scene photos."

Russo sighed. "Why do you always try to get the protocols changed, Soul?"

Soul's laughter floated on the night air. "Because I'm the best. Because of what I am. Agree, Rus'. You know I'm right."

"Fine. An intern will deliver the file to LaFleur's private chambers before you get back to base."

Rick smiled tightly, his eyes on the house across the street. The "private chambers" comment said a lot about his entire stay at Spook School.

"She agreed," Soul said. Brute flinched. Rick held his own recoil in. She had appeared right next to them without a sound, even with his and Brute's keen hearing. He remembered what she had said to Russo, "Because of what I am." And he wondered, not for the first time, what Soul was.

When he let himself into his quarters, the file was on his desk beside his MP player, which was loaded with the counter-spell melodies he played during the full moon. The private chamber was a twelve-by-twelve space in the back of the Quonset hut that held Spook School's paranormal supplies. He slept away from the trainees' barracks for a lot of reasons: because of Brute and Pea, who were deemed too dangerous to sleep near humans, and who refused to sleep in cages—not that he blamed them. And because he was too dangerous to be around humans at the full moon; Rick refused to be caged too. Because PsyLED was afraid that he might snap some full moon and bite his partner, he would never be a solo investigator, never be paired with a human or witch. His nonhuman unit was already established—a de facto triumvirate—if he didn't kill Brute first.

Brute went to his bed—a cedar-chip-filled mattress on the floor in the corner—walked in a circle three times, lay down, and closed his eyes, Pea curled against his side. Rick showered and took the file to his own bed—a two-inch-thick mattress that had seen better days, on a corroded metal, folding bed frame. He hadn't complained. He'd take what he could get, hoping to salvage something of the law enforcement career he'd lost when he contracted the were-taint.

He opened the file and started through it. The first thing he noticed was that there were only four mug shots, not five. There had been five witches at the crime scene, he knew that by the scent patterns. He flipped through the arrest reports and discovered that the coven leader had gotten away and the other coven members had refused to name her. Rick closed the file. *Delicate and volatile . . .* That could mean most anything.

He flipped through the arrest interviews and quickly discovered that one of the witches was Laura McKormic, the wife of Senator McKormic, a hard-line Republican from the state of Georgia, and an avowed witch hater. Now Rick knew why Russo claimed that the situation was delicate. Politics.

Laura McKormic rang a bell different from politics, however, and Rick booted up his old laptop to Google her. According to news reports, Laura had been killed in a one-car accident forty-eight hours after the arrest, but Rick could find no coroner's report and no accident report. That meant she was likely the woman bitten at the scene and was hidden away in a private asylum—a werewolf, a danger to herself, her family, the public, and mostly, her husband's career. Female werewolves who survived the initial bite went into immediate and permanent heat, and insanity was never very far behind. Rick closed the laptop. He had personal knowledge of just how bad that could be for the bitches themselves, and for the humans who came into contact with them. He reached up and scratched the scars on his shoulder. That had to be why Smythe wanted the name of his friend, the witch who had provided the counterspell for his own were-shifting problem. To help Laura find a measure of peace from the binding of the were-taint.

From his pallet, Brute whined and thumped his tail. Slowly Rick turned his head to Brute and met the wolf's eyes. Brute was watching his hand on the scars. The wolf dropped his head to his paws and whined again. Rick frowned. He recalled little of his time with the Lupus Pack, under their control, but it had all been bad. Beatings. And worse. Stuff Rick chose not to remember. Some of it at Brute's hands back when the were had been able to shift to human. But Rick had been there when Brute came into contact with the angel Hayyel. Maybe the angel's presence had affected both of them, because having Brute in the corner of his bedroom didn't seem as awful as maybe it should have. Rick slid his hand away from the scars, ridged and numb, and yet somehow burning. Brute's eyes followed.

"Full moon is coming," he said, and Brute whined again. Rick closed the folder, dropped it to the floor, and turned off the lamp. Rolled over and pulled up the blanket. "Go to sleep."

Morning was back to basics, which meant breakfast in the farmhouse kitchen. From the yard, as he climbed the steps, Rick could hear dishes clatter and classmates chatter. He wondered who would try to cause trouble this time. The cook frowned on weres and had tried to keep his entire unit out of the kitchen, saying that, "Animals should eat outside." Some of Rick's fellow trainees weren't much better. Brute and Pea beside him, wearing red and blue PsyLED K9 harnesses, Rick entered the big room and moved to the left of the doorway, out of silhouette—instinct, to get a wall at his back.

Mary, three tables down, looked over the rim of her coffee cup and nudged Walker. "Our were-animals are here," she murmured. "I had hoped they'd be out of the program by now."

Walker pursed his lips. "I tried."

Rick reached up and touched his face. The fading bruises were no longer painful, but they had been a virulent yellow in his shaving mirror this morning. "Not animals," he said, loudly enough to be heard by the other trainees. The room went silent and Mary blushed scarlet, the telltale of pale-skinned redheads. The other trainees swiveled their heads toward him, then to the couple. Rick stared Walker down and said, "A PsyLED unit. My unit." He pretended not to see Brute's ears prick up, and kept his eyes on Walker. He dropped his voice to a low growl and lied through his teeth, "And the next time you try to kick Brute, I'll either let him eat you, or I'll take you down. No chance to sucker-punch me again." Brute chuffed and smiled at Walker, showing way too many teeth. "You may have me by forty pounds, but you won't get back up."

The other trainees looked from the guilty couple, to the table holding the instructors and mentors, and then back to Rick. From the corner of his eye, he saw Soul put her hand on the arm of his jujitsu teacher, holding the man still. Rick winked at her, and her brows went up in surprise.

"It's okay. He's lying," she murmured, her words audible to Rick only because of his enhanced hearing. "And the wolf is perfectly in control."

Two tables down, a blonde named Polly stood to see Walker. Into the uneasy silence, she said, "You tried to kick his partner? If LaFleur doesn't take you down, I will."

Brute chuffed quietly at the term *partner*. Pea chittered and sat up on the wolf's back to see better, sounding pleased.

The girl beside Polly leaned back in her chair and said, "And I'll help." She looked at Rick. "I knew he was hassling you. Sorry I didn't step in." She raised her voice so the instructors couldn't pretend not to hear. "I don't tolerate bullies."

Some of the tension Rick carried melted away as both girls patted an empty place at their table. "Come on, gorgeous," Polly said. "You can eat with us." She flicked a look up at Rick. "And your ugly, bruised handler too."

Rick shook his head at the ribbing. "Go sit with the nice ladies, Brute. Be charming. I'll bring you a plate." The wolf rolled his eyes up and Rick said, "Yeah, I know. Six eggs over easy, half a chicken, raw, and apples, quartered. Come on, Pea. Let's go through the line."

Rick tossed the grindylow to his shoulder and turned his back on the wolf, going to the buffet. While loading up three plates, he watched in the mirrors over the serving table as Brute padded to the table and sat beside Polly, who was a dead ringer for a young Gwyneth Paltrow. Brute rested his head on her thigh and looked up at her with puppy-dog eyes. Both girls went all mushy and started petting him.

It was ridiculous. Brute got more female attention than he did. And it wasn't like Rick was ugly, despite the bruises. At six feet even, with black eyes and black curling hair, he'd been known as a ladies' man, a player. Of course, that was part of the reason he'd been bitten by a female black were-leopard, tortured by werewolves, lost his humanity, his job with NOPD, and his girlfriend, but that was another story.

Rick set Brute's plate on the floor, Pea's beside his on the table, and slid into the proffered seat, digging in. The eggs were perfect, and the pancakes, while not as good as his mom's, weren't bad, especially when he poured warm blueberry syrup over them.

"Is he really a werewolf?" Polly asked, her fingers in Brute's fur.

"Yep. The only tame werewolf in the world."

"You tamed him?" she said, her tone going skeptical.

"Nope. An angel named Hayyel did."

"No shit?"

"No shit at all. I was there. Saw the whole thing. Pass the coffee?" The girls exchanged a pointed look and Polly poured him a cup. Rick glanced at the wolf's pale eyes. Brute looked . . . shamed. Rick narrowed his eyes. The wolf was not feeling shame for what he had done in his life. No amount of penance assigned by an angel could make that happen.

The schedule was a twelve-hour day: three hours of physical training and combat sparring, six hours in class, with a break for lunch, then shooting, at which Rick excelled. He grew up on a farm in the South and had practically been born with a gun in his hand. Dinner was at seven, with library study time after. The library was a computer room with no books, but with electronic links to everything: the National Crime Information Center, the National Law Enforcement Telecommunication System, the FBI's Integrated Automated Fingerprint Identification System, the U.S. Department of State's database of biometric facial recognition and iris scans, and databases the CIA had been compiling since 9/11. They also had access to every state's motor vehicle records, criminal warrant and parole records, and wanted information. The computers allowed access to Interpol and most of the law enforcement agencies in treaty nations, not to mention advanced GPS and satellite photo programs that made Google Earth look like a high school science project.

Everything was encrypted and was monitored by advanced artificial intelligence counterterrorism software, just in case someone was running unauthorized searches or a sleeper terrorist was compiling a database for use against the U.S. It was a cop's wet dream. The library alone was reason enough to join PsyLED, and that didn't count all the cool toys stored in the other half of his Quonset hut quarters.

Polly joined Rick there for study. He could tell she was interested, but for lots of reasons, there would be no big love scene to end the evening: it was against the rules for trainees to hook up, Polly had a night-training session, and the biggest reason—Rick could transmit were-taint to a human through sex. The proscription against sex—for the rest of his life—was something he hadn't been able to make himself think about yet. At all. Instead of encouraging Polly, he kept it casual.

Together they researched a bungled crime scene from the seventies and talked shop, while Brute and Pea lay curled in the corner. Later they all went to the farmhouse kitchen for snacks and beer. The nearly full moon was just rising over the trees when they said good night, Polly heading to the admin building to meet her mentor, and Rick to the Quonset hut to get out of the moon-glow.

He nodded to the security guards he passed, his night vision so acute that he could pick them out in their night-black camo. Ernest lifted two fingers from the stock of his weapon and Rick waved back. Ernest was a former PsyLED operative, now fifty-seven and retired, working part-time to keep his hand in. Rick understood that; most cops had problems quitting full-time work, going from service and adrenaline to sitting in front of the TV or playing golf.

As he reached for the door handle, Brute came out of nowhere and slammed into his legs, sending Rick stumbling to the side. The wolf started that horrible, low-pitched growl, the one that made the hair stand up on Rick's arms. Rick stared at the handle. There was nothing there, nothing visual anyway. He bent and sniffed, but smelled nothing except his own scent. He looked at the wolf, who was staring at the door, head down, slightly hunched, as if he was going to pounce.

"Someone went into my quarters?"

Brute nodded, dropping his head once.

Rick ran through the scenarios. He wasn't allowed to carry his side-arm on campus. None of the students were—they weren't on duty, they were in school—so going in alone would be stupid. But if he called for help and no one was in there, he'd look like an idiot. So . . . He took a slow breath and let it out. "Let's be stupid and see what this is." Rick stood to the side of his door, his back against the wall, and turned the knob slowly. Opened it an inch and sniffed. Brute stuffed his snout inside and sniffed too. After a moment, his ruff settled and he looked up at Rick. "I agree," Rick said. "Whoever it was, is gone." He reached in and turned on the switch, flooding the small space with light. No one was there. There weren't any hiding places. And witches didn't have invisibility spells. Or at least that was what he'd been taught. Of course, if they were invisible, how would you know?

They entered slowly, Brute at Rick's side, alert, quiet, intense. "We'll quarter the room. When you smell something, give me the signal." Rick moved around the room, his jeans brushing the wolf's side. Brute kept his nose to the floor, his ears pricked sharply. He sat in front of the small dresser, and again at the closet, which was the signal they had worked out for having found something. Rick opened both dresser and closet, but the wolf showed no particular change in attitude. The intruder hadn't done anything with his clothes, so, why come in here? The wolf stopped at the old bed, the small laptop lying on top. Brute sniffed and sat.

Rick studied his computer. Pea leaped to the bed and raced around the laptop, twittering, almost as if she were scolding it. Rick still had a pair of gloves on his desk from the crime scene and he pulled them on before carefully lifting the screen. He didn't see it at first, and he never would have noticed it at all except for Brute's nose and Pea's verbalizations. A tiny black dot was on the black keyboard where he would rest his palms when not typing.

He had to get someone in here to check it out, but if he was going back into the moonlight, he'd need his MP player and the counter-spell music. He reached to the desk.

It was gone.

Shock swept through him, electric, hot. In an instant he was back at his first full moon, three days in a New Orleans cell, drugged to the gills, as his body tried to turn itself inside out, fighting to shift, struggling to change into the black were-leopard that was his beast. Tried and failed over and over again, held to his human shape by the mangled tattoo-spell on his shoulder and upper chest. The artwork bound him to his human shape, his human form, and stopped every attempt to shift. The full moon meant pain like being struck by lightning, pain like being flayed alive. Mind-breaking pain. He didn't want to shift, didn't want to be a were, but even that would be better than the three days of hell.

His heart thundered. He broke into a hot sweat. The world telescoped down to the desktop, empty of the MP player. Rick reached out and touched the surface of his desk. Gone.

He blew out a breath, heated and hard. He had uploaded the music to a cloud backup system. He could easily download it to his computer for instant listening.

He dialed Soul on his cell. "Someone's been in my room and stole my MP player. They also left something on my laptop. Brute found it." He described the tiny dot and added, "I'm in my quarters. And no, I didn't touch anything except the light switch and my laptop, and I was wearing gloves."

"I'm on my way," she said.

Rick closed the cell. An hour later, his room had been swept for listening devices and video recorders, and the black dot had been confiscated. His room was clean, and Rick finally got to bed. He needed sleep, but he was edgy, restless, and couldn't keep his eyes closed. The full moon sucked. Each one could be the last night of his life, or leave him permanently furry like Brute. That was enough to make anyone jumpy. Finally, Rick opened the laptop, downloaded the counter-spell, and hit Play, the laptop volume so low no human could pick it up. With the music playing in the background, he fell asleep.

At three twenty-two a.m., his cell rang and Rick fumbled for it in the dark. "Yeah," he mumbled.

"Rick. Are you all right? Say something logical," Soul demanded.

"E equals MC squared. Isosceles . . ." He yawned in the middle of the words and swiveled his legs up, sitting. ". . . triangle. 'Four score and seven years ago our fathers brought forth on this continent, a new nation, conceived in liberty,' and so on. Will that do?"

"I just heard back from the lab. The black dot recovered from your laptop was LSD on absorbent blotter paper with a sticky-back. Someone wanted you incapacitated or out of control."

Rick grunted, thinking. "The list of people who might want me to become dangerous, and who know where I am, is confined to the people on campus." He heard Soul's long, drawn-out breath at the accusation. "Mary and Walk—" He stopped, remembering that Chief Smythe wanted the name of the witch who recorded his counter-spell. Thinking about Polly's sudden interest in him—keeping him out late so someone could get into his room? "Mary and Walker. Maybe Polly. And whoever wanted my counter-spell music."

After long moments, Soul said, "We need to talk."

"About Chief Smythe, who wants the name of the witch who made the counter-spell?" Rick let the harsh tone cops use on suspects grate into his voice. "Wants it enough to enroll me here, even though I'm dangerous?"

"We need to talk," she repeated, her voice steely. "I'll be there shortly. Meet me in the kitchen."

"Yeah, yeah, sure." He closed the cell and got up, dressed, and headed out. Brute and Pea were there first, Brute blocking the door, Pea riding on his shoulder. Rick reached for the leash, but Brute growled and shook his head slowly, the human motion utterly un-wolflike. Rick sighed. "Fine. But keep close."

Outside, Rick leaned against the wall in the shadows and waited. Brute, however, went scent-searching. He started right at the door, his nose to the ground, and began a circular pattern, walking and sniffing in an ever-widening spiral. He was about twenty feet out when he stopped, his nose buried in a clump of grass. Even in the moonlight, Rick could see his ruff stand on end.

"Brute?"

The wolf chuffed and breathed in and out in short, sharp bursts. Rick had seen the wolf get scent-lost before, his wolf-brain taking over, leaving the human part of him behind, disoriented and confused. Dog people called it nose-suck, which might be humorous in a toy poodle, Chihuahua, or shih tzu, but not so much in a rottweiler, pit bull, or werewolf.

Pea scrambled down from Brute's shoulder and inspected the tuft of grass with her nose as well. She scampered to Rick, mewling and chittering.

"Brute, are you scenting the person who put the LSD on my keyboard?" Brute didn't react or respond, and Rick knew better than to touch him. Wolves had violent physical reactions to being brought off a scent-binding and he wasn't in the mood to be mauled. "Brute?" He whistled softly and finally the wolf raised his head. His pale eyes were wholly wolf, feral. Rick went still, vamp-still, not even daring to breathe.

The wolf growled so low Rock felt it vibrate in his chest. "Brute? Stand down. Stand down." Pea launched herself across the two yards and landed on the wolf's head with a catlike yowl. Brute yelped. In a moment, they were rolling around on the ground, roughhousing, the scent forgotten.

Rick blew out, letting the adrenaline rush melt away. "Brute," he said, his voice a command. The animals' heads came up fast. They stopped playing, and Rick could see the intellect again in Brute's eyes. "Were you scenting the person who put the LSD on my keyboard?"

Brute dropped his head and raised it. Yes.

"Okay. Can you follow it? And not get scent-lost again?" Rick asked. Brute nodded. A small grim smile pulled at Rick's lips. "Then let's see where it goes."

With Pea riding his shoulder, Brute turned, sniffed, and started running to the back of the Quonset hut, his nose to the ground. Rick followed at a trot. He was halfway around the building when he ran out of the shadows into the moonlight. The moon-call hit him. His breath stopped in his lungs; his muscles cramped in an electric spasm. He hit the ground face-first. The night vanished.

Rick woke slowly, the dark night full of scents. He knew where he was and who was with him by the scent patterns alone—the Quonset hut. Brute, Pea, and Soul were there. Soul was sitting on the edge of his bed; he was lying on the floor. His music was playing, the musical notes of the flute driving back the pain.

Even with the music, his skin burned as if he'd been flayed with stone blades, drenched in gasoline, and set on fire. All he wanted was to go back to sleep, find that dark and pain-free place he'd left upon waking, and stay there until the misery ended. Instead, he said, "That was really stupid." The words were mumbled, but he knew he'd been understood when Soul laughed softly and Brute snorted.

"I do hope that is the last time you forget to carry your music when you go out under the full moon," she said. "I brought my old MP3 player and downloaded your music. Here." She leaned down and draped the cord over his head to rest on his neck, the speaker close by his ear. "Are you up to trying again, or shall the werewolf and I do this alone?"

Rick pushed up with his palms, groaning. His abdominals felt like he'd been stomped on by a herd of rampaging elephants. The rest of his muscles had a fine quiver through them, like his body was carrying an electric current. "Sure." Kneeling, he caught the desk as the room spun. "I feel just peachy. Just let me puke my guts out for an hour and I'll be ready to go."

Soul rested her hands on his shoulders. "See if this helps." The skin below her palms stopped aching. Instantly. From there it spread down his body, soothing and cool. Somehow the sensation made him think of the color green, green water, green grass in a green meadow. In two minutes he was mostly pain-free.

Raising his head, he looked up at Soul. "You're not a witch. Not a were. You measure on the psymeter as a human, but you're not. What kind of creature are you?"

"Creature," Soul *tsk*ed. "Such rude, personal questions. Surely your mother taught you better. Let's find the person who stole your music and wanted to drug you."

Rick cursed, but managed to roll to his feet. All he wanted to do was curl up and sleep, but making the grade at Spook School would be an effort of perseverance, and the three days of the month when he was moon-called were the days the PTBs would watch him most closely. The world lurched and he nearly fell, but Brute came and sat at his side.

After a moment, Rick rested his hand on Brute's head. He had never touched the wolf before, and the long hair was coarse, but the shorter hair near the wolf's skin was softer, and warm. Far warmer than human skin. The heat felt good on Rick's chilled skin. Brute didn't react, didn't look up at him, or snap, or move away. Pea raced up the wolf's back, then up Rick's arm to his shoulder. She nuzzled his cheek and crooned softly. Rick chuckled, his voice hoarse, and adjusted the player's strap.

"Brute. Follow—" He stopped. Soul had said something about his mama and manners. "Brute, would you please follow the scent you discovered outside?"

The werewolf huffed softly and went to the door, taking his warmth with him, leaving Rick's hand cold. He followed the wolf slowly, feeling the moon-call's ache in his bones. But if he wanted to be a PsyLED agent, he had to make it through this full moon, sane and functioning. And the next moon. And the next after that.

He paused at the threshold and took a slow breath, fear skittering up his spine on chitinous legs, sweat trickling in its wake. Stepping into the moonlight took an effort of will. But he followed the wolf back to the scent-marked grass in the moonlight. This time, Brute took a single sniff and started walking, nose to the ground, glancing back only once to make certain Rick was there. Soul close behind them, they moved across the compound, past the farmhouse kitchen. Toward the business offices, the library, and the communication building.

One of the security guards stepped from the shadows and looked them over. It was Ernest, and Soul paused, asking the guard to follow them. They wound through the compound, Brute's nose to the earth, and they reached the administration building. At the foot of the stairs, the werewolf paused, burying his nose in the grass again, breathing in and out with no rhythm, fast, short, long. Soul and Ernest stood silently behind them. Rick could hear the crackling of the guard's radio.

Finally, Brute blew out and turned his head to Rick. The wolf's head was down, his shoulders high, ruff high, ears flat. Whatever he was smelling, it wasn't good. Brute started up the steps to the admin building, setting his paws carefully, slowly, his nose moving back and forth over each step. When he reached the narrow porch, that low-pitched, rumbling growl started, and Rick automatically reached for his weapon. He was unarmed and his hands closed on empty air. Brute snarled, showing fangs. Behind him, he heard the soft whisper of leather-on-steel, as Ernest drew his sidearm and positioned to the left. Soul moved quickly to Rick's right, her feet silent on the wood.

Brute stared at Rick, his eyes almost glowing, trying to communicate . . . something.

"Are you still tracking the same scent from my quarters?" Rick asked.

Brute nodded once, then shook his head.

"Yes and no?"

Brute nodded, showing a gleam of teeth in the night.

Rick asked, "Have you smelled this scent before?"

Brute nodded, his eyes so intense that Rick felt, for a moment, like prey. He had no idea what to ask next. Brute huffed, put out a paw, and traced a jagged shape.

Rick asked, "The full moon?"

Brute shook his head.

Rick said, "It's just a circle."

Brute huffed, his head jutting forward.

"A witch circle," Rick said. "The witch circle at the crime scene. You found the coven leader. Here."

Brute nodded once, slowly.

"She's been here all along?"

Brute nodded and turned back to the door, his eyes, nose, and ears focused on the wood.

"Someone I've never had contact with."

Soul said, "Call backup, Ernest. Now."

The guard didn't bother to reply, but murmured into his mike, "Backup to Admin. Silent, armed approach." To Soul, he said, "I'm carrying only standard ammo."

Soul pulled up her skirt to reveal a thigh holster. She handed Rick a Smith & Wesson .22, still warm from contact with her body.

Holding a weapon, Rick instantly felt better. He released the magazine and checked the ammo. "Silvershot," he said. He slammed the magazine back into place, pulled back on the slide, injecting a round into the chamber. Rick stepped into the shadows beside the door and slowly turned the knob. It wasn't locked.

He pointed to the wolf, and held up one finger, then to himself and held up two fingers, then to Ernest with three fingers. The guard nodded, pointed left. Rick nodded and pointed right. He turned off his music and opened the door. Brute flowed in like a white cloud, hunched down, silent. Rick followed to the right, and felt, as much as heard, Ernest and Soul move left.

Inside, the entry was dark, lit only by the green glow of computer battery backups. Brute didn't need more light; neither did he. They moved through the entry, around the counter, to the doorway in back. It opened to a hallway, offices on either side. Music flowed through the air, the mellow sounds of wood flutes, familiar and calming. His music, stolen from his quarters, the music that Chief Smythe had been so interested in.

The frame around one doorway was bright, and Brute padded down the hallway, nose down, to that door. Rick followed, and the music grew louder. He expected the office to be Chief Administrator Liz Smythe's. Instead, it was Mariella Russo's office, her name in gold leaf on the wood. Mariella Russo, who was on call the night he went to the crime scene.

He stood back and let Ernest take his place. The man reached out and took the knob in hand, turning it slowly. The door didn't creak as it swung open. Light flooded into the dark hall along with his music, amplified, and a stench like rotten cabbage, rotten eggs, and burned matches. Rick covered his nose. Brute padded inside two paces and halted.

The office furniture had been pushed back, exposing the wood floor painted with a witch's circle and pentagram. In the circle was a dark cloud and a body, human, Caucasian, female. Blonde. Rick felt the shock of recognition. Polly. He didn't have to wonder if she was dead. Her abdominal cavity had been ripped open, and the cloud was feeding on her. A demon. Mariella Russo was sitting at her desk, staring into the witch circle, her cupped hands in front of her, holding something that glowed yellow-green.

Soul leaped for the desk, her body leaving the floor in one smooth, sleek movement. Agile. Inhuman. Both Ernest and Rick lifted their weapons in two-hand stances. Fired. Two taps. Ernest's slammed Russo midcenter of her body mass. Rick's shots hit her forehead.

A half second later, the concussion of the shots still echoing, Soul was standing behind the desk, holding Mariella's hands in hers. She eased the thing, whatever it was, from the dead administrator's hands. "Call for a containment vessel," she ordered. But Ernest was already doing so, his voice soft and in control.

Brute whoofed and growled and ended on a faint whine, his eyes on Soul. Yeah, Rick thought, remembering her speed, like a time-jump of movement. She wasn't human. No way, no how. Not with that leap. He walked to the circle and stood beside Brute, one hand on the wolf's head, scratching gently at the base of the upright ears.

The demon raised up out of Polly's naked body and hissed at them, showing a mouth full of sharp, pointed teeth. Ernest turned up the volume of the music and the demon closed its eyes, settling back to the corpse, as mellow as Rick felt when the music protected him from the moon-call. He thought back to the spell at the crime scene. They had called up a moon-demon. Soul lifted her eyes to Rick. "Please go back to your quarters."

Rick ejected the magazine of Soul's .22 and put the safety on before setting the gun on the desktop. He and his unit backed out just as four men rushed into the room, one carrying a cylindrical canister with a rounded top.

The next morning, Rick and the others of his triumvirate were called to the chief administrator's office. Since he hadn't started with the other trainees, Rick hadn't met the CA, Dr. Smythe, but now, the chief was sitting at her desk, her face grave, her salt-and-pepper hair in a short bob, her face set in the no-nonsense expression of a drill instructor. Soul was standing against the window, her arms crossed, shoulders hunched, her stance protective and uncertain, maybe just a bit defiant.

The former cop, the wolf, and the grindylow stood inside the office, Rick's eyes drawn to the pile of things on the CA's desk. It was his nine mil and holster, his backup ankle weapon, stakes, three silvered vamp-killers, his money, ID, credit cards, and the little black velvet jewelry box he'd purchased on his last leave.

He hadn't seen his stuff since that last leave, two weeks ago.

His next leave was days away.

It was two weeks until graduation.

They were booting him out.

Rick's heart dropped. Brute looked up at him and whined. Nudged his hip with his damp nose. Rick put his hand to the wolf's ears and scratched.

"It has been brought to my attention," the CA said, "that you were part of the reason—"

"The only reason," Soul interrupted.

The CA nodded serenely. "The only reason why Mariella Russo's crimes were discovered. We now believe the three students who sup-posedly signed Quit-Forms in the last few weeks did not terminate their schooling, but may have been fed to her demon." The CA leaned back in her chair and templed her fingers at her chin. "We have launched a full investigation. We also understand that you witnessed . . ." She looked at Soul over her fingers. ". . . something that is classified, and must remain so."

Did she mean the sight of Soul flowing-leaping-gliding over the desk to catch the thing in Mariella's hands before she dropped it? Or the containment cylinder? Or—

"But that isn't why I called you here," the CA said. "We have a problem in New Orleans. You are from there, yes?"

Rick straightened. This didn't sound like a you're-fired speech. "Yes, ma'am."

"And you are familiar with Leo Pellissier, the master of the city?"

"I am." He was related to Leo's heir too, but he didn't offer that, not now, not ever.

"We would like you to travel there and deal with the situation." Rick's breath exploded out of him, and he sucked in another. He hadn't been aware that he'd been holding his breath. Smythe looked at Soul and her lips lifted into a faint smile. "Just so you know, Soul is against this. She feels you need more time here. Which is why, if you accept, she will be going with you."

Soul's mouth opened for a moment, then closed. "You could have told me," she said.

The CA chuckled. "If you agree to the assignment, Soul will accompany you into the field and provide both a temporary partnership and the last weeks of your training. You may return for graduation, of course. Soul, please explain the assignment to your in-field trainee. If he accepts, collect the necessary gear from the Quonset hut, and credit cards for your expenses from financial." Smythe stood and held out a wood box. "I am assuming you will accept. Your temporary badge."

Rick took the box and shook Smythe's hand. He wasn't being booted. He was being given an assignment. Before graduation. "Thank you, ma'am." The CA placed his gear in a paper bag, and had him sign for his personal belongings. Holding the bag and badge, Rick left the admin building with his unit and Soul. They stopped in the sunlight and Soul studied him, shading her eyes.

"They didn't kick my ass out." A smile pulled at his face. He wasn't sure how long since he'd grinned that widely. Probably since he lost his humanity. "I have a present for you," he said. Rick reached into the paper bag and handed Soul the velvet box. "It was supposed to be a thank-you gift, for after graduation. But you should take it now. Sorry it isn't wrapped."

Soul raised her eyes to his and started to speak, but stopped, and took the box instead. She opened it. Inside was a golden apple on a thin gold chain. "A Golden Delicious apple," he said, "for the . . . creature." He laughed as sparks flew from her eyes when he brought up the fact that she wasn't human. "Tell me about the operation."

Magic Tests

ILONA ANDREWS

Ilona Andrews is the pseudonym for a husband-and-wife writing team. They met in college, in English Composition 101, where Ilona got a better grade. (Gordon is still sore about that.) They have coauthored the bestselling urban fantasy series of Kate Daniels. "Magic Tests," the short story that follows, takes place right after *Magic Slays*, the fifth book in that series.

Sometimes being a kid is very difficult. The adults are supposed to feed you and keep you safe, but they want you to deal with the world according to their views and not your own. They encourage you to have opinions, and if you express them, they will listen but they won't hear. And when they give you a choice, it's a selection of handpicked possibilities they have prescreened. No matter what you decide, the core choice has already been made, and you weren't involved in it.

That's how Kate and I ended up in the office of the director of Seven Star Academy. I said I didn't want to go to school. She gave me a list of ten schools and said to pick one. I wrote the names of the schools on little bits of paper, pinned them to the corkboard, and threw my knife at them for a while. After half an hour, Seven Stars was the only name I could still read. Choice made.

Now we were sitting in soft chairs in a nice office, waiting for the school director, and Kate was exercising her willpower. Before I met Kate, I had heard people say it, but I didn't know what it meant. Now I knew. Kate was the Beast Lord's mate, which meant that Curran and she were in charge of Atlanta's giant shapeshifter pack. It was so huge, people actually called it the Pack. Shapeshifters were kind of like bombs: things frequently set them off and they exploded with violent force. To keep from exploding, they made up elaborate rules and Kate had to exercise her willpower a lot.

She was doing it now; from outside she looked very calm and composed, but I could tell she was doing it by the way she sat. When Kate was relaxed, she fidgeted. She'd shift in her chair, throw one leg over the other, lean to the side, then lean back. She was very still now, legs in jeans together, holding Slayer, her magic saber, on her lap, one hand on the hilt, the other on the scabbard. Her face was relaxed, almost serene. I could totally picture her leaping straight onto the table from the chair and slicing the director's head off with her saber.

Kate usually dealt with things by talking, and when that didn't work, chopping obstacles into tiny pieces and frying them with magic so they didn't get back up. The sword was her talisman, because she believed in it. She held it like some people held crosses or the star-and-crescent. Her philosophy was, if it had a pulse, it could be killed. I didn't really have a philosophy, but I could see how talking with the school director would be difficult for her. If he said something she didn't like, chopping him to tiny pieces wouldn't exactly help me get into the school.

"What if when the director comes in, I take my underwear off, put them on my head, and dance around? Do you think it would help?"

Kate looked at me. It was her hard-ass stare. Kate could be really scary.

"That doesn't work on me," I told her. "I know you won't hurt me."

"If you want to prance around with panties on your head, I won't stop you," she said. "It's your basic human right to make a fool of yourself."

"I don't want to go to school." Spending all my time in a place where I was the poor rat adopted by a merc and a shapeshifter, while spoiled little rich girls jeered when I walked by and stuck-up teachers put me in remedial courses? No thanks.

Kate exercised her will some more. "You need an education, Julie."

"You can teach me."

"I do and I'll continue to do so. But you need to know other things, besides the ones I can teach. You need a well-rounded education."

"I don't like education. I like working at the office. I want to do what you and Andrea do."

Kate and Andrea ran Cutting Edge, a small firm that helped people with their magic hazmat issues. It was a dangerous job, but I liked it. Besides, I was pretty messed up. Normal things like going to school and getting a regular job didn't hold any interest for me. I couldn't even picture myself doing that.

"Andrea went to the Order's Academy for six years and I've trained since I could walk."

"I'm willing to train."

My body tensed, as if an invisible hand had squeezed my insides into a clump. I held my breath. . . .

Magic flooded the world in an invisible wave. The phantom hand let go, and the world shimmered with hues of every color as my sensate vision kicked in. Magic came and went as it pleased. Some older people still remembered the time when technology was always in control and magic didn't exist. But that was long ago. Now magic and technology kept trading places, like two toddlers playing musical chairs. Sometimes magic ruled, and cars and guns didn't work. Sometimes technology was in charge, and magic spells fizzled out. I preferred the magic myself, because unlike ninety-nine point nine-nine-nine-whatever percent of people I could see it.

I looked at Kate, using a tiny drop of my power. It was kind of like flexing a muscle, a conscious effort to look the right way at something. One moment Kate sat there, all normal, or as normal as Kate could be, the next she was wrapped in a translucent glow. Most people's magic glowed in one color. Humans radiated blue, shapeshifters green, vampires gave off a purple-red. . . . Kate's magic shifted colors. It was blue and deep purple, and pale pearl-like gold streaked through with tendrils of red. It was the weirdest thing I had ever seen. The first time I saw it, it freaked me out.

"You have to keep going to school," freaky Kate said.

I leaned back and hung my head over the chair's back. "Why?"

"Because I can't teach you everything, and shapeshifters shouldn't be your only source of education. You may not always want to be affiliated with shapeshifters. Down the road, you may want to make your own choices."

I pushed against the floor with my feet, rocking a little in my chair.

"I'm trying to make my own choice, but you won't let me."

"That's right," Kate said. "I'm older, wiser, and I know better. Deal with it."

Parenting, kick-ass Kate Daniels's style. Do what I say. There wasn't even an *or* attached to it. *Or* didn't exist.

I rocked back and forth some more. "Do you think I'm your punishment from God?"

"No. I'd like to think that God, if he exists, is kind, not vengeful."

The door of the office opened and a man walked in. He was older than Kate, bald, with Asian features, dark eyes, and a big smile. "It's a view I share."

I sat up straight. Kate got up and offered her hand. "Mr. Dargye?"

The man shook her hand. "Please call me Gendun. I much prefer it."

They shook and sat down. Adult rituals. My history teacher from the old school once told us that shaking hands was a gesture of peace—it demonstrated that you had no weapon. Since now we had magic, shaking hands was more a leap of faith. Do I shake this weirdo's hand and run the risk that he will infect me with a magic plague or shoot lightning into my skin or do I step back and be rude? Hmm. Maybe handshakes would go away in the future.

Gendun was looking at me. He had sucker eyes. Back when I lived on the street, we used to mob people like him, because they were kind and soft-hearted and you could always count on some sort of handout. They weren't naive bleeding hearts—they knew that while you cried in front of them and clutched your tummy, your friends were stealing their wallets, but they would feed you anyway. That's just the way they moved through the world.

I squinted, bringing the color of his magic into focus. Pale blue, almost silver. Divine magic, born of faith. Mister Gendun was a priest of some sort.

"What god do you believe in?" I asked. When you're a kid, they let you get away with being direct.

"I'm a Buddhist." Gendun smiled. "I believe in human potential for understanding and compassion. The existence of an omnipotent God is possible, but so far I have seen no evidence that he exists. What god do you believe in?"

"None." I met a goddess once. It didn't turn out well for everyone involved. Gods used faith the way a car used gas; it was the supply from which they drew their power. I refused to fuel any of their motors.

Gendun smiled. "Thank you for responding to my request so promptly."

Request? What request?

"Two of the Pack's children attend your school," Kate said. "The Pack will do everything in our power to offer you assistance."

Huh? Wait a minute. I thought this was about me. Nobody said anything about the school requesting our assistance.

"This is Ms. Olsen," Kate said.

I smiled at Gendun. "Please call me Julie. I much prefer it." Technically my name was now Julie Lennart-Daniels-Olsen, which was silly. If Kate and Curran got married, I'd be down to Lennart-Olsen. Until then, I decided Olsen was good enough.

"It is nice to meet you, Julie." Gendun smiled and nodded at me. He had this really strange calming thing about him. He was very . . . balanced somehow. Reminded me of the Pack's medmage, Dr. Doolittle.

"There are many schools in the city for the children of exceptional parents," Gendun said. "Seven Stars is a school for exceptional children. Our methods are unorthodox and our students are unique."

Woo, a school of special snowflakes. Or monster children. Depending on how you chose to look at it.

Magic didn't affect just our environment. All sorts of people who once had been normal and ordinary were discovering new and sometimes unwelcome things about themselves. Some could freeze things. Some grew claws and fur. And some saw magic.

"Discretion is of utmost importance to us," Gendun said.

"Despite her age, Ms. Olsen is an experienced operative," Kate said.

I am?

"She understands the need for discretion."

I do?

"She has a particular talent that will make her very effective in this case," Kate said.

Gendun opened a folder, took out a picture, and slid it across the table to me. A girl. She had a pretty heart-shaped face framed by spirals of red hair. Her eyes were green and her long eyelashes curled out until they almost touched her eyebrows. She looked so pretty, like a little doll.

"This is Ashlyn," Gendun said. "She is a freshman at this school. A very good student. Two days ago she disappeared. The location spell indicates she is alive and that she hasn't left the grounds. We've attempted to notify her parents, but they are traveling at the moment and are out of reach, as are her emergency contacts. You have twenty-four hours to find her."

"What happens after twenty-four hours?"

"We will have to notify the authorities," Gendun said. "Her parents had given us a lot of latitude in regard to Ashlyn. She is a sensitive child and her behavior is often driven by that sensitivity. But in this case our hands are tied. If a student is missing, we are legally bound to report it after seventy-two hours."

Report it to Paranormal Activity Division of Atlanta's police force, no doubt. PAD was about as subtle as a runaway bulldozer. They would take this school apart and grill all of their special snowflakes until they melted into goo in their interrogation rooms. How many would fold and confess to something they had not done?

I looked at Kate.

She arched an eyebrow at me. "Interested?"

"We would give you a visitor pass," Gendun said. "I will speak to the teachers, so you can conduct your investigation quietly. We have guest students who tour the school before attending, so you wouldn't draw any attention and the disruption to the other children will be minimal."

This was some sort of Kate trick of getting me into this school. I looked at the picture again. Trick or not, a girl was hiding somewhere. She could be hiding because she was playing some sort of a joke, but it was highly unlikely. Mostly people hid because they were scared. I could relate. I'd been scared before. It wasn't fun.

Someone had to find her. Someone had to care about what happened.

I pulled the picture closer. "I'll do it."

My student guide was a tall dark-haired girl named Brook. She had skinny legs, bony arms, and wore round glasses that constantly slid down her nose. She kept pushing them up with her middle finger, so it looked as if she was shooting the bird at the entire world every five minutes. Her magic was a strong simple blue, the color of human abilities. We met in the front office, where they outfitted me with a white armband. Apparently they marked their visitors. If there was any trouble, we'd be easy to shoot.

"Okay, you follow me and don't touch things," Brook informed me. "Stuff here is randomly warded. Also Barka has been leaving little tiny charges of magic all around the school. You touch it, it zaps you. Then your fingers hurt for an hour."

"Is Barka a student?"

"Barka is a pisshead," Brook told me and pushed her glasses up. "Come on."

We walked up the stairs. The bell rang and the staircase filled with kids.

"Four floors," Brook told me. "The school is a big square, with the garden slash courtyard in the center. All the fields, like for soccer and football, are outside of the square. First floor is the gymnasium, pool, dance studio, auditorium, and cafeteria. Second floor, humanities: literature, history, sociology, anthropology, Latin—"

"Did you know Ashlyn?" I asked.

Brook paused, momentarily knocked off her course by the interruption. "She did not take Latin."

"But did you know her?"

"Yes."

"What kind of a student was she?"

Brook shrugged. "Quiet. We have an algebra class together, fourth period. I thought she might be competition at first. You have to watch out for the quiet ones."

"Was she?"

"Naaah." Brook grimaced. "Progress reports came out last week. Her math grade was seventeen. One seven. She only does well in one class, botany. You could give her a broom and she'll stick it in the ground and grow you an apple tree. I took botany last semester and she beat my grade by two points. She has a perfect hundred. There's got to be a trick to it." Brook squared her shoulders. "That's okay. I am taking AP botany next year. I'll take her down."

"You're a little bit crazy, you know that?"

Brook shrugged and pushed her glasses up at me. "Third floor, magic: alchemy, magic theory—"

"Did Ashlyn seem upset over the seventeen in math?" Maybe she was hiding because of her grades.

Brook paused. "No."

"She wasn't worried about her parents?" When I got a bad grade in my old boarding school, Kate would make a trip to the school to chew me out. When I got homesick, I'd flunk a grade on purpose. Sometimes she came by herself. Sometimes with other people. Boy kind of people. Of whom I promised myself I wouldn't be thinking about, because they were idiots.

"I met her parents on family day. I was in charge of Hospitality Committee. They are really into nurture and all that," Brook said. "They wouldn't be upset with her. Fourth floor: science and technology—"

"Do you have lockers?"

"No. We have storage in our desks in the homerooms."

"Can we go to see Ashlyn's homeroom?"

Brook stared at me. "Look you, I'm assigned to do this stupid tour with you. I can't do the tour if you keep interrupting."

"How many tours have you done so far?"

Brook peered at me. "Eleven."

"Aren't you tired of doing them?"

"That's irrelevant. It's good for my record."

Right. "If you don't do the tour this time, I won't tell anyone."

Brook frowned. That line of thought obviously stumped her. I worked my iron while it was hot. "I'm here undercover investigating Ashlyn's disappearance. If you help me, I'll mention it to Gendun."

Brook puzzled it over.

Come on, Brook. You know you want to.

"Fine," she said. "But you'll tell Master Gendun that I helped."

"Invaluable assistance," I said.

Brook nodded. "Come on. Ashlyn's homeroom is on the second floor."

Ashlyn's homeroom was in the geography class. Maps hung on the walls: world, Americas, U.S., and the biggest map of all, the new magic-screwed-up map of Atlanta, complete with all the new additions and warped, dangerous neighborhoods.

A few people occupied the classroom, milling in little clumps. I took a second to look around and closed my eyes. Nine people in all, two girls to my right, three boys farther on, a girl sitting by herself by the window, two guys discussing something, and a blond kid sitting by himself at the back of the class. I opened my eyes. Missed the dark-haired boy in the corner. Oh well, at least I was getting better at it.

Brook stopped by a wooden desk. It was nice, large and polished, the sealed wood stained the color of amber. Pretty. None of the places I ever studied at were this nice.

"This is her desk," Brook said.

I sat down into Ashlyn's chair. The desk had one wide drawer running the entire length of it. I tried it gently. Locked. No big. I pulled a lockpick out of the leather bracelet on my left wrist and slid it into the lock.

The blond kid from the back sauntered over and leaned on the desk. His magic was dark, intense indigo. Probably an elemental mage. He had sharp features and blue eyes that said he was up to no good. My kind of people.

"Hi. What are you doing?"

"Go away, Barka," Brook said.

"I wasn't talking to you." The kid looked at me. "Whatcha doing?"

"I'm dancing." I told him. Ask a dumb question . . .

"You're breaking into Ashlyn's desk."

"See, I knew you were smart and you'd figure it out." I winked at him.

Barka made big eyes at Brook. "And what if I tell Walton you're doing that? That would be a spot on your perfect record."

"Mind your own business," Brook snapped.

"He won't," I told her. "He wants to see what's inside the desk."

Barka grinned.

The lock clicked and the drawer slid open. Rows of apples filled it. Large Red Delicious, Golden Delicious, green Granny Smith and every color and shape in between, each with a tiny sticker announcing its name. Even a handful of red crab apples the size of large cherries, stuck between Cortland and Crimson Gold. I had no idea so many varieties of apple even existed. None of them showed any signs of rotting either. They looked crisp and fresh.

I concentrated. My sensate vision kicked in. The apples glowed with bright green. Now that was a first. A healthy hunter green usually meant a shapeshifter. Human magic came in various shades of blue. Animal magic was typically too weak to be picked up by any of the machines, but I saw it just fine—it was yellow. Together blue and yellow made green. This particular green had too much yellow to belong to a regular shapeshifter.

Most shapeshifters were infected with Lyc-V virus, which let them turn into animals. Sometimes it happened the other way and animals turned into humans. The human-weres were really rare, but I've met one, and the color wasn't right for them either. Human-weres were a drab olive, but this, this was a vivid spring green.

"What kind of magic did Ashlyn have?"

Brook and Barka looked at each other. "I don't know," Barka said. "I never asked."

Whatever she was, she didn't advertise it. Totally understandable. Seeing the color of magic was an invaluable tool for law enforcement, for mages, basically for anyone who dealt with it, so much so that people actually made a magic machine, called an m-scanner, to imitate it. My magic wasn't just rare, it was exceptional. I was a hundred times more precise than any existing m-scanner. But in a fight, being a sensate didn't do me any good at all. If I walked around telling everyone about it, sooner or later someone would try to use me and I had to use other means than my sensate ability to protect myself. It was easier to just keep my mouth shut.

Ashlyn could be that kind of magic user, something rare but not useful in combat.

Still didn't explain her obsession with apples, though. Maybe she was using them to bribe her teachers. But then her grades would be better.

The shorter of the three girls to our left glared at me. Her magic, a solid indigo when I came in, now developed streaks of pale celery green. Normally the magic signature didn't change. Ever. Except for Kate.

Hello, clue.

I pretended to look at the apples. "Did Ashlyn have any enemies?"

Barka picked up a pen and rolled it between his fingers. "Not that I noticed. She was quiet. A looker, but no personality."

Brook pushed her glasses up at him. "Pervert."

The girl took a step toward us. "What are you doing?"

"Dancing!" Barka said.

Brook didn't even look in her direction. "Mind your own business, Lisa."

Lisa skewed her mouth into a disapproving thin line, which was quite a fit because she had one of those pouty-lip mouths. Eyebrows plucked into two narrow lines, unnaturally straight hair, carefully parted, pink shiny on those big lips . . . Lisa was clearly the Take-Care-of-Myself type. Good clothes, too. Girls like that made my life miserable at the old school. I was never put together enough, my clothes were never expensive enough, and I didn't stroll the halls broadcasting to everyone who cared that I was much better than they were.

But we weren't at my old school, and a lot has changed since. Besides, she could be a perfectly nice person. Although somehow I doubted it.

"You shouldn't be doing that," Lisa said, entirely too loudly.

If I poked her, would her magic get even veinier? Was *veinier* even a word? "I'm looking for Ashlyn," I told her.

"She's dead," Lisa announced and checked the room out of the corner of her eye.

Don't worry, you have everyone's attention.

"Here we go," Brook muttered.

"How do you know that? Did you kill her?" Poke-poke-poke.

Lisa raised her chin. "I know because I spoke to her spirit."

"Her spirit?" I asked.

"Yes, her spirit. Her ghost."

That was nice, but there was no such thing as ghosts. Even Kate had never run across one. I never saw any ghost magic and I had seen a lot of messed-up things.

"Did her ghost tell you who killed her?" I asked.

"She took her own life," Lisa declared.

Brook pushed her glasses up. "Don't be ridiculous. This whole 'I see spirits' thing is getting old."

Lisa rocked back on her heels. Her face turned serious. "Ashlyn! Show yourself, spirit."

"This is stupid," Barka said.

"Show your presence!" Lisa called.

Yellow-green veins shot through her magic, sparking with flashes of dandelion yellow. Whoa.

The desk shuddered under my fingertips. The chairs around me rattled.

Brook took a step back.

The desk danced, jumping up and down. The two chairs on both sides of me shot to the ceiling, hovered there for a tense second, and crashed down.

Nice.

Lisa leveled her stare at me. "Ashlyn is dead. I don't know who you are, but you should leave. You disturb her."

I laughed.

Lisa turned on her heel and walked out.

"So Lisa is a telekinetic?" I asked.

Brook shrugged. "A little. Nothing like this. The chair-flying thing is new. Usually she has to sweat to push a pen across the desk."

And this new power wouldn't have anything to do with those lovely yellow-green streaks in her magic, would it? Like Ashlyn's apples, yellow green, but not the same shade. Two weird magic colors in one day. That was a hell of a thing, as Kate would say.

"You're not leaving?" Barka asked me.

"Of course she isn't leaving," Brook told him. "I haven't finished the tour."

"When people tell me to leave, it's the right time to stick around," I told him. "Did Lisa have any problems with Ashlyn?"

"Lisa has problems with everyone," Brook said. "People like her like to pick on you if you have any weakness to make themselves feel better."

"She's a dud," Barka added. "Well, she was a dud, apparently. Her parents are both professors at the Mage Academy. When she was first admitted, she made a big deal out of all this major magic that she supposedly had."

"I remember that." Brook grimaced. "Every time she opened her mouth, it was all 'at the Mage Academy where my father works' or 'when I visited my mother's laboratory at the Mage Academy.' Ugh."

"She claimed to have tons of power," Barka added, "but she couldn't do anything with it, except some minor telekinesis."

"Let me guess, people made fun of her?" I asked.

"She brought a lot of it on herself," Brook told me. "Not everybody here has super-awesome magic."

"Like Sam." Barka shrugged. "If you give him a clear piece of glass, he can etch it with his magic so it looks frosted. It's cool the first time you see it, but it's pretty useless and he can't control it very well either. He doesn't make a big deal out of it."

"It's in Lisa's head that she is super-special," Brook said. "She feels entitled, like we're all peons here and she is a higher being. Nobody likes being treated that way."

"Does she get picked on?" I asked.

Barka shrugged again. "Nothing too bad. She doesn't get invited to hang out. Nobody wants to sit with her at lunch. But that's just pure self-defense, because she doesn't listen to whatever you have to say. She just waits to tell you about her special parents. I guess she finally got her powers."

"Did she get them about the time Ashlyn disappeared?"

"Yeah." Barka grimaced. "Then she started sensing Ashlyn's presence everywhere. Who knows, maybe Ashlyn is really dead."

"Location spell says she is alive. Besides, there is no such thing as ghosts," I told them.

"And you're an authority on ghosts?" Brook asked.

"Trust me on this."

Ghosts might be better. I had this sick little feeling in my stomach that said this was something bad. Something really bad.

I could call Kate and ask her what would cause the magic of two different colors to show up. The colors weren't blended or flowing into one another the way Kate's colors did. They were distinct. Separate. Together but not mixing.

Ehhh. There was some sort of answer at the end of that thought, but I couldn't figure it out.

Calling Kate wouldn't be happening. This was my little mission and I would get it done on my own.

I tried to think like Kate. She always said that people were the key to any mystery. Someone somehow did something that caused Ashlyn to hide and Lisa really didn't want me to keep looking for her. "Did Ashlyn have a best friend?"

Brook paused. "She and Sheila hung out sometimes, but mostly she kept to herself."

"Can we go talk to Sheila?"

Brook heaved a long-suffering sigh. "Sure."

"You're leaving? In that case, Brook, hold this for me for a second." Barka stuck the pen he'd been rolling between his fingers at Brook. She took it. Bright light sparked and Brook dropped the pen and shook her hand.

Barka guffawed.

"Moron!" Brook's eyes shone with a dangerous glint behind her glasses. She marched out of the class. I followed her.

We went down the hallway toward the staircase.

"He likes you," I said.

"Yeah, sure," Brook growled.

Sheila turned out to be the exact opposite of Ashlyn. Where Ashlyn's picture showed a petite cutesy girly-girl, Sheila was muscular. Not manly, but really cut. We caught her in the locker room, just as she was going out to play volleyball. It's not often you see a girl with a six-pack.

She sat on a wooden bench by the small wooden room inside the locker room that said *sauna* on it. I wondered what the heck *sauna* meant. It was a first-class locker room; the floor was tile, three showers, two bathrooms, "sauna," large lockers. The clean tile smelled faintly of pine. Special locker room for special snowflakes.

"I don't know why Ashlyn pulled this stunt." Sheila pulled on her left sock.

"Was she worried about anything?"

"She did seem kind of jumpy."

"Did she have a problem with Lisa?"

Sheila paused with the shoe on one foot. "Lisa the Dud?"

Okay, so I didn't like Lisa. But if they called me that, I'd get pissed off really quick, too. "Lisa who senses Ashlyn's 'presence.'"

"Not really." Sheila shook her head. "One time someone left a paw print on Ashlyn's desk. She got really upset."

"What kind of paw print?"

"Wolf," Brook said. "I remember that. She scrubbed her desk for ten minutes."

"How big was the print and when did this happen?"

"Big," Sheila said. "Like bowl-sized. It was about a week ago or so."

Prints that large could indicate a shapeshifter, a werewolf, possibly a werejackal or a werecoyote.

"If anybody had a problem with her, it would be Yu Fong," Sheila said.

"He is the only eighteen-year-old sophomore we have," Brook said. "He's this odd Chinese guy."

"Odd how?"

"He's an orphan," Sheila said. "His parents were murdered."

"I thought they died in a car accident," Brook said.

"Well, whatever happened, happened," Sheila told me. "For some reason he didn't go to school. I heard he was in prison, but whatever. Anyway, he showed up one day, talked to Master Gendun, and got himself admitted as a student. He tested out of enough credits to start as a sophomore. He's dangerous."

"Very powerful," Brook said.

"Uber-magic," Sheila said. "You can feel it coming off of him sometimes. Makes my skin itch."

Brook nodded. "Not sure exactly what sort of magic he has, but whatever it is, it's significant. There are three other Chinese kids in school and they follow Yu Fong around like bodyguards. You can't even talk to him."

"And Ashlyn had a problem with him?" Somehow I couldn't picture Ashlyn deliberately picking a fight with this guy.

"She was terrified of him," Sheila said. "One time he tried to talk to her and she freaked out and ran off."

Okay, then. Next target—the mysterious Yu Fong.

The search for the "odd Chinese guy" took us to the cafeteria, where according to Brook, this uber-magic user had second-shift lunch. Brook led the way. I followed her through the double doors and paused. A large skylight poured sunshine into the huge room, filled with round metal tables and ornate chairs. At the far wall, the buffet table stretched, manned by several servers in white. Fancy.

The students picked up their plates and carried them to different tables. Some sat, talking. To the right, several voices laughed in unison.

To the left, a wide doorway allowed a glimpse of a smaller sunroom. In its center, right under the skylight, grew a small tree with red leaves, all but glowing in the sunshine. A table stood by the tree and a young guy sat in a chair, leaning on the table, reading a book. He was too old to be called a boy, but too young to be called a man, and his face was inhumanly beautiful.

I stood and stared.

I'd seen some handsome guys before. This guy . . . he was magic. His dark hair was brushed away from his high forehead, falling back without a trace of a curl. His features were flawlessly perfect, his face strong and masculine, with a contoured jaw, a tiny cleft in the chin, full lips, and high cheekbones. His eyebrows, dark and wide, bent to shield his eyes, large, beautiful, and very, very dark. Not black, but solid brown.

I blinked, and my power kicked in. The guy was wrapped in pale blue. Not quite silver, but with enough of it to dilute the color to a shimmering blue gray. Divinity. He was either a priest or an object of worship, and looking at him, I was betting on the latter. Glowing like this, he reminded me of one of those celestial beings of Chinese mythology they made me learn about in my old school. He looked like a god.

"That's him," Brook said. "And his guards."

Two boys sat at a second table a few feet away. "I thought you said there were three," I murmured.

"There are—Hui has algebra right now."

I scanned the two guys sitting next to Yu Fong—plain blue—and let go of my sensate vision. His face was distracting enough. I didn't need the glow.

"I'll go ask him if he'll talk to you," Brook said.

"Why don't we go together?" They took the pecking order really seriously in this place.

Brook compressed her lips. "No, they know me."

She made it about two-thirds of the way and then one of Yu Fong's guards peeled himself from the chair and blocked her way. Brook said something, he shook his head, and she turned around and came back to me.

Of course, it was a no. And now they knew I was coming.

Well, you have to work with what you've got.

I raised my hands and wiggled my fingers at the uber-magic guy. He continued reading his book. I waved again and started toward him, a nice big smile on my face. I've seen Kate do this, and if I didn't screw it up, it would work.

The first guard stepped forward, blocking my path. I gave him my cute smile, looked past him, and pointed to myself, as if I was being summoned over and couldn't believe it. He glanced over his shoulder to check Yu Fong's face. I drove my fist hard into his gut. The boy folded around my fist with a surprised gasp. I slammed my hand onto his head, driving his head down. Face meet knee. Boom! The impact reverberated through my leg.

I shoved him aside and kept moving. The second bodyguard jumped to his feet. I swiped the nearest chair, swung it, and hit him with it just as he was coming up.

The chair connected to the side of his head with a solid crunch. I let go and he stumbled back with the chair on top of him. I stepped past him and landed in the spare chair at the table.

The uber-guy slowly raised his gaze from his book and looked at me. Whoa.

There was a kind of serious arrogance in his eyes, a searing intensity and determination. Living on the street gives you a sixth sense about those things. You learn to read people. Reading him was easy: He was powerful and arrogant, and he imposed control on everything he saw, including himself. He had been through life's vicious grinder and had come out stronger for it. He would never let you know what he was thinking and you would always be on thin ice.

I touched the surface of the table with the tip of my finger. "Safe."

There was some scrambling behind me. Yu Fong made a small motion with his hand and the noises stopped. I'd won the right to an audience. Wheee!

He tilted his head and studied me with those dark eyes.

I smelled incense. Yep, definitely incense, a strong, slightly sweet smoke. "I always wondered how would one address an object of worship? Should I call you 'the lord of ten thousand years,' 'the holy one,' or the 'son of heaven'?" Dali, one of the shapeshifters, was teaching me the beginnings of Asian mythologies. Unfortunately, that's as far as we got, since I only just started.

"I am not an object." His voice was slightly accented. "You may call me Yu."

Simple enough.

"Is there something you want?" he asked.

"My name is Julie Lennart." Might as well go with the big gun. Most people didn't know the Beast Lord's last name so if he recognized it, it would be a good indication that he was some sort of magic heavyweight.

"It is a weighty name for someone so small." Yu Fong smiled a nice easy smile. He would smile like that while he watched a cute puppy play with a butterfly or while his flunkies were torturing his enemy. Take your pick. "The Beast Lord commands fifteen hundred shapeshifters."

"More or less." It was more, but he didn't need to know that.

His dark eyes fixed on me. "One day my kingdom will be greater."

Ha-ha! Yeah, right. "I'm here with Master Gendun's knowledge and at his request."

He didn't say anything. The metal table under my fingers felt warm. I rested more of my hand on it. Definitely warm. The cafeteria was air-conditioned and even now, with magic up, the air stayed pretty cool, which meant the metal table should've been cold.

"A girl disappeared. She was a small girl. Shy. Her name is Ashlyn."

No reaction. The table was definitely getting warmer.

"She was scared of you."

"I don't kill little girls."

"What makes you think she was killed? I didn't say anything about her being killed."

He leaned forward slightly. "If I take notice of something that offends me, I choose to ignore it or kill it. I ignored her."

Boy, this dude was conceited. "Why did she offend you?"

"I've never threatened her. She had no reason to cringe in my presence. I don't expect you to understand."

I thought hard on why he would find an obvious display of fear offensive.

"When she cringed, you felt insulted. You had no intention of hurting her, so by showing fear, she implied that your control over your power was imperfect."

Yu's eyes widened slightly.

"I'm the ward of the Beast Lord," I told him. "I spend a lot of time with arrogant control freaks."

The table under my hand was almost too hot to keep touching it. I held on. "Ashlyn annoyed you. You said you ignored her. You didn't say anything about your bodyguards. Did they do something to Ashlyn to make her disappear?"

His face was the picture of disdain, which was just a polite way of saying that he would've liked to sneer at me but it was beneath him. I've seen this precise look on the Beast Lord's face. If he and Curran ever got into the same room, Kate's head would explode.

I waited but he didn't say anything. Apparently Yu decided to not dignify it with an answer.

Thin tendrils of smoke escaped from his book. The table near him must have been much hotter than on my end. That had to be something because the metal was now hurting my fingers.

"If I find out that you hurt Ashlyn, I'll hurt you back," I said.

"I'll keep that in mind."

"Do. Your book is smoking."

He picked it up. I slowly raised my hand, blew on my skin, and got up to leave.

"Why do you care?" he asked.

"Because none of you do. Look around you—a girl is missing. A girl you saw in class every day got so scared by something, she had to hide from it. Nobody is looking for her. All of you are just going on with your business as usual. You have all this power and you didn't lift a finger to help her. You just sit there, reading your book, comfy behind your body-guards, and demonstrate how awesome your magic is by heating up your table. Somebody has to find her. I decided to be that somebody."

I couldn't tell if any of this was sinking in.

"True strength isn't in killing—or ignoring—your opponent, it's in having the will to shield those who need your protection."

He raised his eyebrows slightly. "Who said that?"

"I did." I walked away.

Brook was staring at me.

"Come on," I told her, loud enough for him to hear the derision in my voice. "We're done here."

In the hallway I walked to the window and exhaled. The nerve. All that power, all that magic boiling in him, and he just sat there. Didn't do a thing to help Ashlyn. He didn't care.

Brook cleared her throat behind me.

"I just need a minute."

I looked outside at the courtyard, enclosed by the square building of the school. It was a really large courtyard. No place to hide, though: benches, flowers, twisted stone paths. A single tree rose toward the north-ern end of it, surrounded by a maze of concentric flower beds, spreading from it like one of those little handheld puzzle games where you have to roll the ball into a hole through a plastic labyrinth.

"You're wrong," Brook said behind me. "You know what, we all got problems. Just because I didn't look for Ashlyn doesn't make me a bad person. Do you have any idea how competitive the Mage Academy exams are? Getting the right credit is taking up all my time. And I don't even know you! Why do I have to justify myself to you?"

The flowers were in full bloom. Blue asters, delicate bearded irises, cream and yellow, purplish spiderwort—I had a lot of herbology in my old school. Normal for early June. The tree had tiny little buds just beginning to unfurl into gauzy white and pink petals.

"It's not like I even knew her that well. I don't see why I should be held accountable for whatever problem made her hide. If she'd come to me and said, 'Brook, I'm in trouble,' I would've helped her."

"What is that tree?"

"What?"

"The tree down in the yard." I pointed to it. "What kind of tree is it?"

Brook blinked. "I don't know. It's the dead tree. You can't get to it now anyway, not with the magic up, because the flower garden is warded. Listen, I'm not proud that I didn't look for Ashlyn. All I am saying is that maybe I didn't look for her and I probably should have, but I was busy."

I bet it was an apple tree. Some apple trees bloomed late, but most of them flowered in April and May. It was June now.

"How long has that tree been dead?"

"As long as I can remember. I've been in this school for three years and it was always dead. I don't know why they don't cut it down. Are you listening to me?"

"It's flowering."

Brook blinked. "What?"

"The tree is blooming. Look."

Brook looked at the window. "Huh."

Perfect hundred in botany. Apples in the drawer. Wolf print on the desk. Terrified of a boy who creates heat, because where there is smoke, there is fire. Blooming apple tree that has been dead for years.

It all lined up in my head into a perfect arrow pointing to the tree.

"Can we get down there?"

Brook was staring at the tree. "Yes."

Two minutes later I marched out of the side door into the inner yard and down the curved stone path. I was fifty feet from the tree when I sensed magic in front of me. I stopped and snapped into the sensate vision. A wall of magic rose in front of me, glowing lightly with pale silver. A ward, a defensive spell designed to keep out intruders. Currents of power coursed through it.

Some wards glowed with translucent color, both a barrier and a warning that the barrier existed, and walking into it would hurt. This one was invisible to someone without my vision. And judging by the intensity of the magic, touching it would hurt you bad enough to leave you writhing in pain for a few minutes or knock you out completely.

I turned and walked along the ward, with Brook following me. The spell followed the curved flower bed.

"What's the point of the ward?"

"Nobody knows," Brook said.

"Did you ever ask Gendun?"

"I have, actually. He just smiled."

Great.

Ahead, a two-foot-wide gap severed the circle of the ward. I stopped by it, looked through, and saw another ward. This was a magic maze, with rings inside rings of wards and in the center of it all was the apple tree.

"She's watching us," Brook hissed.

"What?"

"Second-floor window, on the left."

I looked up and saw Lisa looking at us. Our stares connected. Lisa's face had this strange mix of emotions, part realization, part fear. She had figured me out. She understood that I saw the ward somehow and I knew about the apple tree, and she was afraid now. It couldn't be me she was scared of. I wasn't that scary. Was she scared that I would find Ashlyn?

A bright green glow burst from Lisa's back. It snapped into the silhouette of an eight-foot-tall wolf. The beast stared at me with eyes of fire.

My heart fluttered in my chest like a scared little bird. Something ancient looked at me through that fire. Something unimaginably old and selfish.

The wolf jerked and vanished. If I had blinked, I would've missed it.

"Did you see that?"

"See what?" Brook asked.

So I had seen it with my sensate vision.

Lisa turned away and walked off. My forehead felt iced over. I swiped the cold sheen off my forehead and saw sweat on my hand. Ew.

Things were making more and more sense. I turned to Brook. "Do you have a library?"

She gave me a look like I was stupid. "Really? Do you really need to ask that question?"

"Lead the way!"

Brook headed to the door. Just as she reached for it, the door swung open and Barka blocked the way. "Hey!"

Brook pushed past him and marched down the hall, clenching her teeth, looking like she would mow down whoever got into her way. I followed her.

Barka caught up with me. "Where are we all going so fast?"

"To the library."

"Is it on fire and they need us to put it out?"

"No."

Barka must've run out of witty things to say, because he shut up and followed us.

The library occupied a vast room. Shelves lined the walls. With magic coming and going like the tide, the e-readers were no longer reliable, but the library stocked them, too. If you needed to find something in a hurry, the e-readers were your best bet. You just had to wait until the magic ebbed and the technology took over again.

Sadly the magic showed no signs of ebbing.

I walked through the library, checking labels on the shelves. Philosophy, psychology . . .

"What are you looking for?" Brook snapped. "I'll find it faster."

"Greek and Roman mythology."

"Two ninety-two." Brook turned and ducked between the bookshelves. "Here."

I scanned the titles. *Encyclopedia of Greek and Roman Myths.* Score!

Brook's eyes lit up. "Shit! Of course. The apples. It's so plain, I could slap myself for being so stupid."

"You got it." I yanked the book from the shelf and carried it to the nearest desk, flipping the pages to get to the letter *E*.

"What's going on?" Barka asked.

"She found Ashlyn. She is in a tree," Brook told him.

"Why?"

"Because she is an Epimeliad," I murmured, looking for the right listing.

"She is a what?"

"An apple dryad, you dimwit," Brook growled.

Barka raised his hand. "Easy! Greek and Roman was three semesters ago."

"Epimeliads are the dryads of apple trees and guardians of sheep," I explained.

Barka leaned again the desk. "That's a bit random."

"Their name comes from Greek *melas*, which means both apples and sheep," Brook said.

"This explains why she's scared of Yu Fong," I said. "He's all about heat and fire. Fire and trees don't play well together."

"And someone left a wolf print on her desk. Wolves are the natural enemies of sheep," Barka said.

"Someone was trying to terrorize her." Brook dropped into the chair, as if suddenly exhausted. "And none of us ever paid attention long enough to see it."

"It was Lisa." I scanned the entry for the dryad. Shy, reclusive, blah-blah-blah . . . No natural enemies. No mention of any mythological wolves.

"How do you know?"

"She has a wolf inside her. I saw it. That's why her powers are stronger. I think she made a deal with something and I think that something wants Ashlyn."

They looked at each other.

"Just what kind of magic do you have, exactly?" Barka asked.

"The right kind." I pulled a chair out and sat down next to Brook. "If Lisa had made a deal with a three-headed demon or some sort of chimera, I could narrow it down, but a wolf, that could be . . ."

"Anything," Brook finished. "Almost any mythology with a forest has a *canid*. It could be French or Celtic or English or Russian or anything."

"Can any of you remember her saying anything about a wolf? Maybe there's a record of books she checked out?"

"I'll find out." Brook got up and made a beeline to the library desk.

I flipped through the book some more. Dryads weren't too well-known. They were just supposed to be these flighty creatures, easily spooked, pretty. Basically sex objects. I guess Ancient Greeks didn't really have a lot of access to porn so it must've been fun to imagine that every tree hid a meek girl with big boobies.

Somehow I had to untangle Ashlyn, and not just from that apple tree, but from this entire situation. I didn't know for sure if Lisa had made some sort of deal with the creature. I could be wrong—it could be forcing her. The only thing I knew for sure was that I alone didn't have the strength to take it on in a fight. My magic wasn't the combat kind and that thing . . . well, from the intensity of the wolf's magic, it would give even the Pack's fighters a pause.

Sometimes I wished I had been born a shapeshifter. If I was Curran, I'd just bite that wolf's head off.

Curran. Hmm. Now there was a smart thought. I pulled a piece of scratch paper from the stack on the library desk, wrote a note, and read it. He would do it. After I pointed out all of his shortcomings, he would do it just to prove me wrong. I felt all happy with myself.

Brook came back with a disgusted expression on her face. "Apple trees. She checked out books on apple trees."

"That's okay. Barka, can you take this note to Yu Fong?"

He shrugged. "Sure. I like to live dangerously." He took the note out of my fingers. "Later!" He winked at Brook and took off.

"You're going to fight the wolf," Brook said. "You are the stupidest person I've ever met. We need to take this to adults now."

"I think Gendun already knows what's going on. He wouldn't have missed the tree coming to life. He didn't seem frantic about Ashlyn's disappearance and he said that the locating spell indicated she was on the grounds. I think that I'm meant to solve this one myself."

"He would be putting your life in danger." Brook shoved her glasses back up her nose. "And Ashlyn's."

"I can't explain it. I just know that I'm trusted to do this on my own." Maybe it was something only I could do. Maybe Ashlyn would trust another girl her age, but not an adult. Maybe Gendun was just clueless. I had no idea. I just had to get Ashlyn out of that tree.

When I was stuck in my old school, there were times I would've hid in a tree if I could have. I knew Kate and Curran and even Derek, the dimwit, would come to rescue me. But I knew none of my school friends would. Sometimes you just want a kid like you to care. Well, I was that kid.

"I'm coming with you," Brook announced.

"I don't think this is a good idea," I told her.

She pushed her glasses up at me.

"Fine." I grinned. "Get yourself killed."

I waited in the courtyard on one of the little benches on the edge of the wards, reading my little book in plain view. I'd borrowed it from Brook. It was explaining how the universe started with a giant explosion. I understood about two words in it, and those were *the* and *and*.

The day was dying down. Most students were long gone and those who lived in the dormitory had left campus, too. Strangely, no teachers came up and interrogated me or demanded to know when I was planning on leaving. That only confirmed my suspicion that Gendun knew all along what I was up to. Maybe he had some sort of secret adult reason for handling this problem through me. Maybe it was a test. I didn't really care. I just waited and hoped the magic would hold.

The dusk had arrived on the wings of a night moth, silent and soft. The sky above me darkened to a deep, beautiful purple. Stars glowed high above, and below them, as if inspired by their light, tiny fireflies awoke and crawled from their shelter in the leaves. Late enough.

I put my book on the bench and started toward the wards. The magic still held, and when I focused, using my sensate vision, the glowing walls of the wards shimmered slightly. I walked along the first gap and paused. I was pretty sure I'd be followed. Lisa alone might not be capable of remembering all the gaps in the invisible fence, but a wolf would follow his nose and my scent.

I'd have to ask people in the Pack how to make my scent signature stronger. If I had had dandruff, I'd scratch my head, but I didn't. I dragged my hand through my blond hair anyway and moved on, walking along the next ward to the narrow gap.

I weaved my way through the rings of defensive spells, taking my time, pausing at the gaps, until finally I emerged in the clear space around the tree. Blossoms sheathed the branches. Delicate flowers with white petals blushing with faint pink bloomed between tiny pink buds.

I hoped I was doing the right thing. Sometimes it's really hard to figure out what the right thing is. You do something, and you wish you could go back in time for five seconds and undo it or unsay it, but life doesn't work that way.

Nothing ventured, nothing gained.

I pulled a Red Delicious apple from my pocket. The skin of the fruit was so red, it was almost purple. I crouched and rolled the apple gently to the tree's roots. It came to rest against the trunk.

The bark of the tree shifted, crawled. . . . A bark-sheathed leg separated from the trunk and stepped into the grass around the tree. The toes touched the grass and the bark melted into human skin. A moment, and a short petite girl crouched in the grass. I caught my breath. Ashlyn's hair had gone completely white. Not just blond or platinum. White.

She picked up the apple. "Red Delicious."

"Hi, Ashlyn."

She glanced at me with green eyes. "Hi. So you found me."

"It wasn't very hard."

A spark of magic flared beyond the wards. Ashlyn cringed, her eyes wide. "It's coming!"

"It will be okay."

"No, you don't understand! The wolf is coming."

Lisa walked up to the outer ward.

"She's here!" Ashlyn squeaked. "Go away! You'll get hurt."

"Trust me."

Lisa dashed through the wards, running fast, following my trail. I stepped in front of Ashlyn.

Lisa burst out of the ward maze and stopped. "Thank you for showing me the way."

I kept myself between her and Ashlyn. As long as Lisa concentrated on me, she wouldn't look behind her to see who was following her through the ward. "What is the wolf?"

"You saw him?"

"Yep."

Lisa sighed. "It's a forest spirit. It's called Leshii."

"It's a creature of the forest?" Ashlyn gripped my arm. "But why does it want to hurt me? It's like me."

"It wants your blood," Lisa said. "It's weak, and your blood would make it stronger."

"It wants to eat me?" Ashlyn whispered.

"Pretty much. Look, I never had a problem with you. I'm just tired of being Lisa the Dud."

"How did you make the deal?" I asked her.

"I let it out of the Mage Academy," Lisa said. "My dad showed it to me. The mages trapped it during the last magic wave and gave it some trees, to keep it alive while they studied it, but the trees weren't enough. It wants a forest and I want people to take me seriously. It's a win-win."

"Except for Ashlyn, who will be eaten alive. No biggie," I said. Bitch.

"What am I supposed to do?" Lisa's voice went up really high and I saw that same fear I glimpsed earlier. Except now it was in her eyes and written all over her face. "I didn't know what it wanted when I took it out. The deal was, I carry it out inside me and it gives me powers. I didn't know it was going to kill her!"

"Are you a total moron? That's the first thing they teach you in any school," I growled. "Never make deals with magic creatures. It's a spirit of the damn forest! Do you know how powerful it is? What the fuck did you think would happen?"

"I'm tired of listening to you," Lisa snarled. "This is over. Nobody asked you to stick your nose where it didn't belong. I told you to leave and you didn't listen. You can't fight it. And now you're both going to die, so who is a moron now, huh?"

"You're a terrible person," Ashlyn told her.

"Whatever . . ." Lisa's arms snapped up and out, as if she was trying to keep from falling. A scream filled with pain and terror ripped out of her. A phantom wolf burst out of her chest, huge, shaggy, glowing with green magic. It landed on the grass, towering over us. Its fur turned gray. The wolf's cavernous mouth gaped open, suddenly solid. Monstrous fangs rent the air.

"Now!" I yelled.

Yu Fong stepped through the ward into the clearing. His irises glowed with orange and in their depth I saw tiny spirals of flames.

The wolf spun to face him.

Magic unfurled from Yu Fong like petals of a fiery flower. It shone with scarlet and beautiful gold and shaped itself into an outline on a translucent beast. It stood on four muscular, strong legs, arms with huge claws rippling with flames. Scales covered its body. Its head belonged to a meld of Chinese dragon and lion, and long whiskers of pure red streamed on both sides of its jaws. Spikes bristled among its crimson mane and its eyes were pure molten lava. Within this beast Yu Fong smiled, a magic wind tugging at his hair.

Wow. He was a dragon.

The wolf charged, aiming for Lisa. Yu Fong stepped into its path, knocking Lisa out of the way. She fell on the grass. The dragon opened its mouth. Flame burst with a roar, like a tornado. The fire engulfed the wolf, and the shaggy beast screamed, opening its mouth, but no sound came.

The wolf lunged at Yu Fong, biting at the dragon with its enormous teeth. Yu Fong clenched his fists. A wall of towering flames shot out from the dragon and wrapped itself around the wolf.

Heat burned my skin.

The wolf writhed in the cocoon of flame, biting and clawing to get free. Yu Fong's face was serene. He leaned back, laughed softly within the beast, and the fire exploded with pure white heat, singeing my hair.

Ashlyn hid her face in her hands.

The wolf burned, crackling and sparking. I watched it burn until nothing was left except for a pile of ashes.

The dragon melted back into Yu Fong. He stepped to the pile of flames and passed his hand over it, so elegant and beautiful, he seemed unreal. The ashes rose in a flurry of sparks, up into the sky, and rained on the courtyard beyond the wards, settling to the ground like beautiful fireflies.

"Well, that's that," Brook said, at the outer ward. "Ashlyn, I have this blanket here for you."

Yu Fong stepped toward us, and Ashlyn took a step toward the tree.

"Don't be afraid. I won't hurt you," he said, his voice soothing. "Come, let's get you dressed."

Around us, the world clenched. The magic vanished, abruptly, like a flame of the candle being blown out by a sudden draft. The wards disappeared. The garden seemed suddenly mundane.

Well. How about that?

Yu Fong escorted Ashlyn away from the tree, guiding her toward Brook.

Lisa got up. Her legs shook. She shuddered and limped away, into the courtyard. I didn't chase her. What was the point?

Brook draped the blanket over Ashlyn's shoulders and gently led her away. I sat down on the grass and leaned against the trunk of the apple tree. I was suddenly very tired.

Yu Fong walked over and looked at me. "Happy, Julie Lennart?"

"It's Olsen," I told him. "I only pull Lennart out of my pocket for special occasions."

"I see."

"Thank you for saving Ashlyn."

Yu Fong reached for the nearest apple branch and gently pulled it down, studying the fragile blossoms, his inhumanly beautiful face framed by the blooms. Somebody should have taken a picture. It was too pretty.

"Of course, now you owe me a favor," he said.

Jerk. No, you know what, forget it. He wasn't pretty. In fact, I've never seen an uglier guy in my whole life.

"The satisfaction of knowing you saved Ashlyn's life should be enough."

"But I didn't just save her life. I saved yours, too," Yu Fong said.

"I would've handled it."

The look he gave me said loud and clear that he thought I was full of it. "I expect to collect this favor one day."

"Don't hold your breath."

"I imagine I'll have plenty of opportunities, since you will be spending a lot of time here," he said.

"What makes you think I'll be studying here?"

"You've made friends," he said. "You will be worried about them." He let go of the branch and walked away. "I'll see you tomorrow, Julie Olsen."

"Maybe!" I called. "I haven't decided yet!"

He kept walking.

I sat under the apple tree. Somehow leaving Ashlyn and Brook to his tender mercy didn't give me a warm and fuzzy feeling.

I was pretty sure I could get admitted into this school. It wouldn't be that hard.

I was right. Kate had set me up.

But then again, maybe it wasn't such a bad thing.

An Introduction to Jewish Myth and Mysticism

STEVE HOCKENSMITH

Steve Hockensmith is the author of the *New York Times* bestseller *Pride and Prejudice and Zombies: Dawn of the Dreadfuls*. His first novel, the mystery/Western hybrid *Holmes on the Range*, was a finalist for the Edgar®, Shamus, Anthony, and Dilys awards and spawned several sequels. His next novel, an occult-themed mystery, will be released in 2013. He is a Waspy Midwestern goy but hopes that's not too obvious when you're reading his contribution to this anthology.

FRIDAY, 9:47 A.M.

Everyone in the class noticed the woman come in. They would've noticed a gnat flying in. Room 202 wasn't particularly big and it wasn't particularly full.

The woman took a seat at the back and quietly began to cry.

Professor Abrams went on lecturing in the slow, deliberate, deadpan way that made it so hard for undergrads to drag themselves out of bed for History 340: An Introduction to Jewish Myth and Mysticism. But a little worry-furrow creased his forehead even as he droned on about the Golem of Prague and its influence on later stories of Jewish *übermenschen*.

For once, he ended class early—at 9:49 as opposed to 9:50. Then he walked to the back of the room and sat next to the woman. She was fortyish, with short, black hair salted gray here and there. Her cat-eye glasses were perched on a button nose speckled with faded freckles.

Some of the students knew her. Professor Mossler. Her class on

Hollywood during the Depression was a lot more popular than anything Professor Abrams ever taught.

"Karen," Abrams said, "what's wrong?"

Mossler stole an embarrassed glance at the students filing from the room.

"Robert's back," she whispered. She began wiping the tears from her red, puffy eyes. "Cynthia saw him moving things into his house this morning."

"Oh." A flush of color came to Abrams's already swarthy face, and when he spoke again his words had something they usually lacked: emotion. "I'm so sorry, Karen. Have you called the police?"

"You know what they'll say. As long as he stays away from me, there's nothing they can do. And when he finally decides *not* to stay away . . ." Fresh tears trickled over Mossler's cheeks. "What do I do? Things can't go back to the way they were. I can't live like that. If he won't leave, I'll have to. I'll have to give up everything I've worked for and pack up and—"

"It won't come to that."

"How do you know? How can you say *what* might happen this time?"

Abrams drew in a deep, *deep* breath, as if trying to suck in enough air to last him the rest of his life. When he exhaled, there was a smile on his face. It was a "*C'est la vie*" smile—small, sad, resigned.

"Tell you what," Abrams said. "You already had plans to see Wally and Leslie this weekend. Go. Enjoy. Forget Robert. When you get back, maybe things will look different."

"That's your advice? Go on a road trip? 'Enjoy'?"

Abrams nodded. "Yes. That is my advice. While you're gone, I'll poke around. See what I can do."

He placed his hands over hers.

Mossler looked down at them in surprise. Then she tilted her head and gave Abrams the kind of look a mother gives her four-year-old when he offers to protect her from the bogeyman.

"Oh, Andy . . ." she said.

She didn't go on, but it was obvious what her words would have been if she had.

What could you *do?*

They talked a little longer after that, only getting up to leave when students started drifting in for the next class. Mossler had a lecture of her own to give downstairs, in one of the big halls. After that, she was going to take her friend's advice. She would hop in her Prius and get out of town.

"It'll be good practice," she said. "I mean, if I'm going to run away, I might as well start getting used to it."

Abrams shocked her by leaning in to give her a hug. He usually wasn't the hugging type.

When the awkward embrace ended, she left.

Abrams sat back down. He didn't move—didn't even blink—until another professor spoke a few minutes later. The man was behind the table at the front of the room.

"Will wonders never cease? The eminent Professor Abrams seems to be auditing one of my classes!"

"Oh . . . sorry, Paul," Abrams said, chuckling dutifully as he rose to go. "You caught me daydreaming about a new course I'm planning."

From there Abrams went straight to the nearest grocery store, where he bought two bottles of wine and a six-pack of beer.

FRIDAY, 5:53 P.M.

There was a knock on Robert Ramsey's door. Half of him thought it would be the police. No part of him at all was expecting Andy Abrams.

"What are you doing here?"

Abrams held up a six-pack of beer that was missing a bottle. "We're your welcoming committee."

"Unbelievable." Ramsey snorted and shook his head in disgust. "I wouldn't have thought you had the balls to come here."

Abrams shrugged. "Yet here I am. Can't I come in for a talk? Man to man?" Abrams gave the six-pack a little wiggle. "Beer to beer?"

His eyes were droopy, his words slurred. Ramsey could tell he'd already put away a lot more than that one missing beer. The little guy was lit.

Even when things had been at their worst, Ramsey had never feared Andy Abrams. He saw no reason to start now.

"Suit yourself."

Ramsey reached out, plucked a beer from the six-pack, then turned and stalked off into the house.

Abrams followed.

The first hour or so was all stilted chitchat. They sat in the living room, surrounded by dusty boxes and jumbled furniture fresh from the U Store It, and talked about everything except what mattered. Ramsey's wanderings during his yearlong "sabbatical." The history of American labor he was working on. The college kids he'd rented his house to who'd seemed nice at first, but you know how that goes. . . .

Abrams nursed his beer, taking a sip every five minutes, saying just enough to keep the other man talking. He'd needed the booze to goose up his nerve, Ramsey figured, and now he was letting his host catch up. Fine.

Abrams had taken *her* side—had been one of the key players on what Ramsey thought of as Team Bitch. So he was happy to down the little bastard's beer now. Abrams owed him a lot more than a few Leinenkugels.

"Tell me what you've been up to, Andy," Ramsey said when he finally tired of talking about himself. "Still working on that book about how Dracula was really Jewish?"

Abrams offered him a prim little smile. All Abrams's smiles were prim and little. Like the man himself.

"That's not *quite* the gist of it, Bob. It's an overview of Jewish vampire traditions stretching from the *Testament of Solomon* and the Lilith myths all the way to . . ."

Abrams paused and looked back at the picture window behind him. The blinds were drawn, and no more light bled in around the edges. Outside, night had fallen.

He turned back to Ramsey.

"You don't really want to hear about my book, do you?"

Ramsey barked out a bitter laugh. "You called my bluff. No. I don't want to hear about it. To be honest, Abrams, I could never take you seriously as a historian. When you first came along, all I could think was,

'Where did Conklin dig this stiff up?' Yeah, you always had the nitty-gritty down cold. The dates and people and places. The details of daily life in thirteenth-century wherever. Enough to convince Conklin and Katz and the rest you were something special. But you always managed to make it so deadly *dull*. And then when you started mixing in that Kablahblah nonsense—"

"Kabbalah," Abrams corrected mildly.

Ramsey kept talking as if he hadn't heard.

"—it was just insulting. That stuff doesn't have any place in a history department. I mean, no one was going to let me teach a course on Santa Claus and the Easter Bunny."

"That's a rather offensive analogy, Bob."

"And the really amazing thing," Ramsey plowed on, "is how tiresome you still were. You'd think all the pseudo-magical hoo-ha would've made you interesting, in a pathetic kind of way. But no. You were still the biggest bore in the department. I mean, no wonder you're interested in vampires. You could suck the life out of anything."

"I'm sorry you feel that way, Bob."

A muscle just under Ramsey's right eye twitched.

Nobody called him "Bob." He was Robert Ramsey. *Professor* Robert Ramsey. Or at least he had been once.

"Karen always felt that way about you, too, by the way," he said. "I'm sure she's been all sweetness and light to your face. She needed your help with Conklin and the tenure committee. But do you know what she used to call you, *Andy*? When it was just her and me snickering in bed?"

Ramsey let the question hang there a moment, hoping to savor Abrams's humiliation. But the man refused to squirm.

"Oh . . . are you waiting for me to guess?" Abrams said. "I assumed it was a rhetorical question, Bob."

The muscle twitched again.

" 'Mr. Spock,' " Ramsey said.

Abrams enraged him by having the gall to look pleased.

"Really? How ironic." He held up his right hand, his middle and ring fingers parted to form a V. "Did you know that the Vulcan salute is actually based on an ancient Kabbalistic blessing meant to evoke the Hebrew letter—?"

"Oh, shut up, you pedantic twerp."

If passive-aggressive wouldn't get Ramsey the reaction he wanted, he'd just drop the "passive."

He took a quick swig of his beer, then jabbed the bottle at Abrams like a pike.

"I know your secret, Abrams. I've known it all along. I saw the way you used to look at Karen, when you thought I wouldn't notice. You're not *all* robot."

"I think you're confused, Bob," Abrams said. "Mr. Spock wasn't a robot. Perhaps you're thinking of Mr.—"

"You want her for yourself," Ramsey spat. "That's why you pried her away from me. But you'll never have her. Not for a second. She could no more love you than she could love an encyclopedia. And when I get her back, there you'll be, eating your shriveled heart out because *I'm* the one she . . ."

Ramsey locked his bottle to his lips again even though there was nothing left in it but foam. He had to shut himself up.

Coming back had nothing to do with Karen—that's what he'd meant to tell everyone. He just wanted to stop drifting, get as much of his old life back as he could. Karen wouldn't be a part of that. Couldn't be. He'd accepted that . . . he would say.

And now, one day back and he'd already said otherwise. Already said too much. All because a backstabbing S.O.B. had showed up on his doorstep with some beers.

Why did people always mess with him? Why did they push him like this—and then blame *him* when he pushed back? It wasn't fair. *It wasn't fair.*

"Damn it!" Ramsey leapt up and threw his bottle across the room. It smashed into a framed Le Chat Noir poster propped against the wall. He took some satisfaction from the way the explosion of glass made the little man on the couch flinch.

Abrams said nothing for a moment. He just tipped back his head and took his first real drink since coming inside. When he was done, his bottle was empty, too. He bent over to place it oh-so-gently on the floor, then looked up into Ramsey's eyes.

"You're wrong on a few counts, Bob," he said calmly. "I didn't have to pry Karen away from you. She ran, remember? And you're not getting her back. Ever. Because now she's with me."

To this, Ramsey said the only thing he could.

"Huh?"

Abrams nodded, another small, tight smile pinching his thick lips.

"It's ironic, really. All those jealous rages of yours. The suspicions. The accusations. The paranoia. It was a self-fulfilling prophecy. Eventually, you weren't being paranoid. Karen *was* having an affair."

Ramsey took a step toward Abrams. He was still in shock, but he managed to grate out a slightly more articulate reply this time.

"What?"

"Oh, come on, Bob. What do you need—a syllabus? I've been shtupping Karen for a couple of years now. It started not long after you split her lip the first time. It was me who convinced her to move out. Me who suggested going to Katz. Me who said it was time for a restraining order. Me who took those e-mails and letters to the police."

Ramsey took another step toward the smugly smiling man sitting on his couch. He could feel the old, familiar rage boiling up inside him. He even had a name for it: "The Hulk." That's what he called it whenever he was apologizing to Karen. It was something alien, something other, something he couldn't control.

"Just . . . don't get me angry," he would say. "You won't like me when I'm angry."

"Gee, Bob," Abrams said to him now, "you're not about to Hulk-out on me, are you?"

Ramsey clenched his fists so hard his fingernails bit into his palms, breaking the skin.

"Why are you doing this?" he growled.

"So you can see what life's going to be like for you if you stay. Everyone knows you're a psycho, Bob. None of your old friends will have anything to do with you. I mean, there's Cynthia and Jason right on the corner, practically across the street, and have they dropped by with balloons and cake? No. Because you're an outcast. Totally alone. All you'll get if you stay is the knowledge that at any minute you could walk around a corner and bump into me and Karen strolling hand in hand. Maybe we wouldn't call the police, Bob, but it would be our—"

"*I am not Bob!*"

Ramsey wasn't even aware of the last few steps to the couch. It was as if those seconds had been snipped from a film he was watching. One moment he was standing, the next he was on the floor, sitting on Abrams's chest, his hands wrapped around the man's throat.

"Do I look like a Bob? Is this what Bobs do? If I'm Bob, why am I in Robert's house? Huh? Do you see what Bob is doing to you? I wish Bob would stop, but what can I do? *I'm Robert!*"

Abrams flailed, squirmed, kicked. But not hard. Just enough to make Ramsey squeeze more tightly, bang Abrams's head against the floor with more force, until there was no reason to keep squeezing or banging or anything.

Abrams lay still beneath him.

Ramsey rolled over onto his back, stared up at his hands, sobbed. He didn't cry long, though. After a couple minutes, he stumbled to the kitchen in a daze and got one of his own beers from the fridge. One slurp sobered him up. By the time he was taking his second, he knew what he had to do.

SATURDAY, 12:01 A.M.

There was a knock on Robert Ramsey's door. It was loud, insistent. Maybe it started off soft, but if so Ramsey hadn't heard it over the sound of running water.

He was in the bathroom washing the dirt from his hands. He turned the water off and waited for the knocking to stop.

It didn't.

He thought he'd been careful. Karen's old flower bed was around back, flush against the house, blocked from view by bushes and the tall wooden fence around the yard. He'd worked by the light of the moon, though it was a cloudy night and the world around him had been little more than gray blurs in blackness.

But maybe the neighbors had *heard* him. There's not much you can do to muffle the sound of a shovel biting into earth.

Ramsey crept into the hall and peeped at the picture window in the living room, thinking he might see red and blue lights flashing through the blinds. The police would need a warrant, wouldn't they? They couldn't just come barging in, no matter what someone had seen or heard . . . right?

But there were no flashing lights, and when Ramsey sneaked to the window and peeked at the street all he saw out front was the old Corolla he'd have to move soon with the key he'd taken from Andy Abrams's pocket. The porch was out of his line of sight.

And still the knocking didn't stop.

He had no choice. Whoever it was—nosy neighbors, stoned students trying to get into the wrong house, his former tenants dropping by to tell him what a tool he was for kicking them out—he'd have to shoo them away, fast. He couldn't let anyone draw attention to his house or the car parked out front.

It occurred to him as he walked to the door that it might be Karen. Perhaps she'd found out that Andy was coming to see him. What a nightmare that would be. Or what an opportunity . . .

The knocking got louder.

"All right! I'm coming!" Ramsey faked a yawn as he reached for the doorknob. "You woke me up in the middle of the most beautiful dr*AHHHH*!"

"Hi, Bob," Andy Abrams said.

His clothes were dirty and disheveled, and there were clumps of sod in his dark, curly hair. But there were no marks around his throat, and his face had lost the purple-blue hue it had the last time Ramsey had seen it. Which had been, of course, the last time Ramsey had *expected* to see it.

"Mind if I come in?" Abrams asked. His tone was relaxed, his expression pleasant.

"Uhhhhhh . . . sure."

"Thanks."

Ramsey let Abrams move past him into the house. Then he leaned out and scanned the street and the neighboring homes. No one seemed to have noticed the freshly exhumed man standing on his porch.

Ramsey closed the door and joined him in the living room.

"Andy, I . . . I don't know what to say."

"I know." Abrams smiled blandly. "Awk-ward!"

"Yeah. Look. I wonder . . . Do you know . . . Is it clear to you that . . . I mean . . . What do you think happened?"

"Oh, I remember everything, if that's what you're trying to ask. It's not like I woke up in the flower bed thinking, 'Golly, what am I doing *here*?' But don't worry. I'm not mad."

"You're not?" Ramsey said.

Abrams gave him an "awww, pshaw" swipe of the hand. Pebbles and dirt slid from his sleeve.

"Perish the thought. I was prodding you, Bob. Testing you. And you simply reacted according to your nature . . . which I think we've established pretty solidly now is 'psychopath.'"

Ramsey gritted his teeth. "I am not a psycho."

Abrams shrugged. "The proof is in the pudding, Bob. And up until ten minutes ago, it was in your backyard. But as I said—no hard feelings. Just pack up, get out of town, and we'll forget the whole thing."

"You really expect me to believe that you wouldn't tell the cops I . . . You know. Lost my temper?"

"Sure. Don't look a gift mitzvah in the mouth, Bob. And anyway, what choice do you have?"

Ramsey had been moving across the room as Abrams spoke, pretending to pace nervously. He stopped when his feet began crunching over silvery slivers on the floor—remnants of the frame glass he'd shattered earlier in the evening. He crouched down and picked up part of the beer bottle he'd smashed it with.

The neck.

The edges were jagged, sharp.

"What choice do I have, Andy? *What choice do I have?* Why don't I show you?"

Abrams put up his hands and took a step back. "Please. No. Not like that. The strangling, Bob! The strangling wasn't so bad!"

Ramsey rushed him.

It was a lot messier this time. And louder. But it was more definitive, too. No one was going to wake up from *that*. And there was an advantage to murdering a man twice in the same night, Ramsey discovered.

You only had to dig the grave once.

SATURDAY, 2:24 A.M.

There was a knock on Robert Ramsey's door.

Ramsey opened his eyes and found himself staring up at the ceiling. He blinked and blinked and blinked again. Then he remembered.

He'd collapsed back onto his bed, exhausted, after finishing up out back. He was only going to rest for a minute, he'd told himself. Then he'd get up and move Abrams's car.

Only he'd fallen asleep instead. And now a dream about a knock on the door had—

There was another knock. Loud and long and very, very real.

It wasn't a dream. Someone was at the front door.

It couldn't be, Ramsey thought. *It couldn't be. It couldn't be. It couldn't be.*

Yet he couldn't make himself get off the bed and go check. He couldn't make himself move at all, except to turn his head to look at the clock.

2:28—still knocking.

2:33—still knocking.

2:37—the knocking stopped.

Ramsey heaved a sigh of relief.

Then someone tapped on the window just above his bed.

"I hope you don't mind if I lecture a bit here, Bob," Andy Abrams said. "But it seems like my message just isn't getting through."

The window was closed and the blind drawn, thank God, so Ramsey couldn't see him. But he could picture him. And what Ramsey pictured made him want to puke.

"Do you know what *dybbukim* are, Bob?" Abrams said. "I assume not. I might have mentioned them to you once, at a party or something, but you probably stopped listening. Jewish mysticism—not your thing, I know. So here's a little refresher: A *dybbuk* is a malicious spirit that attaches itself to a living host. Sort of like a psychic parasite. And sort of like you, Bob. What you did to Karen. Haunting her, hurting her, sucking her dry. I thought I'd give you a taste of it. That bad, *bad* penny that keeps turning up. Not fun, is it?"

Another rap on the glass jolted Ramsey off the bed.

"I hope you're listening, Bob. I hope you're taking notes," Abrams said. "Oh, Karen was never unfaithful to you, by the way. I just made that up to get your goat. And boy howdy, did it! Ouch! Vick's isn't going to do a thing for *this* sore throat, let me tell you. It's worth it, though. Karen is a very special lady. So smart, so funny. And cute as a button. I do admit I've had my eye on her. You had me pegged there. She stirred something in me that had been asleep for a long, long . . . Well. I've strayed off topic, haven't I? Summation time. Listen closely. This *will* be on the final exam.

"You've got to get over this jealous-possessive-crazy thing, Bob . . . because I'm going to keep dropping in on you if you don't. Go forth and sin no more, that's my message to you. People *can* change. It's hard, it takes time, but it happens. So try. Please. If you find you can't hack it . . . I don't know. Maybe castrate yourself. Or at the very least join a monastery. But you've got to knock it off with the stalking. Do you hear me, Bob? Hmm? Scream or something so I know you're listening. Bob? *Bob?*"

Abrams was leaning in close to the window, listening intently, one ear to the glass. Which is why he hadn't noticed Ramsey slipping out the back door and coming up behind him.

He didn't ask to be strangled this time. Didn't complain about the aluminum softball bat in Ramsey's hands. He never saw it coming.

Ramsey brought the bat down over Abrams's head like he was Abe Lincoln splitting a log. The head didn't act very loglike, though. It was more like a watermelon taking a whack from a mallet. There wasn't much of it left by the time the body was dragged inside.

Ramsey deposited Abrams on the kitchen floor, then went out to the garage for his power tools and a tarp. When he was done an hour later, he loaded up Abrams's Toyota and went for a little spin. There were four suitcases in the trunk.

One he left in the woods north of town.

One he left in the lake south of town.

One he left in the quarry east of town.

One he left at the dump west of town.

The car he left at Kroger.

It was a long walk home, made all the longer by the need to keep to alleys and yards and shadows. But at last, at exactly 5:30 A.M., Ramsey was able to collapse back onto his bed and close his eyes and rest.

SATURDAY, 5:31 A.M.

There was a knock on Robert Ramsey's door.

MONDAY, 9:41 A.M.

Everyone in the class noticed the woman come in. It was Professor Mossler again. The students who'd seen her last time—who'd resisted the urge to sleep in through Professor Abrams's Friday-morning lecture—stole quick, nervous glances at her as she took a seat at the back of the room.

They needn't have worried. There would be no scene, no awkwardness this day.

She wasn't weeping. She was beaming.

Professor Abrams smiled back at her. It was a big smile, too. A grin, even. Which seemed wrong. Professor Abrams wasn't a grin kind of guy. Not usually anyway.

He'd seemed perkier all morning, though. Livelier. As if he'd been sleepwalking around campus for who knew how long but had finally awakened.

What the students couldn't have guessed was this: Abrams already knew the good news Professor Mossler had come to tell him.

That their friends Cynthia and Jason had been keeping an eye on Robert Ramsey's house.

That the day before, they'd noticed the front door open for hours.

That Ramsey's car and U-Haul were gone from the driveway.

That when they risked a peek inside, they found the house cleared out, deserted.

That Robert Ramsey had apparently changed his mind about moving back in.

That Robert Ramsey was gone.

Professor Abrams was wrapping up an animated talk about the *ibbur*—a benevolent spirit, the flip side of a *dybbuk*—when one of his students raised her hand and asked about Jewish views of the afterlife. Her roommate, a Reform Jew, had told her that she didn't believe in heaven or hell or immortality of any kind. How could Jews believe in ghosts if they didn't believe in life after death?

"Things change," Professor Abrams said with a shrug. "Jiminy Cricket, do they change."

Well, when did that happen? another student wanted to know. They'd discussed all kinds of immortal creatures from Jewish folklore. Not just spirits like *ibburim* and *dybbukim* but angels, the demon-goddess Lilith, the Wandering Jew . . .

"Let me stop you right there," Professor Abrams said. "Yes, Lilith and the angels and cherubim we've discussed. Maimonides, Mendelssohn, Kant, Cohen and the long debate over the soul—all that we're getting to. The Wandering Jew, on the other hand, we *haven't* talked about nor will we. Anyone know why?"

Professor Abrams looked around the room. No one raised a hand.

" 'The Wandering Jew,' " he said, "is the story of a Jewish man who supposedly taunted Jesus when he was on his way to be crucified. As punishment, the man was subjected to a peculiar curse: He couldn't die. He would roam the earth until Christ returned. He would be immortal . . . if you can be said to be immortal when you've got an expiration date."

The professor paused to see if he'd get a chuckle. Only Professor Mossler obliged him.

"Thank you," he told her with another grin. "Now. There are two reasons the Wandering Jew isn't relevant to a class on Jewish myths. First off, it's not a Jewish story. It's a story Christians tell about a Jew. Second—"

Abrams stopped and checked his wristwatch.

"Oh, my. Where does the time go? I'll see you all on Wednesday."

He headed for the back of the room, still smiling, as his students gathered up their things and left.

He never did say what the second reason was.

VSI

NANCY HOLDER

Nancy Holder is a *New York Times* bestselling and multiple Bram Stoker Award–winning author, and a short story, essay, and comic book writer. She is the author of the Wicked, Crusade, and Wolf Springs Chronicles series. *Vanquished*, in the Crusade series, is out now; *Hot Blooded*, the second book in the Wolf Springs Chronicles, will be out soon. She has written a lot of tie-in material for "universes" such as Buffy the Vampire Slayer, Teen Wolf, and many others, and recently won the Scribe Award for *Saving Grace: Tough Love*, based on the show by the same name. She lives in San Diego.

Birds trilled through Boston, and jocund dawn was on its way. Claire and Jackson had already been well into overtime when their informant placed their fugitive here, now; and in the grab-game, it was arrest while the iron was hot or give the glory to someone else. And so.

"I have her at the door. She's A and D. She's going upstairs; she's out the back door; I am in pursuit!" Jackson told Claire via earpiece. He was laughing.

"What the hell?" Claire shouted into her mic. *He's telling me she's armed and dangerous and he's laughing?*

Positioned behind a dead apple tree in the weed-choked yard of the duplex, she stepped on a dollop of dog poop—*nice*—with her service weapon out just as a completely naked woman of a certain age (and size) soared over the balcony railing, which was decorated with a set of jumbo Christmas lights, and landed ten feet away from Claire.

Bingo. Claire would have to thank the police sketch artist who had provided them with Linda Hannover's likeness. He had captured every nook and cranny of her tired, doughy face.

Ms. Hannover's landing stuck, although she wobbled. Claire was amazed the woman hadn't broken an ankle. In her right hand, the suspect clutched a turkey baster. The baster didn't look loaded but you could never be too sure.

"FBI. Don't move," Claire said.

The woman teetered a moment as Claire approached. She was very large, and very naked.

"Oh, Jesus, oh, sweet Jesus," the woman said, taking in Claire's FBI vest, helmet, and, presumably, her gun.

"Drop the baster," Claire said.

Ms. Hannover did not comply. Instead, she wheeled around to an open side gate—Claire's original ingress—and zoomed through it. Whapping it shut behind her, the suspect took off like a bat out of hell. Claire was astounded. The lady was *hauling*. She had to be on drugs.

"FBI! Freeze!" Claire bellowed at her. She always said "FBI" as much as possible to give it as many chances to sink in. Resisting arrest always added so much more paperwork.

Ms. Hannover did not freeze.

Claire vaulted over the gate, nearly landing on a rusted, broken tricycle. Claire gave chase—hell, she wasn't even thirty, and she was in fighting trim—but she watched with awe as her naked criminal made it to the sidewalk and hung a left. Ms. Hannover's bare feet slapped on the pavement.

Somewhere, a dog barked and a car engine started up. In a second Bureau car, Santos and Park, their backup, threw open their doors and aimed guns at Claire's bad girl.

Still, Ms. Hannover ran. She might have made it as far as the crosswalk if Claire hadn't tackled her. Claire's face smacked against Ms. Hannover's naked behind and her left elbow ended up in more dog poop. Didn't these fine citizens curb their dogs? Or wear *anything*?

Then she saw the spotless boots of Jackson approaching, stopping at Claire's eye level and madame's ass.

"FBI. Don't move, ma'am," Jackson said, so much more professional than laughing. Claire was going to chew his balls off for breakfast.

"Oh, *Jesus*," the woman said, as Claire extracted herself and whipped out her handcuffs. Then Claire read Ms. Hannover her rights, and together they hauled her to her feet. Ms. Hannover remained silent until

Claire was finished. Then she started panting and said, "Jesus, who's going to cook my goddamn Thanksgiving turkey?"

Claire and Jackson traded incredulous looks. "You should have thought about that before you started cooking methamphetamines in your spare bedroom," Jackson said.

"Yes, unfortunately, it's your goose that's cooked," Claire added, with a straight face.

"It's not cooked. And it's a turkey. It's going to spoil," the woman said, sounding confused. And high. Higher than the rising sun.

The backup team approached with a double-extra-large FBI Windbreaker and Special Agent Santos wrapped it around Ms. Hannover with some difficulty, trying to snap up the front without getting sued for sexual harassment.

"My son was messing around with that stuff," Ms. Hannover argued as they walked her to their car. "That's his room."

"Your son is serving twenty-five to life for murder," Jackson said.

"My nephew is staying in Sweetie's room while Sweetie's in prison," Ms. Hannover prevaricated. Her teeth were very pointy, as in maybe filed down on a whim or for some trick's big bucks, or as a result of some pimp's payback back in the day before Ms. Hannover lost the will to limit her caloric intake to only three double cheeseburgers at a single sitting. Claire realized that lack of sleep was making her snarky. As a rule, she had nothing against people who liked their food.

"Sweetie told his cell mate that *you* committed the murder," Jackson added. She'd been read her rights. She hadn't asked for a lawyer. Things were looking good.

"I'm going to be in jail on Thanksgiving." She chuckled and grinned at Claire with those freaky teeth. "I won't have to cook but *you* will, honey." She broke wind against the Windbreaker.

"She's riding with you guys," Jackson told Santos. He wrinkled his fine freckled nose at Claire's assorted dog poop stains. "Maybe *she* should, too."

Santos narrowed his eyes at Jackson, promising payback, and escorted Ms. Hannover to the backup car. When Jackson and Claire got back to their own government-owned vehicle, Claire folded a towel and sat sideways with her feet on the ground as she scraped off her shoe. Behind the wheel, Jackson pulled all kinds of little-boy "ew" faces that she ignored entirely. She started cleaning her elbow with a fresh wet wipe.

"You were laughing," she said to him.

"She caught me unawares," he said. "Door opens, I see her in the buff, she bolts."

"And you've been an agent for what, six seconds?" In truth, he had more time in the Bureau than she did. They'd partnered up in fugitives three years ago, and before that, he'd done years and years in white-collar crime—while she'd had just a handful of assignments as a new agent.

He shrugged unapologetically. "Whatevah," he said, in his Southie accent.

"I wonder if she thought no one in the neighborhood would see her running naked down the street? Was she hoping to blend in?" Claire said.

That set them both to laughing.

"Did you see her *teeth*?" Claire asked. "Maybe she used to be a goth."

"When—1953?" Jackson shot back.

Claire shook her head. "A woman that size, leaping off a second-story balcony. I'd think she'd break an ankle. And she was so *fast*."

"PCP. It's a beautiful thing," Jackson replied. "So, you all packed?" he asked, changing the subject only slightly.

Claire's merriment faded. "This is bogus. Advanced evidence collection techniques on Thanksgiving? For two weeks? It's got to be code for something else."

Jackson rolled his eyes heavenward. "The aliens have landed. Finally."

"What about people with kids?" she pressed. "Or elderly parents? What was the Bureau *thinking*, scheduling this now?"

"Maybe they're only taking people who won't be missed."

"Oh, *thanks*," she snapped.

Jackson was quiet a moment. Then he slid a glance at her. "Maybe a couple of weeks apart will help. Have you given any more thought to the therapy idea?"

She pulled another wet wipe from the pack—they bought them by the case at Costco—and scrubbed at her ick-encrusted elbow. Then she wadded the towelette and slipped it into their little black trash holder.

"Peter and I don't need couples counseling. And we don't need 'help.' Things are fine."

"It really helped Santos and his third wife. Or was it his fourth?" Jackson deadpanned.

"We're *fine*," Claire said through gritted teeth.

"Claire, I'm your partner," Jackson said gently, and his voice slid perilously close to the edge where they should not go. She was married to Peter, and even if she hadn't been, fraternization was not cool. There was no way she wanted to jeopardize her career because Jackson was handsome and funny and observant. And tall with lanky legs and blond hair shot with silver. And had periwinkle blue eyes, periwinkle being her favorite color. They were both superstars on the fugitive task force—which was why they were the "lucky" ones being dumped with Advanced Forensics Techniques over Thanksgiving—and for kids like them who got all A's in The Job, the straight and narrow was the only way to fly.

"I'm all packed," Claire said. "I'm ready to go."

"I'll miss you," Peter said, kissing Claire good-bye the next evening. Her assignment was all very cloak-and-dagger: Night before Thanksgiving, car at eight, not to take her to the Boston field office but to an undisclosed location.

"I'll miss you, too," Claire said, but she was still focused on his forced tone of voice. His fakey-fake smile. She was an FBI agent. She knew lying when she saw it, heard it. He was actually happy that she was leaving. Not simply relieved, the way people are when things are not great at home and a business trip gives you both a break. He had something planned. He had dark brown curly hair and big coffee-colored eyes, and he worked out. Maybe some hottie grad student at MIT, where he taught physics, was coming over to cook a goddamn Thanksgiving turkey for poor Dr. Anderson, whose careerist wife was abandoning him at such a special time of year.

Peter didn't even like turkey.

Their kiss left much to be desired, and then the car slid up to the curb like a shark. Jackson was in the back, in a really great black suit, white collar, and tie. Blond hair, tanned, he took the FBI look to a whole new *GQ* level. Claire had on a killer black jacket, white silk blouse, black wool pencil skirt, black heels—not too high for the job, very flattering.

"You okay?" Jackson said by way of greeting. She didn't bother answering. One lie today was enough.

"This is all very drama-drama," she said. "We could drive ourselves. We both have take-homes." As in, Bureau cars they could drive home when they went off-duty.

"Which makes it even more mysterious and, therefore, cool," he replied. Then he nodded knowingly as they glided away. "Aliens."

Not aliens.

"Holy shit, are they kidding?" Jackson murmured, as the next PowerPoint slide popped up on the screen. In the image, the vic, who in life had been very beautiful, was lying on her side in a room with ugly beige wallpaper. She was wearing a pink turtleneck sweater and blue jeans, and clutching a copy of Thoreau's *Walden*. Fingertips in blue latex had moved the sweater neck away from the vic's skin, revealing two deep punctures. Next slide: Luminol had been applied to the punctures, and the long-exposure shot revealed the telltale glow of blood, also showing a few droplets on the floor beside her. Only instead of glowing blue, as it should have, the blood was a brilliant purple. "We surmise that when the vampire attacks, it deposits something into the victim's bloodstream that causes this reaction to the Luminol," Dr. Alan DeWitt, their forensics instructor, explained in a flat monotone that boggled Claire's mind. How could anyone sound that detached when they were discussing an attack by an actual bloodsucking vampire?

Until the car had arrived in Salem, Massachusetts, Claire hadn't known that the Bureau had a Special Forensics Unit located there. Jackson hadn't, either. The nondescript brick building was situated near a Walgreens. According to some last-ditch, furtive net searching on her non-Bureau smartphone, the Walgreens was not too far from the correct location of Gallows Hill (as opposed to the recreational area that was still listed as the actual site). Nineteen people had been hung for witchcraft on Gallows Hill in 1692. Her first thought had been that maybe their secretive little group was going to do some kind of forensics on the bodies of the victims. Learn historical forensics techniques or something like that.

She sure hadn't thought they were going to learn how to detect vampire activity.

After being welcomed to the SFU by Mark Nash, the Special Agent in Charge, they'd been sent to a classroom with individual, college-style desks in two rows of six. Claire wondered at all the rush, as if there was some pressing need to learn vampire evidence collection as fast as possible—as if the information would spoil if left out too long, like Ms. Hannover's goddamn turkey.

Told not to eat or drink anything, Claire and Jackson made sure to sit in the first row, dead center. First impressions were everything.

Dr. DeWitt didn't spend a lot of time on preamble. All he had said was that the Bureau had conclusive evidence that vampires walked among the living; that there had been three attacks from Boston to Portland, Maine; and that it seemed to be the work of an individual vampire, classified, therefore, as a serial killer. And that they were there to get trained in evidence collection so they could figure out his pattern, apprehend him, and process any additional vampire-related crime scenes that presented themselves. Such evidence collection being referred to as VSI. Vampire Scene Investigations.

A vampire. A goddamn vampire. That was pretty much the consensus of the entire class.

"You owe me fifty bucks," Claire said to Jackson.

"I think vampires count as aliens," Jackson retorted.

The PowerPoint kept going. They saw another vic with telltale puncture marks. Another pretty girl. Third vic, cute girl again. Same type of holes, luminous with Luminol. They watched a computer simulation of how the fangs must be shaped, how they would enter the body. The closest analogy was a rattlesnake. Which, bleh.

They discussed the process of exsanguination—having all your blood sucked out of you. Dripping. If you lifted vampire prints, they would glow, too. However, there were no prints found at any of the crime scenes, so Claire raised her hand and asked how they knew that prints glowed. DeWitt told her to hold that excellent question. There were theories as to why so much glowing, but that would also wait for when they got into blood chemistry. As well as profiling the perp, who clearly had a thing for beautiful girls.

They were going to stay on-site, the male agents doubling up. Claire, as the only female, would have a room to herself.

"Now we have a body to examine," DeWitt announced, as he turned off his projector.

He didn't say which body. There seemed to be an assortment of them—at least three victims. Claire was eager to see any and all of them.

"Before we do, I want each of you to provide a buccal swab," he went on.

Claire and Jackson traded frowns. Buccal swabs provided personal DNA. Of course they'd both had extensive physicals, bloodwork, and even drug tests for the FBI, but here, now, requesting a swab rang an alarm bell. She also realized why they hadn't been allowed to eat or drink anything, and why class had begun that night—so their first swabs would be valid control samples. Still, Claire raised her hand.

"The purpose for this, sir?" she asked.

"Health precaution," he replied. "Since we're not certain how vampirism is transmitted, we want to monitor the well-being of everyone on the team."

Transmitted? Her mind ran ahead to the possibility that vampirism might be a communicable virus, and so their vics might contain said virus, that being why the blood glowed purple.

While she pondered that, DeWitt handed a box of swab kits to the agent at the end of Claire's row. The agent hesitated. There were a few cases before the courts of police officers refusing to comply with requests for DNA samples by their departments. Civil liberties, violation of privacy. Not everyone wanted everything in an accessible database.

But the hesitation was two seconds at best. He took one and passed it on. The next guy did, too.

And then it was her turn. DeWitt was watching her. She grabbed one and handed the box to Jackson, who did the same. All the agents opened them and performed the six swipes inside their cheeks, repeated on the other cheek. They put the swabs in the sterile vials and closed them.

"Last name, first name, please," DeWitt instructed them. Claire wrote ANDERSON, CLAIRE and Jackson wrote JACKSON, BRIAN and she and he passed them in.

"Now we'll examine the body," DeWitt announced.

Everyone rose from their spotless government-issue desks. Note-taking had not been permitted. Nor were cell phones, which had been locked up in a safe until their owners were driven back to their homes. Apparently, everything the agents would be learning would be kept in one place and one place only—their heads. That posed no problem. FBI agents were used to memorizing lots of information and keeping secrets. They knew things that might break civilians, cause widespread panic. Biochemical warfare, terrorist plots, close calls with nuclear power plants. Maybe it was just as well that Peter seemed disinterested in what she did when she wasn't with him.

Almost as disinterested in what she did when she was with him.

In a little rush of anger, she was glad she wouldn't be able to tell him about vampires. She hadn't realized just how angry she was with him. How not fine they actually were.

By tacit agreement, Claire and Jackson scooted directly behind DeWitt as he left the classroom, as close to Source Vampire Data as possible. Other, slower, perhaps less enthusiastic agents queued behind them. Then the thirteen of them walked down a chilly hall, and passed a door with a sign that read *HIC LOCUS EST UBI MORS GAUDET SUCCURRERE VITAE.* That was the traditional Latin phrase often seen on plaques in autopsy rooms: *"This is the place where death rejoices to help those who live."* So one would assume that was where the body was, but they weren't going in there.

"We'll get to that later," DeWitt announced.

He turned a corner and Claire saw two federal marshals standing on either side of a fire door. DeWitt showed them his badge and used a card swipe. Although everyone had been checked in at the main desk when they'd arrived, the marshals studied each ID card as each agent in turn waited at the door.

There was a concrete staircase on the other side of the threshold. After DeWitt, Claire and Jackson started down, Jackson making no effort to conceal how excited he was, like they were going on an amusement park ride. Claire found that she was kind of tense. That was how it often was between them on cases—Jackson all yippi-kai-yai-oh and Claire pondering, speculating, absorbing. She wondered if Peter thought she was a drag because of her reserve. But really, all he liked to do was go to wine tastings and read. He wasn't exactly Mr. Excitement. That had always been okay with her. Her job was excitement enough.

She didn't want to be thinking about Peter right then. A real vampire was a game-changer. This was history in the making.

Cement stairs gave way to uneven cobblestones, and the walls changed from modern brick to very old, pitted blocks of stone that smelled of mold and dust. They moved into a tunnel, and Claire saw a metal door painted black at the other end. Also, two more marshals and another card reader. The marshals were impassive, and all the VSI students had fallen silent. Claire could feel the tension building in the air.

As DeWitt took off his ID badge and swiped the lock, Claire glanced over at Jackson. Her partner bared his teeth and mimed biting her. Everything was a joke to him, except her happiness. He became unhappy when he sensed that things were going even less well than usual at home. She knew that deep down in her heart, where she kept her secrets. And she also knew, right then and there, that she was very close to telling him that she loved him for it. In the icy hall at their very bizarre forensics school. Or maybe this impulse was just an extra little splash of adrenaline kicking into her system. Because all this was pretty goddamn incredible.

The door fwommed open and DeWitt stepped outside. Claire went next, into another world of ivy, tombs, weeping angels, and headstones. A cemetery. And more marshals, planted like statues around the graveyard, dressed for trouble in raid jackets. An owl hooted. She saw her breath.

There were some murmurs throughout the ranks, but Claire kept quiet. DeWitt walked purposefully along a gravel path. On the nearest headstone, the name written there was illegible but the date was *1692*. If she remembered her hasty phone search facts, that was the year of the Salem witchcraft trials. Maybe the occupant had been hung by the neck until dead because her next-door neighbor's cow stopped giving milk.

Claire didn't know what all this had to do with vampire forensics, but DeWitt was on the move now, like a bloodhound. Sure enough, about twenty seconds later, he stopped in front of an aboveground tomb the size of a potting shed. Klieg lights blazed around it, and guards formed a living wall around it. With a bit of a flourish, DeWitt turned and faced the expectant group.

"We'll be going down into the crypt in groups of four. Count off, please."

"Crypt," Jackson said, raising his eyebrows. "I don't know about you, Claire, but this sure beats mashed potatoes and stuffing."

Jackson was observer number one, and he snickered when Claire announced that she was number two. Numbers three and four were two agents from Maine. After donning gas masks—DeWitt slapped one on, too—the five entered the illuminated interior of the tomb. The floor had been swept clean. Klieg lights and what appeared to be battery-operated air filters were whirring away. There were four old stone sarcophagi, sitting about waist-high, which had been opened, and Claire glanced inside the nearest one. Stove-in wooden planks, bones, fibers, from a long time ago.

"We tested the contents of these coffins," DeWitt said through his transmitter. "Bodies are fully human, and appear to be seventeenth- and eighteenth-century. The sarcophagus you're examining, Agent Anderson, was the one concealing this trapdoor."

She followed his pointing finger, spotting the trapdoor in question. It was open, and on the exposed underside of the access hatch, a cross had been inlaid with iron, now very rusty. The cross would have been flush with the ceiling of whatever lay beneath it.

DeWitt climbed through the hatch and clanged down a contemporary set of portable metal stairs. Claire and Jackson followed after, Claire in her skirt and heels, and then the two guys from Maine. The walls of the tiny chamber were pitted and limey. More super-bright lights illuminated a wormy, weather-beaten wooden coffin perched on top of a stainless steel sheet, on top of another sarcophagus. Its lid sat across the tiny room on several pieces of what appeared to be linen, on a metal cart.

"We're unclear about pathogens, so make sure your masks are secure," DeWitt said through his mic.

"Before securing the masks of any children traveling with you," Jackson murmured, as he, Claire, and the Mainers walked to the side of the coffin and peered inside.

A man who appeared to be about forty years old lay as if sleeping. His cheeks were ruddy and his face was full. He was covered up to his neck in the same linen as the coffin lid rested on, but something protruding from his chest tented the fabric. DeWitt lifted the linen, and Claire saw old-timey clothes in tatters and a wooden stake plunged through the chest, exactly where the heart should be.

"Vic number four?" said the taller of the Maine agents.

DeWitt shook his head. He reached into his pocket and pulled on blue latex gloves. Then he approached the body and gently pulled back the left side of the upper lip. The canine was long, and very sharp, as if it had been filed.

"We believe that this is a vampire," he said.

For a few seconds, Claire's mind went blank, as if it simply couldn't process what he had just said. Then errant thoughts filtered in about naked Ms. Hannover and her pointy teeth. Leaping over a balcony railing, flashing—literally—down the street.

"I smell money," Jackson said. "Fifty bucks."

"How did you find him?" Claire asked, ignoring Jackson.

"It was an accident. A lucky one," DeWitt said. "About five years ago, there was an incident in the graveyard—kidnapping across state lines, murder—so we had jurisdiction. We were collecting evidence. In addition to the blood of the human kidnapping vic, we got a faint purple glow in the cemetery dirt. We didn't know what it was, and we sprayed the cemetery down. The glow was strongest on the ground around the sarcophagus on top of the trapdoor. We kept following the trail. And habeas corpus."

"Damn," Jackson said.

"We took fingerprints, too," DeWitt said. "There were two distinct sets on the trapdoor, and on this coffin, with the purple glow. We've documented them with long-exposure photographs, same as the punctures."

"So these were the prints you were talking about in class?" Claire asked.

"Yes," DeWitt said.

"But there were no fingerprints at the crime scenes," Jackson said.

"Yes. Our serial killer vampire is very careful. He cleans up after himself. Except he doesn't know about the Luminol."

Claire stared down at the vampire. "So back to this body. You conjecture that Vampire One came down here with Vampire Two and, what, staked him?"

"I thought when you staked vampires they turned into dust," said the shorter agent from Maine.

"There's no evidence to support that," DeWitt said with a straight face. "We've drawn some blood and taken tissue samples. We don't have the proper language to describe the results. You'll be going over those samples tomorrow."

"Is he alive?" Claire asked, grimacing down at the vampire. The tent of linen was neither rising nor falling, so it didn't appear that he was breathing.

"Again, that's open to interpretation," DeWitt said.

"What happens if you remove the stake?" Jackson asked.

"We don't know. We haven't done it. We debated for a long time about if we should remove the body from the crypt. We ultimately decided against it." He stared down at the vampire with a little smile on his face and shook his head as if to say, *You rascal.* "We don't know why he's here."

"Why are *we* here?" Claire asked. "Why were we selected for this case?"

"'Cause FBI fugitive task forces are a dying breed," Jackson said. Which was true. Marshals had the corner on the fugitive biz these days.

"KSAs. Knowledge, skills, abilities. Each of you has been selected to be here because of your stellar performance records," DeWitt said. "We're hoping that once we show you everything we've learned so far, you'll come up with some theories about the perp. The vampire at large," he elaborated. "We're wondering if our perp is the same vampire who accompanied our friend here. Maybe he staked this vampire to put him in some kind of stasis. To immobilize him. Maybe this is a vampiric coma, or imprisonment. We conjecture that the stake acts as a kind of restraint."

"So maybe this vamp is a vic," Jackson said.

DeWitt cracked a small smile. "That's a theory. There's so much to learn, wouldn't you agree? Two weeks isn't nearly enough time."

Claire and Jackson went back up tombside and talked to the Maine agents while the other two groups took their turns discovering that the Truth wasn't out there; it was about ten feet below. By then it was nearly midnight, and they were dismissed and sent off to their quarters. Jackson asked to come to Claire's room after they both got settled in to talk for a while, and she figured they weren't in high school and they did have a lot to talk about, so she said yes.

"Damn," he said, as he shut the door. Her room had a bed, a small dresser, a desk and a chair, and an overstuffed chair. He sat on the desk chair and she took the more comfortable one. *"Vampires."*

They shared a look. And Clare got nervous, because not only was she really glad he'd asked to come in, but she'd been hoping that he would.

"Vampires," she concluded. "Can you believe it?"

"Just watch. We're going to end up as a task force," he said. "We twelve. We're going to have T-shirts that say VSI. They're going to transfer us to the basement of the J. Edgar Hoover Building in D.C. like those guys in *The X-Files*. People will laugh at us."

"That should pose no problem for you. You're already big on laughter," she pointed out.

"She had a *baster*," Jackson said.

"I might have shot her."

He nodded. "I'm sorry, Claire. It's been a weird time in my life."

Her ears pricked up at that and felt an unsettling little blip in her chest. "Girlfriend?"

Steadily gazing at her, he replied, "You know I don't have a girlfriend."

It was stupid to be relieved. Stupid, and wrong.

"Is your grandma sick?" she probed, trying to get him to share.

"It's just family stuff," he said. "My sisters and I inherited a house in California from our aunt and we're trying to decide what to do about it."

He's thinking about moving, she translated. She hadn't known about all these feelings for him—okay, she'd known she *had* feelings, just not that they ran this deep.

"Hey, so how'd you meet Peter?" he asked, naming the elephant in the living room, and she blessed him for it.

"A party. Engagement party, actually." She looked off in the distance, remembering. "He knew the groom. I went to college with the bride. I almost didn't go."

There was a pause. She looked back over at him, to find him staring at her with undisguised longing. His cheeks reddened and he got up.

"I'd better go to bed." He pulled a face. "Two weeks is a long time to sleep with some guy you don't know."

"You have my sympathies," she said lightly.

"Which I'll keep in a jar on my desk," he said. He walked to the door and put his hand around the knob. Then he paused. "Ms. Hannover today. Do you think *she* was a vampire?"

"Daylight. They can't walk around in it," she reminded him.

"The Cullens can walk around in it," he said. "It makes them spar-kle. And *Dracula* went out in daylight in the original novel, too."

She blinked. "You know a lot about vampires."

"We all have our fetishes. Isn't yours Orlando Bloom?"

She reached over to the bed and made as if to throw a pillow at him. He laughed and opened the door. "Actually, I was just speed-reading the material on vampires they left on our pillows. Me and my snuggle buddy." He looked at her bed. "Didn't you get yours yet?"

"No," she said. "Maybe they forgot me because I'm in here by myself."

"Agent Anderson?" a voice said in the hall. He came into the door-way. Young, agent-y or clerk-y looking. "I have a file for you."

He held out an interoffice memo jacket, and Claire took it. Signed for it.

"Thanks," she said, as the guy hovered.

"Yes, ma'am." He gave Jackson a look, turned, and disappeared around a corner.

"That'll be your vampire dossier," Jackson said. "Don't forget to hang up your garlic and crosses," he added as he headed out, too. "Per-haps ze count vill walk tonight."

That creeped her out, but she didn't show it. Then she shut the door and stared at it, and wondered what Peter was up to tonight. For some-one so diligent about her career, she'd been very sloppy about Peter. They'd just kind of ended up together. She was pretty sure the reason they'd gotten married was to make her conservative Catholic father happy. Which was a pretty weak reason.

We were in love, she insisted. *We are in love.*

Then she got ready for bed, climbed in, and started reading about Nosferatu, Sookie Stackhouse, and Vlad the Impaler. And despite how wound-up she was, she fell asleep.

She dreamed about waking up because someone was in her room, but she couldn't make herself open her eyes. So she drifted in a sea of apprehension for most of the night, and woke in the morning to nothing new but the reflection through the window sheers of steady rain. But as she lowered her gaze and studied the ground, she couldn't shake the sensation that the rain had just washed fresh footprints away.

Footprints pointed straight at her window.

"Blood type AB. I guess that makes sense. ABs can get blood transfusions from all four blood types. Lower than average levels of serotonin," Claire read to Jackson, as they studied their blood sample readouts. It was their fourth day of training, and they were sitting in a lab off the autopsy room. The agents had been paired off, and everyone was discussing results. It was still raining, and gloomy.

The three vics were in cold storage in that room, but today the VSI students were analyzing vampire blood that they themselves had drawn. The vampire in the coffin had not appeared to feel anything when the needle went in, and no one had any reasonable theories about why his blood hadn't coagulated inside him long ago. Also, about whose blood it actually was that they were studying. If the vampire drank the blood of his victims, what happened to it?

"Lower levels of serotonin have also been found in the brains of murderers on death row, accounting for increased aggression," Jackson said, reciting from their class lecture.

"There are caps on short tandem repeats of DNA strands," Claire continued.

"Which suggests increased life span," Jackson said. "Caps allow for little to no unraveling of the strands."

"Time for swabs," DeWitt announced, holding the box out to them.

They'd had one swab a day since arriving. Claire was becoming increasingly apprehensive. Was there concern that something was happening to them?

"I don't like this," she murmured to Jackson as she unwrapped the swab. "Do you think they're withholding information from us? Even experimenting on us? I mean, we didn't even volunteer for this. This could be construed as a form of coercion."

"It could," Jackson said. "You want to see Nash?"

"Yes," she said. "Absolutely."

Then the lab door opened and Nash himself poked his head in. He looked straight at DeWitt and then the class and said, "It's time."

"Let's roll," said DeWitt. "I'll brief you all while you're suiting up."

In near-unison, the ten other agents in the room rose from their chairs and made for the exit. DeWitt went with them. Claire looked around in confusion, then began to get up, too.

"Claire," Jackson said in an odd tone of voice, "you and I are staying behind."

"What? What's going on?" she demanded.

"Jackson, Anderson, in five," Nash said, closing the door.

"Do you trust me, Claire?" Jackson asked, locking gazes with her. "Please, trust me."

"Tell me what's going on," she insisted. "Why are we staying behind?"

"You'll find out everything in a few minutes," he said.

"You bastard. I *don't* trust you. You've been holding out on me." She glared at him. "You're my *partner.*"

He looked upset. "I know, Claire. I know and I'm sorry, but it's going to be okay now."

"Okay *now*?" she asked, her voice rising. "What hasn't been okay?"

Jackson stood up. He said, "Let's go see Nash."

They went down a hallway and faced Nash's door. Jackson rapped on it sharply. Nash opened it, and Claire did a quick sweep of the interior. American flag, portrait of the POTUS, commendations.

"Take a seat, please," Nash said to Claire and Jackson as he sat down behind his desk. Nash picked up the folder. "Agent Anderson, I need you to stay calm."

She sat down. A million scenarios ran through her mind: She had done something to cause a civilian's death. She had a fatal illness. She was becoming a vampire. The vampire had risen and was terrorizing Salem.

And: By his demeanor, Jackson knew a hell of a lot more about what was going on than she did.

"The perp," she said. "The vampire. He's struck again?"

Nash nodded, his expression somber. "Yes. He has."

Then why are we in this room? she thought. *Why aren't we with the rest of the team?* "Let's roll" obviously meant lights and sirens. As in, get your tail to the crime scene. "Suit up" meant vests and helmets. A violent confrontation.

Jackson gave her a look and she kept her mouth shut.

Nash flipped open the folder. The topmost picture was the first vic they'd seen onscreen, the one in the pink turtleneck sweater. Second vic. Third vic. Purple glow at the puncture sites. And then a form she recognized as DNA test results.

Like any decent bureaucrat, she was a champ at reading upside down. In one box, MATCH was typed and in the "subject's name" box, ANDERSON, CLAIRE.

"*Match?* What's this?" she demanded, reaching for the document. Nash kept his hand splayed over it, preventing her from taking it. Her blood pressure spiked. *Bad news. Frame-up,* she thought. *Setup.* But how or what, she had no idea.

"Listen to him," Jackson said, his voice that gentle voice he used, connecting with her, helping her focus.

"I'm going to be blunt," Nash said. "We've had a prime suspect in this case for some time."

"Not me," she said, reaching again for the piece of paper. Nash kept a firm hold of it.

"The suspect had access to your DNA and planted it at each of the three crime scenes your class has discussed," Nash told her. "Hair follicles. To make you look like the guilty party."

Stunned, she looked at Jackson. "The swabs—"

"We've been taking swabs so we could ensure that you are not a vampire, and we arranged this school so we could keep you under observation if and when he killed again," Nash said plainly. "If he hadn't struck within the two weeks, we would have extended the duration of your training.

"You're not a vampire," he added.

Dumbfounded, she could only sit and listen. A terrible feeling was spreading throughout her body—Claire was smart and she could piece things together, which was why she was so good at what she did. But she couldn't fathom that she was drawing the correct conclusions.

"The perp was careful. He wore gloves and booties, and he wiped down the scenes. But he obviously did not consider that when he bites his victim, he leaves behind a vampiric marker we can catch with Luminol. And he didn't do a perfect cleanup job. He's not a professional criminal, just a killer. But we had to be sure of you."

She looked from him to Jackson, handsome, kind Jackson, whose cheeks were blazing, and who looked ashamed.

"Be sure of me," she said.

"Because you know the vampire in question," Nash said.

"No," she said, feeling dizzy.

"We think the reason he's been killing these women is because they resemble his mother. We have cause to believe that the vampire in the tomb is his father, and that he killed his father after his father killed his mother because she was unfaithful to him. In the seventeenth century."

"He," she said, swallowing hard, not wanting to think about who had easy access to her hair follicles.

"The perp—the son of the vampire in the crypt—began his attacks approximately two and a half years ago—after he became convinced that you were being unfaithful to him." He looked at Jackson.

"I discussed our relationship with Agent Nash," Jackson said to her. "We're partners. Nothing unprofessional has passed between us." He leaned toward her. "I went along with all of this to clear you, Claire. And to make you safe."

My husband is a vampire. My husband is the vampire. My husband is a serial killer.

She didn't know how long she sat there. She became aware that Nash was holding out a shot glass of whiskey to her. She took it and tossed it back.

"The ten other agents in your class know all this," Nash said. "DeWitt is the agent in charge of the task force."

"This was a sting operation," she said shakily, "in case I was the guilty party."

"We got a search warrant for your condo," Nash continued. "We found a diary your husband's been keeping. It's written in Romanian, which, as you know, is not a problem for the Bureau. The entire document has been translated. If what it says is true, Peter Anderson has had several dozen aliases, and he's hundreds of years old."

"I need a moment," she said, feeling ill. "I need a bathroom."

Jackson moved to help her up. She waved him away and pulled herself to her feet. Then she swayed out of the room and made it down the corridor to the bathroom. On her knees, she threw up. Then she tumbled against the cold metal of the stall and began to hyperventilate.

"Claire," Jackson said, opening the door and hoisting her up. He wrapped his arms around her. "They've gone to get him."

"Oh God, oh God," she murmured against his chest.

"They recruited me a month ago," he told her. "All they told me was that they thought your husband was involved in a crime, and that he was planting DNA evidence to make you look guilty. But they didn't tell me it was murder, and they sure as hell didn't tell me anything about goddamn *vampires*. If they had, I would have staked that son of a bitch first chance I got."

She hitched a breath, and he leaned his cheek against the crown of her hair. He did not kiss her. "As soon as we arrived here at FSU, and I found out what exactly was going down, I pitched holy hell. Nash and DeWitt came down on me hard. You were under surveillance before we got here, and it's been going on here, too. Hell, I've been standing outside your window at night myself, to protect you."

"You faked me out," she said accusingly, pulling out of his arms.

"I'm a hell of an FBI agent," he affirmed, stuffing his hands in his pockets. "But I'm an even better . . . friend."

"Did he kill someone tonight?" she asked. Her voice sounded as if it belonged to someone else. It sounded like someone who was about to completely lose it.

"An undercover cop has been posing as a coed at MIT," he said. "She fits the resemblance pattern of his victims, and he moved in fast. She was supposed to go over there tonight. I'm guessing he made his move, and that's why the team went out."

Anger surged through her, burning away some of the trauma. "So, what, was he building up to murdering me?"

"Escalation is consistent with what we know about serial killers," he said.

"Is it consistent with what we know about vampires?" she countered.

He held her. "I don't know, Claire. Life was simpler when it was just basters."

"I want to be there," she said. She swallowed down all her emotions except for grim determination. "For the takedown. I have to be there."

They got him.

They didn't kill him.

They dragged him out of her condo in the pouring rain. He was hissing like a rattlesnake, his fangs protruding, hands cuffed, manacles and chains around his ankles, but otherwise he looked like Peter. Handsome, not evil, not a supernatural creature. MIT, red wine, and reading, and with a little cheating on the side.

"Murderer," Claire said, keeping to the shadows beneath an eave as they fitted a hockey mask over his face and forced him into a van. The growing neighborhood crowd was being held back, prevented from seeing anything. Acting as a curtain, the rain aided and abetted. She was sick, and livid, and a tiny bit ashamed. It was because of her feelings for Jackson that he had been triggered. Triggered *this* time, Jackson had reminded her. They'd translated his entire diary. She was only one of many wives, and he had wound up murdering most of them.

"I'm sorry I had to lie to you," Jackson said.

Half an hour later, when they brought Peter into an interview room at the Boston field office, Claire insisted on standing behind the one-way mirror as Jackson and Nash interrogated him. DeWitt was with the team. Jackson had asked to be there, and Nash and DeWitt had thought it was a good idea. See if they could shake up the enraged, jealous, psychotic husband.

Peter was no longer wearing his hockey mask. Claire was alarmed. She didn't know why they'd removed it. Jackson had taken off his wet FBI raid jacket. Raindrops clung to his silvery blond hair.

Claire stood beside Lisa Shiflett, the undercover cop who had posed as Peter's winsome Thanksgiving feast. Shiflett was trying very hard to appear unfazed, but it was clear her near-miss of dying at the hands of a vampire had unnerved her.

"Crosses don't work on them," she said quietly to Claire. "At least, they didn't work on him."

Claire remembered the iron cross in the ceiling above Vampire Number Two. Peter's *father*. Maybe in the old days they had worked. When people had faith.

"Why were you planting evidence to frame your wife for murder?" Jackson asked Claire's husband as Nash looked on, seemingly oblivious to the one-way mirror where Shiflett and Claire observed. Jackson leaned across the table and glared at Peter. Peter was still cuffed, his ankles still manacled.

"I want a lawyer," Peter said to Nash. Ignoring Jackson.

"Dream on," Nash said, moving toward him. "You're not even human. You have no rights."

"Escalation is consistent with serial murder," Jackson said, still looming over the perp. "I would assume you were building up to killing Claire."

Peter—the vampire—looked up at Jackson and smiled thinly, and Shiflett caught her breath.

"I can't believe it's the same guy," she said. "He was so . . . elegant, you know. He just *charmed* me. Like in those Stookie Stackhouse books."

"Sookie," Claire said faintly, her eyes riveted on Jackson as he gazed levelly at Peter. He was too close. Being in the same room with Peter was too close.

"Maybe you were going to make it look like a suicide," Jackson continued. Knowing him as well as she did, Claire detected the tremor of fury in his voice as it crackled through the interview room speaker. "She murders all those girls out of, say, jealousy, then takes her own life."

Peter just chuckled. Then he said, "I could rip out your throat right now, if I wanted to." He looked at Nash. "Both of you. You'd be dead before you knew I'd done it."

Shiflett took an involuntary step backward, but Claire moved protectively toward the mirror.

"I don't think you can," Jackson retorted, remaining where he was. "I think that vampire super-strength thing is just a myth."

"One way to find out," Peter said, and Claire thought about her weapon. Nash and Jackson were unarmed. For obvious reasons, you didn't take guns into interview rooms. But she could shoot Peter through the mirror.

And if it came to that, she would.

"Maybe younger vampires are stronger than older vampires," Jackson said, still not backing down. Claire wanted to press the speaker button and tell him to move away. "You were pretty young when you staked your father. But it's been a few centuries since then. Since you're so old now yourself . . . maybe you don't have it anymore, Count Dracula."

Peter shifted in his chair, guilt and rage pouring off him. That was the crime he was upset about—killing his father. "My father? I don't know what you're—"

"We read your diary, scumbag," Jackson said, holding up a photograph of the cover of a plain brown leather journal.

Peter quietly stared at the picture in Jackson's hand. Claire considered that Peter's prints on it probably glowed after an application of Luminol. The thought made her tremble.

"*And* we've got custody of Daddy Dearest in the Salem crypt," Jackson said.

Peter visibly reacted, looking frightened.

"I'm so freaked out," Shiflett muttered. She looked at Claire. "Not meaning to be rude, but was anything different . . . anatomically? I mean, was there anything about *him* that struck you as odd?"

Claire shook her head. That answered one question: The cop hadn't slept with Peter. Claire was glad . . . for Shiflett's sake.

"So the stake, Peter. If we pull it out, does your dad come back to life?" Nash asked, walking toward him. Adding a little pressure.

And Claire cracked a little smile. Because the question coming as it did after the cop's question, plus Peter's name, made it a doozy of a triple entendre.

"Why should I tell you?" Peter asked.

"Because we're going to shove one into you," Jackson said. "As big as a goddamn turkey baster."

Claire snickered. Shiflett looked at her with astonishment. Claire shrugged.

"FBI humor," Claire said.

"But how can you *laugh*? You're married to him," Shiflett said. "You lived with him, and had sex with him, and all that time, he was a vampire. And he was murdering girls. Sucking out their blood."

"You don't need to remind me," Claire said. "Anyway, we hardly ever had sex."

"Good." The cop blanched. "If anything like that ever happened to me, I don't think I'd come out of it okay."

"Then you'd better not ever get married," Claire said, and this time she chuckled.

"Ha-ha," the cop said weakly. "Wow." Then, "So, you want to go out for coffee once this is done?"

"Sure, but I need to make it a quickie." Claire actually winked.

This time the cop smiled back, just a little. A little was good.

"I've already made calls," Peter said. He lifted his chin and looked straight at the mirror. "I have relatives, Claire," he said. "I have *brothers*."

"*Love* the *flaccid* posturing," Jackson said.

"Bring it, *sucker*," Claire said back at Peter, wondering if he had super hearing or eyesight. Maybe he could see her standing there. She hoped he could. "*I've* got eleven VSI agents backing me up."

And as soon as Peter was history, and forensics school was over, damn straight they were all moving to Washington, D.C., to work in the basement of the Hoover building. Laughter and all.

And somehow . . . Jackson.

The Bad Hour

THOMAS E. SNIEGOSKI

Thomas E. Sniegoski is a *New York Times* bestselling author of the young adult series The Fallen as well as the popular urban fantasy books featuring angel-turned-private-investigator Remy Chandler. *The Fallen: End of Days* is the latest in the Fallen series, and *In the House of the Wicked*, the next of the Remy Chandler books, was released in August 2012. Tom lives in Massachusetts with his long-suffering wife, LeeAnne, and their French bulldog, Kirby. Please visit him at www.sniegoski.com.

NOW

The trees bordering the winding back road bent in the breeze, forming a natural canopy that prevented the light of the nighttime heavens from reaching the road below.

Still, it seemed darker than usual in Tewksbury, Massachusetts.

"Bascomb Road should be right up ahead," Remy Chandler announced. He leaned forward in the driver's seat, peering into the night, straining to find the street sign that would signal his destination.

"Yep, here we are," he said, taking a right onto Bascomb and then a quick left into the parking lot of his client's property.

There was a shifting of weight in the shadows of the backseat, and Remy gazed into the rearview mirror to see Marlowe's dark brown eyes staring back at him.

The Labrador retriever whimpered, his eyes temporarily leaving the rearview mirror to take in his surroundings.

Remy pulled the car into a space in front of a large wooden building,

his headlights illuminating a handcrafted sign that read, KINNEY KEN-
NELS AND OBEDIENCE SCHOOL.

"You ready?" Remy asked, putting the car in park.

"*No,*" the dog answered in the language of his species, eyes once
again meeting Remy's in the mirror.

Eyes filled with the question of why it was necessary to come to such
a horrible place.

NINE HOURS AGO

Remy sat behind the desk in his Beacon Street office putting together an
expense report for a client whose job he had finished the previous week.
Marlowe snored in the grip of sleep, lying on the floor beside Remy's chair,
flat on his side with his legs stiffly outstretched as if he'd been tipped over.

It was a slow day at Chandler Investigations, which wasn't unusual,
and why Remy had decided to bring his four-legged pal to work with
him. Some paperwork, maybe a few follow-up phone calls, and then he'd
be free for the rest of the day.

Unless something unexpected came up.

Some of the more interesting examples of the unexpected he'd experienced over recent months passed through his thoughts as he double-
checked some math on the report: investigating the possibility of a demon
incursion in a Southie housing project, making sure that a cache of
Heavenly armaments didn't fall into the wrong hands, a lunch meeting
at the Four Seasons with the archangel Michael to discuss his possible
return to the Golden City, and of course there was the time that he had
to avert the Apocalypse.

Not the types of jobs usually associated with a typical private investigator, but Remy Chandler was far from typical.

Remiel, as he had been called when serving in the angelic forces of
the Lord God, was of the Heavenly host, Seraphim, a warrior angel who
had fought valiantly in the Great War against the forces of Lucifer Morningstar. It was that war that had soured Remiel to the ways of Heaven,
and he had abandoned the Kingdom of God, choosing instead to live on

the earth with the Creator's most amazing creations, losing himself amongst them for thousands of years; suppressing his angelic nature, doing everything in his power to be one of them.

To be human.

But that had proven to be far more difficult than he had expected, as things of a supernatural nature had a tendency to find him, even though he did everything in his power not to be found.

He opened his desk drawer to remove the stapler, the clattering of items in the drawer disturbing the Labrador lying ruglike at his feet.

"Why noise?" Marlowe asked in annoyance.

"I'm sorry," Remy responded, using the gift of tongues common to all those with an angelic heritage, and one that Remy didn't mind using, especially when dealing with the four-year-old black Labrador.

"Didn't mean to disturb you, Your Highness," Remy joked as he stapled the sheets together.

"Noisy," Marlowe grumbled again, then settled his head back down on the hardwood floor with a disgusted sigh.

Remy laughed as he found an envelope in another drawer, and a sheet of stamps in the drawer beside that one, making as much noise as he could to play with the puppy a bit.

"Bite you," the dog said, sitting up and glaring at him.

"You wouldn't dare," Remy warned, fighting the smile that tugged at the corners of his mouth.

The dog sprang to his feet, his thick tail wagging so furiously that Remy couldn't understand how it was that the dog didn't take flight.

"Joke," Marlowe said, shoving his large blocky head into Remy's lap, looking to have his floppy ears scratched. *"No bite—joke."*

"You're such a bad dog," Remy said, as he lovingly petted the animal.

"No bad dog," Marlowe argued.

"Oh, yes, you are," Remy said. "Only bad dogs threaten to bite their masters."

Marlowe stood on his haunches, resting his front paws on Remy's thigh so he could lick his best friend's face. *"No bite, joke!"* Marlowe barked. *"Joke! Joke! Joke!"*

The private eye laughed, trying to avoid the dog's pink, slobbering tongue.

The door into the office suddenly opened, and both Remy and Marlowe turned to see who had interrupted their play.

An older woman strode in as if she owned the place. She was tall, close to six feet, wearing a lambswool jacket and faded blue jeans. Her white hair was pulled back tightly in a long braid, her blue eyes slightly magnified behind her silver-framed glasses.

"Sounds like somebody has a bit of a discipline problem," she said with a hint of a smile, as she closed the door behind her.

Seeing a new face was all he needed. An excited Marlowe bounded happily across the office to greet what he was certain would be another best friend to add to his collection.

"Stop," the woman suddenly commanded, hand outstretched.

And Marlowe did just that, coming to a complete stop, staring up at her with large, attentive eyes.

"Sit," she said, motioning with the same hand, slowly lowering it.

And Marlowe did that too.

"It appears he has the aptitude for the basics," she said, looking to Remy, who was now coming around the side of his desk. "I'm guessing a lack of consistency in discipline might be the culprit."

"Ya think?" Remy asked, as Marlowe scurried away from the woman, to cower behind him.

"I've never met a dog that I couldn't train," she said, staring at Marlowe as if he was a challenge. Then she looked back at Remy, and started toward him, hand extended. "Jacqueline Kinney," she said.

"I'm Remy Chandler," Remy responded, taking her hand and shaking it. It was rough and callused. "What can I do for you?"

Marlowe continued to watch the woman, scooting closer to press against his leg.

"I'd like to hire you, Mr. Chandler," she said, looking around the office.

"What seems to be your problem, Ms. Kinney?"

"Jackie," she told him. "Call me Jackie."

"Okay, Jackie." He gestured for her to take the chair in front of his desk as he went around to take his own. Marlowe remained close to him, as if some strange static charge had caused him to stick. "Why don't you tell me what's wrong?"

"Thanks," she said as she lowered herself down into the seat. "For the past month or so, someone has been trying to disrupt my business, and my life."

Remy slid a notepad over in front of him and picked up a pen for writing notes.

"And why do you think that?"

She dug into the pocket of her coat and removed a folded piece of paper. "I found this in my mailbox not long before the problems started," she said, as she leaned across the desk to hand the wrinkled paper to Remy.

BEWARE THE BAD HOUR it read in capital letters, obviously written by an angry hand.

"And you have no idea who could have left this?" Remy asked.

Jackie shook her head. "I didn't even know what it meant, and thought it might be one of my staff pulling a joke."

"I'm guessing it wasn't?"

"No, they had no idea, or where it came from, and honestly, I threw it in my desk drawer and never gave it another thought—until the problems started."

"Problems?" He set the note down and picked up his pen.

"It started really as a kind of feeling . . . an uneasiness in the air, I guess, and I wasn't the only one to feel it. I run an obedience school and kennel, and the dogs staying in the kennel seemed to feel it too. They began barking and carrying on twenty-four-seven. In all my years of boarding dogs, and I've been doing this for a long time, I've never seen animals act that way. It was as if they could sense something coming."

"The Bad Hour?" Remy suggested.

"Maybe." Jackie shrugged. "Whatever that's supposed to mean."

"Has there been anything other than this strange uneasiness that you and the kennel dogs have been feeling? A physical threat, maybe?"

"The uneasiness was just the beginning," the older woman said, nodding. "It wasn't long before I started to sense a presence . . . and then it started to show me that it was there, and what it could do."

"A presence?" Remy questioned. "Do you mean like a ghost, or an evil spirit or something?"

"I wouldn't know what to call it," Jackie said. She was sitting taller in her chair, her breathing coming quicker. Whatever it was, it was clearly frightening her. "It likes to slam doors and slide furniture around in the middle of the night. I hear barking inside my bedroom, but I don't have a dog of my own."

Suddenly, Remy heard that familiar alarm bell start to go off inside his skull; the one that signaled this was likely one of those cases. The *weird shit*, as his closest friend, Boston homicide detective Steven Mulvehill, liked to call them.

"And your business? You say you run a kennel?" Remy asked as he jotted down some random thoughts.

"Kennel and obedience school," she answered proudly. "I've been in business for close to thirty years."

"And the presence is affecting that as well?"

Jackie nodded grimly. "I teach obedience classes in an old barn, but I had to cancel my summer classes because none of the puppies would go into the building."

Remy was looking at his notes, unsure exactly how to proceed.

"Ms. Kinney . . . Jackie, it's not that I'm unsympathetic to your situation, but I'm really not too sure how a private investigator would . . ."

"My father had a collection of Civil War memorabilia that I was trying to sell a couple of weeks ago. I met a gentleman who was interested in some of Dad's things, and as we were talking, I mentioned my situation to him. He said you're the best person for my problem. He said that cases like this . . . of a more unusual nature, were your specialty."

Remy frowned. "This gentleman," he said. "Did he happen to have an interest in weaponry?"

"Yes, he did," Jackie said. "He purchased some of my father's cutlasses. His name was Francis . . . I didn't get a last name. He paid cash."

Remy nodded. Francis was once the guardian angel Fraciel, until he was banished to earth after siding with the Morningstar during the War. Fraciel, now going by the earthly moniker of Francis, had seen the error of his ways, and had begged for the Almighty's forgiveness. Instead of imprisonment in the Hell prison of Tartarus, God had shown unusual mercy and had sentenced Fraciel to guard one of Hell's entrances on earth, as well as to act as one of God's own personal assassins.

The former guardian angel had a love for medieval weaponry—all weaponry, really—and often hired himself out to the highest bidder when the Almighty didn't have anybody that needed smiting, so he could afford to expand his collection.

Remy often found Francis's skills quite beneficial for some of his own more dangerous cases.

"Was Francis wrong in sending me to you, Mr. Chandler?" Jackie asked.

Remy thought for a moment. In spite of how Marlowe seemed to feel, there was something about this old dog trainer that Remy liked. And since his schedule happened to be open at the moment, he figured what the heck.

"No, that's perfectly fine," he said. "I'd be happy to take your case."

"*No, make leave,*" Marlowe said in a doggy grumble as he continued to cower beside Remy's chair.

Remy reached down to pet his dog's head and said, "Since your problem seems to focus around your property, I'll need to go there."

"Of course," Jackie agreed. She stood, ready to leave, looking relieved, as if a huge weight had been lifted. "In fact, why don't you come tonight?" she suggested. "Our first class of obedience training for new dog owners actually begins tonight. Bring your boy there, and mingle with the class while you're doing your thing."

Marlowe peeked around the corner of the desk to watch the woman leave.

"Who knows?" Jackie said with a hint of a smile. "Maybe you'll learn something."

NOW

Remy opened the back door of the car for Marlowe to get out.

The dog just sat there, looking everywhere but at him.

"Come on," Remy urged. "Let's go."

The dog lowered his head, still not looking at Remy.

"*No,*" he said with a throaty grumble. "*Not going . . . not a bad dog.*"

"I didn't say you were a bad dog," Remy said. "I just want you to get out of the car."

"Bad dogs go school," Marlowe said. *"Not bad dog. Good dog."*

"Of course you're a good dog," Remy said. "Who told you that only bad dogs go to school?"

The black Lab turned his dark brown gaze to his master's. *"You say."*

"Me?" Remy asked. "When did I ever . . ."

And then he remembered. Ever since Marlowe was a pup, Remy had been teasing the dog about his rambunctiousness, threatening to send him to obedience school if he didn't learn to behave.

"Marlowe, I was only kidding," Remy tried to explain, climbing in beside his friend.

"No kidding," the dog said, refusing to make eye contact again.

"Really, it was just a joke." Remy started to ruffle the dog's ears. "Like when you said you were going to bite me back at the office."

"Joke?" Marlowe asked, daring to look at him again.

"Just a joke," Remy soothed. "I swear . . . you are not a bad dog."

"No school?"

"Well, we still have to go in, I'm afraid," Remy explained. "We have to see what we can do about helping Jackie."

"Jackie scary," Marlowe said.

"Yeah, a little, but she still needs our help."

"Wait here?" Marlowe asked.

"No, I think you need to come in with me," Remy said. "We have to pretend we're here for school, so we can figure out who's trying to hurt Jackie's business."

"Jackie scary," Marlowe said again.

"Yes, I know she's scary, but it doesn't change the fact that she needs our help, all right?"

Marlowe didn't respond.

"So are you getting out of the car?"

The big dog sighed heavily, and stood up on the backseat.

"There's a good boy," Remy said as he got out of the car, Marlowe leaping to the ground behind him.

"We're gonna have to put this on you." Remy showed Marlowe the leash, then leaned in to attach it to his collar. "Now remember, you're going to have to help me out."

The two walked side by side toward the large barn. The sound of dogs barking from the kennel at the back of the sprawling property was carried on the night wind.

Remy stopped to listen, hearing the panic in the raised voices of the kennel dogs. Yeah, they most definitely had to do something about that.

"So I know you're a good dog, and you're very smart, but you're going to have to pretend that you're not. Do you understand?" Remy asked as they started toward the barn again.

Marlowe stopped and stared at Remy as if he were crazy.

"We're supposed to be going to classes to learn things that you already know, so you're going to need to pretend not to know them."

"Pretend stupid?" Marlowe asked.

"Exactly," Remy said. "Pretend stupid."

Several other dog owners and their pets were making their way down the path toward the barn, and Marlowe watched as they passed and went inside.

"Stupid dogs go school. Marlowe smart. Pretend stupid."

"That's it," Remy said, giving the leash a slight tug as they headed toward the barn entrance. "We have to look like everybody else so we don't stand out. Got it?"

"Got it," Marlowe answered.

They reached the door to the barn and Remy took hold of the handle, pulling it open for the dog to enter.

Marlowe sat down, staring.

"What are you doing?" Remy asked.

"Being stupid," Marlowe replied as he continued to stare at the open door.

"Okay, let's pull back a bit on the stupid and get inside," Remy said, trying to keep the annoyance out of his voice.

He could have sworn that the Labrador rolled his eyes as he passed by into the barn.

Marlowe trotted into the building with Remy close behind him.

The dog was immediately on alert as he took in his new surroundings. The smell of urine washed over his senses, and he suddenly realized how bad some of these dogs really were.

Following his nose, he glanced over to see a woman kneeling down with a handful of paper towels mopping up the floor as a white poodle stood innocently by, feigning disinterest.

"He does this when he's frightened," the middle-aged woman in the New England Patriots jacket tried to explain to Remy. "Guess it's obvious why we're here," she said with a nervous laugh.

Marlowe knew that it wasn't fear that made the dog pee inside the barn; it was the desire for his scent to be the strongest, marking his territory. He pulled Remy over toward the poodle as the woman quickly disposed of the damp towels, tossing them into a nearby plastic barrel. She kept the dog tight to her side, although he struggled to get closer to Marlowe.

"He isn't very nice," the woman said to Remy. "They say he needs to be socialized better. I hope these classes work."

"What's his name?" Marlowe heard Remy ask.

"Vincent," she replied, still holding the poodle back.

Bad dog better name, Marlowe thought as he extended his muscular neck toward the defiant poodle.

He heard Remy making small talk with the woman as he fixed the poodle in his sternest of stares. *"No pee,"* he growled at the white, curly-haired dog.

"I pee . . . mine," the poodle retorted, his entire body quivering with excitement.

"Not yours," Marlowe corrected.

"Mine!" the dog barked, straining on his leash.

With a *harrumph,* Marlowe went to the spot where the dog had just relieved himself, sniffed it, then positioned himself over the damp floor.

"Not yours," Marlowe said again, letting a quick stream of his own urine spray upon the spot.

"Marlowe!" Remy yelled in horror as he watched his dog urinate on the barn floor.

The dog looked at him with an expression that said, *What's the problem?*

"What the hell are you doing?" Remy asked, dragging him over to one of the many paper towel dispensers bolted to the walls around the barn.

"Teaching," the dog explained.

"Yeah, this one escapes me," Remy muttered softly. He pulled a handful of towels from the roll and returned to the scene of the crime.

"How were you teaching by pissing on the floor?" Remy asked him as he started to sop up the still-warm puddle.

"Said room his. . . . Not his," Marlowe explained.

"So you showed him that the room wasn't his by peeing on his pee," Remy finished.

"Yes," Marlowe barked happily.

"You know what, no more teaching, okay? Let's leave that to Jackie."

Marlowe didn't really care for that, but agreed for the sake of higher learning.

Remy tossed the wet paper towels into the barrel, and took a moment to absorb the vibe in the room. Jackie had talked about feeling a presence, something that had prevented her summer puppy classes from happening, but all he could sense at the moment was the nervous anticipation of people desperate for their dogs not to do anything embarrassing.

He watched as a large man in baggy shorts and a red hoodie was dragged by an equally large Saint Bernard to see a cream-colored French bulldog, owned by a mother and little girl, that didn't appear at all interested in the other dogs, focused instead on killing a spider that had been trying to cross the room. There was an attractive young woman with a slightly older companion whose eyes were glued to a BlackBerry. She was trying to calm a shivering German shepherd mix who seemed terrified of the other dogs. An older couple—probably retired—stood off by themselves, a howling dachshund held tightly in the woman's arms.

"How old?" asked a voice nearby, and Remy spun to face a woman with a coal black dye job, drawn-on eyebrows, and a turquoise velour sweat suit. She held a small, puffy-furred black dog protectively in her arms that silently studied him and Marlowe with deep, dark eyes. Remy didn't know what kind of dog it was, maybe a Maltese, or some kind of terrier, but it was cute in that ankle-biting kind of way.

"Excuse me?" Remy asked.

"Your dog," she said, looking down at Marlowe. "How old is he?"

"Oh, he's four," Remy replied.

Marlowe pulled on the leash, trying to get closer to the woman, as well as the dog in her arms. She backed up quickly as if afraid, holding her little dog closer to her.

"Sorry," Remy said, hauling Marlowe back. "He's perfectly harmless."

"This one isn't," the old woman said, eyes darting to her little friend, who remained perfectly calm and silent cradled in her arms.

"Bit of an attitude?" Remy asked with a smile.

"You might say that," she answered coldly.

There was silence then, and Remy tried to fill the uncomfortable moment by again looking around the barn. Nothing seemed out of the ordinary. Even extending his preternatural senses, Remy experienced nothing more than anxiety from the dog owners in attendance, and their pets.

"You shouldn't be here," the older woman said suddenly.

"Excuse me?" he asked.

"You shouldn't be here," she repeated, her expression showing as little emotion as the tiny black dog she held in her arms.

"I really don't understand what . . ."

"He's too well behaved," she added, motioning with her chin to Marlowe, who was sniffing the air, taking in all the various scents. "Maybe an advanced class would be better for him."

"Maybe," Remy said, petting his dog's head. "But I think a refresher course might do him some good."

A chorus of dog barks suddenly filled the air of the barn, and Remy glanced over to see Jackie Kinney entering through a back door, striding across the wood floor, clipboard in hand. He was amused by the air of confidence she exuded as she stopped in the center of the room, her eyes falling upon each and every person, and their dog. Like General Patton about to address his troops.

"Good evening," she said, her voice booming with authority. "First off, I'd like to thank you all for choosing the Kinney Obedience School for your dog's education, and for having the wherewithal to realize that a dog needs training if it is going to be a part of your family . . . a part of your day-to-day life."

She looked around the room again, this time only making eye contact with the dogs. Remy could have sworn that the majority averted their gazes, surrendering dominance, as her stare touched them.

"*I'm scared,*" Marlowe grumbled, as Remy gently stroked his blocky head with the tips of his fingers.

Jackie raised the clipboard. "Before we get started, I'd like to take attendance."

The trainer began to read from the list, ticking off the names of the owners and their dogs as they responded.

"Remy Chandler and Marlowe?" she called out, and before Remy could respond, Marlowe let out a booming bark to let her know that they were there.

Jackie smiled at them, checking off their names.

"Anyone whose name I didn't call?" she asked, her eyes darting around the room for people she might have missed.

"Patricia Ventura," the woman standing behind Remy called out. "Patricia Ventura and Petey."

And that was when Remy felt it. There was a sudden change in the atmosphere. The air seemed to get heavier, colder. It was obvious that the others were feeling it as well because they began to look about, talking amongst themselves. The dogs became uneasy, some beginning to whine.

"*What happening?*" Marlowe asked.

"I have no idea," Remy answered as he watched Jackie, her face wearing an expression of supreme unease. She was staring at a point somewhere behind him, at something that seemed to have frozen her in place. Remy started to turn, as the lights began to flicker, a sound like an angry hive of bees filling the room.

The barn then went completely dark and somebody cried out, the dogs all reacting in a cacophony of high-pitched yips and booming barks.

The lights momentarily returned, before they started to flicker again, and Remy saw that Jackie was gone, her clipboard lying abandoned on the floor, the door at the back of the barn swinging in the evening breeze.

The room was in chaos with dogs barking crazily, straining at their leashes, as their owners struggled to maintain control. The owners could feel it too: the presence of something unnatural. Remy watched as a few of them dragged their dogs toward the exit, and he started across the room to the swinging back door. Then he noticed that Marlowe was still by his side and he stopped.

"I want you to stay here," he told the dog, kneeling at eye level.

"Help you," Marlowe said eagerly. *"Find scary Jackie."*

"No, I need you to be a good dog and stay here," Remy replied firmly.

"Good dog?" Marlowe asked with a tilt of his head.

"Yes, a good dog will stay here and do as he's told."

He saw that Marlowe was about to argue, but then the dog sat down just inside the door.

"Good boy," Remy said, darting out into the night. "I'll be back."

The cold nighttime air felt charged, but it was the frenzied barking of multiple dogs in the distance that told Remy where to go.

He moved across the back lot, past an obstacle course of some kind, and toward a larger, single-story structure that was the kennel. The closer he got, the louder and more frantic the dogs became. Remy listened to the barks, hearing the panicked message in their cries. They all had one thing in common: they were all concerned for Jackie's safety.

He reached the back of the kennel, and saw the open door. That strange sensation still clung to the air, and he followed its trail into the building, senses on full alert.

It was even louder inside, the dogs frantically carrying on in response to what was playing out before them. Remy came around a section of cages, catching a glimpse of the woman in the blue sweat suit with the jet-black dye job, standing over the unconscious form of Jackie Kinney.

He stepped into the aisle and caught the woman's attention. A look of surprise passed across her features, before she looked back to the unconscious woman on the floor.

"Huh," she said, eyes fixed to Jackie Kinney. "Petey was right, it was you."

Remy cautiously moved closer.

The older woman looked at him from the corner of her eye. "He said that we had to do this now, or we wouldn't get the chance . . . that you were here to stop us."

He stopped moving, watching as her lipstick-covered lips twisted in a crazy smile.

"Did you see the look on her face when I said our names?" the old woman asked Remy. "Patricia Ventura and Petey." She returned her intense stare to Jackie, still lying motionless upon the ground. "It was like she'd seen a ghost."

Strangely, the dogs in the kennel stopped barking. Remy could feel their eyes upon him, as they stared out through the mesh of their cages.

"Are you Patricia Ventura?" he asked her.

She nodded. "I am."

Something moved in the shadows by the floor, and Remy watched as the tiny black dog approached Jackie's body, its small shape suddenly shifting and blending, seeming to absorb the shadows around it, transforming into something monstrous that reached down with a black, clawed hand to the unconscious dog trainer, hauling her up from the floor.

"And this is Petey," Patricia said.

Remy lunged toward the creature that seemed to be composed entirely of shadow. As much as he hated to do it, he tapped into the nature that resided deep within, drawing upon the power of Heaven at the core of his being, coaxing the Seraphim forward to help him deal with the fearsome threat he was about to confront.

Through a warrior's eyes, Remy watched as the creature called Petey reacted, its movements quicksilver fast. Jackie's body was cast aside, and Petey came at him, immersing him in the darkness of its mass.

The black of the beast seeped through his clothes, and into his flesh, permeating his very soul, and Remy felt an anger—*a rage*—that threatened to overwhelm him, and to unleash the full fury of the angelic essence that was held in check within the human guise that he wore.

An angelic essence that, if roused to anger, could burn the world to a cinder.

Marlowe was a good dog, he really was, but still he stood at the open door, tempted to go farther. The Labrador lifted his snout and sniffed at the air. His Remy was there on the wind, but there was something else as well.

Something that made the hackles of black fur around his thick neck stand on end, something that could only mean that his Remy might need him.

Marlowe started to go forward, but heard his master's words again warning him to stay where he was. If he was a good dog he would do what his Remy asked of him.

He hesitated momentarily, not wanting to be bad, but could not help himself.

Remy had dropped to his knees, arms wrapped tightly around himself as he tried to keep the destructive potential of his angelic nature inside.

It was so angry right now; it wanted to come out. . . . It wanted to come out and burn the world and everybody on it. And then it wanted to move on to Heaven.

"I call it Petey," the old woman said. She was wringing her hands, old eyes fixed to the living shadow as it expanded and contracted in the air beside her. "But I know it isn't really him."

Jackie Kinney was starting to come around, her moans just a precursor to the horrors to come, Remy was sure. He had to get control of himself, to push the power of the Seraphim back down deep inside himself where it couldn't do any harm before he could help her.

But it was just so damned angry.

"I think it was the grief that called it," Patricia began to explain. "My grandfather from the old country called it the Bad Hour . . . some kind of spirit or demon or whatever, that came when the anger . . . when the grief was just too strong to control."

Through burning eyes Remy watched the living shadow churn and shift its form to that of the little black dog again, before transforming back to its more monstrous shape. It then surged down to the woman moaning on the ground and snatched her up, holding her body aloft in the grip of shadow.

The kennel dogs had started to react again, snarling and baring their teeth through the screened doors of their kennels. It was apparent that they too had been touched by the anger exuded by the black beast . . . the thing called the Bad Hour.

"It was her that did it," Patricia accused, eyes fixed to Jackie hanging in the air in front of her. "She was responsible for all of this."

The living shadow let out a fearsome growl, shaking the dog trainer's body like a rag doll. Jackie moaned in both pain and mortal terror.

"How?" Remy managed, still fighting to keep his more volatile nature in check. He needed to know what this was all about. Maybe in knowing he would find a way to defeat the beast, as well as the anger that crippled him.

"I trusted her," Patricia said with a quiver of rage in her voice. "I trusted her with my Petey and she killed him."

The old woman was crying now, and the shadow thing—this Bad Hour—extended a tendril of darkness to her, tenderly stroking her face, as if savoring her tears and sadness.

"My mother was dying, and I had to go to her, to be with her. . . . I knew that it wouldn't be long, that I was going to say good-bye to her. She was the last of my family, my brother and sister had been gone for nearly two years. . . . We were all that was left, Momma and me . . . and Petey."

The little dog appeared briefly in the mass of shadow again.

"I'd never had children, so Petey was my child . . . my baby." She was wringing her hands faster now, more violently, as if trying rub them clean of some stubborn stain.

"Momma was in the hospital and I knew that Petey wouldn't be allowed there. . . . I needed a place for him to stay, where somebody would take care of him until I got back."

Patricia clenched her fists and strode toward Jackie hanging in the air, to confront the trainer.

"This woman . . . this cold-hearted bitch promised to take care of my baby, swore to me that she'd look after him . . . and she lied."

Remy saw that Jackie's eyes were now open, a tentacle of darkness wrapped tightly around her throat.

"No," Jackie managed, her voice nothing more than a tortured whisper. "It . . . It was . . . accident."

Patricia shook her fists at the woman. "Don't you dare say that," she hissed, the flush of her cheeks showing through the heavy makeup. "Don't you dare!"

The Bad Hour flowed tighter about Jackie, bending her limbs in impossible ways, threatening to break her into pieces.

"I trusted you," Patricia shrieked. "I trusted you and you killed my Petey."

Jackie struggled pathetically in the grip of nightmare.

"So . . . sorry . . ."

"No," Patricia bellowed, turning her gaze from the woman. "It's too late for that. . . . You did what you did and you have to pay. . . . I have to pay."

The older woman seemed to grow smaller, collapsing in upon herself.

The Bad Hour reached out again with one of its limbs of shadow, touching the woman as if lending her some of its strength, feeding her anger.

"I know the story she told, I've heard it over and over again inside my head, but it doesn't matter one little bit." Patricia studied the trainer hanging helplessly before her. "You weren't looking out for him. . . . You weren't being careful, and you let him get out of his crate, and he was so scared. . . ."

Patricia became overcome with emotion, choking back her tears as she again recollected what had led them all to this.

"He . . . He was probably looking for me . . . wondering where I had gone . . . why I had left him in this . . . place. . . ." She dropped to her knees, weak from grief. "So scared that he didn't even think of the road outside . . . of the cars. . . ."

Patricia stared at her balled fists; they were trembling with fury.

"You told me that he was dead when you found him, that the car that struck him hadn't even stopped. . . ."

She looked at Remy then, and he saw in her eyes the depths of her sadness, of a grief so strong that a monster such as the Bad Hour could have feasted upon it for centuries.

"Can you imagine hearing that?" she asked him. "Hearing that about your baby?"

Remy couldn't imagine it, and the Seraphim fought harder, surging to escape the prison of flesh, blood, muscle, and bone that had kept it locked away for centuries.

The Bad Hour was growing, feeding off all the emotion in the room. This was its power, to feed upon the anger, to use it to grow its strength. There was no wonder why it hadn't yet dealt with Jackie, Patricia's emotions still so very raw . . . so strong.

So delicious.

"I tried to get past it, but I couldn't. . . . I kept imagining him there, lying in the road, wondering why I had left him as he died." She was sobbing now, the grief completely overwhelming her as it had continued to do since Petey's death.

And the Bad Hour grew stronger, taking the little form of Petey, stoking the fires of her grief.

Patricia suddenly went quiet, wiping the tears from her face as she carefully rose from her knees.

"And now we've come to this," she said, seeming more in control. "At first I was afraid . . . scared of what I had called up. . . . I tried to warn you with a note that it was coming, so that you could prepare. . . . I think I did it more for myself, hoping that it might satisfy my anger, my hunger for revenge if you knew something was coming . . . but it did the opposite and made me want to see you suffer all the more."

Patricia stared at her adversary, with dark, cold eyes. There was a piece of the Bad Hour behind those eyes, of that Remy had no doubt.

"How should we do this?" the woman then asked. "How do I make you pay for your sins? Do I let Petey drag you out into the street so that you can be hit by a car and die there alone . . . or do I let it just rip you apart while I watch?"

The Bad Hour seethed, writhing in anticipation, feeding off the woman's escalating fury. This was what it had been waiting for, and though it had savored her tears and rage, this was what it was all about.

The coup de grace.

Remy felt as if his skin were on fire, the Seraphim bubbling just below the surface. The Bad Hour's influence was still upon him, but he had to try to stop this . . . to halt what was about to happen.

"And if you do this," Remy asked, still managing to hold on to the leash that kept the power of Heaven inside him in check. "If you toss her in the street to be hit . . . or rip her apart . . . what then?"

Patricia seemed confused by the question, the darkness in her eyes temporarily fleeing. "She'll have paid for what she did to my baby . . . to me."

"But then what?" Remy asked. "Petey will still be gone. . . . The grief will still be as real."

The Bad Hour did not like what he was saying. A mass of solidified shadow whipped out from its boiling mass to strike him savagely to the floor. It took all that Remy had to maintain his grip upon his divine nature, to retain his humanity in the moment.

"You'll still have to deal with the guilt that you're carrying," he told her, lifting his face to look at her.

The old woman seemed startled.

"My guilt?" she asked incredulously. "Why would I have any guilt? It was she who . . ."

"You left your baby," Remy said, rising, hoping to weaken the Bad Hour's hold upon her, to redirect some of that anguish and rage upon her.

"I had no choice!" Patricia bleated, the tears starting to flow again. "My mother was dying and I couldn't . . ."

"Your mother was your major concern," Remy said, regaining a slight bit of control over the angelic essence roused to anger by the demonic spirit. "Petey had to come second."

"But I loved him," the woman sobbed.

"I never said that you didn't," Remy told her. "But a decision had to be made, and you made it."

"I couldn't take him with me. . . . I was staying at the hospital just in case . . . for when the time came," Patricia said, remembering.

"You made a decision to have somebody else care for Petey," Remy said, driving the point home.

"She had excellent references," Patricia said. "I even called some of the people to ask about how their dogs were treated."

"You did everything you could to be sure that Petey would be cared for," Remy said.

"I did."

"But something happened," Remy stressed. "Something horrible."

"She killed him!" Patricia screamed, and the miasma of darkness that was the Bad Hour seemed to grow even larger, starting to engulf the still struggling Jackie Kinney as she was hanging in the air. The dog trainer fought against the living shadow as it attempted to flow into her mouth and nose.

The dogs were on the brink of madness now, throwing themselves against their cages.

"No, it was an accident," Remy bellowed above the din, trying to keep his own emotions in check so as not to rouse the angelic fury within himself.

"She was responsible for my baby . . . for his life, and now he's gone because of her!"

"And that's all true," Remy said. "But it doesn't mean that she did anything on purpose. Yes, she's responsible, but she didn't kill Petey. You're as guilty of his death as she is."

Patricia looked to the living mass of darkness that had practically enveloped all of Jackie Kinney, the look upon her face telling him that perhaps his words had managed to permeate through the thick cover of anguish, and sadness.

The cloud of black receded, and Jackie began to cough uncontrollably as she was able to breathe again.

"You're right," Patricia said, as the Bad Hour angrily tossed the trainer to the floor. The living shadow began to transform, taking the shape of the little black dog, lying upon the ground, its limbs twisted and broken as if having just suffered some major trauma—as if struck by a car.

"No," Patricia screamed at the sight, trying to look away, and as she turned her head, the dog began to pathetically cry out, and Remy could understand the words and emotions being conveyed.

As could the old woman.

She killed me, said the Bad Hour, using the form of Petey as its mouthpiece. *If it wasn't for her I'd still be alive. . . . You would still have me to love. . . .*

The words were burrowing their way inside her, rekindling the fire that Remy thought he'd begun to extinguish.

Jackie had managed to struggle to her knees and Remy found himself crawling over to the woman, blocking her from the next assault that was about to occur.

"Leave her alone," Remy roared, as some of his Heavenly might slipped from his control. The kennel was suddenly filled with an unearthly glow, and wings of golden fire erupted from his back, expanding to fan the growing darkness away from them with their Divine brilliance.

The Bad Hour lost its little dog shape, returning to that of living darkness. And just as it flowed toward them, about to encroach upon the barrier of Divine light that had been placed between it and its prey, there was a flurry of movement, and Remy saw Marlowe bounding to his aid.

Both the Bad Hour and Patricia reacted to the dog's sudden appearance, recoiling from his frantic barking.

The Labrador charged at the Bad Hour, with not even the slightest hint of hesitation, his jaws snapping at the living shadow, attempting to bite the thing that was threatening his master.

"Marlowe, no!" Remy said, torn between leaving Jackie and going to his best friend's side.

The living darkness swatted at the attacking beast, knocking Marlowe across the room where he landed upon his side. The Bad Hour surged at the Labrador, and Remy tensed to leap into the fray to prevent his dog from being harmed, when he heard another voice.

"Stop this," Patricia commanded, a sudden strength in her voice that had not been evident before.

Marlowe jumped to his feet, moving back toward the kennel cages, the dogs within them still carrying on. The Bad Hour hung above him like a frozen wave of oil, its master's command halting it in mid-attack.

The demonic entity spun angrily in the air, turning its fluid mass to confront the old woman.

"No more," she said with a shake of her head. "This is done now. . . . We're not going to hurt anybody else."

The Bad Hour again transformed itself into the injured Petey, but Patricia looked away.

"Don't show me that anymore," she said. "Petey is gone, and as much as that hurts me to admit, nothing's going to bring him back."

The Bad Hour did not care to hear this, swirling around the older woman, trying to get her to look at it, trying to get her to reconsider her words.

But Patricia refused.

"I'm done with this," she said. "Done with feeling this way . . . done with all the violence that my pain has caused. . . ."

The Bad Hour's roar was deafening as it gripped the old woman in hands crafted in shadow.

"I'm done with you," she said, looking into the bottomless hollows of its empty eyes.

Something seemed to pass between them, a conversation not meant for anyone else.

"I know there's a price to pay," the old woman said, still looking into its churning face. "I knew that when I called you to me, and it was a price I was willing to pay.

"And one that I'm still ready to pay to send you back to the Hell that I summoned you from."

The Bad Hour roared once again, feeding upon the anger exuded by the older woman that had caused it to grow larger, and larger still. It held her in its nightmarish grasp as a terrible mouth formed upon its indistinct shape and it lowered itself down onto her, swallowing her up in one tremendous bite.

The thing of darkness hovered there above the kennel floor, digesting its latest meal.

Remy watched the shapeless thing, curious as to whether or not its hunger had been sated. The demon surged toward him with a thunderous growl, and a rush of air, but Remy stood his ground, still managing to keep the angelic power inside him under control.

The Bad Hour kept its distance, as if the glow of Heavenly fire radiating from Remy made it reconsider what it might do.

Then the revenge-fueled beast suddenly turned its amorphous head to one side, and with a sound akin to a chuckling laugh, the undulating mass of darkness seemed to collapse in upon itself until only the tiniest dot of the deepest black remained.

And that was soon gone as well.

Confident that he could now control it completely, Remy pulled back upon his angelic nature, quickly returning to his human guise, and checked on the health of the dog trainer. Her pulse was steady, and she didn't appear to be physically injured in any way, but she moaned in the grip of delirium, repeating the words *I'm sorry* over and over again.

The dogs in the kennel had ceased their barking, as if sensing that the danger had passed, and Remy turned to see Marlowe cowering in the corner by the open back door as if preparing to flee.

"What are you doing?" he asked.

"Bad dog," Marlowe said, hanging his head in shame.

"Why are you a bad dog?"

"Not listen," Marlowe said. *"Remy told Marlowe to stay . . . good dogs stay."*

Remy smiled, raising his hand to motion the dog to come to him.

"You're not a bad dog," Remy told the Labrador as he came, muscular tail wagging crazily. "You're a very good dog."

"No more school?" the dog asked.

"No more school," Remy repeated with a laugh, the dog lovingly licking at his face and ears.

As only a good dog could.

Pirate Dave and the Captain's Ghost

TONI L. P. KELNER

Toni L. P. Kelner coedits urban fantasy anthologies with Charlaine Harris—including the one in your hands right now. She is also the author of the "Where are they now?" mysteries and the Laura Fleming mysteries. Kelner was awarded a Romantic Times Career Achievement Award for the Laura Fleming series, and an Agatha for Best Short Story. She's also been nominated for the Anthony, the Macavity, and the Derringer awards. You can find more of her bragging on Facebook, on Twitter, and at www.tonilpkelner.com. "Pirate Dave and the Captain's Ghost," her contribution to this anthology, is the second short story featuring Joyce and her beau, Pirate Dave. "Pirate Dave's Haunted Amusement Park" was published in the Harris/Kelner anthology *Death's Excellent Vacation*.

"Hello?" I said into my phone. "Is that Pirate Dave, the hottest vampire to ever sail the seven seas?"

"Arrrr!" he growled in reply, which was a lot sexier than you might think. Or maybe growls are just more appealing to werewolves.

We indulged in a few moments of witty banter, then David said, "Not that I'm not delighted to hear your voice, Joyce, but I thought the full-moon run was tonight."

"I went out for a while but the weather isn't that great." Before he could remember that the chance to run with other werewolves had been the part of the seminar I'd most been looking forward to, I said, "Have you looked over that list of ideas for the park?"

Our home and business was Pirate Dave's Adventure Cove, an amusement park in Bartholomew Lake, New Hampshire. I adored the place, but it needed major updating to bring in more business. With the park closed for the winter, David and I had had plenty of time to discuss options. Unfortunately, those discussions could be awfully loud— fortunately, the makeup sex was worth it.

"I'm not docking the *Brazen Mermaid*," he said flatly.

"Look at the numbers. When you add up insurance, maintenance, and operation costs, and compare that to how many guests actually ride—"

"How can we have a Pirate Dave without a *Brazen Mermaid*? It's the park centerpiece. It's on our logo!"

I sighed. "Fine. But check out my other ideas, okay?"

"I will. Tell me, how have you been getting along with the other wolves?"

"Good. Great. Making lots of friends. And today I found out how I became a werewolf."

"Didn't we already know that? You were bitten."

"Yes, but it turns out that only people with were blood can Change after being bitten. Vanilla humans aren't affected. Well, other than blood loss, scarring, and a newfound fear of canines, of course. But if the bitee has enough werewolf in the family tree, his or her body will try to Change at the next full moon." I didn't mention what happened if the person didn't have enough were blood—the slideshow had been pretty gruesome.

"Then you have werewolf kin?"

"I guess so. I should find out where it came from." My parents were dead, but there was a family Bible and other records.

David paused just long enough to be significant before asking, "Would finding your ancestry link you to a pack?"

"God, no! I'm still footloose and fancy-free."

"Ahem."

"From the werewolf perspective, that is. No pack affiliation."

"And nobody has been bothering you about that?"

"No, they're all on their best behavior. With representatives from so many packs, they kind of have to be. Anyway, I haven't had a problem with a single wolf."

"You're sure?"

"Absolutely. But I need to get going. There's going to be a midnight buffet—"

"It's only eight."

"But sometimes they run out of food." With werewolf metabolisms, especially when said werewolves had been on a run, that was definitely a possibility.

We exchanged mushy words, then I hung up with only the slightest twinge of guilt. I hadn't exactly lied to David—the other werewolves really had started out friendly. It was the ghost of Captain Bob who didn't like me, and it was only a matter of time before he found my cabin so he could haunt me some more.

The week had started out well, despite my initial qualms. Though I'd been a werewolf less than a year, I was already making waves in the Lupine-American community: I'd survived a bite, which was unusual; I'd refused to affiliate with a pack, which was unheard of; and I was living in glorious sin with a vampire, which was appalling. Given that, it hadn't been easy to meet other werewolves.

And as much as I loved my red-hot, red-headed lover, I did occasionally want somebody else to talk to. Sure, I had human buds back in Boston, but there were so many things I couldn't discuss with them that it was hard to keep a real relationship going. Plus I'd nearly starved when I tried to go out to brunch with some girlfriends—even at an all-you-can-eat place, they'd eaten next to nothing.

So when I got the letter inviting me to the Talbot Seminar, I didn't hesitate. The annual weeklong event was sponsored by the Pack Council to help interpack relations and share what they called "wolfen wisdom," so all packs were asked to send representatives. It had been decided that I was a pack of one, so I was representing myself. The politics didn't interest me. What did was the chance to meet other werewolves, go on runs, eat without worrying about how my appetite looked to normals, and learn more about the supernatural world in which I'd found myself. Plus it was only a two-hour drive away, in Pine Tree, Vermont.

The venue was the Cahill Resort, an isolated, werewolf-owned operation. There was a big main building that held all the public spaces, and guest cabins nestled in the woods. The decor was big on logs and faux rustic accents. I had a cabin to myself, but didn't plan to spend much time in it. I'd come to socialize. And at first, the seminar was everything I'd hoped it would be.

Sure, there was some curiosity from the other wolves, but it wasn't overly rude. I didn't mind talking about David, and when I pointed out the advantages of dating a man who'd spent centuries perfecting his techniques, some of the other wolves looked intrigued.

With that out of the way, we wolves compared notes, gossiped, and ate massive amounts openly. It was great. At least it was until the second day, when Dr. Angie Hogencamp took the stage in the auditorium.

Her program bio described her as a supernatural researcher, though I didn't know if that meant she researched supernatural creatures, conducted research by supernatural means, or both. The first presentation was the aforementioned discussion on why some biting victims became werewolves and some didn't, which was interesting, and the nasty slideshow didn't stop us from enjoying a hefty mid-morning snack.

Then Dr. Hogencamp took the stage again for the second session. "We have a very special guest today. Captain Robert Antonelli, a former ferryboat captain from my hometown, is going to talk about his experiences."

She stepped back from the podium and waved her hand, inviting the speaker to come forward. At first I thought the man had walked through an entrance in the back wall I hadn't seen, but no, he'd walked *through* the wall. In fact, I could see the wall through him—he was translucent.

"Jesus," I heard somebody behind me say. "It's a ghost."

I tried to look blasé, as if I encountered ghosts all the time, but the fact was I hadn't even known there were ghosts. I was too new to the werewolf world to know which other supernatural denizens actually existed.

The ghost was tall, though hunched with age, with a weatherworn face and a bit of a potbelly. Though the nautical cap on his scraggly gray hair could have been from any age, his khakis and polo shirt were modern, so I guessed he hadn't been dead that long.

"You can call me Captain Bob," the ghost said, his voice surprisingly normal. He surveyed us as if looking over a particularly unimpressive batch of naval recruits. "The doc here invited me to come tell you what it means to be a dead man walking. Or floating." He slowly lifted from the floor until the tips of his deck shoes were at the height of the microphone.

When he was satisfied he'd caused enough of a stir, he settled back down again on the floor of the platform and went on to describe his life after death, or maybe *instead* of death.

Ghostly abilities were pretty much as advertised: floating, walking through walls, making unearthly noises, appearing and disappearing. Some ghosts were big on haunting, ranging from being tied to a location but able to interact with people to just replaying a moment in time. Captain Bob seemed disdainful of what he called anchored spirits—he said he went wherever he wanted and could even appear however he wanted, as long as it was a look he'd had in life. He demonstrated by changing shirts and pants. On the other side of the spectrum, he seemed embarrassed to admit that he couldn't affect the physical world the way some ghosts could—I had a hunch he would have enjoyed playing poltergeist-y tricks.

After he covered the basics, he invited questions, the first of which was from wolves afraid they were being secretly spied on by ghosts. Captain Bob leered a bit for form's sake, but pointed out that werewolves could see ghosts and that there weren't many free-range ghosts around.

Then came the question that caused me so much trouble. Shannon, a gal who liked the same TV shows that I did, said, "Can you tell us how you died?" I'd been wondering the same thing, but thought it might be impolite to ask—supernatural life has situations that aren't discussed by Miss Manners.

Captain Bob said, "I'm happy to tell you—I want to put it out as a warning."

The ghost's appearance shifted, and instead of a normal see-through man, he looked like something out of a splatterpunk flick. His throat was so thoroughly savaged that his head was barely attached, and gore drenched his clothes. Only the lack of scent kept the auditorium full of werewolves from reacting to that much blood.

Captain Bob spoke, which just seemed wrong given the horrible damage. "This is how I looked just before I died. If you don't remember anything else about this session, I want you to remember that this is what a vampire does to people."

I froze, and I could tell most of the eyes in the auditorium were on me.

Being dead didn't mean that Captain Bob couldn't sense awkwardness, and when he looked at Dr. Hogencamp for an explanation, she whispered something in his ear. "For the love of God, what kind of woman would live with a vampire?" he demanded.

"That would be me," I said.

The people to either side shrank away as Captain Bob wafted in my direction, his head bobbling along. I wouldn't have expected werewolves to be so squeamish.

"Are you insane?" he asked.

"Is that a rhetorical question? Because if I were, I probably wouldn't know it."

"Then why are you living with a monster?"

"I'm a werewolf and you're a ghost. It's pretty much monster central casting around here."

"There's monsters, and then there's monsters," he said, as if that meant something. "How long do you think it'll be before that bloodsucker does something like this to you?"

What was I supposed to say? A week from next Friday? "I've already been bitten almost that badly."

"You see? Vampires are killers!"

"Oh, it wasn't a vampire who bit me. It was a werewolf." The wolves around me suddenly found other places to look, and in retrospect, I realized it probably wasn't the smartest thing to bring up. It wasn't as if the other werewolves didn't know that I'd been mauled by a rogue, but they didn't like to have their noses rubbed in the fact. It embarrassed them.

I don't know what stupid thing I'd have said next if Dr. Hogencamp hadn't come fluttering down the aisle. "Captain Bob, please come back to the platform." She was waving her arms as if she could blow him in the direction she wanted him to go. He seemed completely unaffected, but did go with her, though not without turning to glower at me.

Unsurprisingly, there were no further questions, so we broke for lunch.

I didn't enjoy my food. Nobody spoke to me while I was in the buffet line, even though I was right behind a woman I'd traded iPhone apps with over breakfast, and when I went looking for a table, every chair was suddenly filled or saved for somebody else.

Eventually I found an empty table, and sat to choke down my lunch. Had I been human, I probably would have lost my appetite, but shunned or not, I was still a werewolf. Nonetheless, I only toyed with my second dessert, and looked up happily when I noticed somebody was standing next to me. The pleasure didn't last long. It was that damned ghost. At least he'd changed back to his non-gross form.

"Fattening yourself up for the vampire?" he asked.

"Who are you calling fat, tubby?"

He sucked in his gut or performed some sort of ectoplasmic trick to make it look as if he had. "I want to talk to you."

Since nobody else was lining up to chat, I said, "Pull up a seat."

He glared at me.

"Sorry." I pulled a chair out for him, and he floated into it as if actually sitting.

"Listen," he said, "maybe I came on too strong before, but you don't know what you're dealing with. Vampires are vicious killing machines."

"And how many vampires have you met?"

"I've never *met* any, unless you count being murdered as a social event."

"People get murdered every day, and nobody blames all humans. So is it too bizarre to accept that some vampires are nice?"

"How many vampires have *you* met?"

"Just one," I admitted.

"And that makes you an expert?"

"I don't claim to be, unlike some people." I got up, and when Captain Bob followed me, I said, "What are you doing?"

"Sticking around until I can talk some sense into you." He grinned. "Call it a haunting."

The day could not get any better. "Do you mind if I go to the little werewolves' room by myself?"

"Go ahead—I'll wait."

And he did. When I came out of the restroom, he followed me to the auditorium and sat down in the empty chair next to mine. Since nobody had taught exorcism, I knew of no way to get rid of a ghost and had to settle for ignoring him.

The afternoon session was a lot drier than the morning ones. Apparently Dr. Hogencamp and her late husband had researched all kinds of supernatural bloodlines, not just werewolves, and had investigated whether witches' power was inherited and why some people became ghosts after death. Their conclusion was that supernaturals had something extra in their genetic makeup, which she referred to as the "arcane gene."

She got more technical after that, talking recessives and dominants and trauma-induced phantomization, which apparently meant that a person who died horrifically had a better chance of becoming a ghost. After the first hour, I zoned out and started playing solitaire on my iPad. Only I couldn't even enjoy that because Captain Bob kept pointing to cards to show me what I should play. Nor could I doze off because every time I shut my eyes, the ghost noisily cleared his throat, which both woke me up and left me wondering what he had in his throat to clear.

Finally the session ended, and we went to dinner. It was just a quick bite because it was the night of the full moon. Unlike in the movies, werewolves can Change anytime, and into any number of forms. I personally can't manage anything that isn't canine, but before I'd become lupine non grata, I'd heard a funny story about a kid who Changed into a reindeer. Technically, we don't even have to Change on the full moon, except the first time. But it is traditional, so the seminar's activities included a fun run through the resort's extensive grounds.

After a cozy dinner alone with Captain Bob, I ducked into the bathroom, waited until the ghost was momentarily distracted, then snuck off to my cabin to Change. I usually run as a dog to avoid arousing fear, loathing, and wildlife control officers, but this time I went with a classic wolf. It's good for all seasons, it's slimming, and I'd be able to blend in with the other wolves.

That was the plan, anyway. Except that when I joined the wolves frolicking on the front lawn, it took about three minutes for the captain to figure out which wolf was me—I wasn't sure if it was a ghostly talent or if another wolf squealed. Either way, as soon as he latched on to me, the other wolves found other places to be.

I ran into the forest as fast as I could, but Captain Bob had no problem keeping up, and when I ducked between trees and through underbrush, he went through it all as if it weren't there. Or as if he weren't there. Basically he sucked the fun out of the run, so after a frustrating hour, I decided it was time to give up.

Since the last thing I wanted was to lead him to my cabin, I doubled back twice and shifted forms three times to be reasonably sure I was safe. Once I was again among the two-legged and dressed I called David, and tried to convince both of us that I was having a good time.

After I hung up the phone, I tried to decide if I should go to bed and skip the buffet, go to the buffet and eat so much food that there wouldn't be enough to go around, or just pack up and go home. I hadn't made up my mind when there was a knock on the door. At first I was afraid it was Captain Bob, but I then remembered that he couldn't touch anything and opened the door to find Dr. Hogencamp.

"Hi."

"Joyce, isn't it? I don't know if you remember me from today's presentations, but—"

"It's not a session I'm likely to forget."

"I suppose not. If you don't mind, I'd like to talk to you."

"Sure, come on in."

This was the closest I'd been to the woman. She had a sturdy build and tight gray curls, and she was wearing glasses, which was unusual for a werewolf. The Change cleaned up a lot of health issues, which is part of why we live so much longer than humans. Now that I noticed it, she didn't smell like a werewolf, either.

"Dr. Hogencamp—"

"Call me Angie."

"I'm probably being inexcusably rude, Angie, but I don't know the proper way to ask this. What are you?"

"Just human."

"Isn't that against the rules?" One of the first things that had been impressed upon me when I was Changed was the importance of keeping the existence of werewolves secret. American society was still coming to terms with gays and lesbians—throwing werewolves into the mix would have been a bad idea.

"I'm in a unique position. My husband, Carl, and I were bitten by a rogue, just as you were, and the local pack found us and told us about werewolves and the other supernatural beings. But only Carl Changed. We didn't understand why and that led us to discover the arcane gene. We found that Carl had an incomplete penetrant."

"That sounds painful."

"An incomplete penetrant of the arcane gene. He barely survived the Change."

"What about you?"

"I don't have the gene at all. Still, I can continue the research, even now that Carl has passed away."

I wasn't sure how long he'd been gone, so didn't know if I should express sympathy or not, so I went with a noncommittal nod.

"I imagine you noticed that in my discussion of the arcane gene, I didn't mention vampires."

I hadn't, actually—I'd been too busy wondering if I could use an electric fan to try to blow Captain Bob away.

"The fact is," Angie said, "I don't know much about vampires. Nobody does, except presumably other vampires."

"You could ask Captain Bob. He seems to know it all."

"I'm sorry about that. I had no idea he would take your living arrangements so personally." She did look honestly embarrassed. "I consider your relationship with a vampire a valuable opportunity. I've studied werewolves, and have spent considerable time with witches and ghosts, but I've been unable to make any kind of connection with a vampire. I was wondering if you could tell me about your experiences."

"I guess. What do you want to know?"

"I'm most interested in reproduction."

"When a Mama vampire loves a Daddy vampire very much . . ."

Angie blinked.

"Just kidding," I said. "I assume you mean how to create another vampire, not vampire sex."

Again she blinked. Apparently she was also missing the sense of humor gene.

"Basically, the vampire drains the human almost to death before allowing the human to suck on him. His blood, that is. The human then dies, but after three days, rises as a baby vampire."

"Very much according to legend," Angie said. "Do you mind if I take notes?"

When I shook my head, she pulled paper and pen out of her shoulder bag and scribbled intently. "How does the vampire choose the human who will become his offspring?"

"I really couldn't say. The relationship is pretty intense, like a marriage or a parent-child relationship. Even when they go their separate ways, there's always a connection."

"I assume the human has to have the arcane gene."

"I don't know. From what David has said, vampires can bring over anybody they choose. He thought it was odd that werewolves can't."

"But surely the gene is required," Angie said, more to herself than to me. "What about the vampire's nutritional needs? How often does he need to feed? How does he approach his food sources?"

That was the start of a supremely aggravating hour. Angie wanted to know how much David drank at a sitting, whether he preferred a given blood type, how long he slept, whether he was affected by silver, if garlic bothered him, if he could see himself in mirrors . . . All the old vampire tropes and a bunch that were just silly. Sparkles? Really?

The worst part was that I didn't know half of what she wanted to know. David and I had never focused on our biological details, other than recreational ones.

Finally Angie shut her notebook, clearly not satisfied. "I really need to talk to a vampire myself. Could you ask your boyfriend if he'd meet with me? Do you two live nearby? I could go home with you after the seminar."

"I'll ask, but I can't guarantee anything. He's a private kind of guy."

"This is for science!"

Since David predated most of what we knew about science, I really didn't think that would be a compelling argument to use on him.

There was another knock on the door, and I jumped again. "Ghosts don't knock, right?"

"Captain Bob can't," Angie assured me.

"Excellent." I pulled open the door and there stood the best-looking man I've ever seen. Tall, incredibly well-built, piercing blue eyes, with gorgeous red hair pulled back in a short ponytail. In other words, it was Pirate Dave, and there was only one appropriate way to greet him.

"What in the hell are you doing here? I wasn't even supposed to tell anybody where it is because it's only for werewolves. And Captain Bob and Angie, but they're invited! I am going to get in so much trouble."

In response, he took me in his arms and made me forget the seminar for a good five minutes. A very good five minutes. We might have gone for half an hour if Angie hadn't cleared her throat.

"Oh, sorry." I waved David inside the cabin and said, "David, this is Dr. Angie Hogencamp. She's been researching supernaturals, and spoke at the seminar early today. Angie, this is David Freeman, the owner of Pirate Dave's Adventure Cove."

"Dr. Hogencamp," David said, bowing over her hand.

"I cannot tell you what a treat this is," she said, blushing. "Joyce has been telling me all about you."

He raised an eyebrow in my direction.

"She's only interested in your genes," I told him. "Not the pants, the genetic kind."

"I have so many questions," Angie said. "Do you suppose—"

"Another time, perhaps. I'm here to take Joyce home, and since we need to be back before dawn, we should leave right away."

"Oh, you can't leave now!"

"As Joyce pointed out, I wasn't invited. Even if I had been, I wouldn't stay at a gathering where she'd been made to feel unwelcome."

"I never said I felt unwelcome," I protested.

"You didn't need to," he replied.

Angie said, "I know there have been some problems, but please, let me talk to the Council. I'll convince them to let you stay, and to make sure the other wolves mind their manners."

"What about Captain Bob?" I asked.

"I'll talk to him, too. I'll fix everything. Please, don't leave!" She nearly ran out of the cabin.

"Do you want to stay?" David asked me.

"I'm not sure. I really was having fun at first, but then Captain Bob showed up, and—"

"Who is Captain Bob?"

"That's going to take some explaining." I'd just finished when Angie showed up at the door again, beaming.

"It's all arranged. The Council invites you to join them in the dining hall so they can introduce you as an honored guest."

David lifted his eyebrow again, which meant it was up to me. I was torn between wanting to make a dramatic exit and wanting to make friends. Remembering the boring days I'd spent alone while David slept decided me. "We'd love to come."

I took a few minutes to change into something nicer and fix my hair—a gal can't show up in a ratty sweat suit when she's accompanying a gorgeous pirate. Then David tucked my arm inside his, and let Angie lead us to the dining room.

I think it safe to say that we were the center of attention when we walked in the door. The Pack Council was waiting to greet David with the solemnity and nervousness I'd always imagined that government leaders feel around ambassadors from hostile countries.

Once introductions were made and hands were shaken, they invited the three of us to join them at the head table. David didn't eat, of course, but he sipped some wine to be polite. Conversation started with small talk, then moved on to admiration for their respective kinds. It was all very civil, and nobody bit anybody else, and I was bored stiff.

So I ate. Being at the head table meant that we got a waiter instead of having to go through the buffet line, but I headed for the line anyway when the waiter was too slow with third helpings.

A group of my buddies from earlier hailed me on the way back, so I ended up at a table with them. It wasn't quite as relaxed as it had been before, but they were trying. And Shannon caught me up on *Project Runway*, which I appreciated. When I suggested some of them might want to make a trip to the Adventure Cove the next summer, they looked enthusiastic even before I promised free passes.

The group in turn invited me to join them in the bar, but I decided to stick close to David. So I was enjoying a final dessert and checking email on my iPad when Captain Bob floated over. At least he looked normal, and not like an extra from *The Walking Dead*.

"I guess I should apologize," he said.

"Don't bother. You wouldn't mean it, and I wouldn't believe it."

"Fair enough." He looked toward where David was still schmoozing with the Council. "I can't believe they're allowing a vampire around civilized people."

I wasn't sure if either werewolves or ghosts really counted as civilized, but since my cheesecake was really good, I could be magnanimous. "It was Angie's idea, not mine."

"I know—if anybody but the doc had asked me to stop bothering you, I'd still be at it."

I owed Angie a drink. To distract him from haunting, I asked, "How did you two meet anyway?"

"She and Carl were the first people to spot me after my death. They were in the cemetery looking for ghosts when I rose."

"And you were the new ghost on the block?"

"I was the *only* ghost on the block. We're rare—we have to have the arcane gene and either suffer a traumatic death or die with some sort of unfinished business. Weren't you listening during the doc's talk today?"

"Yeah, not so much."

"Wasting time playing games," he said in disgust.

"Hey, you were the one telling me which cards to put where."

"Is it my fault that you couldn't see moves that were right in front of you?"

"Did you ever consider playing your own game?"

"I would have if I could have."

"Oh, right. Sorry." I didn't want to feel bad for the old so-and-so, but I sort of did. How sad was it when a guy couldn't even play solitaire? The other werewolves weren't exactly eager to hang with him, so Angie and I seemed to be the only ones who talked to him. "Hey, how does Angie see you anyway? I thought you needed the arcane gene to see a ghost."

"If that were true, why would there would be so many ghost stories? Any human can see me if in a receptive frame of mind."

"Like at a séance?"

"Or in a house believed to be haunted, or late at night."

"Or in a cemetery."

"Exactly. Plus the doc got a witch to make her an amulet to help her see ghosts."

I wondered if I could get an amulet to keep me from seeing ghosts. Then I had a thought. "Hey, Bob—"

"Captain Bob!"

"*Captain* Bob. You said you can appear in any of the forms you had in life, but how do you know what you looked like when you were dying? Were you attacked in front of a mirror or what?"

He squirmed a bit. "No, it was dark and I didn't see anything. I don't know how I can take that form without actually having seen it. The doc can't figure it out, either."

"I guess it's no weirder than me being able to Change into any breed of dog. 'There are more things in heaven and earth, Horatio, than are dreamt of in your philosophy.'"

"My name isn't Horatio!" he said, but I was fairly sure he was kidding.

"So why do you look so old?" I asked.

"What do you mean? This is how I looked before I was killed."

"I get that, and you look pretty good for a man your age. What were you, seventy-something?"

"Sixty-six," he said, glaring.

"And you didn't look a day over sixty," I lied. "It's just that if I could control my appearance, I'd go for something younger."

I saw the wheels turning, and he started shifting outlines. The result was a lot more scenic. He was still tall, but no longer stooped. The potbelly was gone, and his barely-there gray fuzz had become a full head of dark brown hair. Without the wrinkles, I could tell that he had cheekbones to die for.

"Is that better?" he asked.

"Whoa! Captain Handsome!"

He looked absurdly pleased, but when he saw David and Angie coming toward us, switched back.

Angie was chattering away, and I could tell David was just managing to stay polite.

He said, "I will try to make time to answer more of your questions, but it's time for Joyce and me to retire for the night." He gave me a look that I had no trouble interpreting.

All thoughts of cheesecake fled, replaced by anticipation of beefcake, and we beat a hasty retreat to our cabin. It turned out that David had missed me as much as I'd missed him.

Afterward, we got David safely ensconced in the cabin's closet. It was a good-sized one, and after I took my stuff out and found him a pillow and blanket, he said it was perfectly acceptable. He used a bit of rope I'd had in my car to tie the door shut from inside, just in case somebody got the bright idea to open it in the middle of the day.

Since everybody had been up late for the run and buffet, there were no sessions scheduled until the afternoon of the next day and I'd planned to sleep in. So I was still asleep when someone yelled my name. I jerked awake and sat straight up—luckily I was wearing an oversized Adventure Cove T-shirt that covered all the essentials, because Captain Bob was standing next to the bed.

"You're a heavy sleeper," he commented.

"You promised to stop haunting me."

"This isn't haunting. The doc sent me to invite you to breakfast."

"Are you kidding?" I looked at the clock by the bed. "It's eight o'clock."

"Which is breakfast time."

I wanted to blow Angie off, and I really wanted to blow him off, but I knew he wouldn't leave until I agreed. Besides, breakfast sounded good.

"Fine. Just go away and I'll get dressed."

"I'll wait for you outside." He looked around the room. "Where's your boyfriend?"

"None of your beeswax."

"Cranky in the morning, aren't you?"

I threw a pillow through him, and climbed out of bed to get showered and dressed.

When I joined Captain Bob outside, he led me away from the main building and said, "The dining room isn't open yet, so the doc ordered breakfast in her cabin." Angie's cabin was the mirror image of mine, if you subtracted the vampire in the closet and added a boatload of food on the table.

"Good morning," she said. "I hope this is enough to eat."

"It's a good start," I said, my mouth watering from the tantalizing aroma of bacon and eggs.

"Then, help yourself. I'm not a big morning eater." She wasn't kidding. All she had on her plate was a piece of toast. "I hope you don't mind me waking you so early, but I knew you'd be free. David has to sleep during the day, right?"

"He's a real bear if he doesn't get his full day's rest."

"Then he can get by on less sleep?" she asked eagerly, reaching for a notepad.

"Just a joke. When the sun comes up, he goes down, and doesn't wake again until dark."

"Fascinating. Another thing . . ."

I stifled a sigh, and dug into the food. At least it was fresh, even if the questions were stale. Angie asked me the exact same things as she had the day before, and I still didn't have answers. Did she think I'd quizzed David the night before so as to be ready for her? It was so boring that I was yawning like crazy, and I could barely keep my eyes open wide enough to see the plate in front of me.

By the time I reached the obvious conclusion that I'd been drugged, it was too late to do anything about it except pass out.

I woke up in a cage. It wasn't the first time that had happened, but this instance was considerably more frightening. I smelled death.

Superior sense of scent is part and parcel of being a werewolf, even when in human form, but it isn't always a good thing. Somebody had died in that cage, maybe several somebodies. I smelled werewolf, and human, and beings I couldn't identify. It was all I could do to keep from whimpering.

Okay, I lied. I whimpered.

The cage was enough to make any werewolf whimper. It was bare of furniture or comfort and the mesh of which it was built was woven so tightly that no dog on earth would be small enough to escape.

The room in which it stood was just as bleak. The walls and floor were bare concrete, and there were tables and shelves covered with medical and chemistry equipment, a computer, a bookshelf of serious-looking tomes, and a refrigerator. Add it all together and you got a low-rent animal research facility, but the only lab rat was me.

A few minutes later, in walked Angie.

"Oh good, you're awake. I knew that drug would work on werewolves, of course, but I had to estimate your weight so I wasn't sure how long you'd be out."

"And you drugged me why?"

"To get you here, of course." She got a bottle of water out of the refrigerator, put it into a contraption on the side of the cage, and pulled a lever that lifted a section of mesh just enough to allow the bottle to roll inside before slamming shut again.

"You've done this before," I said, reaching for the water. The bottle was sealed, which was thoughtful. I wouldn't have taken it from her otherwise.

"Many times. At first we had such a hard time getting people to talk to us, and an even harder time getting them to allow us to examine them. Then I designed the cage, and Carl said he didn't think even he could get out of it. As it turned out, he was right."

"You put your husband in here?"

"He was going to leave me! After I'd stuck with him through his Change! Do you know how much I cooked for that man? And how hard I worked to become a werewolf, too? I let him bite me over and over again! Then we started hunting witches, but none of the ones we found had any idea of what to do, no matter what we did to convince them."

I really didn't want to know what their persuasion techniques had been.

"The best we could do was to get one to make me the ghost amulet. That was our next idea, you see. Becoming a ghost sounded like a viable alternative."

"I don't think your definition of *viable* is the same as mine."

"I know, I couldn't very well sleep with my husband if he couldn't touch me, but we didn't know that most ghosts are insubstantial, or even the proper way to make one. We had half a dozen failures before we got it right."

"Captain Bob?"

"That's right. He wasn't really killed by a vampire, of course, though Carl did try to make it look as if he had been. At first we thought it had been a waste of time, too, because the form has too many limits. Then I did a routine case study on him and realized that he had a witch in his family—that's when we began to suspect the existence of the arcane gene.

"Next I traced Carl's family tree and found a great-uncle who was a werewolf, but I had nothing. There was no way I could become a were-wolf or a ghost or a witch."

"Is that so awful?"

"To see all the possibilities and not want powers of my own? Not to mention the lengthened life span."

"It's not all wine and roses," I said. "We have weaknesses, too. We have to hide what we are, and we lose more babies than we can carry to term, and—"

"I never wanted children. I just wanted Carl. But I got older while he stayed young. He started spending more time with the pack and less on our research. I hadn't given up, but he didn't care anymore. All he cared about was that bitch!"

It wasn't even an insult, really, since she was talking about a werewolf.

"She was another bitten werewolf," she said, "and he claimed he was just easing her into the life." She snorted. "I didn't need to be a werewolf to smell her on him. Soon he all but abandoned our work. All he cared about was rutting in the woods with his new mate."

"So you killed him."

"Thanks to our research, I knew exactly how to drug a werewolf. He didn't taste a thing, any more than you did. Once I had him in the cage, it was easy." She brushed off her hands as if she'd just wiped a dirty table. "If he'd been patient, we could have been together forever thanks to you."

"I'm not sure what you want me to do. I'd be glad to bite you." I couldn't quite keep the growl out of my voice when I made the offer.

"That's sweet, but no, it's your boyfriend I want to bite me."

"Excuse me?"

"David's going to make me a vampire. Then I can continue my

research forever. I wonder if a vampire can taste the arcane gene in a person's blood. . . ." She actually pulled a pad out of her pocket to jot a note.

"You're keeping me hostage to make David change you?"

"That's right. As soon as I rise, I'll tell him where you are."

I saw a flaw in her plan, but unfortunately, she already had it covered.

She said, "I know he'll try to use his vampire glamour on me, but it won't work. The last witch I trapped claimed to know all about vampires, but what she really knew was how to protect herself from them. I was quite vexed. Still, the potion she made is coming in handy now, isn't it?"

"It won't work. David swore that he'd never offer anybody else the Choice."

"I'm sure that was before he met you. I've seen the way he looks at you, just like Carl used to look at me. He'll do anything to get you back."

"He'll find me without your help." She probably didn't know about a vampire's sense of smell—it was as good as a werewolf's.

"I don't think so. This lab is extremely well hidden, thanks to another research subject. I'm still not sure exactly what he was, but the fellow had a gift for hiding things. Carl's little friend came sniffing around after his 'car accident' but she never found a thing." She frowned. "I'd have gotten rid of her, too, but I was afraid it might look suspicious. At any rate, I doubt any werewolves will even try to find you—you've got no pack."

"But David will never give up."

"Try to be logical, Joyce. There's no time for that. Remember what you said about werewolf weaknesses? You're already hungry, aren't you?"

As if in response, my stomach rumbled; even with the stench, my stomach growled. I must have slept through a meal or two.

"If he bites me tonight, I'll rise in three days. You can certainly go that long without eating as long as you have water, but how much longer than that could you last? A human can survive a month, but research shows a werewolf starves much more quickly. If you're injured, it's even faster." She smiled, and the sight nearly made me wet myself. "You're not injured now, but if your vampire doesn't bite me tonight, you will be."

She left me another dozen bottles of water, then went through a metal door, and of course locked it behind her. I immediately investigated my cage more thoroughly. It was still secure and I was still hungry.

Despite Angie's scheme, I wasn't overly afraid. David would no more abandon me than he would snack on puppies. He'd bite Angie if that was what it took. It was what came afterward that worried me.

Would his sense of honor force David to take care of Angie once she became a vampire? As I'd told her, the bond between a creator and creation was close. If David broke that connection to kill her, it would hurt him emotionally, if not physically, and if he didn't, then presumably the three of us would be living together for the foreseeable future. It would be like rooming with a mother-in-law, if your mother-in-law was a serial killer.

Considering the logistics of the situation didn't improve my mood. I didn't have any idea what time it was, either, which meant I couldn't even begin to guess how much longer I was going to be in that cage. That naturally made me hungrier and thirstier, and I was trying to decide if I dared risk drinking another bottle of water when somebody arrived.

To my disappointment it wasn't David. It was Captain Bob.

"Where's the doc?" he demanded. "The vampire is on his way to the meeting site."

"How should I know? Why don't you ask someone who isn't locked in a cage?"

"It's for your own good—once she exterminates the vampire, you'll be safe from his influence."

"There are no words for how stupid you are. She's not going to kill David. She wants him to bite her."

"And when she's got what she wants, do you think she'll let him live?"

"You mean she—" Of course she'd kill David! She wouldn't want to be under the thumb of a stronger vampire. There were no words for how stupid *I* was, but I didn't need them. I howled, like a wolf who'd lost her mate, and I Changed to a wolf without even meaning to. Again and again I threw myself against the bars of the cage.

It was idiotic, of course, and when I finally calmed down enough to Change back, I was hungrier than ever.

Captain Bob was watching me.

"Go away," I said, my throat raw.

"You really love him."

"Damned right I do, and now he's going to die because of me."

"It's his own hellish actions—"

"Blow it out your ass, ghost boy! If it weren't for my wanting to go on a play date, David would never have come to the damned seminar and Angie would never have gotten near him. That makes it my fault. I suppose you'll be right there, cheering her on. Maybe she'll let you watch when she kills me, too."

"She won't kill you. As soon as the vampire is dead, she'll let you go so you can be with your own kind."

"What makes them my kind? It was a werewolf who nearly killed me, not a vampire. Speaking of werewolf bites, you might want to check out the ones on your neck."

"It was a vampire—"

"I've seen plenty of vampire bites, and they don't look like that. Take a good look at yourself in the mirror. Maybe your friend Carl tried to make it look like a vampire bite, but I bet even you can tell the difference between wolf teeth and vampire fangs."

"Carl was my friend."

"He was Dead Bob's friend—he didn't give two cents for Live Bob." I threw up my hands in disgust. "Believe what you want. It's not like I'll be around to care. Angie won't leave a witness."

"Witness to what? Killing a vampire is no crime."

"How about the other murders she's committed?" I took a deep breath. "I can smell at least three humans who were kept in this cage, plus two of what I think were witches. Werewolves, too. What happened to them? Carl was in here, too, and you know he's dead."

"He was in a car accident!"

"Don't tell me. I bet his body was completely destroyed."

"So?"

I didn't have the energy to argue with him, not with the scents of so many deaths seeping into my pores. I just turned my back on him, and when he came into the cage, shut my eyes and put my fingers in my ears.

Eventually he got tired of talking to somebody who wasn't in a receptive frame of mind. I waited until I was sure he was gone to cry.

Another interminable period of time passed while I tried to figure out some way I could get at Angie before she killed me, but when the lab door opened, I had nothing. I didn't even want to look at her. I only opened my eyes when I smelled David. At first I honestly thought I was dreaming, but no dream I've ever had got that scent right.

I leapt up. "Is Angie . . . ? Did you . . . ?"

"She's dead."

"What happened?"

He didn't answer because he was busy ripping the cage open, and after that, we were both busy for several minutes. Just having him still alive—well, as alive as I'd ever known him to be—should have been enough, but my stomach was growling constantly by that point.

"Sorry," I said.

He just smiled and picked me up to carry me outside. Breathing the untainted nighttime air was intoxicating. In fact, the air was better than untainted. I smelled werewolves. And chicken soup!

Somebody pushed a cardboard container of hot soup into my hand, and I inhaled it. Only when I was wiping my lips with the back of my hand did I realize that it was Shannon who'd handed it to me.

Other werewolves I recognized were going into and out of Angie's lab, which was apparently under an old barn out in the middle of nowhere. Whatever spell she'd used to hide the place had been broken.

Shannon gave me another container of soup, saying, "Remember, you're not human. You don't have to go slow."

I took her at her word, and slurped down that and the next two portions without hesitating. Only then did I say, "David, I think you can put me down."

"Must I?" he said, but did so and promptly wrapped his coat around me. I wasn't cold, but I did appreciate having his aroma to inhale. I wasn't sure I would ever get the stench of that cage out of my nose.

"What happened?" I asked again. "Captain Bob said you'd gone to meet Angie."

"I did, but Angie was in no hurry. She said she just wanted to ask more questions before letting me feed from her, but I don't believe that she ever intended for me to bite her. She thought that if she drained my blood herself and drank it, the effect would be the same."

"Would that have worked?"

He shrugged. "The wolves found us before she could try. She shot one with a dart gun, possibly what she'd intended to use on me, and they killed her before she could fire again."

"Then how did you find me?"

"A friend helped."

To my complete shock, Captain Bob floated into view.

"Since when are you a friend?" I asked.

"Since I helped save your life!"

"You helped Angie drug me in the first place."

"I helped save your boyfriend, too."

"You also helped lure him into Angie's trap—still no points."

He thought for a minute. "I told the wolves to bring you food."

"Really?" Maybe we were friends after all.

The rest of the wolves stayed at Angie's lair to explore it and decide what part of her research was worth saving. In a surprisingly short time, they dismantled the place and destroyed any evidence of supernatural beings. Of course, that meant destroying evidence of the murders, too, but Angie and Carl were both dead, so it seemed like the best choice.

While all that was going on, David drove me back to the Cahill Resort—it was too close to dawn for us to be sure of getting home. Captain Bob came along, cheerfully criticizing David's driving. At least he had enough manners to leave us alone when we got back to my cabin.

There was only half an hour left of darkness by then—enough for me to either eat again or thank David properly for rescuing me. I think I made the right choice.

With David in the closet for the day, I took an obscenely long shower and then went down to the main building to see if the breakfast buffet was open. It wasn't, but when the staff saw me, they started bringing me food. I don't think French toast had ever tasted so good, and luckily for me, it was just the appetizer.

Other werewolves started arriving for breakfast after a while, and a good number stopped to say hello. Some were shy, some expressed concern and sympathy, and one was bold enough to make jokes about what I'd been through. It was all good. They'd rescued David and me. They might not be my pack, but they were my friends.

After people started heading off to seminar sessions, Captain Bob floated in.

"I thought you'd be getting some rest," he said.

"Too hungry to sleep."

He looked at the empty plates around me. "So I see."

"You're just jealous."

"Maybe, but at least I never get heartburn. And I only fart when I want to."

"There's no fart like an old one," I replied, and he chuckled. "So what changed your mind about David?"

"You love him. I thought it was Stockholm syndrome or something like that at first, but you weren't abused or hypnotized. You just love him. I couldn't take him from you."

"Thank you."

He smiled, I smiled back, and it was very sweet.

Of course he had to spoil it by saying, "Why you picked a vampire to love I'll never know."

I wasn't going to try to explain it to him. "One more question. How did you talk the Council into riding to the rescue? They'd known Angie a long time—it couldn't have been easy to convince them that she was a murderer."

"It took some doing."

"Yeah?"

"First I showed them my death bite, and told them what you'd said about mouths. One of the alphas is a dentist and once she took a good look, she could tell a werewolf had killed me after all."

"And that did it?"

"Not completely. They were willing to investigate, but they can't do anything without forming a committee. So I pointed out that if they didn't stop Angie, there was going to be a vampire nearby who knew pack secrets."

"That must have lit a fire under their tails."

"It got them moving, but not fast enough to save your boyfriend. For that, I had to get tough."

"How does a ghost get tough?"

"I threatened to haunt them."

"They went for that? I mean you can be annoying, but you aren't that bad."

"Wanna bet? You remember how I can take any form I had in life? I picked the worst form I could think of."

"A teenager?"

"A baby. And I had colic for my whole first year."

"Remind me to never get you mad at me."

"Been there, done that."

I started yawning, and decided I could use a nap after all. I went back to my cabin and ended up sleeping most of the day, and woke up with David beside me. It was very nice.

The rest of the seminar wasn't bad, either. I attended a few more sessions, with presenters who were considerably less creepy than Angie, and Captain Bob stuck around to make sure I paid attention. The meals were convivial, and nobody seemed to mind David showing up every evening, especially after the Council invited him back the next year to talk about vampires.

There was a gala the final night, which was the first time David and I had danced together. I was wearing a new dress that was tight in all the right places, and he looked absolutely mouthwatering in a suit I'd had no idea he owned. Much to my delight, he'd kept up with the latest dances and had some serious moves.

Most of the attendees were leaving the next morning, but we had to leave that night to make sure we got home in time to get David back to his own light-proof bedroom. So even before the gala ended, we changed out of our party clothes, packed up, and loaded everything into my car. I'd been looking for Captain Bob all evening, but it was only when I was locking the door to the cabin that I spotted him sitting on the hood of the car.

"Just the ghost I wanted to see," I said.

"How many ghosts do you know?"

"One is enough. Did you ever dress as a pirate for Halloween or a costume party? I mean, as a grown man."

"I might have."

"Could you switch into that costume?"

"Why?"

"Just bear with me."

He frowned, but his clothing morphed into an impressive pirate captain's costume: a royal blue frock coat with gold trim, a wide-brimmed hat, and big black boots. It was more foppish than David usually wore in his pirate guise, but not so close to Disney's Captain Hook as to raise copyright issues. Best of all, he looked really good in it—if he'd been wearing a chintzy beard or a painted-on scar, it would have spoiled my plan.

"Perfect!" I said.

David raised an eyebrow.

"I've got an idea." Said idea had been percolating for the previous couple of days, but until I saw Captain Bob in costume, I hadn't known if it would work. "Captain, have you given any thought to going back to the sea? Or at least to a lake? You see, Pirate Dave's Adventure Cove has this pirate ship that nobody rides."

"Nearly nobody," David put in.

"Fine, nearly nobody rides. So I was thinking, how about a haunted pirate ship?"

"With me providing the haunting?" Captain Bob said.

"Why not? With the proper set dressing and some spooky music, and maybe some special effects, people would be in the right mood to see you." I didn't know how we'd convince our workers that Captain Bob was a special effect instead of a real ghost, but that was just a detail. "I bet it would be a big hit."

I could tell David liked the idea, but Captain Bob had to make a show of looking doubtful.

"Why would I want a job?" he said. "You can't pay me, and you can't expect a man to work for nothing. Not even a dead one."

"What would you say if I told you that there are computer programs that are voice activated?"

"Really?"

"So if somebody set it up for you, and lent a hand now and then, you'd be able to surf the Web, post on Facebook, whatever you wanted. In fact, if you promise to stay out of my bedroom, I'll even help you play solitaire."

"I'm in," he said, and jumped into the front seat of the car.

"I'm riding shotgun, ghost boy," I said.

"What do you care? You're just going to roll down the window and ride with your head hanging out anyway."

David silently endured our bickering for a solid fifteen minutes of driving before roaring, "Enough!" Belatedly I realized I should have consulted him before inviting Captain Bob to move in.

Before I could decide between an apology or a bribe, David said, "If you two don't behave yourselves, I'm going to turn this car right around!"

I snickered, and Captain Bob snarked, "At the rate you're going, we'll never get there anyway. You drive like my great-aunt!"

"Number one, I'm older than your great-aunt. Number two, I sailed ships across the Atlantic and the Caribbean, so it's safe to say that I know more about navigating than a ferryboat captain."

As they continued their discussion, I decided that while Captain Bob wasn't the new BFF I'd pictured, he was going to work out just fine.

HOME IMPROVEMENT
UNDEAD EDITION

Charlaine Harris &
Toni L.P. Kelner

What could be scarier than the first day of school? Take a crash course in the paranormal from editors Charlaine Harris and Toni L. P. Kelner in An Apple for the Creature, featuring thirteen all-new tales out of school.

Your schooldays are supposed to be the happiest days of your life – until you start thinking of your worst school nightmares: not knowing which is your classroom door, finding yourself naked in Assembly! But those fears will pale in comparison to these thirteen original stories that take academic anxiety to whole new realms.

You'll need more than an apple to stave off the creatures in these spooky scholastic stories!

Jo Fletcher
BOOKS

www.jofletcherbooks.co.uk

www.jofletcherbooks.co.uk

Jo Fletcher
BOOKS

BRINGING YOU A WHOLE NEW WORLD OF BOOKS

VISIT US AT OUR WEBSITE, OR JOIN US
ON TWITTER AND FACEBOOK FOR:

• Exclusive interviews and films from your favourite
Jo Fletcher Book authors

• Exclusive extra content

• Pre-publication sneak previews

• Free chapter samplers and reading group materials

• Giveaways and competitions

• Subscribe to our free newsletter

www.jofletcherbooks.co.uk
twitter.com/jofletcherbooks
facebook.com/jofletcherbooks